Review

Naiveté and dreams of fame are quickly dashed in this exciting anthropological mystery by Stefan Vučak. *Towers of Darkness* is an exposé style story, questioning the ethics of the ivory towers of the most respected academic institutions. Fighting for his career and even his life, Larry Krafter does not back down and the action builds steadily as the plot plays out. This is truly an amazing look at how greed and position affect people in all professions at all levels! Well written with strong characters, plenty of action, and a wide net of law enforcement closing in on the culprits, *Towers of Darkness* is sure to please as you can't wait to see what happens next. Great story!

Readers' Favorite

I0592731

Books by Stefan Vučak

General Fiction:
Cry of Eagles
All the Evils
Towers of Darkness
Strike for Honor
Proportional Response
Legitimate Power
Autumn Leaves
All My Sunsets
F/X-26
28th Amendment
Night Sirens
Broken Rose

Shadow Gods Saga:
In the Shadow of Death
Against the Gods of Shadow
A Whisper from Shadow
Shadow Masters
Immortal in Shadow
With Shadow and Thunder
Through the Valley of Shadow
Guardians of Shadow

Science Fiction:
Fulfillment
Lifeliners

Non-Fiction:
Writing Tips for Authors

Contact at:
www.stefanvucak.com

TOWERS of DARKNESS

By

Stefan Vučak

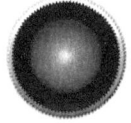

Note:

This is a work of fiction. All names, characters, places, and events are the work of the author's imagination. Any resemblance to real persons, places, or events is coincidental.

Stefan Vučak ©2011
ISBN-10: 0-6484731-0-4
ISBN-13: 978-0-6484731-0-7

Dedication

To Bož ... and his own struggle to achieve

Acknowledgments

My thanks to: Greg Durocher from the U.S. Geological Survey; Nick Jones from the Wyoming State Geological Survey, for information on coal geology and mining. For information on fossil dating, particular thanks goes to Dr. Jeffrey D. Stilwell, Applied Paleontology and Basin Studies Group, Monash University, Melbourne.

Valuable information was sourced from *Forbidden Archeology*, Michael A. Cremo, Bhaktivedanta Book Publishing, Inc., 2005.

Note: The International Anthropological Society is fictitious and not a real body.

Cover art by Laura Shinn.
http://laurashinn.yolasite.com

Chapter One

Nothing could soften the sun's harsh glare. An occasional ragged cloud streamed high in the sky's blue deeps, and a whispering cool breeze sometimes drifted silently across the ugly black gash of the Karringa open-cut mine. Neither helped hold back the eighty-four-degree bite, and it was only eleven o'clock. Hands clasped behind his back, polarized shades over his eyes, Ferguson stood tall outside the drab, gray fibro prefab hut of the temporary admin office. With a black glazed meerschaum pipe locked firmly between his teeth, his steel gray eyes were fixed on the overburden wall that hung sixty feet above the freshly exposed bench some two hundred yards on his right.

The sub-bituminous coal layer he wanted lay a farther forty feet below the bench. That's why he stood there, stoically sweating under his blue hardhat and open-neck white shirt, waiting for the cast blast that would heave a seventy-yard section of overburden into the pit floor now denuded of coal. Dozers would then push the remaining overburden and the thin lignite layer that sat atop the Upper Smith Seam, onto the resulting cast pile. The exposed coal bed would then be ready for extraction.

Opposite him, working in the shadow of the looming north-south overburden wall, two tracked bucket wheel excavators were chewing at the open coalface that fed coal to enormous Caterpillar 797B rear dump trucks with a capacity of 380 short tons, which they took to one of four storage silos for washing and blending before being flood loaded into rail cars from the loop silo, then transported to coking processors or ever-hungry power stations around the state. Ninety-five feet below the open seam, a dwarfed excavator worked the main prize, the Lower Smith

1

Seam of anthracite, a dense, lustrous coal hard as rock; deep and costly to get at, but well worth the expense.

Karringa was a new mine in the Powder River Basin working the Fort Union Formation bed, already crowded by over a dozen operators of various sizes around Gillette. Ferguson had stood here, watching when they drilled the first group blast into the open plain. When the dust settled, the dozers moved in to clear the virgin soil, which made way for further, deeper blasts until they hit the Roland Seam, enabling the excavators and trucks to take over while finishing touches were done to the holding silos and rail line. A tough eighteen months for everybody getting this far, but the sweat and curses were paying off. He didn't give a toss about the other mines, inasmuch as they were taking away coal that should properly belong to him, or at least his Relans Mining Corporation parent. He only cared about Karringa and his extraction quotas, always going up.

He often contemplated dragging Stanton from his comfortable Gillette office and show the hardboiled general manager what it took to meet his ridiculous quotas. He threatened, but never carried through on his promise. An old coal hand himself, Stanton knew very well what it took, and that's how they played the game. Ferguson grumbled and wouldn't have minded having Stanton on the receiving end of today's cast blast, but he went on with his job anyway. There were never enough men, equipment, time or money for either of them to satisfy the head office. Once the new sixty-five million dollar dragline excavator was installed, its 120 cubic yard bucket eliminating the slower dozer push key pass, it would enormously speed up pre-production. In two months the monster dragline would be assembled and ready to do some paid work—excavating virgin overburden, always the messiest part. Stanton might ease off then, however dubious the prospect. Probably issue another quota increase. Despite their squabbles, the two of them got along. While Stanton remained buried in his Gillette office worrying about capacity expansion and takeovers, Ferguson would keep Karringa producing.

Even with his ongoing operational problems, he had little to complain about. He might bitch about Stanton's unreasonable demands, but nothing compared to what the pitmen called him. 'Mustard' Ferguson, mustard the bastard, and he relished the accolade. Getting coal out of unforgiving ground not willing to give it up for the asking, took determination and tough, no-nonsense men who shunned all forms of subterfuge and obfuscation. Anyway, damn them, they got paid, and paid well for what they did. Too bad Katarina had not been as understanding, if only a little. Things might have been different then, but he was a miner who loved his job more than he loved her. At least that's how she put it. He could not explain the fire burning in him when he worked his mine, not in words she would accept or understand. Then again, she had always been a big city girl, and he hoped New York would make her happy. The fire of love that burned for her within him still burned, but without her to fan it, he feared it would eventually smolder away. Life was shit.

He sucked on his pipe and puffed out a gray cloud of aromatic rum-flavored tobacco smoke. Anytime now, he thought comfortably. Strictly speaking, he shouldn't be out here at all, but he wanted distraction from cold figures, charts and paperwork, a reminder of what the whole thing was about. He could never afford to lose that connection, or he would end up like Stanton. Besides, as mine manager, he could stand wherever he damn well pleased.

On cue, a wall of dust rose fifty feet directly behind the overburden bench face, followed by a sharp crack of high explosive core charges going off. In a ripple of blasts, dust and debris walked back along the bench toward the burgeoning overburden wall, the effect bodily heaved the bench layer onto the worked pit floor. He waited for the dust to clear, then nodded with satisfaction. A fair amount of overburden still showed, mostly the useless soft Roland Seam lignite layer, a characteristic of this formation. It would not take the dozers long, two days at most, to clear the rubbish and expose the main seam. As usual, Cower had done a good job, but he expected nothing else. Blast casting was an art as much as a science, and Cower was one of the best. When he considered the time, effort and money consumed by a blast, he could not afford an amateur.

Ferguson chewed on his pipe stem and walked into the prefab, nodded to Sandra clicking away on her keyboard, and strode toward his office tucked against the back wall. The faces behind the arrayed desks never looked up from their work. The administrative building next to the new car park near the mine entrance would not be ready for another two weeks at least, no matter how hard he badgered the construction project manager.

Inside his cramped office, he emptied the pipe into an ashtray, sat down, and absently glanced at the wall-mounted air-conditioner, wondering what a properly equipped office looked. Getting out of this prefab would be a welcomed change, and not only for him. The men also looked forward to having a proper canteen, relaxation and service facilities. Karringa was not a UMWA shop, thank God, something he and Stanton firmly agreed on, resisting any attempt by smooth-talking greasy reps to make it into one; troublemakers, all of them. There would be no strikes, walkouts or protracted wrangling because the game room walls were painted beige rather than blue, or the cutlery not the right shape. In his view, the best thing a union rep could do for the men and the mine was to stand in front of a cast blast.

* * *

Bruster revved the hundred-ton dozer and drove the angled blade into the broken thirty-foot lignite bed, separated from the sub-bituminous layer by ten feet of rock, shale, and compacted sand. The huge Caterpillar D11 dozer-ripper hardly paused as it bit into the layer, pushing a fifty cubic yard bite of sandstone, shale, crystalline rock, rooted siltstones, and brown coal toward the already cleared overburden spoil that now covered the pit floor. He reversed the dozer, swung it around, and lowered the blade. A dozer on either side of his machine belched black diesel smoke as they worked to clear the overburden the cast blast had left behind. Exacting work, but repetitive. Still, better than driving a dump truck. The only thing he had to worry about was driving his dozer over the lip of the bench. It wouldn't do anything for his bonus or Mustard's humor.

He wished for a cold beer and a smoke as he engaged the drive and the dozer lurched forward with a bellow from the powerful engine. About to push into the exposed lignite, a flash of light made him blink. He stepped on the brake and tilted his head, staring at the exposed face, but could see nothing except a seam of soft coal and broken gravel. He stepped off the brake and something glinted again. Muttering an obscenity, he put the dozer into neutral and climbed out of the cabin. Bruster jumped off the thick metal track and walked toward the coalface.

He peered at the wall and quickly found what caused the flash of light. Embedded in the coal three feet from top of the layer, protruded a black bone. Smudged, but still bright, a partially exposed ring of twisted yellow metal formed a bracelet around the bone. He leaned forward and reached up to poke the fragment with a stiff forefinger. There was no give, of course, the bone lying solidly encased in the seam.

He placed his hands on his hips and shook his head.

"Well, if that don't beat all."

As he stared at the bone, he figured the thing had to be ancient, buried this deep below ground. The boys often came across curiosities, which they kept or sold at one of the Gillette curio shops, but a worked bracelet this deep? Maybe he should take the thing and sell it. It could be gold and the money would come in handy. If he got caught, he would likely lose the bracelet, his job, and possibly end up with a fine or prison term for his trouble, not counting getting blacklisted. It simply wasn't worth the hassle. Besides, he had a wife and family to think of to risk petty theft over a lousy few bucks. The curio shop owners always underpaid. His old lady wouldn't be amused if he got caught either. No, better do this right. Maybe Mustard would give him an added bonus for the find; if the bastard felt generous, that is.

He tilted back his yellow hardhat and ear protectors, and pulled out a cellphone. Selecting a listed number from the menu, he pressed the call button. Dozers rumbled around him, but he hardly noticed them.

"What is it, Bruster?" Cower answered after two rings, his voice distracted. Bruster figured the man was probably evaluating the effectiveness of the last cast blast.

"I got something here you should see, chief."

"I see you taking a break beside your dozer instead of clearing away that shit like you're supposed to."

Bruster's mouth twitched with bleak humor. Cower wasn't a bad guy to get along with, for a company staff puke, provided you did your job. He had little time for idlers, at least on mine time anyway, until you got him to Sanford's Grub & Pub in Gillette. There, old Cower could tank up and mix it with the best of them. Not actually old, but that's what everybody called him. On the job, though, the man had no sense of humor at all.

"Ain't taking no break and you really should see this."

There was a moment of silence followed by a long sigh. "Okay, five minutes," Cower said and the line went dead.

Bruster smiled, waved to Gulio working the dozer on his left and started walking toward the belching machine. The dozer stopped.

"What's up?" Gulio asked in a chesty voice, leaning out from his seat.

"Found something interesting and Cower is coming over for a look. Keep clear of this part of the bench, okay?"

"What you got? Blackbeard's treasure?"

"Just a piece of bone."

"Okay, I'll keep clear. You flagging it?"

"You bet," Bruster said and walked back to his dozer.

He climbed into the cabin, reached behind the thick padded seat, and pulled out two three-foot yellow poles. Jumping down, he unfurled the little triangular red flags and planted the poles into the detritus in front of the buried bone. With the flags set, he climbed onto the dozer and went back to work. Plenty of overburden still remained to be cleared.

A few minutes later, Cower drove up in his battered pickup and stopped at end of the makeshift road the dump trucks would use to shift coal once the overburden was removed. He waved a yellow flag to keep from being run down and approached Bruster's dozer. The miner cut power, eased the machine to a stop, and climbed down.

"Okay, Bruster, what's the big deal?" demanded the burly mine engineer, clearly in no mood for games.

Bruster pointed at the flags hanging limp on the poles and walked toward the face without looking if the engineer followed. When he reached the flags, he stopped and pointed at the seam.

"This isn't another gag, is it?" Cower scowled at the miner and peered at the exposed coalface.

"Look up."

Frowning, Cower searched the top of the brown lignite seam, his eyes invariably drawn to the glint of yellow metal. He saw the exposed bone and drew back with a start.

"Holy shit!"

Bruster knew exactly what Cower must be thinking: A bracelet on a bone sticking out of an Eocene lignite layer? The bracelet implied human bone, clearly impossible. The Fort Union Formation consisted of late Oligocene and early Eocene lignite over a Paleocene sub-bituminous bed that was mined, the lignite quality being too poor to be worth extracting, at least the stuff here was. If this piece of bone was real, it had been buried for thirty or forty million years! The bracelet, however, meant intelligent workmanship.

Cower's shoulders sagged and he groaned. After a moment, he pushed back his red hardhat.

"Why me, Lord? Why today? As if I haven't got enough problems on my hands already."

"Is this trouble, chief?" Bruster asked. The engineer slowly looked at him.

"Trouble? I don't give a crap about that bone. I'm worried about delays and cost overruns, Ferguson ranting at me, blaming me for everything that goes wrong. A whipping boy, that's what I am. An unappreciated, underpaid whipping boy. I'm sorely tempted to tell you to bury the thing and forget it, but I'm not going to. Plant more flags twenty feet on either side and don't go near the thing. Stick some flags on top of the seam as well. I'm not going to thank you for calling me, by the way. You've just ruined a great day for me."

"Do I get a finder's reward?" Bruster ventured half jokingly.

"Yeah, you'll get a reward. You get to keep your job! Now get back into that dozer and start earning your pay."

Bruster grinned and walked off, not minding Cower's kill 'em on sight attitude.

* * *

With three dozers snarling around him, Cower stared at the piece of bone, shook his head in wonder, and slowly made his way back to the pickup. He leaned against the hood and dragged out his cellphone. The mine manager had to know about this and he winced at the expected blast. It took a couple of rings before a deep, confident voice answered.

"Ferguson!"

"It's Jackson, boss. I'm at the new cast blast bench and you need to come down right now."

"What's the matter? A dozer run over your foot?"

"I wish, but I'm afraid it's a bit more serious. One of the guys found what looks like a human hand bone wearing a yellow metal bracelet stuck in the lignite seam."

"Ah, shit," Ferguson growled after a pause.

Cower sympathized. Both their days were shot.

"Yeah, that's what I said."

"You know what this is going to do to my schedule? Stanton will go orbital."

"We still got four days before we're ready to start shifting coal here, boss. The sub-bituminous bed will be exposed on time."

"Except for your find," Ferguson complained bitterly. "Right now, I'm not anxious to handle another headache, but you were right to call me. I know the company policy regarding anthropological items, but you could have been a pal and pretended not to see the thing. I could also pretend you never called, but I'm not going to. And you know what? It started being such a great day too."

"That's what I told Bruster who found the thing," Cower said.

"This isn't a prank the guys pulled, is it?" Ferguson demanded. "If it is, I'm not going to be very amused."

"Looks real to me, boss."

"It would. All right, we'll simply have to work around it. Flag the area, then wrap the bone in some plastic and place a tarp over the whole thing. Better post a security guard over there twenty-four-seven until further notice."

"Already flagged, boss, but are you sure about security?"

"What do you think? I'm on my way," Ferguson snapped and switched off.

* * *

Larry Krafter reached the corner of 12th and Lewis Street, and ambled confidently toward the broad entrance steps of the new Anthropology Building, so much more comfortable than the old place on Ivinson Avenue. He looked around the almost deserted grounds, seeing an odd student making his way along narrow lanes between the campus buildings. They could be here for anything: remedial classes, summer courses, research or a wandering visitor. But at eight in the morning, he didn't consider that likely.

Thick glass panels slid aside and he gave a small sigh of relief as he entered the air-conditioned interior. Although early, it already pushed seventy-five and promised another hot day. He enjoyed summer, August always lovely, especially when winters in Laramie seemed to be getting longer each year. Climate change or merely a natural 100,000-year weather cycle linked to the sun's increased magnetic activity? He couldn't say and didn't particularly care. It wasn't his department, but he did acknowledge that man's mounting industrial pollution output wasn't doing the atmosphere much good. Still, compared to the annual volume of gases ejected from Earth's 160 or so active volcanoes, to him, man's contribution seemed rather paltry. However, climate scientists were on a roll. Why spoil a good thing by pointing out inconsistencies?

He took the broad stairway to the third floor and made directly for the Paleoanthropology Lab. The short summer break before the start of the fall semester gave him an opportunity to pursue one of his pet research programs. Somewhat outside his immediate field, as it dealt with geology, but as a biological paleoanthropologist, the extremely thick and extensive coal seams in the Powder River Basin and the south-eastern Montana beds, had puzzled him, and had sorely worried geologists all over for years.

Some of the seams were forty meters thick, most of it nearly pure. So, why did this basin have so much coal when similar basins in Wyoming hardly had any? Geologically, there simply should not have been enough organic feed material during the Eocene and Paleocene epochs to produce the volume of coal held there. Extensive crustal deformation during that period could have buried all the other coal beds. Nobody could account for it. Krafter hoped to find out one way or another by analyzing deep core drilling data from mining companies and the USGS, no matter how long it took. If necessary, he would do some drilling himself. An amusing diversion from his more serious work: establishing the facts behind population migration into the Americas.

Krafter bypassed the research labs and lecture rooms, and walked deliberately toward his small office halfway down the wide corridor. A cramped six-by-eight-foot cubicle with no window, he should be insulted, but as a very junior Assistant Professor on the university totem pole, he considered himself lucky to have it. He could have ended up with a corner desk in one of the senior faculty offices. Just the image of being under such constant surveillance and condescending fatherly advice made him cringe. In his view, most of the old fuds on the faculty hung on by a thread and should have been pastured off long ago. He unlocked the drab off-white door, walked in, and flipped on the light switch. A double fluorescent strip flickered into life and Krafter immediately walked to his desk shoved hard against the far wall.

He pulled back a dark gray cloth ergonomic chair and pressed the power button on his tower computer. Ignoring the two metal filing cabinets behind him, the ceiling-high bookshelf fitted against the wall on his right, stuffed full of student files, magazines, binders, and professional books—he ought to take time to weed out junk that invariably accumulated during an academic year before the fall semester started—and a corner cupboard, he waited for the 17" LED screen to finish displaying the startup sequence. Finally done, the cursor arrow blinked steadily beside columns of icons, waiting for him to do something, like logging on.

As part of his usual morning routine, he activated Outlook and check the email list. There were several from his students, but a red flag message from Dr. Perkins caught his attention. The subject line simply read 'Come and see me'. He wondered what the old relic wanted, but despite the imperative, it couldn't be anything too important or the man would have rung.

As Assistant Director, Perkins ran the Paleoanthropology Lab, its research programs, graduate and undergraduate classes, and of course, the grants system so badly needed by resident researchers, including Larry's. Although he didn't have the final say in everything, that privilege belonged to the Anthropology Department director, Krafter made it a policy not to antagonize Perkins unnecessarily. Besides, he kind of liked the forty-six-year-old codger. To him, being only twenty-six, anyone over forty was already half fossilized, in mind and body. Perkins was tenured and could afford to be demanding, unreasonable, and a general pain when it suited him.

Krafter clicked on the email line and quickly scanned the message. A human bone unearthed in a Roland Seam at a Gillette coal mine? Perkins had to be kidding. Most of the Fort Union Formation was Paleocene, fifty million years or more! According to accepted evolutionary models, man did not walk this Earth until some 400,000 years ago. At least *homo sapiens* did not. As for the ape-like creatures before then, inference and guesswork. No one knew, not definitively. The bone had to be someone's idea of an elaborate gag and a waste of university time. Perkins was probably having one of his little jokes and jerking his chain.

He clicked on the first JPG attachment and stared thoughtfully at the sharp image. A bone and a bracelet, all right, solidly embedded in brown coal. If this was a gag, somebody went to an awful lot of trouble to make it look real. How did they encase a piece of bone in coal strata? The second attachment showed a close-up of a partially crushed bracelet. Intricate fine lines and seemingly random geometric patterns clearly indicated sophisticated workmanship. It looked very real to him.

Skeptical and unable to accept what he saw, Krafter nonetheless felt a tug of curiosity and a desire to expose what had to be a case of elaborate intrusive burial, but buried under ninety feet or so of overburden? Of course, the overburden no longer there, having been blasted away, and with it, any evidence of possible strata tampering. The blast made the integrity of the find highly questionable. Somebody *could* have planted the thing.

The last two attachments were an e-ticket with Great Lakes Airlines for a return flight to Gillette and a motel reservation. It wasn't hard to guess what Perkins wanted, but Krafter felt uncomfortable at the dubious honor accorded him. Well, the university paid for this, and a change of scenery would do him good. Then he noticed the departure time: 11:25 this morning! What the hell was the rush? He bit back his indignation when the perfectly obvious answer struck him.

Karringa Mine was an active working, and they were being more than generous to invite the University of Wyoming to look at the find *in situ*. They could simply have dug the thing up and handed him a cardboard box, thereby destroying any validity the find might have had, if it still had any. As a scientist, he respected the sacrifice Karringa made, provided UW did not drag its ass, if *he* didn't drag his ass, or he *would* only get a box, if he were lucky.

Incredible as it seemed, what if the thing was real? As a progressive paleoanthropologist straining against the shackles of orthodoxy and powerful personalities who dominated the field, he didn't have to have things spelled out. Human evolutionary theory would take a massive hit, as would all those creationist nut groups, not that scientific evidence meant anything to them. His name could go down in history books alongside Leakey, or more likely, as a fraud like Professor von Zieten, if his detractors had their way. It would certainly get him noticed, something every academic craved, but would it be the right kind of exposure this early in his career? He was running ahead of himself and knew it. Get the facts first, then see what happens. A little dreaming of glory did no harm.

He printed the email message and attachments, and walked quickly down the silent corridor toward Perkins' spacious office, his footsteps echoing on the hard linoleum floor. He would have to hustle if he wanted to catch that flight, and glory would have to wait a while longer. After a solid knock on the wood-veneered door, followed by a muffled 'Come in', he opened the door and stepped through. Wide windows splashed soft light against a deep gray carpet and turned the packed bookshelves beside him a rich amber. A broad pale beige executive desk fronted the door, behind which stood a row of five four-drawer steel cabinets.

In his usual summer outfit, a navy blue T-shirt with a UW logo on the left breast, Adam Perkins lifted his brown-cropped head from the computer screen and gave a noncommittal grunt.

Krafter did not need to be a mind reader to know what Perkins thought. It would be about his attire. Krafter preferred to dress casually. His scuffed black jeans, a purple open-neck shirt with rolled-up sleeves, runners that were long past their use-by date, didn't project an image of a serious faculty member. He rather enjoyed projecting an impression of a rebellious young scientist, regardless of the frowns this had earned him from some of the stuffy faculty. His students didn't mind his youth, and in these protest-marching times, that counted for more than being garroted by a tie.

"Ah, Larry, you obviously read my email," Perkins said. "If you'd had your cellphone on yesterday, we could have avoided this scurrying around."

Krafter winced slightly at the rebuke, only mildly disconcerted. He told Perkins on Monday that he wanted to take yesterday off and would be out of touch. Besides, the old duffer could have used his landline number if the thing was so important. Jerking his chain, that was it.

"I read the email, all right, but I don't understand why the university is interested. You know my thinking on human evolution is considered somewhat radical, but finding a supposedly intact *ulno* or *radius* bone with an attached bracelet in an Eocene layer is preposterous. It's got to be."

Perkins lifted both eyebrows. "Somewhat radical? Extreme, would be more accurate. As I told you before, that kind of thinking will land you in trouble one dark day. You're pushing the established envelope too hard and risking derailing a bright career. Be warned."

"My papers are backed with solid evidence," Krafter pointed out defiantly, somewhat tired of Perkins' veiled conservatism. Anyway, the man was only a bureaucrat and simply didn't understand. "Bollinger and Maddson are wedded to outmoded ideas and refuse to treat the evidence objectively."

"Of course they refuse to be objective!" Perkins snapped. "Accepting your findings would mean acknowledging that a lifetime of work was nonsense and would embarrass not only them, but the universities they represent."

"Their position *is* nonsense!"

"Just because you've got evidence, doesn't mean you cannot be discredited. You need thirty years of orthodoxy before you can be radical. Your problem is that you lack those years. Take it from me, I know. Even though Professor Walsh agrees with you and supports your theory, and he carries the weight of Oxford behind him, even he is cautious embracing your extrapolations on Pacific migratory patterns. Remember my warning," Perkins said mildly and wagged a finger at him.

Krafter wasn't convinced and it showed on his face. Perkins sighed in resignation.

"You simply don't get it, do you? I don't mind seeing your unshakeable confidence, or display your sense of immortality and impatience with stuffy academic protocols. That's healthy at this stage of your career, although others might not agree with me.

But you need to temper your rashness or your career will wither. You need to learn prudence and wisdom in the crucible of experience."

"Yes, sir," Krafter said stoically. He'd had these father-knows-best speeches before, and he had seen that crucible close-up.

Perkins cleared his throat. "As for the Karringa find being preposterous, that might be, but we have a responsibility to find out, and you're one of my experts on Powder River Basin geology and anthropology. We'll treat this with an open mind, examine the evidence by sticking to established scientific principles and ascertain the cold facts. There is no room in this laboratory for prejudicial indulgence. Isn't that what you've been telling your undergrads?"

Stung by the admonishment, Krafter sat up. "I might be pushing the envelope, but Karringa is way outside it! It's got to be."

"That's why you're going up there to find out. Of course, if this is beneath you and you prefer to shuffle papers all summer, I can always give it to Wethermans." Perkins said and a faint smile touched his mouth.

Krafter blanched at the very idea of Associate Professor Paul Wethermans in one of his impeccable London suits anywhere near the Karringa find, or any other find, for that matter. The two clashed and disagreed on almost everything, their ideas and objectives diametrically opposed. Wethermans belonged in old-school anthropology and archaeology, whereas Krafter challenged recognized authorities. Wethermans valued his position and career, sucked up to powers that be and published regurgitated dogma comfortably regarded by his peers. Krafter doubted the man ever had an original thought. He knew Wethermans saw him as a dangerous and provocative reactionary who should never been awarded a PhD. To frustrate the locked mind of his critic and other detractors, Krafter got even by producing flaw-lessly researched papers that *Science* and *Nature* peer reviews failed to discredit, regardless of their dislike for the content.

Perhaps the unstated snobbery Wethermans oozed when-ever he talked or moved that grated on Krafter. The man came from a moderately wealthy family—uranium mining somewhere in Crook County—and never let people forget it. He ought to have stuck with daddy's business instead of becoming a hack ac-ademic. Krafter knew he shouldn't be so thin-skinned and he had more powerful adversaries to deal with.

"That was cruel, Dr. Perkins," Krafter said stiffly, and the lab head chuckled.

"Relax, Larry. I only wanted to see you squirm. You don't have time to argue this and I don't have time to indulge you. I suggest you go home, put something decent on—you're repre-senting the university—pack a bag and catch that flight. I spoke to the mine manager yesterday and you're expected. We don't want to disappoint him because you're stuck in an ideological vacuum. When you get there, make sure you photograph every-thing, and I mean everything. Once the bones are removed, Kar-ringa will have the site dug up and those photos and films will be the only corroborating evidence left to support stratigraphic da-ting. When you get the material here, we'll carry out a rigorous analysis and announce the find. Do it by the book."

"I get to publish the paper?" Krafter demanded, unwilling to be railroaded into doing all the grunt work and have Perkins reap the glory, controversy more probably. As a rising academic, and he liked to consider himself as one, getting published was every-thing. Any notoriety that came his way would merely be a bonus.

Perkins spread his hands in surrender. "The thing is all yours, but be careful what you wish for."

* * *

17

When Krafter left, Perkins leaned back in his chair and smiled with wry amusement. The boy had no respect for authority or the cultured image he should project. He had sponsored Krafter's PhD program and sat on his convocation, liking the seditious streak and a sharp, incisive mind the youngster displayed, although some did not. His thesis, *An analysis of early Pleistocene humans in the Americas*, caused an understandable stir in the paleoanthropological community around the world, but Krafter's research was solid and the evidence irrefutable.

Krafter contended that by the time the Beringia land bridge migrations across the Bering Strait took place, those people found North America already populated. Modern man not only inhabited the Americas 60,000 years ago, but did so originally by moving north from South America and left verifiable artifacts that biostratigraphic and radiometric dating had validated—however unpalatable the results for some and damaging to established dogma of the accepted human evolutionary path.

The fact that existing migratory theory was based on tenuous, sweeping assumptions, and a pitiful handful of unearthed fragments and campfire campsites, meant no never mind to the establishment, whose view is that science only grows, it does not backtrack. If a new discovery showed that modern science had made a major mistake and massive backtracking is indeed required, the discovery must be wrong, and that's what Krafter's critics maintained.

If Krafter's migratory theory hadn't been enough, he stirred the pot properly by announcing that the Clovis asteroid could not have wiped out the North American indigenous population 12,900 years ago as claimed by most researchers. Although significant portions of the continent and its wildlife were wiped out by the resulting firestorm, contrary to currently held belief, most inhabitants survived. Krafter maintained that this was largely due to an already established population base that took root 60,000 years ago. The continent's varied geography made it impossible for the catastrophe to wipe out everything, and his analysis of the Black Mat Layer seemed to support his theory.

If nothing else, his papers made for interesting reading.

The boy's problem was not his research or methodology, but lack of opportunities to expand himself and his horizons. Although a great institution, the University of Wyoming was simply inadequate for Krafter's inquiring mind, and Perkins intended shoving his protégé out of his comfortable nest at the earliest opportunity. The Karringa find could be exactly the opportunity he looked for to make Krafter stretch his wings. Like Icarus, he needed to be mindful of the heat.

Perkins understood the workings of a rebel mind. He'd had several options along his own career path to become a pure scientist, but he found early that he wanted to run things, be an administrator, and very good at it. Rick Larson was retiring as department director, and Perkins already had the nod from the university Trustees and the president to replace him. That would be good on a personal level, but his job was not only to look after the university's interests, but also nurture rising talent. If Krafter remained here, he would wither and die, something Perkins would make sure did not happen.

He understood completely the younger man's parochial position as he picked up his mug and stood up. A good cup of coffee would get his mind back into gear and off Krafter's bone.

* * *

Wings steady, the twin-engine Beechcraft turbo-prop sank quickly toward the Gillette-Campbell County Airport's north-south runway. The pilot feathered the props and Krafter removed his earplugs. Shouldering the horizon on either side loomed the Bighorn Mountains in the west and the Black Hills in the east. Gillette itself lay four miles farther south from the airport on the gently rolling Powder River Basin plateau. As the aircraft came in, he noted the huge black gashes of open pit and strip mines, and marveled at the volume of coal here. He knew the raw numbers, but they lacked the visual impact. Most of northeastern Wyoming was one giant deposit. If they dug for another hundred years, there would still be coal left.

The aircraft touched down with a scrape of tires and the empty grassland on either side of the runway rushed by. The Beechcraft turned right onto a taxiway and bumped its way toward a small L-shaped terminal building. A security guard met the passengers as they alighted, while baggage handlers pushed caged trolleys toward the idling aircraft. Carrying a black leather bag of toiletries and change of clothing, Krafter squinted at the bright blue sky, enjoying the pleasant warmth, and followed a ragged group of eight fellow passengers into the terminal, ending the comfortable fifty-minute flight.

He collected his tools suitcase and wheeled it through the double sliding glass panels, and raised a hand at the first cab waiting in a row of three. The yellow cab pulled up beside him and the driver stepped out, manhandling the suitcase into the trunk without being asked. Krafter got into the front seat and strapped in.

When he got in, the cabbie immediately pulled away and headed for the US-16 entrance.

"Where to, buddy?" he demanded, pausing to check the traffic before entering the highway.

"Americas Best Value Inn," Krafter told him and settled back, his ears still buzzing from propeller noise.

"Right. First time in Gillette?"

"First time."

"You a mining engineer or something? You don't look to me like a mine grunt."

"Actually, I am a professor at UW."

"Laramie, eh? Not much action up here, doc, not unless you're in the mining business."

"Just doing a bit of archaeology."

"A fossil hunter, eh? There are a couple of interesting curio shops in town, doc. You might care to take a look at one. Miners sometimes find a neat piece of something or other in a coal seam and the tourists, when one does show up, lap up the stuff."

"I'll keep it in mind."

The driver nodded and Gillette's sprawl grew larger, the engine making a drowsy hum to the whisper of tires. Nothing stirred on the lonely stretch of highway. The town had some light industry, coal, and a bit of uranium mining, and that was it.

Krafter considered the idea of visiting one of those curio shops, but probably wouldn't get a chance to do it. Whatever he bought might make a distracting item on his mantelpiece at home, but as a serious object of study, without an evidence trail or photographs where found, the thing would be useless. Still, his return flight wasn't until 11:20 tomorrow and there might be time to look around, provided he finished his work at Karringa.

The cab crossed the rail line at E. Echeta Street gently curving left into E. 2nd Street, and pulled into the driveway of a blue and white double-story motel, stopping under the lobby portico. Two sedans stood parked in an otherwise empty lot. The driver got out and unloaded the suitcase.

Outside, Krafter stretched his arms and breathed deeply of the crisp air, a fine day for digging.

The cabbie slammed the trunk shut and walked up to him. "That's fifteen-fifty, doc."

Krafter handed over two tens. "If you're not busy, can you wait ten minutes? I need to get to Karringa Mine."

"Karringa, eh? I'll wait for you, doc. You'll want a ride back?"

"I will, but I don't know how long I'll be there."

"No problem." The cabbie dug out a business card and held it out. "Call when you're ready."

"Say, that's great…Markus," Krafter said, reading the name on the card. "Thanks."

The cabbie grinned. "Wouldn't want a greenhorn like you getting lost. Bad for business."

"It shows, eh?" Krafter said and pointed at his equipment bag. "Might as well put the suitcase back in. I'll be needing it."

"You got it."

Inside the small but modern reception office, Krafter showed the young receptionist his booking printout. While she checked her computer, he filled in the registration card.

"Room 109, sir," she chirped and slid a brass key held on a large fish-shaped metal plate. Stamped on it in bold gold letters was the room number and the Best Value Inn address, with the usual blurb to mail the key if found.

"Thanks."

"Have a pleasant day," she said mechanically and went back to her computer.

Krafter pocketed the key, picked up his black bag and walked toward the narrow stairs. In the orange-carpeted corridor, he checked which way the numbers went and turned left. Unlocking his room, he dropped the bag beside the small writing table pushed against a draped window, and reached for the phone. Checking the number and name he had written on a slip of paper at UW, he quickly dialed.

"Trantor Coal Company, Karringa Mine, Sandra speaking."

"Hi, Sandra. This is Professor Larry Krafter from the University of Wyoming."

"Professor Krafter! We've been expecting you, sir. Do you wish to speak to Mr. Ferguson?"

"No, thank you. I don't want to disturb him, but if you could please tell him that I'll be there in about twenty minutes, that would be great."

"Of course, sir. I'll let him know."

Satisfied that Karringa had things organized, he locked up and hurried down the stairs, not bothering with the elevator. After handing in the key, he walked out quickly and got into the waiting cab.

Markus kept a running commentary of Gillette's sterling attractions, such as the Heritage Center, Skatepark, Powder River Symphony and the like, all the way up US-16 and Wyoming 59 going north that linked every mine. They passed the small Dry Fork Mine and the cab slowed when a prominent green sign indicated the Karringa exit half a mile ahead.

Krafter didn't mind the tourist info and hardly paid attention, his eyes fixed on glimpses of mine workings on his left. Half-mile-long trains hauled loaded cars to Gillette and beyond. Seeing it from the air simply did not convey the emotional impact and overwhelming scale of what went on here.

A uniformed security guard stepped out of his little fibro hut when the cab crossed the rail line and pulled up in front of the boom gate. Krafter got out and waited beside the cab.

"Can I help you, sir?" the guard inquired pleasantly, right hand hovering close to the holstered handgun.

"Professor Larry Krafter to see Mr. Ferguson."

"Ah, been expecting you, sir. If I can have some identification, please?"

Krafter pulled out his wallet and handed over the UW ID badge. The guard glanced at it and nodded.

"Please wait here, sir. Someone will be along shortly," he said and walked back into the hut.

When Krafter turned, Markus had already unloaded the suitcase. Krafter paid him off and Marcus climbed into the cab.

"Don't forget to call!"

The car reversed, turned around, and sped toward W-59. As Krafter stood beside the suitcase, feeling conspicuous, he studied what he could see of the mine layout. A wide concrete road led toward a three-story building and two smaller single-story structures next to a full parking lot. Judging by the utility trucks and vans, the complex still under construction. Some two hundred yards farther down stood four tall concrete silos. On their left a shorter silo fed coal into a rail car. Beyond the buildings, he could see a length of exposed overburden wall, excavators, and moving trucks. The air had a distinctive smell of coal and raw oil.

A battered white Ford pickup came roaring up the road and squealed to a stop next to the security hut. A stocky, powerful man, clean-shaven, black hair disheveled, stepped out and walked toward the boom gate. The security guard came out and followed.

The man stopped before Krafter, grinned, and stuck out his hand. "Jackson Cower. I'm the mine engineer," he said pleasantly and pointed at the suitcase. "That's all you got?"

"Everything I need is in there, Mr. Cower," Krafter responded, liking the rugged-looking engineer.

"Call me Jack, Professor."

"And I'm Larry."

"Fine." Without turning, Cower held out his hand. The guard gave him a blue badge with an alligator clip and Cower offered it to Krafter. "Keep it pinned on at all times."

Krafter clipped the badge to his shirt pocket and reached for the heavy suitcase.

"Here, let me have that," Cower said, grabbed the suitcase, and with a grunt, heaved it into the pickup. "What's in there? Bricks?"

Krafter grinned as he walked toward the pickup. "Photo equipment and my toolkit."

"Could have fooled me. Okay, let's go. Thanks, George." Cower waved to the guard and got into the car. When Krafter got in, the car turned around and headed down the road.

"Quite a setup," Krafter commented, eyeing the workings.

"It'll be more comfortable once they finish all the construction," Cower growled. "We'll see Ferguson first, then I'll take you to the find. Afterward, you can decide what to do with the thing, but don't wait too long as we got to clear the seam."

The pickup rounded a gentle left bend and slowed as they

approached a collection of four prefab huts beside a small make-shift parking lot full of all types of cars, most of them the worse for wear. Krafter gaped at the open strip mine spread before him.

"Wow," he said reverently, and Cower grinned.

"They all say that, but compared to some of the more established workings up the road and south of Gillette, Karringa is still small cheese. Come back in two years and you'll really see something."

If this was small cheese, Krafter could only imagine what a couple of square miles of exposed coal seam looked like. Where did all that coal go?

Cower got out and walked toward the largest prefab. Krafter hurried after him. Inside, the open plan interior filled with half a dozen occupied office desks, computers, filing cabinets, a potted plant or two, seemed bigger than he expected. Some of the staff looked up and gave him the usual examination one gave a stranger. Cower stopped before a wide desk and nodded to a pretty brunette.

"Sandra, please tell the boss that Professor Krafter is here."

Krafter saw her looking at him with an appraising eye. He had seen such looks from some of his students: undergrads and master's candidates. He knew his features were hard, his form tall, and his body muscled. He wasn't attending aikido training for nothing. A vain thing, he knew, but he also knew that he was young enough for it to matter.

"Of course," she said, picked up her phone, and pressed a button on the multi-function keyboard. "They're here…Right." She replaced the phone and looked up. "You can go right in."

Cower nodded and strode toward one of two offices tucked against the back of the prefab. Without bothering to knock, he opened the right door and walked in. When Krafter stepped in, Cower closed the door after him. The man behind the cluttered desk stood up, took a pipe out of his mouth and offered his hand.

"Glad you could make it, Professor," he boomed in a powerful voice accustomed to command. "Please sit down. You will have to excuse the primitive conditions, but we're still setting things up as you might have seen."

Krafter clasped the firm dry hand and squeezed lightly. "This is comfort compared to some of the digs I've been on, Mr. Ferguson."

"Just, Amos, doc. I must say, you don't look at all like my image of a distinguished professor," Ferguson added, sat down, and stuck the pipe into his mouth.

Krafter looked directly into the deep gray eyes, chiseled clean features, determined carriage, and wasn't at all fooled. The mine manager was intelligent, worldly-wise, used to dealing with company politics and tough plain men. Krafter pulled back a dark blue cloth chair and made himself comfortable. Ferguson was clearly busy, but his genuine friendliness put Krafter at ease.

"Beard, flowing white hair and thick glasses?"

Ferguson laughed. "Something like that. No reflection on you, however. On the contrary, after Dr. Perkins told me you were coming, I did a bit of digging up on you."

"And you're still nice to me?"

Ferguson laughed again and Cower chuckled. "You seem to know your business and that's all that matters to me. Given some of your controversial papers, which is again your business, what we have here should be right up your alley."

"I've seen the photographs you sent to Dr. Perkins, but I admit to being dubious about an apparent human bone dug up in an Eocene Roland Seam."

"I don't blame you, but this isn't a gag, doc, or I wouldn't have bothered calling the university. The thing might hold some interest for the academia, but it's a damned nuisance for me, and it's stopping scheduled work. As you know, the whole Powder River Basin has yielded some interesting archaeological pieces from time to time. This one happens to be somewhat more interesting than most, and we have a policy to cooperate with UW."

"A forty-million-year-old human bone? I'll say it's more interesting. How much time will you give me to look things over?"

"You have twenty-four hours. After that, my dozers move in, ready or not."

"Fair enough. Once I see the site, I'll have a better idea what I am up against. I understand Trantor Coal and your parent, Relans Mining Corporation, waive all rights to ownership?"

"That's right. We made our legal position clear to Dr. Perkins."

"Fine. In that case—"

"Jack will take you down to the site. The area has been flagged off and make sure you stay there. There are dozers clearing the overburden and I don't want an industrial accident on my hands having you run over."

"I understand, sir, and I appreciate your cooperation," Krafter said and stood up.

"By the way, have you had lunch or anything? We have a canteen in one of the huts here that's pretty good, and runs all day."

"Thanks. I wouldn't mind taking you up on that a bit later, but I want to see the site first, if that's all right?"

"Not a problem. Take him away, Jack, and bring him back in one piece."

"You got it, boss."

Back in the pickup, Cower drove quickly along a narrow track toward the newly cleared overburden wall. Krafter could clearly hear the throaty bellow of bulldozers at work.

"What we're driving on now is old overburden spoilage," Cower said without turning his head. "Once we clean out a section of seam, we cast blast a new section of overburden into the worked pit floor, exposing more seam which keeps us in business. We crab up and edgewise all the time, and we'll keep doing it until we've worked the entire lease or Relans manages to get us more."

"What do you do to the land after all the coal's been dug up?"

"We re-vegetate it; plant trees, grassland, and make ponds. There is no way to make the ground look exactly how we found it, not after all the tons of coal that's already been removed. That won't happen for a while. I don't know what other companies are doing, but here, we'll rehabilitate the land as we go. Besides, trees will make the place smell better." Cower smiled at some private joke Krafter didn't get, and re-vegetation was environmentally a sound idea. The whole area now looked like something out of Dante's *Inferno*.

A couple of hundred yards ahead, Krafter gaped at the towering dragline excavator and its monstrous arm that would maneuver the actual bucket. Temporary metal sheds presumably held parts and human facilities. Among parked cars and trucks, people walked about, antlike in the shadow of the metal giant. He glanced at Cower, who smiled.

"We've been waiting for that beast to be assembled for the last nine months. It should be up and running in about six to eight weeks. Once it's up, its job will be clearing virgin overburden."

As he stared at the machine, Krafter realized that in mining, everything was big.

The pickup stopped and Cower invited Krafter to get out. They walked about forty feet straight ahead until they reached a cliff face. Cower pointed across the worked pit floor below.

"On the other side is the new overburden bench being cleared and where we found the bone."

Krafter peered at the three dozers pushing rock, shale, and lignite over the already blasted overburden, exposing the black coal bed, ready for extraction. Fifty yards or so farther back loomed a ninety-foot wall of rock and dirt, marked by clearly defined colored strata layers. Behind the dozers in the partially cleared bed, protruded a small island of rock and lignite, surrounded by little fluttering flags. In the clearing stood a hut. A uniformed security guard walked casually within the flagged perimeter. Krafter was about to ask why the need for a guard when the obvious answer presented itself. Thorough, Ferguson clearly understood the importance of the bone. On his left, a bucket wheel excavator, looking huge despite the distance, worked the already exposed coalface, feeding a stream of enormous trucks. The very air hummed with power and machinery noises.

Cower walked back to the pickup, climbed onto the flat tray and opened a large steel chest. He lifted out a yellow coverall and heavy boots.

"Take off your shirt and pants, and put these on," he ordered and threw down a yellow hardhat. "Don't walk around without it." He also held out a pair of orange ear protectors. "You might need them."

Krafter changed, pinned on his visitor badge, and donned the hardhat. The tough steel-capped boots were a size too large, but he wasn't about to complain. Cower put on a hardhat and squeezed himself into a yellow vest with white vertical luminescent strips, then grabbed the heavy suitcase. He jumped down, heaved down the case and started walking toward the cliff face that angled slightly right along a narrow track that led to the cast bed.

A seventy-foot descent, Krafter was glad he didn't have to lug the suitcase. The sound of working dozers very loud and the air stank of diesel fumes. They were busy pushing soil way on his right and unless he deliberately walked out of the flagged area, he figured he would be okay. Krafter moved quickly over the uneven newly exposed coal bed as he followed the engineer to the fibro hut, clearly there to provide the guard some shelter.

"Good afternoon, Mr. Cower," the heavy guard said politely

and nodded, then looked curiously at Krafter.

The engineer put down the suitcase and flexed his fingers. "How's it going, Marv?"

"No sweat, Mr. Cower."

"This is Professor Krafter from the University of Wyoming. He's here to look at our find."

The guard touched his hat. "Pleased to meet you, sir."

"Okay, doc. This way," Cower said and walked behind the hut.

Pulse racing slightly, hands sweating, Krafter hurried after him. Not many paleoanthropologists got to see a history-breaking discovery like this and he appreciated the unique opportunity. The sites he'd been to so far were caves, burial grounds, and remnants of ancient campsites. Everything had to be inferred and extrapolated from scraps of cloth, pottery or bits of charcoal, akin to looking at history through a thick pane of frosted glass. What he would see now was not an extrapolation, but something real and tangible—he hoped. The idea that he might be a victim of some practical gag still lingered at the back of his mind. When he rounded the corner, he stopped in shock and stared. Instead of an ancient revelation, the only thing he saw was a large green tarpaulin draped over a broken nine-foot high lignite face.

Cower smiled at Krafter's startled reaction and started climbing the face along a narrow ledge. "We need to take that down. Care to give me a hand?"

Getting over his surprise, Krafter scrambled after him. Of course they would have the thing protected and covered. Cower removed two heavy steel H beams holding down the tarp and grabbed a corner. Krafter got the idea and took the other corner. They lifted the tarp and heaved it over the edge.

Krafter clambered to the bottom and hurried eagerly toward the plastic-wrapped object protruding slightly from the solid coalface. The bent bracelet, it had to be gold judging by the buttery color, shimmered and flowed under bright sunshine, and the dark gray bone seemed to beckon in a promise of further revelations. Impatient to get his hands on it, to touch it, to connect with impossible history, he turned to Cower and nodded approvingly.

"Excellent thinking, Jack, covering the thing," he said warmly, voice raw with emotion as time held open a bridge to him.

"Well, we didn't want the boys pawing it," Cower growled, sensitive to what this moment meant for Krafter.

Krafter smiled, leaned forward and peered closely at the bone and bracelet, his mask of detached professionalism back in place. It looked exactly as the photographs showed. He could dismiss the photos easily enough, modern graphics software could fake anything, but they were detached, impersonal, nothing to connect with. Being here, looking at the real thing altogether different and his guts tightened.

Lignite beds everywhere were natural plant fossil treasure troves. If a piece of bone can be found here, he wondered what other priceless evidence was casually destroyed by lumbering machines in mines and excavations the world over. Whether he liked it or not, this find appeared genuine, however impossible. Modern humans walking the Earth millions of years ago? That took some swallowing. Hell, half a dozen evolutionary cycles could have come and gone in that period. Would successive cycles necessarily produce the same human form? Then again, man's skeletal engineering and appearance dictated by adaptive function, not aesthetics. Why couldn't an ancient hand bone have the characteristics of a modern *radius*? They both served the same mechanical purpose.

He stepped back and studied the exposed overburden wall towering on his left, and squinted at the various strata. He would need samples, lots of them, and his stock of specimen flasks might not be enough.

"Will you be okay here, doc?" Cower ventured as he peered

at Krafter's vacant, absorbed expression.

Already in a world all his own, Krafter turned. "It will take me a while to set myself up and film everything, but I'll need help to dig out the bone. That will have to be done as a solid block. I don't want it removed from its casing of coal. I could also use something like a cherry picker to get soil and rock samples off the main overburden wall strata."

"No problem. Get Marv to call me when you need someone."

"Thanks for everything, Jack. I mean it."

"My pleasure. Have fun."

They shook hands and Cower walked to the guard who stood there watching them. Cower said something to him, slapped his shoulder and hurried toward the trail leading up the cliff.

"Care for a soda or a drink of water, Professor?" Marv asked diffidently.

"Say, that would be great. Some water, please, and call me Larry."

"Yes, sir. Be a minute," Marv said and disappeared into the hut. A few moments later, he came out holding a glass of water.

Krafter took a long swallow and sighed. "You got a fridge in there?"

"Mr. Ferguson wanted us to be comfortable."

"Us?"

"There are six of us on four-hour shifts."

A twenty-four-hour watch? Krafter was impressed. He finished the water and handed back the glass.

"Thanks. I needed that."

Keen to start work, he moved to his suitcase, laid it down, opened it and pushed back the lid. Methodically, he started removing the contents. He mounted a JVC memory card camcorder on a small telescopic tripod. He then lifted two extendable metal measuring rods, followed by a 30cm by 30cm steel box that contained his glass flasks set in a foam cushion. He used glass exclusively to avoid contaminating the samples, other materials invariably leaving a molecular trace that could compromise sensitive dating techniques.

In this case, dating the overburden wall and the lignite would not be a problem. The U.S. Geological Survey and the Wyoming State Geological Survey offices had undisputed dating data for the entire area, but he had to be thorough and wanted independent validation. He then took out a plastic box that had his working tools: small hammer, trowel, brushes, and pegs. The last things were two meter-long graduated poles, each able to be extended in sections to five meters.

Done, he carried the camera tripod to the flagged perimeter. Switching on the camcorder, he slowly panned the entire site, taking plenty of close-up shots. Setting the camera to its photo mode, he took stills of everything. Glancing at Marv sipping a Sprite, the guard seemed to be watching the proceedings with interest.

Krafter took the graduated poles to the overburden wall, mindful of the roaring dozers, and stuck one into the ground. From his toolbox, he took out a hammer and two galvanized pegs, which he drove into the wall, then laid the other pole across them, making an inverted L. He shifted the camera closer to the face and took more shots, lingering over each strata layer as he panned up. Humming contentedly, unaware that he was doing it, he repeated the process with the lignite face holding the bone. In his element, buoyed by the discovery and eager to share it with the world, Perkins' warning forgotten. This was anthropology he loved and the reason he went into it.

Finished, he delicately removed the plastic wrap, careful not to touch the bone, totally absorbed in what he was doing. Using more pegs, he placed a metal measuring rod above and below the find, then took more film and pictures.

Glancing at his watch, surprised to see it almost three p.m. He had been at it for two hours. Happy with his work, he walked to the guard.

"Marv, please call Mr. Cower and ask him if I can have two men with drilling equipment. I also need a large padded packing box, approximately two feet a side."

"Will do, Professor," Marv said and reached for his cell-phone.

As he waited for the men, Krafter went back to the overburden wall and started taking samples, diligently labeling each one, recording everything on film and his notepad. Samples from higher up, he would do after he got the bone out. After a few minutes, he heard a car and looked up. A white pickup appeared on top of the cliff and two men stepped out, looking small from the coal bench level. They opened the tray door and dragged out a small pneumatic drill and portable compressor. Between them, they lugged the stuff down.

"Where do you want to start digging, doc?" the shorter of the two demanded when they got to the hut and Krafter pointed to the top of the coal seam.

"We'll start there. I want to go down above the bone and remove loose stuff as we go."

"Okay, and this is for you," the main said and held out a small brown paper bag. "Compliments of Mr. Cower."

Puzzled, Krafter took the package and opened it. Wrapped in cling wrap was a thick sandwich. He looked at the man and laughed.

"That was very thoughtful of him."

The small man shrugged. "He didn't want you dying on us, doc." With a glance at his partner, they manhandled the compressor and drill up the face.

Krafter unwrapped the sandwich and took a hungry bite, turkey and cheese by the taste. Munching, he climbed after them. While they set themselves up, he leaned over the edge to check the position of the bone. Sandwich in one hand, he used a rock to scratch lines in a rectangular U where he wanted the cuts. Not very technical, but it would do the job. After he scrambled back down, he wrapped the protruding bone with the original plastic wrap. Silly when he thought about it, as the thing could not get contaminated further from having more coal dust over it. An instinctive reaction and he could not ignore his training. Importantly, he didn't want the sample contaminated by touching it, leaving behind all sorts of fatty deposits and fluids, albeit in microscopic quantities. Enough to potentially compromise the dating process.

The short man started the generator and the other picked up the drill. Krafter put on ear protectors he'd been given and waited.

"Go in six inches at a time!" Krafter yelled over the racket and the man nodded. He took two more hurried bites of the sandwich. From what he had seen, the cast blast shock had pretty much reduced the lignite seam to manageable rubble—for a bulldozer, but not loose enough to dig with a shovel. He hurried to get the camera and his toolbox, leaving the sandwich on the ground, and climbed to the top of the mound.

The drill made a horrendous pounding noise as it bit into the soft coal, and the drill bit went in with hardly any resistance. Replacing the bit with a broad spade attachment made short work of loosening the debris. Krafter turned off the camera, slid his index finger across his throat, and the compressor died. He took off the ear protectors and nodded.

After taking close-up shots, he used his hammer and trowel to lift out solid pieces of brown coal and fine debris. Two more drilling sessions produced a foot-deep cavity. Painstaking examination of excavated material revealed nothing but coal. He looked at the two men and pointed at the hole.

"What I want now is a groove along the edge of the hole a foot or so deep. We'll then cut beneath the bone fragment and lift out the whole thing. Can you do that?"

The two men exchanged glances and shrugged.

"Piece of cake, doc," the short man growled.

The groove done, the men brought down the equipment and quickly cut into the seam some eight inches below the bone, the job made slightly harder as the driller had to hold the heavy drill at shoulder level. Using the drill shovel bit, they levered the block of coal until it gave way with a crack and muffled groan as it lifted slightly. Krafter filmed everything, watching anxiously as the men carefully extracted the block and placed it next to the hut. On the ground, the block of coal looked pathetically insignificant. At the same time, it also represented professional danger and inevitable controversy. Krafter wondered whether getting to write the paper on the find, he had gotten the short end of the deal.

"Doc?"

Krafter looked up and swung his head to where the short man pointed. At the back of the hole protruded a smooth convex shape.

"What's that?" the man asked.

"Not sure," Krafter murmured, walked to the face, frowned and bit his lip.

He recognized the thing and quickly unscrewed the camera from the tripod and stepped to the cavity. One of the vertical drill grooves had come dangerously close to the protrusion. Hardly able to contain himself, he carefully took shots from several angles. Using a trowel and brush, he delicately removed loose material, leaving no doubt in his mind. He had himself a skull. This was incontestable proof that even his most vitriolic critics could not refute. There was always a possibility that the hand bone could be something other than human, however unlikely—why put a bracelet on an animal—but no one could dismiss a skull, if it *was* human. It might be anything, but judging by the shape he could see, it definitely looked *sapien*.

Bollinger and Maddson, eat your heart out.

"More digging, doc?" the short man asked with a wry smile.

Krafter gave him a sheepish grin and nodded. "I'm afraid so.

Cut a groove another six inches below the edge as deep as you can go. Okay?"

With the cut done, he hammered out the pieces, checking for more bone fragments. Immensely satisfied, wanting to shout with glee at the discovery, he took the camera and his tools to the top again while the men heaved up the equipment. After marking out a square around the skull's position, he ordered the men to start cutting. The work finished in minutes, Krafter had himself another block of coal.

Elated but weary, he checked his watch: 4:30. No wonder he felt tired…and still hungry. He picked up the remains of his sandwich and resumed munching. There could be more bones in the seam, but he'd had enough for the day. Even if he found nothing else, his reputation was made, one way or another. Would Perkins support him when it might mean the find could threaten his own position and tenure? He wanted to think that his superior was above such foolishness, but could he bank on that? His critics were also supposed to be objective scientists, but it didn't stop them from being foolish. Could he expect *any* support from UW? This was the ugly side of academia, a side he only dimly understood, and liked even less. He didn't know anything right now and useless getting anxious.

Without being told, the two men went back to the pickup and returned with two packing cartons.

"You guys are mind readers," Krafter told them warmly, stuffing the sandwich wrapper and bag into his pocket.

"Mr. Cower always allows for contingencies," the short man said with a grin and opened his box. Krafter was pleasantly startled to see inside sheets of three-inch gray padding foam.

"Excellent!"

He picked up the box and brought it beside the skull block. After lining the bottom and sides with foam, he had the guys lower the block into the box. He squeezed more foam into the gaps, placed a layer on top and folded the flaps. The other block received the same treatment. Confident that the boxes would survive handling and a flight intact, he walked to Marv and pointed at the cartons.

"Do you mind if we leave them in the hut overnight?"

"Not a problem, Professor. They'll be secure here. Finished?"

"For the day," Krafter said and exhaled loudly. "I haven't worked this hard in a while."

"Doc, if you want to do more digging tomorrow," the short man pointed out, "we'll leave our stuff here also, if that's okay?"

"Good idea. My thanks for everything."

"Part of the job, doc. If you're going back, we'll give you a lift. Your clothes are in the pickup."

"Great! Let me put my tools away and I'll be right with you."

Krafter left his tools suitcase in the hut, having removed the SanDisk memory card from the camcorder, not wanting to take any chances with it. He followed the two miners up the cliff. Standing beside the pickup, he changed and climbed into the cabin. Grimy, and his hands were streaked black, a shower at the motel would fix that. When he sat down, he let out a long breath and the short man grinned at him as he started the engine.

Sandra looked up as Krafter walked into the prefab office and beamed.

"Did you have a good day, sir?"

"Outstanding. Is Mr. Ferguson in?"

"I'll let him know you're here." She picked up the phone and punched a button. "Mr. Ferguson? Dr. Krafter is here…Very well." She nodded and gave him another sunny smile. "You can go right in."

"Thanks." He dug out Marcus' card and gave it to her. "Can you please call this number and ask Marcus to pick me up? If he's not available, any cab will do."

"Of course. Will you be staying long in Gillette?"

"Afraid not. I'm flying back to Laramie tomorrow morning."

"Oh. Will you be coming back?"

Krafter gave a short laugh, puzzled at what she was getting at, his mind totally distracted by the day's events. "Not unless you locate another bone."

"Well, good luck."

He nodded to her, walked to the mine manager's office, knocked once and opened the door.

"Ah, Professor! All done?" Ferguson extended a hand at a chair and Krafter gratefully sank into it, feeling as if he had been worked over. And he believed he was fit! His *sensei* would be disappointed.

"Almost, and we've unearthed another find, a possible human skull."

"A skull? I imagine the thing is invaluable."

"Priceless, but it might be a mixed blessing when I publish."

"Your headache. I'm just glad that you had a successful day. What are your plans now?"

"Well, I thought that tomorrow, I would dig farther around the immediate site. There could be more bone fragments, but I'll be out of your hair before ten regardless. I also need to take some strata samples off the overburden wall."

"We run two eight-hour shifts here. If you want to come in early, someone will be here to help you."

"You're very generous, Mr. Ferguson, and thanks. I'll do that."

"It's settled, then. I'll inform security to expect you."

Chapter Two

The cab took a right from E. 3rd Street into E. Lewis, and accelerated smoothly with the traffic toward the University of Wyoming campus. Warm and sunny, only a few clouds marred a pristine blue sky. Krafter's legs and shoulders ached from unaccustomed exercise, but he also felt a deep glow of satisfaction. His muscles might be protesting and his mind buzzed with torrents of ideas, work required to clean and date the bones, an announcement paper to be written and submitted, and inevitable skepticism and ridicule to be faced, but none of that could remove the overwhelming fact of his discovery.

His critics can scoff and rant, and that is all they could do. The bones would be available for independent inspection to anyone, even Bollinger, if the venerated sage wanted to tear himself away from Harvard's hallowed halls. Maddson might condescend to make an appearance from Stanford, but Krafter didn't care. He would post everything on the UW website, for some to either gloat or grind their teeth. For others outside the field, they would read his publication and wonder not only at the find itself and the impact on human origins, but also at the childish goings on of the anthropological community. The very image of Bollinger and Maddson grinding their teeth with seething frustration made Krafter eager to make his announcement.

Regrettable that two such otherwise fine minds refused to apply the scientific method and accept factual evidence when presented to them, all for the sake of protecting reputations. He found it even harder to understand acquiescence of this behavior from respectable institutions such as Harvard and Stanford, until he remembered what Perkins once said. Universities were run by people who would rather give up a child than have their wedded ideas and theories discredited.

If he wanted to survive and succeed in his chosen field, the quicker he shed his naiveté and idealism, and developed a hard shell of predatory self-interest, the better. Krafter always found this aspect of academic politics and professional infighting unsettling, blighting the credibility of the entire scientific establishment. Tested in the same crucible himself, Perkins had quietly taken him aside and gently instructed him in the finer points of career assassination. Krafter would be wise to brush up on Sun Tzu's maxims. Perhaps a graduate course could be introduced in the art, he mused wryly.

At least he knew the face of his enemies.

But those lessons were theory, and Krafter found real life altogether different. Unlike karate or aikido where one practiced in a dojo, a street attack had little resemblance to the stylized moves executed against fellow students. Only a game…

The thing was, he didn't want to play it. Not with their rules. He wanted to be a scientist, reaching into the unknown, adding to the sum of man's knowledge, and expected his peers to behave accordingly. Give him a technical challenge or a puzzle uncovered at a dig, he was in his element. Dealing with the human dimension always left him feeling inadequate, out of his depth. Perhaps Perkins had something when he advised brushing up on Sun Tzu. After all, science was blind and impersonal, without prejudice or jealousy. It took men to inject that.

Philosophizing was okay, but right now, he had work to do, glad to be back home.

After a very early start that morning, when all he wanted was sleep, muscles protesting, he took a cab to Karringa Mine and the shift boss gave him two men to do more digging. As he drove Krafter to the motel last night, Marcus laughed at the idea of picking him up at six-thirty in the morning. There were limits, he said, but he did arrange for someone else to come. Krafter could hardly blame the man. After a shower and a quiet dinner, watching dusk fall, he wondered if Sandra had offered to take him out and he was too obtuse to take the hint. Well, he had blown it properly, but he wouldn't have cheated on Elena in exchange for one diverting evening.

As he stood on top of the lignite seam beneath a clear sky, breathing crisp air and the prospect of making further discoveries, got his blood pumping. Unfortunately, apart from unearthing two finger bones and a single vertebrae, nothing else remained of the skeleton. If anything had been there the cast blast or the bulldozers probably removed it. Krafter was not disappointed. What he had already more than made up for not finding anything else. Ferguson dismissed his profuse thanks, but he suspected the mine manager was glad to see him go, something he understood perfectly. He didn't know whether operational delays caused by his presence had cost Ferguson and the mine money, but Krafter would make sure that Karringa remained enshrined in history books forever.

As it reached the corner of 12th Street, the cab pulled in front of the Anthropology Building. He paid the driver and the two of them manhandled the specimen boxes and his suitcase inside. Giving him a wave of acknowledgment when Krafter thanked him for his help, the driver got into the cab and drove off, trailing a thread of blue smoke from the exhaust pipe.

Krafter took out the cellphone from his jacket pocket, selected a number from the contact list, and pressed the dial button.

"Dr. Perkins," Krafter's mentor answered after four rings.

"It's Larry, Adam. I'm downstairs, but I need help with some boxes."

"I'll have someone down with a flat trolley," Perkins said and switched off.

Several students wandered by, going into the building and coming out, giving him and his assorted baggage curious stares along the way. A lot of them were munching sandwiches or fruit and Krafter hoped he would not have another day without lunch. Looking at the students, he didn't recognize anyone. It wasn't surprising. He mostly taught undergraduate classes and a couple of master's subjects, and did not expect to see somebody he knew. His youngsters would have disappeared for their summer vacations without waiting for the ink to dry on the last exam paper or assignment. Dressed like a kid himself, he still saw his students as youngsters. But then, a vast gulf existed between an undergrad and a PhD, no matter how young looking.

The elevator doors opened and a familiar lab technician emerged pushing a trolley. He spotted Krafter and nodded.

"Hi, Spiro!" Krafter called out as he picked up his suitcase and black bag.

Thin, single, in his early thirties and very competent, Spiro wrote science fiction stories in his spare time, several published. He knew as much about paleoanthropology as some PhDs. When Krafter asked the older man why he never went for his master's, Spiro simply smiled his engaging small smile and shrugged. He enjoyed what he did, and seeing what went on among the faculty, he didn't care much for it. Krafter couldn't argue with him there, but pointed out that unless he was content to remain a technician, a master's degree would come in handy. Spiro never said anything and did not apply for the course.

"Afternoon, Professor. Doing a bit of traveling?"

"Digging," Krafter said and placed the bag and suitcase on the trolley. Spiro tried to lift one of the specimen boxes and grunted in surprise at the weight. "Here, let me help you with that." Krafter picked up one end and they heaved the box onto the trolley. Spiro made sure the second box was secure, and pushed the trolley toward the elevator. Krafter could tell the man was curious, but showing admirable restraint, refrained from doing the obvious. Krafter promised himself to get Spiro working on cleaning the specimens, which should satisfy his curiosity.

On the third floor, Krafter told Spiro to go to Lab Three and the technician raised his eyebrows, waiting for Krafter to correct his mistake. Most specimens brought in from the field were cleaned and prepared for detailed analysis and dating in Lab Two. Lab Three was a restricted area, off limits to most students, that stored Dr. Larson's personal haul of fossils, mineral specimens, and hominid fragments, including replicas of some world-famous skulls. Charles Dawson's *Piltdown Man* forgery always came in handy as a lecture exhibit on what unforgivable paleoanthropology and lust for glory was all about. Why the director didn't store his junk in the university's Anthropology Museum with the rest of the collections, thereby freeing up valuable space, Krafter couldn't say. The man was the director, so go figure.

"We need to have this locked up," he told him by way of an explanation.

Krafter stopped before a heavy gray door and watched Spiro tap in an access code into the security pad. When the lock clicked, Krafter pushed the trolley into the specimen room.

"I'll check if we've got any empty lockers in the storage room."

Krafter frowned. "Should be," he said and watched Spiro walk toward the end of the room.

Krafter looked around at the arrayed glass cases and display cabinets, and wondered why Larson insisted on having the lab secured. No one hardly bothered coming to see the collection, the Museum's being far more extensive. Who cared about a copy of Leakey's *Lucy*.

"We got a couple of lockers just right for the job, doc," Spiro called from an open doorway. Krafter took off his suitcase and bag and pushed the trolley toward the room.

A miniature vault in its own right, the windowless room held ceiling-high cabinets built into the three walls, full of open benches holding assorted cardboard boxes and metal drawers. Against the back wall, Spiro had already opened two large airport-style luggage lockers. Pushing a box into each one, Krafter locked the cabinets and pocketed the keys. Heeding Perkins' advice, he had learned caution, although he still considered the whole thing silly. Silly or not, he definitely didn't want his discovery sitting in Lab Two open for anyone to paw over, especially Wethermans.

After stashing the suitcase and bag in his office, he took a deep breath and went down the corridor to face his mentor. He knocked and walked into his master's lair.

"Ah, Larry, good to see you again," Perkins said and invited him in with a wave of his hand. "How was the flight back?"

Krafter made himself comfortable and stretched his legs. "Great Lakes slapped me with a hefty excess baggage charge, but otherwise, nothing to complain about."

"Put in a claim," Perkins growled indifferently and Krafter sagged.

By the time Admin processed the paperwork, he would be lucky to see any money in three months. What were all those UW computers doing, having a lube and wax? Did some service center in India handle it and they were mailing the damned check?

"Amos Ferguson called about an hour ago," Perkins went on. "You seem to have made quite an impression on him."

"Oh?"

"Yes. He admired the way you handled the whole thing. Very professional."

"Nice of him to say so, but we're the ones owing him and Trantor Coal one huge thanks."

"Agreed, and I've sent a letter to them and Relans Mining corporate saying that." Perkins paused and stared at Krafter. "It seems you scored big this time, Larry, but I wonder if you're ready to face what's about to happen. I know we talked at length last night, but there is no doubt in your mind that what you have is genuine? I would hate for UW to be embroiled in a scandal. Especially now when Dr. Larson is having problems with the Trustees."

"We're solid. Seeing that bone and bracelet sticking out of

the coalface, any thoughts I might have had about deliberate intrusive burial has vanished. It simply could not have been done. Apart from some blast damage, the coal seam was undisturbed. I tell you, Adam, we're going to make history here."

"Mmm. There are others, you know, who won't share your enthusiasm and will resent any attempt at rewriting history we already know."

"Anyone who cares to look at my films and specimens is free to prove me wrong."

"Oh, they'll try. Count on it. They will cry fake without bothering to look at the evidence. Controversial finds generate a correspondingly controversial response."

Krafter looked confused. "What's going on here, Doctor? Instead of celebrating a momentous discovery, you're acting as if I've dug up a bomb and it's about to blow up in our face."

"Crude as your analogy is, it's not far off the mark. All I'm saying, be prepared to defend what you've got."

"The bones speak for themselves. Everything else is professional jealousy." Struck by a sudden notion, Krafter sat up. "What about Dr. Larson? Will he back me if things get ugly?"

"He may be old school, but he'll be objective. He might not like what you have, but he cannot ignore it. It doesn't necessarily mean that he'll commit the department totally. Anyway, I'll stand by you."

"Thanks, I appreciate that. My detractors can scoff and rant, but the bones exist. They are tangible."

"My boy, the Shroud of Turin is a fake and proven to be one, yet people still believe. The Church had Galileo locked up for heresy because he dared show that Earth was not the center of creation. Not that the Church will lock *you* up for finding those bones," Perkins added with a faint grin. "Although they might be tempted. Still, whenever something threatens established dogma, you're in for a fight. This is true today as it was four hundred years ago. Don't think the Renaissance brought enlightenment and heralded rational scientific expression. The Bollingers and Maddsons of today are no different from Pope Paul V."

"I'll publish my findings and they can tear me down if they can."

Perkins sighed. "You're not going to be swayed from your path, and perhaps you're right. In full strength of your mental powers, supremely confident in your abilities, why should you cower before minds closed to new concepts and discoveries? If you're not prepared to fight for your beliefs now, you never will. Then again, you've got solid evidence to back you up, always a major inconvenience for any decrier. I still think it unlikely that you know what you're getting yourself into exactly. Well, you have to have your trial of fire sometime. Remember my warning."

Krafter was not entirely sure what Perkins tried to tell him, but he had no time to philosophize.

"Because I'll upset Bollinger's breakfast, I'm supposed to forget the whole thing?"

Perkins chuckled. "You'll be upsetting more than merely his breakfast and you know it. Very well, let the battle be joined. What have you done with the specimens?"

"Locked in Lab Three," Krafter said with a faint smile. He didn't have to elaborate. "I would prefer Spiro to work with me on this if he's free. He's a good technician."

"That should be all right," Perkins mused. "Where do you plan sending your announcement paper?"

"I'll give *Nature* the first bite. If they create a fuss, *Science* can have it, or I'll post it on every professional website I know."

"You may have to yet. Will you be sending a copy to the International Anthropological Society?"

"Maybe the full paper, once it's published, but not the announcement," Krafter said cautiously. His views of that organization were public and not altogether flattering.

Like its sister organizations, the American Anthropological

Association and the World Council of Anthropological Associations, the IAS started off as a good idea. From an informal alliance where biological anthropologists and paleoanthropologists met and exchanged ideas and papers, the thing had grown into a quasi-accreditation body that now attempted to vet all university research and sought to peer review every paper submitted to prestigious journals in order to control, and if necessary, suppress theories and discoveries that did not fit the accepted mainstream norm as defined by the IAS.

The governing committee consisted of recognized, respectable academics from eminent institutions the world over, who genuinely started off with good intentions, mainly to prevent blatant fraud and bogus papers plastered on the Internet being taken as fact. It also saved universities time, money and resources involved in organizing laborious and sometimes-onerous peer reviews. Krafter knew what was paved with good intentions.

Starting as an open review forum, the IAS had become an all-encompassing censor of everything that did not conform to ideas and arbitrary standards set by the governing committee members. The situation now so bad, many academics scorned the Society and published on the Internet when their papers were rejected by a journal due to negative IAS endorsement; thereby creating the very problem they sought to prevent. The more insidious aspect of the Society and the creeping influence its accreditation program had on universities everywhere, was that anthropology PhDs were 'encouraged' to seek membership, without which getting grants and a tenured position could become problematic. Outright blackmail, of course, and a transparent policy to keep emerging postdocs and established academics in check. Many university boards didn't think much of the idea either, resenting this intrusion into their bailiwick.

The IAS approached Krafter when he published his disturbing doctoral thesis, and two subsequent papers asserting that modern humans coexisted with their more primitive brethren, inviting him to seek membership and endorsement, hinting strongly that pursuing questionable research contradicting established and proven theories would be frowned upon. Proven theories indeed! All very polite and seemingly innocuous, but Krafter got the message loud and clear. He hoped that in a landfill, their letter fulfilled a higher purpose. He had more of the same since and all received similar treatment.

Perkins smiled wryly and nodded. "I don't have much time for the IAS either, although I'm an accredited member. The Society in its current form will invariably fail. It has to, and you know it. Freethinking academics everywhere scorn all forms of gratuitous control, even the necessary mechanisms imposed by universities. With institutions, however, it's a beneficially symbiotic relationship. The IAS, on the other hand, is a malignant cancer that attacks original discourse and progressive research. Nevertheless, for the time being, the Society exerts malicious influence and has to be taken seriously. I don't know whether you have read that article by some science reporter wit in New York, I can't recall the name, who labeled the IAS an anthropological Inquisition? I loved it, but it was received with predictable results."

Krafter nodded. "I remember. IAS demanded a retraction, never made, of course, while most academics applauded the article. Uncomfortable with the label and the image it presented, I don't think the Society has ever gotten over it and the name seems to have stuck."

"Yeah." Perkins smiled. "I need to remember to cancel my membership. Anyway, you'll be dating the samples?"

"The Powder River Basin has been dated to death already and I'll use available data for base stats," Krafter said. "I want some fission track and potassium-argon tests done to satisfy my own curiosity and have independent corroboration."

"Even on the bones?"

"Especially on the bones. Although I realize that a K-Ar test has large plus or minus factors, this shouldn't matter too much here. Fission track will give me good supporting data for the overburden layers, but I want to forestall any comments about sloppy dating. Not for something like this."

"Probably a good idea. Who do you have in mind to do the analysis?"

"I'm considering using either the Geochronology Laboratories at Melno Park, the Geochron Labs at Billericia, or possibly the New York's Union College fission track lab. I heard they do good work."

"You don't want to use Stanford's facilities?"

Krafter's expression turned nasty. "And have Maddson snooping around before I'm ready to publish?"

"I suppose," Perkins said and sighed. "The University of Arizona's Geochronology Lab isn't bad."

"You worried about cost if I use private labs?"

"I'm always worried about cost, Larry. I approve of your desire for independent validation, though."

"I simply want to preclude cries of bias if I use UW's facilities."

"I agree. You know, it might be a good idea to post your test data and a short film on the department's open website, with an invitation to major universities to review the find."

"I intended doing that and I'll append a URL as a reference in my paper."

"Okay, my boy, when you have it ready, let me see it." Perkins stood up and grinned. "Now, show me what you've got."

* * *

Sharp shadows cut through the canyons of towering skyscrapers and tore at a cloudless sky. A film of brown smog hung over the city, generated by countless cars winding their way along choked boulevards, filling the streets with blaring horns, police sirens, and fetid smells.

At 1200 Avenue of the Americas, there was nothing to distinguish the stately old three-story building from others around it. The gray stone façade looked tired, blackened by exposure to decades of New York's relentless grime and pollution. It might have looked tired on the outside, and a pedestrian walking by wouldn't have given it a second glance, but like its occupants, the building was more than it seemed.

As Raymond Kessler walked toward them, the heavy glass entrance panels slid aside. He nodded to Vicky sitting behind her curved reception station. She flashed him a polite smile, then bent her head to stare at the computer screen, her fingernails clicking on the keyboard. Beside the doorway stood a sloping wooden stand covered with International Anthropological Society pamphlets, publications and professional periodicals. Tucked against the corner, surrounded by three ultramodern chairs, a glass-topped coffee table held an untidy pile of newspapers. Soothing pearl down lights illuminated large abstract paintings adorning the cool green walls.

The reception area looked tastefully sophisticated, designed to reflect the image of the organization it represented. A young executive type looked up briefly as Kessler sauntered toward the elevator, then resumed his reading of *Nature*. Kessler frowned when he saw the cover. He stopped before the polished steel elevator door, his feet soundless on the soft dark gray carpet, and pressed the white Up triangle. It turned red. An elevator moved quickly down from the first floor and the door hissed open as the request triangle turned green, accompanied by a pleasant *ting*.

Two large potted plants flanked a spacious desk as Kessler stepped out onto the third floor. Behind it, two tall windows provided ample natural light and a cramped view of the city skyline. Brenda lifted her narrow face, framed by shoulder-length straw-colored hair that had a mysterious luster all its own, and immediately held out a handful of yellow message slips.

"Professor Fuijuma will not be able to make the two p.m. teleconference."

She did not offer an explanation and Kessler didn't ask for one. Fuijuma would not be calling and that's what mattered. An explanation as to why served little purpose, and Kessler preferred not to waste his energy on things he could not influence.

"Anything else?" he demanded in a strong voice emanating from a trim five-foot-eleven frame as he flicked through the messages.

"Mr. Neil Reed from *The New York Times* has requested an interview…again."

Hearing the name, Kessler looked at her severe features and scowled. Reed was a major pain, and several of his articles were less than complimentary to the Society, but the man was an influential science and technology reporter. It would not be wise to irritate him unnecessarily, regardless of how much irritation he caused in return. Some evils had to be endured. Kessler was tempted not to see the reporter, but then, he would miss an opportunity to present the irritating weasel a more favorable picture of the IAS.

"Give him a slot," he growled.

"Very good," Brenda said and waited for her boss to refocus. "The minutes of the last meeting are on your desk. There is one additional item on today's agenda."

"Oh?"

"Professor Larry Krafter. The item was included by Dr. Ted Horowitz."

Kessler allowed himself a frosty grin. If the IAS president had not brought it up, he certainly would have. Brought into the Society from his last position as Chief Operating Officer at Bio-Chip, a small, but critical Silicone Valley integrated chip manufacturer on which a number of civilian corporations, NASA and the U.S. military relied for some of their advanced custom com-

ponents, his job description was to make the International Anthropological Society a force to be taken seriously among the
learned community. His salary a measly $180,000 a year, but he
wasn't in it for the money, being already independently wealthy
from Microsoft and Oracle shares his old man gave him on his
twenty-first. Hell, his dividends netted more than his salary. A
radical departure from the corporate sector, he saw the Society
as a unique challenge, but he'd had those before.

Fixing sloppy operations in ailing companies was always demanding and sometimes not appreciated by the client. It was a
challenge to turn IAS's cigar-and-brandy club atmosphere enjoyed by the core group of academics who had started it all, into
a body now recognized by most institutions the world over as an
authority on all matters anthropological. After all, what did stuffy
academics know about running promotions, hardcore marketing,
and grinding down opponents?

He brought with him a solid business case, a management
plan, objectives and tactics to achieve them, not the least to become a university accreditation body and an anthropology research filter. With it, of course, came the enforcement mechanisms, something that did not sit comfortably with every Executive Committee member or national branch. One did not come
without the other, he had pointed out calmly, and gotten his way
purely on the weight of his resume. He'd had few open complaints since, but rumors of covert tactics employed by the Society were growing. Character assassination of a fellow academic
was encroaching on hallowed turf, the sole prerogative of IAS
members, and a growing number of them could not stomach
what he was doing.

Well, tough cookies.

His smile turned into a frown as he turned and walked toward his office. He strode past the matte gray ceiling-high door
of the Treasurer, opened the door to his office, stepped into the
subdued opulence spread before him, and absently pushed the

door shut behind him. His large black desk faced the relatively narrow rectangular room. With two large windows on his right, the room always had plenty of light. A wide tray beneath them housed a lush creeper of some sort. Brenda told him more than once what the thing was, but he never remembered. Simply not information he needed to know. Apart from an oak bookshelf and a bar cabinet tucked between the windows, the office was unadorned. He revolted at the idea of plastering a wall with diplomas, certificates and awards so treasured by the learned, preferring results to speak for him. Tucked into the far left corner stood a round table surrounded by four padded chairs.

He walked behind his desk, eased himself into a black leather ergonomic chair and faced the LED screen. When he logged in, he quickly scrolled down his email list. He checked the time, a few minutes still before the teleconference, and scowled at the number of messages requiring his attention. Brenda could handle most of them, and she would end up doing the work, but she required direction and decisions that, as CEO, only he could provide.

As he stared at the message list, he decided that he'd had his break and it was time for some paid work. Lunch at Freshco's particularly pleasant, and the rack of lamb superb: soft and tender, just shy of being medium rare. A fine glass of Australian cabernet sauvignon during the meal, followed by a snifter of Otard cognac, topped off a diverting hour and twenty minutes.

At one-fifty-five, Brenda walked in carrying a black mug of steaming coffee and a white folder tucked beneath her left arm. Without saying anything, she placed the mug on his desk and strode to the conference table. She took out two sheets of paper from the folder and arranged them opposite the chairs. Sitting down on the corner chair, she reached for the speakerphone. Dialing quickly, she set up the conference call. It was now a matter of waiting for everybody else to ring in. Kessler took a sip of black coffee, one sugar, and rapidly scanned through the last meeting's minutes and today's agenda.

Someone knocked and the door opened. A short, portly individual, white hair severely trimmed, dressed in a dark blue silk suit and striped orange tie, walked in, nodded to Kessler and made for the table.

Kessler studied the taciturn little man with fondness. Ethan Prowse was a constipated humorless son of a bitch who would take pennies out of a beggar's hat, but as the Society treasurer, he was priceless. Without his firm stewardship and tight fiscal management, the Society would still be a gentleman's club. It took Kessler a hard year to convince the Executive Committee and the more influential contributing universities, that the Society would only begin to exert influence on academic establishments worldwide if it provided a differentiating value-add service. The Fellowship and accreditation programs being the most important, followed by its influential and telling policy of centralized peer reviews. Everybody needed to remember that they were competing with the likes of the American Anthropological Association and the World Council of Anthropological Associations. Those people would not surrender their positions easily. The squabbling academics were subject to the same human frailties and ambitions as any power or prestige seeker, and Kessler had exploited that knowledge fully. The corporate world he had grown up in had been a hard taskmaster.

Jealous of their standing and protective of their accepted theories, the academics were in agreement on one thing. They wanted to control dissent in the ranks and stifle what they saw as threatening research. That meant controlling university grants and what they published. Convincing prestigious magazines such as *Nature*, *Science*, *The Physical Review Letters*, and others to submit papers to the Society for external peer review took time and many arduous meetings. The runs were now on the board and the Executive was well pleased with themselves and him.

Several members called in, interrupting his thoughts. He

stood up and sat next to Prowse.

It was never easy to arrange a teleconference with the fifteen executive members. Spread across institutions all over the world, time differences were a major problem. Full meetings were only held every two months and sacrifices had to be made. Besides, today's call was a local North American branch matter that did not require everyone to be present.

At two p.m. sharp, Brenda tapped the table with her slim silver pen. "Before proceeding, does anyone wish to challenge the minutes of the last special branch meeting?"

"The financial audit; when is that going to be available?" Dr. Theo Duncan, head of Columbia U's Anthropology Department, demanded in a sonorous voice, sounding twitchy and impatient even over the phone.

"Price Waterhouse will have the report available by end of September, Doctor, as previously reported," Prowse replied in a precise, deliberate manner, with all the emotion of making an entry in a spreadsheet.

"Gentlemen, let's not get sidetracked here," Ted Horowitz interjected soothingly and Kessler nodded in approval. The Princeton anthropology department chair a natural leader, skilled at bringing about consensus and smoothing differences among prickly members. No longer a researcher, the silver-haired stocky man was everyone's image of a sage academic. It took Kessler only one meeting to recognize a formidable intellect, but only in his own field. The corporate world would have eaten him up.

"But—"

"Mr. Prowse is hardly going to abscond to South America with the Society funds, Theo," Horowitz announced dryly and titters came from the speaker.

Brenda glanced at Kessler, who nodded.

"In that case, the first item on the agenda is the delayed quarterly contribution by Texas State U. Professor Hartman?"

There was some throat clearing and a sound of shuffling papers. "An administrative oversight, Mr. Prowse."

"An oversight that seems to be malignant, Professor," Prowse snapped. "Texas State U's contributions figure prominently in our budget and projected expenditure plans. Timely receipt of due monies would be appreciated."

"You'll get your money, Ethan. It's not as if you're shy a couple of million or something."

Kessler hid a smile. Contributions from affiliated universities around the world, not substantial in themselves, and levied on a means tier basis, amounted to almost twelve million in direct annual revenues. This was petty cash to budgets he handled at Bio-Chip, but considerable for the Society. The funds sustained over a dozen endowed Chairs and provided numerous scholarships and grants for the more needy institutions. Done for public consumption, of course. A significant bulk of those funds, hence Professor Dunkan's insistence for an external audit, went into promoting the Society and its activities. You cannot be an influence if no one knows you exist, Kessler had argued.

"That's not the point, Professor," Prowse responded stiffly. "Just send me an email when the funds are deposited."

Brenda looked up from her notepad as she finished jotting down the salient points for the special branch minutes.

She was not only Kessler's personal assistant, but to enable her to sit in on executive meetings, he made her the Society Secretary. As such, she was privy to many academic secrets, innuendos and scandals, all useful items at keeping recalcitrant members in line. Although not a listed expenditure item on the balance sheet, dirt gathering cost money. When an executive member failed to vote a certain way, a quiet phone call, revelation of an embarrassing secret or two, and order was restored. Simply how business was done everywhere.

"The second item—"

"Let's leave that for a minute, Brenda," Horowitz cut in,

"and move on to Professor Larry Krafter, which is the objective of this meeting."

"Anyone second the motion?"

"Seconded!" Bollinger declared with obvious relish.

"Very well," Brenda said. "Doctor Horowitz?"

"Just a moment." Kessler lifted a finger and turned to Prowse. "If you don't mind, Ethan? A family fight."

The IAS treasurer nodded stiffly, got up and walked out. Kessler glanced at Brenda and nodded.

"Go on, Dr. Horowitz."

"Thank you, Brenda. If you haven't read the current issue of *Nature* by now, I suggest you do so. Although none of us could have missed what the papers everywhere had to say about Krafter's discovery. We're faced with a grave crisis of identity, gentlemen, and we need to respond promptly and decisively."

"The young whippersnapper is a fraud!" Bollinger declared hotly, daring anyone to contradict him.

"If he is, it was done with unmatched skill," Maddson added thoughtfully. "Even if what he found is genuine, something I don't accept for a moment, he must be totally discredited before any serious study is attempted and the situation gets out of hand. If his discovery becomes accepted, it could ruin all of us."

"We're all in agreement on that, Karl," Horowitz said soothingly.

"What if the find *is* genuine?" Hartman ventured. "Simply because the evidence doesn't fit neatly into the current evolutionary model, does not automatically assign him to the fringe bin. Current theories are based on scant evidence and questionable assumptions at best. They could be partly wrong."

"Well said, Gene, but do you want to set off a revolution that could overthrow two centuries of paleoanthropological research?" Horowitz demanded. "If we accepted Krafter's discovery, it could very well place our own positions in jeopardy like

Karl said, and seriously compromise the universities we represent. A single career is a small price to pay to preserve what we have struggled for and achieved."

"If what he has is truth, airing dusty cupboards is something that's been long overdue. And isn't truth what we're all striving for?"

"You cannot be that simplistic or naïve, Gene," Bollinger boomed over the phone. "You may be prepared to throw away a lifetime of work, your Nobel Prize and reputation is secure, but I'm not so willing to trash mine. Krafter must be crushed, and crushed in a most exemplary manner. It will serve as a warning and an example to others."

"Although I don't share Ryan's enthusiasm completely," Horowitz said with a light chuckle, "he is right about Krafter having to be silenced. We all have similar finds gathering dust in our basements, and that's where I want to keep them. I for one don't want to rewrite history. After all, our version isn't exactly a contrived lie. We simply haven't disclosed all of it."

"That omission is more than a minor oversight, and perhaps it's time we did something about it," Hartman added quietly.

"We'll discuss philosophy some other time, Gene. Raymond, you know what needs to be done."

Kessler pursed his lips. "Are you sure you *want* to do this?"

"What do you mean?"

"Instead of targeting Krafter openly, reel him in. Announce a multi-university team that would study his find and jointly publicize the results in due course. We would control the process rather than react to it."

"You want us to obfuscate?" Bollinger demanded querulously.

"Defuse the situation," Kessler countered.

"Too dangerous," Horowitz said promptly. "He needs to be quashed now."

"Very well." Kessler thought the decision unwise, but he

didn't set policy here. "What are my parameters?" he asked, working possible options in his mind. One in particular might be more effective than any smear campaign.

"Destroy his credibility."

"Understood. Initial press releases will go out today. Major periodicals will be warned not to accept his papers, or to forward them to us. All member institutions will be alerted to treat his discovery with utmost skepticism. I'll take further steps as required. In the meantime, we'll dig into his past."

"Sounds like a good start," Horowitz commented approvingly.

"We've done this once or twice before, Ted," Kessler reminded him wryly.

"I want to go on record protesting this unwarranted attack on a colleague," Hartman declared bluntly. "You're stifling a legitimate discovery. We should at least examine what he found before retaliating."

"The legitimacy of Krafter's find cannot be entertained, Gene," Bollinger said smugly.

"This is riding roughshod—"

"We'll proceed with the smear campaign," Horowitz declared firmly, allowing no dissent. "Any seconds?"

"Seconded," Dunkan snapped.

"The motion is carried," Brenda said softly, jotting into her notebook. "Returning to the agenda—"

"It is *not* carried!" Hartman thundered. "You're planning to besmirch a fine young scientist simply on the basis that his discovery is an upsetting inconvenience. This is not what the Society stands for! This is outright thuggery and I won't be a party to it. What's more, I'll fight you on this, Ted. You have my resignation, effective immediately. You can forget about that quarterly contribution from Texas U!" The line went dead.

After a stunned moment, Horowitz cleared his throat. "Okay, Brenda. What's next?"

General business finished quickly, everyone chewing over what Hartman did and what Kessler was about to do. Hartman had allowed his hot temper to get the better of him and he would eventually come around. If he did not, necessary steps would be taken.

When the meeting broke up and Brenda left, Kessler returned to his desk and spent several minutes staring out a window. He had no qualms following Horowitz's order. Purely a question of practicality and self-preservation. Morals hardly came into it. Besides, whose morals was he supposed to follow? Vatican's? When The Entity sanctioned assassination to keep an awkward papyrus scroll from surfacing, the Vatican was not exactly an authority on morality. His own morals? Nothing personal. Simply business.

His previous job brought him into contact with a number of intelligence agencies, and all of them had procedures in place to protect themselves and their work. The Society no different, even if it had to be dragged into acceptance of that reality. Although GSM and other cellular networks had built-in encrypted voice/data algorithms aimed to protect users from intrusive eavesdropping, intelligence services everywhere required telco providers to divulge the encryption key generator—to protect citizens against criminal elements who would otherwise take advantage of the service. At least that's how it was explained. The reason, of course, much more basic. If paranoid intelligence and policing agencies could not spy on their own citizens and each other, they would be out of business.

Sending out letters and emails was all good, but treating the Krafter problem demanded that little bit extra, and Kessler had just the thing.

NSA recognized the national interest work that BioChip did, and gave key company executives and engineers modified High Technology Computer PDA smartphones with an additional encryption chip and military-grade software that used a variation of the RSA 4096/AES 256-bit random key that changed every second. Key exchange with the network and receiving cellphone done using a modified Diffie-Hellman 4096-bit algorithm. As the NSA man said with a tight smile, no use giving them a supposedly secure phone that CIA and NSA could break. Sometimes the government had to protect itself from its own intelligence services.

When Kessler left BioChip, he somehow neglected to return the cellphone.

He took out the HTC PDA, pressed the menu button, selected the Secure icon, then dialed a number. The key exchange with the switching system's authentication center ensured that the connection was made, but the system was inhibited from recording the event and passing it on to the billing module. In effect, he had a device that could make free calls anywhere in the world.

He never met the operative he called and never would. Likewise, 'Striker' didn't know who Kessler was either, and both preferred that it remained that way. Given the nature of the proposed job, Striker might have his suspicions, but that's all he would have. A lot of people were sufficiently annoyed with Professor Krafter to want something done about it. Maybe he should solicit contributions from members for this part of extra IAS service, Kessler mused sardonically. Before engaging Striker, he was assured the operative employed similar security precautions. That had been enough.

"Identify," an electronically altered voice demanded after two rings.

"Raven," Kessler answered calmly, his own voice changed beyond recognition by the encryption software.

"Proceed."

"Are you available for an assignment?"

"State your problem."

TOWERS of DARKNESS

* * *

FORTY-MILLION-YEAR-OLD HUMAN BONES CAUSE UPROAR
MODERN HUMANS WALKED WITH DINOSAURS
ANCIENT SKULL A FARCE, REPUTABLE ANTHROPOLOGISTS
MAINTAIN
GOD DID CREATE EARTH 6,000 YEARS AGO!
SCIENTIFIC COMMUNITY DEBUNKS PROFESSOR'S CLAIM

Krafter pulled back the gauzy curtain of his bedroom window and peered out. About a dozen mostly middle-aged and elderly protesters dressed in somber clothing were still going up and down the sidewalk in front of his house, chanting and waving placards. They had been at it since early morning and it looked like staying until he came out. At first, he thought nothing of it, but the increasingly vocal group had drawn neighbors and the morbidly curious, until the street resembled a rowdy football crowd. Everyone cheered when two police cruisers showed up, their red and blue lights flashing. He did not think it amusing and finished his breakfast deep in contemplation. Not long afterward, a KCWC-TV van eased through the throng and technicians quickly set up their camera, waiting for a story to develop.

After cleaning up and switching off the television, most channels devoting time to learned and often ignorant comments about his discovery, he toyed with the idea of driving to UW and avoid a possible confrontation with the people outside. He did not expect things to turn ugly, but it would take only one nut out there to throw a punch or a brick, and there was no telling what might happen. He simply had not anticipated this level of personal protest and felt nervous at the prospect of facing the crowd. He wasn't looking for a fight and the police would keep everyone in check, he hoped.

To hell with it! No placard-waving idiot was going to make him run. He would walk to UW as planned. Nevertheless, his stomach tensed as he opened the front door, locked it, and faced the waiting mob.

"There he is!" someone shouted and suddenly, there was silence.

Trying to look determined, Krafter slowly walked toward the street.

"Blasphemer!" a voice screamed. A woman began chanting *Rock of Ages*.

"Repent! It's not too late!"

"You have sinned against God!"

When he reached the sidewalk, a reporter stepped up to him and shoved a black microphone into his face.

"Professor Krafter, everyone wants to know only one thing. Are those bones truly forty million years old?"

Krafter paused and looked at the bright-eyed reporter, realizing that the worldly-wise man did not care at all for the truth. He was after a sensation, wanting to see him unnerved and flustered in front of the protesters. Others picked up *Rock of Ages* and Krafter found himself surrounded. Trying not to show his unease, he faced the reporter.

"My discovery shows something wonderful about man's evolutionary history. It's also a mystery that scientists around the world should embrace and try to solve."

"What you're saying is that man is millions of years older than currently accepted theory suggests. Why haven't others found traces of past civilizations?"

"Evidence of past civilizations does exist, but it's not something that sits comfortably with most anthropologists."

"You're suggesting a conspiracy to hide man's true past?" the reporter demanded eagerly, sensing another controversy in the making.

"All I'm saying is that there is a lot more out there than people realize."

"You're contradicting the Bible!" someone shouted.

Not relishing entering into a complex debate that might inflame the crowd further, Krafter smiled and raised his hand.

"You will have to excuse me. I need to get to the university."

"Professor! One more question!"

Krafter waved at him and turned toward S. 15th Street. Someone showed a placard before him.

"You're spreading lies, disciple of Satan!"

"Burn in hell, unbeliever!"

The crowd reluctantly made way for him and Krafter felt the first stirring of real alarm. Perhaps it had not been such a bright idea to walk to UW. A burly Laramie PD officer pushed his way through, stopped and glowered at the people around him.

"Get back everybody!"

The cop's powerful presence restored momentary peace, but Krafter realized that the situation was still fragile. He decided to walk back to his house when the cop placed a large hand on his shoulder.

"Better come with me, Professor. Don't worry. We'll keep an eye on your house."

The cop scowled at the crowd as he led him to a waiting cruiser. Krafter got into the back seat and gratefully sank against the cloth upholstery. With a surge of power, lights flashing, the cruiser eased through the crowd, then accelerated. He could hear chanting fading behind him and realized that he had experienced firsthand a side of America that had previously been only an amusing newspaper article or TV clip. It was not the chanting or the waving placards that unsettled him, but the raw power of unleashed emotion, which could have turned into instant and unrestrained mob violence. He hoped that some fool wouldn't throw a rock through his window, or worse.

Morose, he wondered how long the siege on his house would last.

* * *

Doctor Larson slammed a copy of *Nature* against a stack of newspapers piled high on his wide polished desk and glared at Krafter with obvious displeasure.

"You published this drivel without conducting a peer review and made this university a laughing stock! Did you read the headlines? And now, I've got placard-waving nut groups marching up and down Lewis Street, demanding that you recant this blasphemous assertion that evolution was responsible for man's creation and embrace God."

Krafter had seen the crowd as the police cruiser stopped before the Anthropology Building. When they spotted him, they surged toward him, but campus police held them back. After the experience at his house, he was in no mood to face them. The way he felt now, he had little time for any crap from Larson either.

"I can hardly be held responsible for that, and I don't see how you can call my paper drivel, Doctor," he said hotly, indignant that his discovery could be so casually dismissed as a blatant forgery, although not unexpected, and disappointed at Larson's reaction. That hurt more than he cared to admit. He knew he should not fret over it, but he took the rejection personally. The university's student-run paper, *Branding Iron*, was enthusiastic about his find, but that was self-serving publicity. "I published verifiable facts, nothing more, validated by independent dating conducted by reputable organizations. I made no claims or attempted to interpret the find. That will be done when I present my full paper."

"There won't be any paper!" Larson snapped. "Young man, if I sanction another publication, I will in effect be saying that this department supports your discovery. It does not!"

"You can't mean that. Everything I stated in my paper is fact! You may not like the resulting controversy, or people marching in protest outside your window, but this university cannot ignore evidence, however uncomfortable for my detractors or sensation-seeking tabloids. Dr. Perkins reviewed all my data, as did Doctors Peel and White, and you saw the skull and bracelet yourself. You didn't consider them forgeries then."

"Dr. Perkins was in error endorsing your announcement paper without clearing it with me," the Anthropology Department Director growled, cooling down somewhat. "When I said a peer review, I meant an external one."

"Was I supposed to send it to Professor Bollinger? You knew I was writing a paper, Doctor. If you had reservations, why didn't you raise them? I'm vilified because I dared challenge accepted theory and my find has become an academic embarrassment. Not only to the anthropological community at large, but for some reason, to you personally. Is this what today's science has become? Being politically correct and bury truth if it threatens careers and reputations? If that's the case, everything this university represents is a lie. If you reject my paper, I'll be labeled a fraud, regardless of my evidence, irreparably tarnishing whatever might be left of my career."

Krafter knew he was laying it on strong, but he couldn't back down now, not to anyone. Wanting to rage at the blatant injustice of it all, he could not believe this was happening.

Larson removed his rimless glasses, frowned and rubbed his face. He glanced at the cover of *Nature* and looked up.

"Dr. Krafter, you may see me as closed-minded, and perhaps you're right, but I am not a free agent, young man. I must deal with issues far outside your concern as an administrator of this department. That imposes constraints not only on me, but on this university as well. Regardless of those constraints, the purpose of this institution is to promote higher learning and discovery without fear, prejudice or favor. Noble words…noble goals, until they touch the men supposed to enforce them. What you said is true and your sentiments should be applauded instead of being hounded by the mindless pack outside. But damnation! It's not that simple.

"The world is far from ideal and the venerated halls of learning don't promote truth, but expediency. You should have learned that by now. Research has to be paid for, and paid for with hard money; money that comes from student fees and federal grants, but only if this institution maintains a reputation and a veneer of respectability, a reputation judged by our fickle peers! I don't mind telling you that in today's bleak reality, esoteric learning is waning, and pure research has given way to industry partnerships that promotes profit, not new discoveries. Industry doesn't want new discoveries if they threaten those profits and entrenched market positions."

Krafter wasn't sure how to take this about-face. "What I have learned, sir, is that even here, the Trustees question the merits of your department. They see money poured into what they consider a useless science when those resources could be more profitably channeled into applied research in support of local industry that maintains the national competitive advantage. What use is anthropology anyway? All the important discoveries have already been made, and man's place on the evolutionary tree firmly established. Right? The world doesn't need disturbing revelations that inflames professional and religious preconceptions. Well, Doctor, I don't give a damn if my discovery upsets that status quo."

Larson frowned. "If I agreed with your criticism, young man, I might as well shut the doors on this department and retire. Man's thinking must soar free or he is nothing. Your discovery is controversial, we both know that, and your enemies will be hunting. You know who they are for you, and your paper has brought others out of the woodwork, as you intended. What rankled wasn't the fact of your discovery, but the tone of your paper! Did you have to be so goddamn smug and dogmatic?"

Krafter blanched at this accusation from the old fossil. Perhaps Larson was merely venting spleen at a convenient target.

"I should have stuck to dry facts, is that it?"

"When you pour petrol on a smoldering fire, you shouldn't be surprised at the inevitable result," Larson said dryly.

"Perhaps there was a touch of hubris in there, which in hindsight, I should have controlled, but I couldn't resist an opportunity to stick it to the likes of Bollinger and Maddson."

Larson grinned and the atmosphere lifted. "Sometimes it's hard to maintain one's objectivity. In your case, though, as a junior professor, it is essential." He chewed his lower lip, took out a tissue and proceeded to wipe his glasses. "Deliberate or not, you created a storm. Now you've got to ride it out. When you finish your follow-up paper, I want to see it. I also want you to send it to the International Anthropological Society for a full peer review."

Krafter sat up in alarm. "What good would that do? You read the headlines. They'll reject it out of hand and any hope I might have of publishing with a prestigious journal will be dead."

"*Nature*, *Science* or anybody else, will send your paper to them anyway. Short-circuit the step. You got away with it this time because it was only an announcement paper. *Nature* will not touch you again without IAS endorsement, and you can use that to poke at them."

"I might as well post it on the Internet now," Krafter complained bitterly.

"Or a newspaper," Larson agreed equitably. "You'll probably end up doing that anyway, but you knew that from the start. Not all reputable journals kowtow to IAS. Pick one of them. Let me know if you need help. Despite what I said earlier, this university will endorse your paper and you'll have to be satisfied with that. You didn't expect IAS to simply lay back and take it on the chin, did you?"

"I'm not presenting a new theory someone can refute, Doctor. I am providing irrefutable evidence of a fact."

"When did irrefutable evidence ever win an argument?" Larson snarled, and then raised a hand in apology. "Look, I know you're right, but you must expect to be challenged. My God, young man! You have a forty-million-year-old human hand and skull!"

"I can handle an informed challenge, but blatant character assassination is something else."

"Welcome to the real world, Doctor. Talking of challenges, the Harvard Anthropology Department has made a submission to independently examine the bones."

"Fine. If they want an independent examination, they can come here."

"Yes, that's what normally happens, but this is hardly a normal case. I want you to send them the bones and original film clips."

"Everything?"

"We have nothing to hide, do we?"

"You know what they're doing, don't you? Once Bollinger gets his hands on them, everything will disappear and they'll be in a position to discredit me completely and say whatever they want. I'll have no way to refute them and I'll end up looking like a fool. Protesting about it later won't do me much good."

"If we deny their request, it will only serve to reinforce their allegations of fraud. Besides, Professor Bollinger knows better than that. He may be a bur in your pants, but he is a reputable scientist. Come on, Larry. Harvard is one of the world's eminent centers of learning and you're painting them as some kind of conspirators."

"I'm simply not comfortable with the idea of giving them everything, that's all. Harvard might be a fine institution, I don't deny that, but I don't trust Bollinger."

"You made copies of your films?"

"Of course."

"There you are, then. You won't be losing everything if he

tries something."

"I can copy my films, but I cannot reproduce the bones."

"That's the way it sometimes goes, young man."

"The request, did it come from Bollinger?"

"No, it's from Professor Chandler, head of their Paleoan-thropology Laboratory."

"I've heard of him. Supposed to be a good researcher with a solid background of discoveries."

"Get it done. I'll email you the details."

"Did anyone else request access to the bones?"

"If they did, it wasn't done through me. Check with Dr. Per-kins."

Uneasy with the entire idea, Krafter returned to his office, his feet heavy. At least the meeting with Larson ended amicably enough. He knew the director had a lot to deal with that was invisible to Krafter, and he appreciated Larson's backing, how-ever grudgingly given. Without it, he might as well pack up and go someplace else. Despite favorable media reaction and guarded approval from many colleagues, he was dismayed at the vitriolic reaction of his opponents. It is not as if he had attacked them personally! As he unlocked the door to his office, he smiled wryly, acknowledging that he still had a lot to learn before he could shed his ideological milk teeth. He sat down, powered up the com-puter and waited for it to boot up.

Reflecting on his talks with Perkins, he had learned one thing, and learned it well. There was no way he would relinquish his entire collection, or trust Harvard's brass-plated good inten-tions. He was no longer that naïve. Making a decision, he stood and walked out. This could spell trouble for him down the line, but he was already in trouble. Despite Dr. Larson's conciliatory words, the old boy was merely covering his own ass and protect-ing UW. He had to know that handing over the bones to Harvard could spell Krafter's professional ruin. To safeguard the flow of all that money into the university, sacrificing one career appeared to be a small price to pay. Well, it wasn't going to be *his* career!

As he strode down the corridor toward Lab Three, he rounded a corner and groaned, not in the mood to play.

"Ah, my dear Professor!" Wethermans cooed, his sleek face wreathed in phony smiles. "Just looking for you, as a matter of fact."

Hot or cold, the man always wore a trendy suit. Tall, tending to fat a little, sporting a Clark Gable mustache, Wethermans fancied himself a socialite, sweating out his time at UW until something cushier and more respectable came along. Krafter stopped and waited. He didn't bother offering to shake hands. They would never be pals—chemistry. The man was a user and an opportunist, and he had no time for him.

"Climbing up in the world, I see," Wethermans murmured with a raised eyebrow. "A splash in the *Laramie Boomerang*, articles in *The New York Times* and *The Washington Post*, and a cover in *Nature*. You even have a spread in the *Branding Iron*, even though that's only a student paper. My, my. I'm disappointed, Larry, that you never bothered to consult me on your find. I could have helped you divert some of the inevitable criticism."

Or driven the knife deeper, Krafter figured. He may be a still-moist PhD, but he could figure out guys like Paul. "You're certainly keeping track, as usual, but I have the matter in hand. Still, I'll keep you in mind when I want my bench cleaned."

Something hard shone out of Wethermans' cool black eyes and the smile slipped.

"We're colleagues, my dear boy, and it's a rough world out there, as you already found. You could do worse than be guided by my experience."

"What do you want, Paul?"

"I am hurt that you keep your collection locked up from everybody. I want to see it."

"Denbow saw it and Peel worked on it. Wade—"

"Geophysicists and geologists! I'm talking about an anthropologist!"

"Wade is an anthropologist," Krafter said sweetly, relishing the ripple of confusion on Wethermans' face, implying that he was not.

A senior professor, Wade had worked alongside Spiro and himself, lovingly chipping away coal from bone with a dentist drill, totally absorbed and fascinated, happy as a little kid making mud bricks. Next to Perkins, Krafter had a lot of time for Wade and his wisdom, acquired over decades dealing with the Bollingers of his world.

Wethermans snorted. "He's a fossil who should be in a glass exhibit like his dusty collection. What you need is a fresh mind to corroborate your discovery."

"Someone like you?"

"You can sneer, but I am skilled in something far more valuable than anthropology, and that's institutional politics. Something you should brush up on, I would suggest."

"Yes, I saw your comments on the department blog. You dismissed my find without ever seeing it."

"Because you refuse people access!"

"Lots of people saw the bones, Paul. I ask you again. What do you want?"

"I want you to show them to me."

"Download the data from the website and you'll see them."

Wethermans colored at the snub, and whatever congeniality he may have felt had long evaporated.

"I only want to look at the damned things! Not steal them."

"You're not on my list of people with a need to know. Now, if you will excuse me, I have things to do."

"You'll regret this, Krafter! One day you'll need my help. Then we shall see."

"That's a hell of a thing to wish on a friend," Krafter said and walked past him. He was being petty and knew it. Showing the bones to him a small thing and might have patched things up between them.

Hell, Wethermans was not a friend and never would be. Why pretend?

Lab Three was empty when he walked in, which suited him fine. He hurried to the storeroom, took out his keys and opened a locker. Enclosed in a large Pyrex container, with most of the residual coal removed, the protruding skull clearly defined. Looking at it, no one could doubt that it belonged to a modern human. Sliding a cardboard box he picked up inside the lab toward the locker, he removed the glass container and carefully lowered it into the box, then packed it with bubble wrap. No one saw him carrying the bundle to his office. Inside, he pushed the box onto the crowded bookshelf next to two other boxes just like it. Far from a perfect hiding place, but he figured it would do until he thought of something better. Then what? He had not planned ahead that far and would need to think about it.

He checked his email list and quickly scanned through the flood of messages. Since the publication of his article, a lot of people suddenly had plenty to say about his find and man's place on Earth. Gratifyingly, some were from fellow paleoanthropologists, mostly cautiously supportive. Invariably, there were the doubters and the skeptics, but he found messages from the religious fringe most amusing. How dare he dispute the Bible? His find was a blasphemy against God and he was in league with Satan himself. May he burn in hell forever. Those were worth a smile or two.

He sat back in surprise when he saw an email from Dennison Walsh, Professor of Social Anthropology at Oxford's Institute of Social and Cultural Anthropology. Fellow of the Wolfson and Magdalen College, Director of Graduate Studies and a page-long list of honorary degrees, Walsh had produced numerous papers on early hominid development and African migratory theories. One of his pet suggestions that man had occupied the Pacific islands, not from South America as is contended, but from south-ern Asia, mirrored Krafter's own research. Both of them were heavily criticized for their views. After reviewing the Karringa Mine films, that Walsh would lend his name in recognition of his discovery took nerve. Krafter reminded himself to send the man a polite email of appreciation, with an engraved invitation to visit UW, or at least view the bones through a video link.

Another message caught his eye and he blinked. Dr. Gene Hartman would welcome an opportunity to discuss Professor Krafter's find if the professor would be kind enough to call. Krafter gaped as he stared at the email. This was patronage of the first order. A Nobel laureate, Hartman was a leading world au-thority on paleoanthropology, head of Texas State U's Forensic Anthropology Center, and Director of the Center for Archaeo-logical Studies. Krafter had read most of his papers, and they both shared the same critics, which immediately made Hartman a pal. This was sweet indeed. At least *somebody* believed that his find wasn't nonsense.

Excited, he picked up the phone and dialed.

"Professor Hartman." The voice cool, cultured and mature, which fitted the image of a learned figure secure in his position.

Krafter breathed a sigh of relief. Despite the email message listing a private number, he was not certain of catching the pro-fessor. After all, the man was unlikely to be sitting in his office gnawing his nails waiting for Krafter to call.

"This is Larry Krafter, Professor. I read your email, sir."

"I am so glad you managed to call, Professor. I still cannot get over your astonishing article in *Nature*, hardly believable. No wonder it attracted the attention it did. I was looking forward to discussing it with you."

"Your interest means a great deal to me, sir."

"Understandable, given some of the things our colleagues are saying about you in the papers, which I don't personally agree with. You have stirred a formidable hornet's nest, Larry. But you knew that before you published. Judging by the reaction from a number of our mutual critics, your discovery has not been received with universal love."

"I admit it wasn't totally the reaction I expected. If I may ask, where do you stand, Professor?"

"My dear boy, breaking new ground isn't for the fainthearted, and you've been there before with your Pacific migration theory. Me, I've had a long and successful career, and I've collected too many of the right awards to be concerned about professional jealousy. If you'll excuse my bluntness, you on the other hand, are vulnerable. I am sure I don't have to explain further. However impossible your find is, I cannot walk away from the physical evidence your announcement paper suggests you have, provided the evidence is genuine, and after viewing the film on your website, I have no reason to doubt it. I want to help you establish credibility by using all the facilities and authority at my disposal and that of Texas State U."

A surge of affection for the man coursed through Krafter. "Professor Hartman, your acknowledgment would indeed give my find enormous standing. My dating data is irrefutable, as are the films I took at every step of my excavation and subsequent examination."

"I'm certain it is as you say, and I have checked the edited movie you made. I am completely satisfied as to the film's authenticity, as should anyone else who bothers to look at it critically. That's not enough to convince a crusty old doubter like me. To indulge my curiosity, what I would prefer, of course, is to see the original movie clips and the specimens themselves. Can you make them available if I came to see you?"

Krafter sat in his chair nonplussed. "You're prepared to come to Laramie?"

"But, of course. I wouldn't expect you to lug priceless artifacts all the way to San Marcos. What do you say?"

"Professor, I have nothing to hide and I have the highest

regard for your reputation and professionalism. I would be honored to have you examine my specimens. Frankly, I could use a supporting voice right now."

"Splendid! Then it's settled. When would it be convenient for me to see you?"

"I can make myself available at any time, sir."

"Would day after tomorrow suit?"

"Friday? I don't see that as a problem, and I'm certain Doctor Larson will be delighted to see you."

"Yes, I am sure. And how is the good doctor?"

"Cautiously receptive, sir."

"Hah! He was less cautious in his younger days, but that's another matter. I'll send you my flight details once I have everything organized."

"I look forward to seeing you, Professor, and I'll email you a URL link where I stored the original film clips."

"Excellent! Thank you, my boy. This should prove very interesting," Hartman said and cut contact.

Puzzled, Krafter wondered what the old boy meant by that, probably a twisted sense of humor. Hartman would denounce him the minute he found anything irregular, but he was unconcerned. He was on solid ground. The main thing was, he had potentially gained another powerful ally. His critics would *have* to sit up and take notice. Pleased at this turn of events, he jerked when the phone rang. Glancing at his watch, he would rather have lunch right now than handle more calls.

"Professor Krafter," he said after picking up, hoping it was only a student.

"This is Neil Reed, Professor, from *The New York Times*. Do you have a moment?"

Krafter nodded, suitably impressed. After a promising academic career at Columbia U, Reed had turned his analytical mind to running a science column, famous for unearthing shady goings on in the learned community and private industry in general, debunking questionable claims and discoveries. A thorn for many, his articles were always eminently readable; a big gun to have trained his way. If Reed sought to discredit his find, he would be holding a short straw.

"Of course, Mr. Reed. I have read some of your exposés with interest."

"No less interest than when I read yours in *Nature*. Tell me one thing, Professor. Are the bones real?"

"You don't waste much time fencing around, do you?"

"I don't have time to fence around, doc. Although not always true, evidence that claims to contradict well known theory invariably turns out to be wrong, and yours is an eye-opener."

"If a new theory or observation is clearly impossible, we should distrust the evidence that supports it. Is that it?"

"Extraordinary claims require extraordinary evidence, as somebody once said."

"The notion that the consensus opinion of a large group of scientists must be trustworthy doesn't apply here, and my find is not a claim, Mr. Reed. However uncomfortable for the establishment, it is a fact, which you saw from the film I took and the published dating data."

"All great truths began as blasphemies, doc. Something that George Bernard Shaw said. I hope what you found is true, because if it isn't, it will come out sooner or later, and believe me, you wouldn't want to be around on that day."

"My material is available to any accredited researcher to see, Mr. Reed."

"Even to someone like me?"

Krafter thought about that. *The Times* was a reputable paper and Reed was definitely qualified, although he only had a master's in astrophysics. Then again, given the army of detractors arrayed against him, it might be very useful to have Reed for a friend, and his word carried a lot of weight.

"Even you."

"I'm downstairs now, Professor," Reed said easily and Krafter blinked.

Was this a ploy to trap him, get him flustered at the prospect of an imminent confrontation? He laughed.

"I would be happy to see you, Mr. Reed. Give me a couple of minutes and I'll be right down."

"See you then."

Well! This was an unexpected development. Three sympathetic and powerful prospects when he expected nothing but ridicule. Maybe not so sympathetic? Hartman sounded genuine, but Krafter could not bank on that, or Hartman's motive. Having Walsh on his side was good, but he lived in England. As for Reed, the man was obviously after a story, either good or bad, depending on what Krafter had to show him. He was selling papers. Okay, he would get his story and perhaps more than he bargained for.

Krafter hurriedly typed a grateful reply to Hartman's email, attached a URL link to the camcorder MTS files, and pressed the Send icon. He did not violate university security doing this, the link being in the restricted part of the faculty website and had no navigational capability for Hartman to trawl elsewhere if he were that way inclined, which he doubted. Why would the old boy bother? He could have created an attachment for the email, but the movie files amounted to more than five gigabytes, almost certainly beyond the carrying capacity of both university message servers. Even if the servers could carry that traffic volume, Krafter did not want anyone downloading the clips.

Downstairs, he paused at the foyer and looked around. A crusty-looking individual of average height, wearing a dark green T-shirt and black trousers, walked toward him and extended a hand.

"Professor Krafter? A pleasure to meet you," Reed said in a surprisingly soft voice; steel beneath the filigree.

He exuded confidence and an air of a hunter stalking prey. His deep blue eyes shone with suppressed humor. Clean shaven, strong featured, his wavy brown hair made him look young. They shook hands, his grip dry and strong.

"I recognized you from your picture," Reed explained with an engaging smile.

"I'm glad you did the recognizing, Mr. Reed," Krafter said, steering his visitor toward the elevators. "I only know you by name."

"And reputation, no doubt. Hopefully deserved."

"That depends on whom you talk to." Krafter said and Reed nodded, still smiling.

"True, I did manage to annoy a few people along the way, but nothing to what you accomplished, Professor."

"It's Larry, okay? I told it like I found it, literally. My detractors cannot ignore that, even if they're not able to explain it."

"That's where you're wrong, doc. They'll do both and try to make it stick."

"Even lie?"

As they waited for the elevator to come down, Reed cocked an eyebrow at him. "What do you think?"

"I don't have to. I know."

"Believe it, and it's already begun. You must have seen the media reports. The only way to fight them is with solid evidence and the glare of publicity. Sometimes even that isn't enough, but truth is a sharp sword, Larry, and you trifle with it at your own risk. Your problem is not lack of truth, but time."

"I don't understand."

"Today, you have a worldwide sensation. Tomorrow, Vatican antics, the Israeli withdrawal from the West Bank, or some domestic nonsense, will occupy the news. With the exception of your fellow anthropologists, your story will be forgotten. Next week, the man on the street won't even remember your name. You must maintain visibility."

The elevator doors opened and they got in. Krafter pressed the three button.

"When I write my full paper—"

"Your reputation will already be shredded, and whatever evidence you've got, ignored. Instead of acclaim and recognition, you will end your days an embittered academic teaching undergraduate geology, if you're lucky. More likely, UW will kick you out to remove an embarrassment and you'll probably wind up teaching hand painting at some kindergarten at best. Unless you get mobbed first."

"You paint a bleak picture, Mr. Reed," Krafter said grimly, his composure unsettled by the reporter's clinical dissection. The bad part, he believed every crummy word of it. "I've already been mobbed," he added and told him about the incident in front of his house.

"There you go. Happens every time. And it's Neil, if you don't mind."

In his office, Krafter offered his visitor the only spare chair he had. Reed did not seem to mind the cramped conditions.

"Am I on record?"

"You don't want to be?"

"Doesn't bother me."

"In that case, you won't mind if I tape our conversation? I don't want to be accused of misquoting anything."

Krafter smiled and waved a hand. "Go for it."

Reed took out a small digital recorder, switched it on and put it back in his pants pocket. "I viewed your movie and read the lab reports—"

"Feel free to call any of them. Of course, they were only testing samples I sent them. I provided location and geological data, but they didn't know the context."

"That your samples held forty-million-year-old human bones? That's a broken chain of evidence, Larry."

"It might appear that way to a layman, but it's not. I didn't need the dating data anyway. The Powder River Basin strata has been reliably dated many times. I was merely taking out additional insurance. If anyone has doubts, further testing can be done from actual lignite samples that encased the bones. None of that is necessary, of course. The films I took at the extraction site provide clear proof of age."

"The site certainly looked real to me. What about intrusive burial? Somebody is bound to raise that one."

"They already have, but through ninety feet or so of soil, shale and rock? There was no evidence of any early mining anywhere around the site. I made sure of that. Besides, you must know that native Americans in Wyoming never used coal as a fuel. The Hopi in Arizona did where it was easy to get at, but not in Wyoming."

"I do know. I checked. Even if what you say is true, you still have a major problem on your hands. Your dig no longer exists. It is now bulldozed. That will make a claim of intrusive burial more believable."

"True, but there are eye-witnesses from the Karringa Mine," Krafter pointed out, not resenting the interrogation. Reed was an investigative reporter interested in hard facts. Krafter only hoped that whatever he wrote, it would be equally objective, and ideally, favorable.

"Mmm, yes, which some will dismiss or discredit. I hope you won't mind a bit of gratuitous advice? What you need to do, Larry, is take the initiative. You need to involve other universities to provide corroboration, and do it now. If you do the normal thing, write your paper, submit it to a journal, wait for a publication slot, if they will publish, you'll be out of business."

"As a matter of fact, I am doing exactly that. Professor Hartman from Texas State U is coming up on Friday to examine the bones. By the way, you can't use that."

Reed nodded. "Hartman is good and carries considerable weight. Well, that's one man in your corner."

"Dennison Walsh, Professor of Social Anthropology at Oxford's Institute of Social and Cultural Anthropology has also backed my find."

"Walsh? He's a heavy, all right. Well, that's two."

"Harvard has asked me to send them the bones for independent analysis."

Reed bit his lower lip and shook his head. "That's not smart. Bollinger doesn't think much of you and you'll be giving him a free get-out-of-jail card to stab you in the back."

"I know, but I've no choice."

"You've been ordered to hand them over?"

"In the interest of inter-university cooperation," Krafter said bleakly and Reed chuckled.

"I wouldn't do it, but it's your game. Now, mind showing me what you've got?"

Krafter grinned and stood up. After all, that's what Reed had come to see.

In Lab Three, he gently placed the Pyrex container on a bench and stepped back, allowing Reed a moment of solitude. The reporter peered closely at the arm bone and gold bracelet, still partially enclosed in coal. After a while, he turned and looked at Krafter.

"Man, the photos don't come close to conveying the emotional impact of this thing. Makes your hair stand on end looking at it. The last time I felt that way was when I saw the John the Baptist Scroll."

"Exciting, isn't it."

"To think this was once a man—"

"A female, actually," Krafter said softly.

Reed peered at him. "How can you tell?"

"There are small anatomical differences between the two that are definitive."

"It could be someone young or the person might've been naturally shorter."

Krafter was impressed by Reed's knowledge, and nodded. "True, but the bone development suggests a female."

"Because of the bracelet?"

Krafter had to smile. "Although indicative, in most early societies, men regularly wore ornaments."

"You're the expert. It's creepy to imagine that someone worked and built something like that bracelet millions of years ago. It doesn't seem possible."

"It isn't. That's what my critics will maintain, and that's why they want to tear me down."

Reed leaned toward the case and pointed at the bone. "What's that little hole there?"

"I removed a cubic centimeter and sent it to the New York's Union College fission track lab, along with soil and rock samples from the overburden strata."

"Ah, I remember reading it in your report; thirty-six-point-four million years, right? Can you explain the vast age?"

"With only a bone and a skull? Hardly. I have a hypothesis, but nothing to back it up with, yet."

"Except that," Reed said, pointing at the case. "Why haven't you cleaned off all the material?"

"That's as far as we'll go. The coal casing provides proof of containment to anyone who cares to look. If we cleaned the bone completely, all I'd have is a piece of mineralized bone with a hearsay evidence history and something very difficult to date even using modern techniques. I've got MRI scans of the hand bone and skull, and that's more than sufficient for any detailed analysis as to species type."

"And the bracelet?"

"It's evidence that the wearer and her supporting social structure were technologically advanced enough to produce such an artifact, and the intricate carvings demonstrate a superior level of abstract thought. The people who made it were sophisticated, probably had an evolved language, government, trade, moral values, and religion. They were nobody's dummies."

"Wow. You inferred all that from a single bracelet?" Reed looked at him in disbelief and Krafter laughed.

"It's not as difficult as you might believe. You need to look beyond the mere fact of the bracelet itself and see the broader fundamentals behind it. It's gold, and that means the people who mined it knew its value, with all the underpinning social implications. There is no gold in Wyoming, and that implies organized trade."

"She may have come to Wyoming wearing the thing," Reed pointed out reasonably.

"She might have, but it only proves my point. We're not talking about an isolated human colony eking out a cave subsistence. There had to be large population groups that interacted and probably cooperated on a social, technical, and intellectual level.

"Once the gold was extracted, it had to be worked and shaped. That takes advanced technology, understanding of metallurgy and highly developed tools. All that has to be underpinned by a broad base of diversified economics. A goldsmith was unlikely to make his own forge and tools, at least not all of them. He would acquire them from a specialist manufacturer or supplier. That's what I meant by diversified economics. Think of the steps needed in our society to produce a car. You're talking about a myriad of interdependent industries. The same thing would have applied to whoever made that bracelet. At a less complex level, of course, but the principal processes are still the same.

"Then you have the geometric carvings. They are abstract renditions. You would consider that a primitive artisan would engrave things familiar to him, if he would engrave anything at all, such as animals, faces, figures, trees, whatever. But this man chose to engrave abstract patterns. It means he was familiar with the concepts he used, and more importantly, the social matrix within which he lived were also familiar to him. A hunter-gatherer or village social group would be too busy surviving to indulge in abstractions. People have to achieve a certain level of economic comfort, social prosperity and stability, security, and learning before their thinking is drawn to esoteric pursuits. That implies an organized, ordered society. See what I'm getting at, Mr. Reed?"

The reporter stood there staring, clearly in shock. After a moment of silence, he cleared his throat and shook his head in wonder.

"I am genuinely impressed, Professor, and I don't impress easily. You've convinced me, without any doubt. That was absolutely top line analysis. I can now see what your follow-up paper might contain and why."

"Anthropology is not merely digging up bones or creating models of primitive dwellings for people to gawk at," Krafter pointed out gently.

"Yeah, I can see that. There is one thing I don't understand. If these people and those who came after them were so advanced, why haven't we discovered more traces of their existence?"

"You must understand the time scale here. The march of geology, shifting continents, climatic variations, natural and social disasters, simple weathering and erosion, they all contributed to wiping out evidence of any past civilization. I might be extrapolating about social groupings I mentioned, but the population base had to be restricted. Disease or extended warfare could have wiped them out. It would take the remnants a long time to recover not only its population base, but also lost knowledge and technology. Unless specific steps were taken to preserve their dead, human bones deteriorate rapidly, leaving no trace that anyone had ever lived."

"Unless preserved, like your find," Reed mused.

"Precisely, but that might not be to our advantage. Consider where my bones were found. Who knows what else lies buried beneath our feet. Leakey and others stumbled on their specimens on the surface, already weathered and contaminated, and dated using the most rudimentary and questionable stratigraphy evidence that incorporated lots of individual bias and assumptions. If you want to make things even more complicated, there is hot dispute in the interpretation of what scant fossil evidence does exist."

Reed frowned. "I thought if a Mungo Man skeleton was discovered that's fifty or sixty thousand years old, that would be pretty much it."

"Yes, but how did that human get to Australia? We're talking about different schools of thought here. On one hand, you've got the replacement model of Christopher Stringer and Peter Andrews that states all humans evolved in Africa who subsequently replaced other early species as they migrated out. Then you've got the regional continuity model advocated by Milford Wolpoff of the University of Michigan, who proposes that modern humans evolved more or less simultaneously in all major regions of the Old World from local archaic humans. Lastly, we've got Günter Bräuer's assimilation model. He's from the University of Hamburg in Germany. He accepts the idea of first modern humans evolving in Africa, but when they migrated into other regions, they didn't simply replace existing human populations, but interbred with late archaic humans that resulted in hybrid populations we know today."

"In which camp do you sit?"

"I am pretty much in the regional continuity school, but I'm not wedded to it and I'm still finding things out."

"I heard about your Pacific migration theory," Reed said dryly and Krafter laughed.

"Many of my colleagues don't like me for it, but they'll come around. What's so complicated about accepting the fact that early man used the southern oscillation event to reach the Americas by taking advantage of the El Nino when the trade winds blow easterly?"

"It upsets people and reputations."

"Yeah, it's a tough world out there. Who said we don't have evidence of ancient civilizations?" Krafter added softly and Reed's head jerked.

"Come again? I missed that."

Given this was within his field of interest, Krafter had dabbled in some of the arcane literature on past cultures and oddball discoveries. Most of them lacked any scientific validity, but as his research expanded, followed by several visits to museums across the country, what he saw had shaken him.

"Between 1786 to 1788, French workmen in the Aix-en-Province quarried limestone. At a depth of fifty feet, they found worked stone blocks, coins, hammers, remains of wood handles and metal tools. In 1830, carvings of what might have been letters were discovered within a block of solid marble from a quarry twelve miles northeast of Philadelphia. The marble block was recovered at a depth of sixty-five feet, and in 1831 the find reported in the *American Journal of Science*.

"On June 22, 1844, the London *Times* reported that a workman at a quarry close to Tweed, discovered a gold thread embedded in stone dug from eight feet. In 1852, *Scientific American* reported that a rock blast at Meeting House Hill in Dorchester scattered fragments, among which were found two pieces of a metallic vessel. When joined, the pieces formed a perfect bell-shaped vase four-and-a-half inches high and six-and-a-half inches at the base, carved with flowers and inlaid with silver. The blown rock was sixteen feet beneath the surface.

"In 1891, the *Morrisonville Times* reported a woman finding a gold chain in a lump of coal. The coal came from the Taylorville or Pane mines in southern Illinois. The Illinois State Geological Survey dated the coal deposit at 263 to 320 million years. An iron cup was found in a lump of coal mined in Oklahoma, dated at

310 million years. I'm only skimming here, mind you. Dig into old scientific publications and you'll be surprised what's there. Our understanding of human evolution is based on fragmentary and highly disputed evidence at best. There is lots more out there than we were led to believe, or are prepared to accept." Krafter paused and smiled at the look of total astonishment on Reed's face.

"You've got to be shitting me."

"Everything I told you is from published sources. You can research it for yourself."

"You spoke of scant and disputed evidence…"

Krafter smiled as he warmed to his subject. "All right. I'll give it to you in one lump. We've got a total of three craniums for *H. Sapiens Idaltu*, one skull for *Rudolfensis*, fragments only of *Rhodesiensis*, and if we go farther back in time to something like *H. Cepranesis*, we've got a single partial skull. Not much to build an elaborate house of cards that represents current accepted evolution."

Reed rubbed his forehead and exhaled loudly. "Phew! You're full of surprises, aren't you? I never knew…"

"That's the problem. Few people do and the information isn't in any published history book. Worse still, what evidence does exist is suppressed, gathering dust in museum basements or private collections. When somebody does challenge the envelope, they're vilified and discredited. Look at what happened to Virginia Steen-McIntyre."

"Wasn't she part of a team that in 1966 did a follow-up study of remains of human habitation in the Valsequillo region, dated to be between 250,000 and 350,000 years old?"

"That's her, and you've got a good memory. In the '70s, the Mexican anthropologist in charge of the Hueyatlaco site had it shut down because everybody *knows* that modern humans are only about 150,000 years old and that the New World was settled some 16,000 ago at the earliest. What the team found was clearly impossible, her colleagues argued. They ridiculed her, accusing her of incompetence and being a publicity seeker. She's not the only one to have suffered professional persecution."

"You got to expect some heat when you rock the boat," Reed said with a disarming smile.

"Heat yes, but not a blowtorch. Universities and museums scoff at the idea of suppressing evidence. People merely have to ask, they say. Sure, but you cannot ask if you don't know what to ask for. You first must to be aware that something exists before you can ask for it. No one gets to hear about those collections because the information is not part of the proscribed anthropology or archaeology curriculum. I don't blame Bollinger and Maddson, to name only two, for this mindset. They're merely a modern byproduct of entrenched ideas and vested interests who have covered up evidence for at least one hundred and fifty years."

"You wouldn't be talking about the International Anthropological Society here, would you?"

"They do come to mind. Privately, and I've spoken to a few, many paleoanthropologists will readily admit to either having or seeing fossils that clearly undermine accepted theories, but when asked to commit themselves in print, you get stony silence. Knowing the truth is one thing, but if talking about it might cost you your job or career, it's better not to say anything."

"That didn't stop *you* from going out on a limb, doc," Reed added wryly and Krafter grinned.

"I didn't know I was on a limb, at least not a thin one, or I might have had second thoughts."

Reed laughed, but without humor. "Man, I need a drink. I came to see the impossible and you've shown me a situation that's almost common. Pardon me for saying this, doc, but I didn't expect to hear something like this from you."

"Because I look young and naïve?"

"Frankly, yes. Looking at you, only twenty-six, you talk like someone much older. But I guess you didn't come by that PhD from a Wheaties box. Mind if I take some shots?"

Krafter waved a hand at the case. "Be my guest."

Taking out a compact digital camera from his pocket, Reed quickly took shots from several angles. He pocketed the camera and frowned.

"Where is the skull?"

Without saying anything, Krafter locked the specimen and took Reed back to his office. He sat down and stared hard at the reporter.

"This is off the record now, okay?"

"Got it," Reed said and switched off the tape.

"Can I trust you, Neil? I mean unreservedly? You've seen enough to satisfy yourself that my find is genuine, and you'll be even more convinced once you view the original films. If I cannot trust you, this is as far as we go. I would rather you tell me now and we part as friends, then later if you intend to shaft me."

The reporter leveled his eyes on Krafter. "Professor, I didn't have to come all the way from New York to get my story. Your website had everything I needed, but a story is more than just a movie and a dry report, especially a story like this. I wanted the human element, which you certainly provided. I had to be sure you were genuine, partly to protect my own reputation and the reputation of my paper, and partly to tear you to shreds if you turned out to be stringing me along. I am a pretty good judge of character, doc. I trust and believe everything you told me, and I would be honored if you could return that trust."

Krafter wanted to believe him, but he carried too many old burn scars, not counting new ones. Despite his willingness to do it alone, he recognized the limitations of his youth and inexperience. When young, one tended to trust in the basic integrity and decency of a fellow human being. It takes painful experience, disappointment and disillusionment before a hard shell of protective cynicism can develop. The problem he had, his shell was still developing and not quite hard yet. But hell, he had to trust someone. He had gotten himself way out of his comfort zone, and despite support from Perkins, he didn't know how to best manage the situation he now found himself in. Even if his trust in Reed turned out to be misplaced, he would only be inconvenienced at most and his shell would harden that much faster.

He reached behind him and picked up the skull box. He placed it on his desk, opened the flaps, and lifted out the glass container.

Reed leaned forward and stared avidly at the partially exposed skull. After glancing at Krafter, he took several hurried shots. Back in his seat, he looked at the skull and smiled.

"I guess you won't be giving Harvard everything after all."

Krafter was not too surprised that Reed had it figured out. The man had been around and clearly knew how the world wagged. He could almost see the hard shell of cynicism shine around him.

"I might be green, Neil, but not that green."

"I would call it being wisely cautious. What are you going to do with it?"

"Have it locked somewhere safe."

"Very safe, I'd suggest. Frankly, Larry, you've given me far more than I ever bargained for. More than lots of people bargained for, and I'm not talking about my editor either. Would you mind if I wrote a think piece on what you've told me? I would need corroborative references to make it authentic."

"I don't mind at all, and I can email you all the references you want. If the Library of Congress doesn't have the original publications, someone is bound to have them on a microfiche somewhere. One question. Why? What's your interest in this, apart from merely getting another story?"

"I told you. You need to take the initiative, maintain pressure and keep your discovery in the public spotlight. Make Harvard and others play the defensive and prove *their* case to be something other than sour grapes. My articles will help you achieve that and raise public awareness. Once the ordinary Joe on the street sees that your bones are far from unique, your critics won't be able to dismiss you so easily. Their weapon is public ignorance, as you already mentioned. You need to take it away from them. They might not be able to explain your find, but they won't be able to dismiss you out of hand either. You will have forced a rethink of man's entire evolutionary path, and that'll be about the best outcome you can ever hope for."

"I would settle for that. I'm not saying that everything we know about human evolution is wrong, but it definitely needs another hard look or two."

"Yeah. The other thing is, I don't have time for the Bollingers of this world riding roughshod over anyone who dares to challenge them. I had a taste of it myself and it burns me up when I see it happen to someone who cannot defend himself. As for those nuts picketing your house, the best way to defuse them is to start throwing mud. If it's one thing people like that love more than God, it's a scandal. Make them start picketing Bollinger and Maddson."

"I'll have to get some mud first," Krafter said with a smile, liking the idea.

Reed reached into his pocket, took out a business card and held it out. "Call if you need anything, and that includes mud. You'll also want this," he said and dragged out a little recorder from his back pocket. He extracted the memory chip and placed the instrument on Krafter's desk.

"It's a little Sony gem I use everywhere I go. It records up to twelve hours of voice data. Like I said, it avoids misunderstandings down the track. I'll mail you the charger. Use it when facing your, ah, brother paleoanthropologists. I'll even throw in a spare memory card," he said and dug into his pants.

Krafter sat back, startled by the offer. "I couldn't—"

"Trust me on this one, doc, and be smart. Okay?"

After a moment, Krafter took the proffered recorder and a cased SanDisk chip. "Thanks."

Reed grinned and stood up. "If you haven't had lunch, I'm buying. I want to know more about your discovery."

Krafter laughed. "Deal! I usually go to the Turtle Rock Coffee. They serve great gourmet sandwiches, and it's within easy walking distance."

"Whatever suits you, doc."

"In that case, let's go!"

Chapter Three

NOBEL LAUREATE ENDORSES PROFESSOR KRAFTER'S FIND!

MAN WALKED THE EARTH MILLIONS OF YEARS AGO!

ANCIENT BONES ONLY 400 YEARS OLD, ACCORDING TO HARVARD

WHERE IS THE SKULL, PROFESSOR MADDSON ASKS

CREATIONISTS HOLD PROTEST VIGIL OUTSIDE THE UNIVERSITY OF WYOMING

IAS AUTHORITATIVELY REJECTS KRAFTER'S CLAIM!

"You published without discussing your findings with me, Professor!" Krafter raged, ready to sob with frustration, his knuckles white as he held the phone.

He could accept that fellow scientists would resist what his discovery implied and fight to prove him wrong, but this was gutter tactics, and libelous! How could Harvard spout outright lies and pretend it was truth!

He expected a natural amount of criticism and a degree of skepticism from fellow anthropologists, but not the level of personal attacks that questioned his professional integrity. Prepared to defend his discovery objectively with what he thought was unassailable evidence, the emotional toll over the past week had drained the will out of him. Every new day, he faced renewed attack, and cracks were appearing in his resolve. Could he have missed something? Surely all those learned figures with decades of research and authority behind them, they could not all be wrong, could they?

"I published nothing, Dr. Krafter," Chandler replied with strained calm, clearly not relishing the exchange.

95

"*The Boston Globe* has your byline!"

"That wasn't my article! What's more, I didn't write it and I don't stand by it."

"You nailed me to the wall without presenting any evidence! You saw the hand bone. How can you say it's only four hundred years old?"

"Will you listen to me, Doctor? I had nothing to do with that damn article!"

Krafter ground his teeth, then took a deep breath and sat down. He had not been this angry and disillusioned since his father threw out his prized mineral collection while he was on a high school field trip. He had spent years gathering the irreplaceable specimens, bought with hours of mowed lawns, car washes, digging around hills and dry streambeds, and bartering with fellow students. What did his old man have to say? He was merely cleaning out the mess in his room. And his old man was a geologist, too! Krafter had never forgiven him for that single piece of betrayal. If he could reach through the phone now, he would cheerfully have strangled Chandler, feeling equally betrayed. By rights, he should sue the bastard for defamation.

"I am listening," Krafter grated with frosty dignity, restraining himself from slamming down the phone by sheer force of will. If he had to face this kind of thing every time he wrote a controversial paper, the struggle wasn't worth it.

"My name was used without permission, and I am equally outraged as you are at this flagrant breach of professional ethics. What's more, I made that abundantly plain to the Anthropology Department Director. My analysis of your sample largely validates your paper in *Nature*, something I made obvious to Dr. Van Neuman."

Krafter snorted. "This was Bollinger?"

"Professor Bollinger is Director of the Peabody Museum of Archaeology and Ethnology, a Fellow of the International Anthropological Society, a Rhodes Scholar, and Deputy Director of

Harvard's Anthropology Department…and my boss. He asked for my data and all your material. I had no choice but to give them to him, on the condition that he discuss my findings with you before making any announcement, which he clearly did not."

"If what you're saying is true, Professor Chandler, he butchered your findings and is guilty of willful misrepresentation." Krafter was far from mollified, but he could see how the mess had developed.

He suspected that this would happen the minute Larson told him to hand over the specimens. Why then did he act so surprised? Beneath his skepticism and clear evidence to the contrary, he still expected decency and honorable behavior from Bollinger. Stupid!

"That's in essence what I told Dr. Van Neuman," Chandler agreed.

"Where is my sample now?"

"I imagine Professor Bollinger still has it."

"I see."

"Professor Krafter, this entire episode is intensely embarrassing for me and I'll seek disciplinary action against Professor Bollinger. I am also writing a retraction for *The Boston Globe* and publishing my findings in *Science* and our *A Journal of Anthropology and Aesthetics*."

The *Journal* was Peabody's own magazine and had limited distribution. A retraction there was a waste of time, but Krafter figured better than a slap in the face.

"I need to tell you that *Nature* rejected my follow-up paper, citing unsubstantiated speculation despite my solid data. How sure are you that *Science* or any other journal will publish yours?"

"I am publishing factual findings," Chandler protested.

"So was I. Have you submitted your paper to the IAS?"

"Yes, I have. Why do you ask?"

"They denounced my research and probably exerted influence on *Nature* to reject my paper."

"Yes, I've seen the tabloid headlines."

"I am speculating here, but I suspect they will do the same with your paper."

"The bastards wouldn't dare. It's censorship, and I am an accredited member!"

"Yes it is, Professor. Now you know how I felt."

"What are you going to do?" Chandler asked.

"Fight it out, of course. Bollinger hasn't heard the last from me, and I apologize for my outburst."

"I understand perfectly, and think nothing of it. It doesn't help, not now, but I'll send you a copy of my paper."

"Thank you. I would appreciate that."

"Goodbye, Professor."

Krafter held the phone, listening to the dial tone. After a while, he replaced the receiver and gave a weary sigh. Reed was right. His enemies were playing dirty at the lowest level and he didn't know how to hit back. Intellectually, he knew what needed to be done. He had to fight them on their own level, using their own tools, but that was a hard ask. He just didn't know how to be vindictive and a bastard. Well, it looked like he would have to learn, and learn in a hurry if he wanted to salvage his reputation. The prospect churned his guts and he ground his teeth in frustration. Did he want to become another Bollinger or Maddson? Where would he draw the line? Would there be a line left after he crossed it?

He graduated with honors at the University of Colorado and pursued his master's in anthropology with single minded passion. Lured by superior facilities at the University of Wyoming's anthropology school, he felt enormous pride, shared by his parents, when the Trustees awarded him his PhD. Higher learning and the pursuit of new truths through discovery and scholarship were beacons he held high and lit his path to what he hoped would be a fulfilling career. In hindsight, it was easy to see where he made his mistake. He had forgotten the human element, something that Reed pointedly reminded him of. Perkins warned him, but he could not accept that people like Bollinger and others existed. He had been naïve and childishly trusting.

When he stood up, his protective shell had hardened almost fully.

Face grim, he walked up the stairs, ignoring friendly greetings from colleagues and students, and made his way to Dr. Larson's office. Laura gave him a pleasant smile when he walked into the outer reception area, but he had no time for idle chitchat now.

"Is he in?"

She blinked at this unorthodox reference to the Department director.

"He is not to be disturbed, Dr. Krafter, but I can make an appointment for you later this afternoon, if you want."

Without looking at her, Krafter hurried toward a polished teak door on her left and grasped the chrome handle.

"Hey! You can't…" Laura jumped up and scrambled after him.

Krafter walked into Larson's spacious corner office and stood there. Tall windows provided an excellent view of the campus grounds and the city outside. Larson slowly lifted his head, placed a pen on the papers before him, and leaned back against the brown leather chair.

Breathing heavily, Laura squeezed past Krafter. "I am sorry, sir. He—"

"Never mind, Laura. The Professor is clearly in a hurry and has a lot on his mind. Would you shut the door, please?"

Laura shot Krafter a poisonous look and retreated, softly closing the door after her. Larson smiled and extended a hand at a visitor chair.

"Might as well make yourself comfortable while we discuss your weighty problem, Doctor."

Krafter had bullied through this far on raw nerve and saw no reason to be humble or apologetic now. Ordinarily, he would never have dared break protocol so crudely, certainly not with Larson, but diplomatic niceties were the farthest things on his current worry list. Strictly speaking, he should have talked to Dr. Perkins, his immediate superior, but this was something his mentor could not help him with. Like Larson said, he had created a storm and now had to ride it. The problem, his grip was slipping.

Krafter ignored the solid wood bookshelves, the antique credenza and glass-topped coffee table tucked into a corner surrounded by soft easy chairs, and sat down, hands held in his lap.

Larson waited for him to make himself comfortable.

"I sense in you a new resolve, young man. Determination and confidence, and I'm not altogether displeased to see this change. Too bad the transformation was wrought under such adverse circumstances, but you had to emerge out of your comfortable chrysalis." He leaned forward and crossed his arms over the desk. "I'm sorry to hear that your house is still picketed," he said gravely.

Startled, and taken aback at having water poured over his powder, Krafter had cooled down sufficiently to swallow his bile and intended spiteful outburst. Although still angry, he relaxed slightly and allowed himself a wry grin.

"I'm hoping they'll lose interest in a couple of days and go someplace else. It's also a bit intimidating having to fight a crowd coming in every morning. I must admit to being a little concerned when I first saw them."

"Mobs are always a nuisance," Larson said seriously. "And violence is usually never far behind. Your reaction is perfectly understandable, but I guess you're not here to talk about group psychology. Shall I sum it up for you? You're outraged at what Professor Bollinger did to you, and shocked that IAS could so coldly stab you in the back. You want to sue Harvard and wring Bollinger's neck. How am I doing?"

"Sounds about right, Doctor," Krafter said and broke into a genuine smile. "I apologize for bursting in on you like this."

"Yes, I can see that you're sorry. At least you had the guts to beard an old dog in his own den."

"Doctor Larson—"

"It's okay, young man. I was glad to see the fire in your eyes. You will need it before this is over. I just got off the phone with Dr. Van Neuman and he's following up on Chandler's complaint. He is yet to confront Bollinger, and apologized in advance for any personal embarrassment this has caused you."

"Big of him," Krafter muttered. "The damage has been done and he knows it."

"Because he does know it, he wants to make up for it. He has extended you an invitation to come to Harvard and discuss your find. He'll be paying all expenses."

"Will Bollinger be there?"

"You didn't expect him not to be, did you? Dr. Maddson will also be there. You'll have two of your most prominent critics in the same room, but you will also have friends. Not everyone is hostile to your discovery. Can you handle that?"

Krafter knew he would be facing formidable opposition without the home ground advantage, but he considered his position unassailable and his facts irrefutable. The cynical part of him sneered. Irrefutable facts have not stopped his detractors so far.

"I can handle it," he said with a resolve he did not entirely feel.

"Good." Larson reached across the desk and picked up a paper. "A letter from the IAS. Strictly speaking, I shouldn't be telling you this, but given the circumstances, it's better that you know. They're not happy with you or this university for publishing unsubstantiated and fraudulent claims based on flawed evidence. Their words. They demand I take disciplinary action against you before you tarnish our fine reputation and the reputation of upstanding anthropologists everywhere."

"You should have asked them what they really thought," Krafter said dryly, not giving a damn, and Larson chuckled.

"Yes. Despite UW's endorsement, they blocked your paper in *Nature*."

"I figured as much. Although disappointing, it comes as no surprise. As a counter, I already submitted my paper to the Public Library of Science and the Paleoanthropological Society. I also posted it on the *American Anthropologist*, the *Anthropological Forum*, and the *Archaeological Newsletter Online* websites. In addition to American newspapers, several international papers agreed to carry it."

"Such as? We don't need tabloid exposure here, Doctor," Larson said severely.

"*Le Monde*, *Das Spiegel* and the British *The Guardian*. They're all reputable."

"Mmm, that's all very well, but you still need more traditional outlets. If you want, I can give you a list of journals who do their own peer reviews. With my backing, your paper should be published promptly."

"Thank you, sir. I would appreciate that."

"Laura will email you the details. You're decidedly cool about this, I must say," Larson remarked, wearing a puzzled expression.

Krafter's features clouded and he sat up. "I'm not cool about this at all, Doctor. My professional reputation is being dragged through the sewer and I'm at my wits end how to fight back. I have never been through anything like this before and I don't know what weapons exist to counter my enemies. For Chrissake, Doctor. I am a scientist, not a character assassin!"

"You have truth behind you, young man. That is the most potent weapon in your arsenal. With determination and perseverance, you will prevail. I'll stand behind you, as will this university. You have powerful friends in Hartman and Walsh, and there are others like them out there. By the way, Professor Chandler noted that you didn't send him the skull for their analysis."

"Why, I'm sure I have," Krafter said sweetly. "I suggest he check with Dr. Bollinger."

Larson stared, then nodded, a faint smile playing at the corner of his mouth. "Yes, probably mislaid somewhere." He plucked another piece of paper off his desk and held it out. "Your e-ticket to Boston. The flight leaves at eight oh-two tomorrow morning. Don't miss it. Unless you want to postpone?"

"No, I don't want to postpone anything, Doctor."

* * *

For the second time in his life, Krafter saw Boston from the air. Bathed in sunshine beneath clear skies, the city skyline stood sharp with only a hint of smog. The Boeing 757 narrow-body jet rocked its wings as it turned on final and descended toward the General Edward Lawrence Logan International airport. When the small jet touched down, the pilot engaged reverse thrust and the aircraft slowed quickly. Krafter stared bemused at the profusion of planes crowding the taxiways and terminals. He hoped that whoever managed this gaggle knew his right from his left.

They pulled into the United domestic hub and everybody stood up, reaching for bags in the overhead lockers. After four hours cramped on a hard seat, Krafter pleased to be out of here. The Beechcraft turboprop at Laramie had a mechanical problem and they took off twenty minutes late. This didn't bother Krafter as his scheduled flight out of Denver wasn't until 10:48, but judging from disgruntled comments, the delay certainly scrambled some passenger's connections. The Great Lakes Airlines attendant apologized profusely for any inconvenience caused, but the poor girl was only a messenger. He spent time wandering around the huge Denver hub before boarding his connection. The sheer crush of people, the noise, lights, glittering attractions and services were overwhelming. He considered himself sophisticated, but Denver International had opened his eyes wide. A big world lay out there and Laramie very much a backwater by comparison.

If he'd had more time, he would have loved to drop in on his parents. Perhaps for Thanksgiving. With the fall semester started, lectures to be organized and given, his summer break was truly over. He only had a couple of classes a week and three tutorial sessions. That still left him with little time to pursue a research program while waging war over his discovery.

He always loved Denver. Its cosmopolitan atmosphere, tempered with easily accessible open spaces of the High Plains in the east and the Southern Rockies in the west, gave him plenty of options for exploring. With a population of only some 600,000, less when he was a kid, it did not crowd like larger cities, and its planned grid system made getting around easy. He grew up in leafy Cherry Creek and his parents still lived in their original sprawling, double-story ranch mansion. They thought of selling up a couple of times and moving into something smaller, but the fact was, they preferred the neighborhood and the house a great investment. A senior geologist with the Resolute Energy Corporation, his father got him interested in things mineral, which eventually gravitated into anthropology.

As Krafter waited to alight, he adjusted his watch to local time from the landing data displayed on one of the overhead screens: 4:55p.m., which wasn't too bad, but his body still insisted it was only one o'clock, having lost time going east. He may have gained time now, but payment would be exacted tomorrow on his way back.

With only a black bag, enough for a single night's stay, he walked into the baggage collection area and looked around. An elderly, gray-haired smallish man held a name card against his chest, looking anxiously at emerging passengers. Generous belly bulging, dressed in black slacks and pale blue shirt, the man nevertheless had poise and authority. Krafter walked up to him and nodded.

"I am Krafter."

The man broke into a broad smile and extended a hand. "At

last! I am Professor Chandler…Mike, to my friends. Welcome to Boston."

"I'm pleased to meet you, Mike," Krafter said warmly as they shook hands. "This is pretty overwhelming to someone like me."

"I'd be happy to trade places with you, Professor," Chandler said cheerfully, steering his visitor down the corridor. "A big city like Boston has its advantages, but I wouldn't mind a slower pace sometime."

"I know what you mean, and please, it's only Larry. I must say, Mike, I didn't expect this welcome, or the invite."

"Even if Van Neuman hadn't told me to take you under my wing, I would have been here anyway. I visited big cities myself and I know exactly what you're feeling. Besides, I had an ulterior motive for meeting you."

"Oh?"

"I wanted to talk to you before our session tomorrow. After what Bollinger did, Van Neuman thought it only fair that you presented your case personally. I hope you're still not mad at me over that article?"

"Forget it. We've both been had."

"Good. By the way, do you have any other luggage?"

"Just this."

"Getting through the Ted Williams Tunnel this time of day is no big deal, but the Monsignor O'Brien Highway will be crowded, I'm afraid. Everybody is wanting to get out of town after a day at the office."

"I didn't intend putting you to any inconvenience, Mike."

"No inconvenience, simply telling you the facts. I've got you in a motel near the Peabody Museum, so you won't need a cab tomorrow. You'll have to walk three or four blocks to get there, though. I need to apologize in advance, but I won't be able to take you back to the airport."

"You don't have to concern yourself. I'm sure the cabbies here know their way around."

Chandler emerged out of the tunnel on I-90 and threaded his way through the traffic, driving with easy skill toward I-93. Boston's skyscrapers glittered in afternoon sunshine. Once they left O'Brien Highway and entered Cambridge Street, the traffic eased off.

Not certain where Chandler stood on this, Krafter discreetly reached into his pocket and switched on his newly acquired recorder, feeling utterly foolish. He did not doubt Chandler's reputation: a double doctorate in archaeology and anthropology from Columbia U, an expert on Mesoamerican history, producing four books on the subject, at fifty-six the man was a respected academic figure. But then, others were also respected figures, which did not mean that Krafter could trust any of them.

Chandler glanced at him, his eyes glittering. "So, how are you enjoying your notoriety?"

"Except for having my house picketed, it's been a mixed bag," Krafter said dryly and Chandler laughed.

"You must have expected this would happen when you decided to publish."

"I expected crowds of adoring fans, not mobs baying after my blood."

"Not many fans in our field, Larry, and mobs are all too easy to come by. I noticed that you reported two finds, a hand wearing a bracelet and a skull. When I made my request to Dr. Larson, I expected you to send me both."

"Professor Maddson has already made mileage of that fact. I didn't send you the skull because I was still working on it, being a definitive sample of a *homo sapien* type," Krafter told the lie easily. "Anyway, you had enough material to do your analysis."

"Mmm. If I were a suspicious fellow, I'd say I was being snowed. Of course, such an unworthy thought would never enter my mind."

"Of course."

"You didn't trust me?"

Krafter looked directly at Chandler. "I didn't trust Bollinger. With all my evidence in his hands, I'd have nothing. He could say whatever he wanted and I would only have my films to fall back on. If the newspapers are right, Maddson has already declared them a fake."

"Yeah, I read the article."

"Do you believe my films were doctored?"

Chandler grinned. "Frankly, the possibility did occur to me. I didn't know you and your discovery was blatantly preposterous. I quickly changed my mind when I saw the hand and the bracelet. There is simply no known way that bone could have been deliberately encased in a coal seam that deep. I also had a couple of physicists and geologists look at it. That lump of coal was solid. I could clearly see unbroken leaf and wood grain across the entire specimen. It is inconceivable to believe that such detail could be faked. Even Bollinger looked white around the gills when he saw it.

"I did have your digital movie MTS files checked by IT, though. If they were doctored, it would have taken the CIA and a Cray computer to do it. I couldn't see how you might have managed that using a PC and a hundred-dollar moviemaking software. And the labs you used to date the stratigraphy samples? I called them to verify the report reference numbers. I might disagree with what your data was telling me, but unless you substituted the samples you gave them, I had to accept the validity of those reports. You unearthed a paleoanthropological oddity that doesn't fit any recognized evolutionary model we know of today. Understandably, it has caused a stir."

"Why didn't you simply publish your findings in the Harvard *Gazette*?" Krafter demanded, exasperated.

"I submitted it, but the article is being, ah, reviewed."

"Bollinger has that much control?"

"Unfortunately, he does."

"Harvard will simply sit back while he buries me?"

"They're is not sitting back at all, Larry. That's why the meeting tomorrow."

"A whitewashing exercise."

"Not by me, it isn't."

"His statement that the bone is only four hundred years old is laughable. An Indian falling down a mineshaft and buried when the thing collapsed around him? It's ridiculous. No scientist will swallow it."

"They would rather swallow accidental burial than admit that modern humans walked in the late Eocene," Chandler pointed out gently.

"It's one thing to have Bollinger and Maddson on my back, but IAS is something else. I thought they were merely butting in gratuitously because my find got some noses out of joint, but they're acting like a policeman here. They demanded that I be dismissed! This is all pretty unnerving, I have to tell you."

"Are you a member?"

"After getting my PhD, I received an invitation to join, but it had a caveat. I was not to pursue research that contradicted established theories."

Chandler nodded. "That sounds about right. I am a member, and so is most of Harvard's Anthropology Department faculty, including Dr. Van Neuman. Strictly speaking, I shouldn't be telling you this, but as a fellow scientist, I don't see any reason why you cannot know. The IAS have issued a circular to all members advising them that showing support for your discovery would be prejudicial to their standing with the Society."

"What? That's coercion!"

"The IAS executive committee has gotten arrogant, Larry. Another problem is that although they make themselves out to be a world anthropological body, individual national branches have a lot of autonomy in what they do. In the United States—"

"Bollinger and Maddson wield the big club," Krafter finished for him.

"They and their cronies, but it could be worse. They haven't got it all their way. Professor Hartman and several other progressive thinkers are on the committee, and so am I, but we don't hold the majority vote when it comes to policy."

"I heard that Hartman resigned."

"He did, which is both good and bad. Good that he stood up for his principles, bad that now there is nothing to stop Bollinger and his crowd using the entire weight of the IAS to quash you."

"Sounds as if you've had rocky dealings with them yourself."

"I am an accredited member, but this experience has given me second thoughts. I wouldn't be surprised if more of my colleagues don't think the same way. Your bones generated not only a scientific controversy, but also triggered a lot of power maneuvering within the anthropological community. It's an old story, Larry. Young liberal scientists like you are chafing under the shackles of conservatism. The problem we both face is that right now, Bollinger's faction controls university departments, grants and patronage. You're seeing what happens when you threatened that power."

"What about Dr. Van Neuman? I cannot believe that he will allow Harvard's reputation to be smeared by Bollinger's antics."

"Van Neuman is an administrator, not a researcher, and he has to tread warily when handling someone with Bollinger's reputation."

"Politics." Krafter sighed and shook his head.

"I'm afraid so. With scientists such as Professor Hartman and Dennison Walsh in your corner…and me, things can't be all that grim."

"You know Professor Walsh?"

"We've had our exchanges. I don't agree with him on everything, especially his assertion on Pacific migration to South America, which you seem to have taken up, but his credentials are beyond reproach."

"I like his theory and how he reached it," Krafter said simply and relaxed into the seat. Chandler only snorted, his feelings plain…merely a professional difference of opinion.

Traffic whispered by and the buildings along Cambridge Street were predominantly two or three-story, most of them businesses, stores and eateries.

Chandler slowed down, turned right into a leafy narrow street and pulled into a small parking lot of the Irving House B & B. Small, modest, the place was nevertheless clean and well cared for.

"Your home for the night," Chandler announced cheerfully as he killed the engine. "The Peabody Museum is practically around the corner. If you want, check in and I'll take you to dinner, or a belated lunch in your case."

Krafter felt uncomfortable, not wanting to impose. "You don't have to—"

"Please, it's refreshing to see a new face and I don't mind dining out. My wife has bridge tonight with her faculty group, so she can't complain if I indulge myself a little."

"Any family, if you don't mind me asking?"

"My boy is at MIT doing nuclear engineering. Rhonda is in Washington, a political strategist for some senator. We don't run their lives and they don't bother us much. It's a live and let live proposition. You?"

"Parents in Denver. No brothers or sisters," Krafter said as Chandler unbuckled his seatbelt.

"I've got a brother. He's a planetary scientist at Caltech. A year older than me, but I was always the stronger one, or more desperate," Chandler said and laughed. "We used to beat each other's brains in before we settled on a business-like relationship. We still get along." He smiled and stepped out.

Krafter retrieved his bag from the back seat and followed his host into the motel office. While an elderly woman processed his registration, he looked around the tastefully furnished foyer clad in dark wood paneling. On his right, wide doors opened to an unpretentious dining area, breakfast from 6:30 a.m. to 10 a.m. according to the sign.

He dumped his bag on the bed of his first floor room and hurried down the stairs, looking forward to eating something. His breakfast of toast and coffee seemed a long time ago now. They served drinks on the United flight, but he declined the offered cold sandwiches. Not at those prices!

Driving back east along Cambridge Street, Chandler glanced at Krafter, then focused on the road.

"I've read your published papers, Larry. Your analyses are sharp, but you're idealistic and inexperienced in academic trench fighting. After all, at twenty-six, you had few opportunities to gain experience. Like many young scientists, your eyes are focused on the horizon of new discoveries and challenges to be overcome, not noticing the grime and dirt of academic life that lies at your feet. Expecting to generate excitement with your discovery, endorsement and approval of your peers, which admittedly you did from many, you're now slammed by the establishment. You're not the first, and others will face the same obstacles in their chosen field, which explains why disillusioned scientists are leaving the halls of stuffy academia for a more fulfilling life of research and financial reward in the corporate world."

"What are you trying to tell me?" Krafter demanded.

After a moment of silence, Chandler sighed. "Keep one thing in mind. There isn't much of a demand for anthropologists in private industry. If you lose your fight, universities everywhere will become even stuffier and gloomier in the shadow of closed-minded conservatism. Let's face it. It was never about science or new discoveries, but power and politics, fought over as bitterly as any brawl in Washington, which my daughter attests to with undisguised relish. I can only hope the encounter tomorrow will not scar you too much. One way or another, you'll see how the grownups handle things."

"I've already seen how the grownups handle things," Krafter agreed moodily. "That's no reason to be gloomy about it. I'll simply have to face it."

"Good. Apart from giving you an impromptu lecture, I pondered whether to have oysters for my entrée or shrimp."

Krafter doubted that Chandler would look concerned over the prospect of choosing an entrée. Despite his brave words, he *was* worried about the meeting tomorrow. He pushed the looming confrontation to the back of his mind. Right now, he needed good food and distracting conversation, regardless of whether it might be a condemned man's last meal.

"Planning on doing any sightseeing while you're here?" Chandler asked, his eyes on the road.

"I would love to, but I don't have the time. This is strictly a business trip and I'm flying back tomorrow."

"Oh, well. Next time."

"There is one thing I do want to see since I'm here; the John the Baptist Scroll."

Scandal still raged over Vatican's sanctioned assassinations to recover the ancient papyrus and keep it from getting published. Given the sensation it caused, Krafter could sympathize why it was done, but he found it difficult to accept that the Holy See, supposedly a pillar of moral standing, would stoop so low. Something the CIA might do, but not the Church. He was not alone thinking that.

Housed at the Peabody Museum, the scroll a coup for Harvard and had become something of a pilgrimage destination not only for the curious, but scholars and theologians from around the world. Unfortunately, it also attracted its share of religious extremists who vehemently denied any suggestion that the Bible was anything other than the literal word of God, regardless of ample evidence to the contrary. Having an old papyrus state that Jesus was John the Baptist's disciple and the second Messiah who would liberate the Jews from Roman rule, Krafter understood why some people might get their dander up over that.

"I'll see what we can do," Chandler said with a grin. "I saw the thing a number of times when they prepared the exhibit. I keep wondering what other embarrassments lay buried in Vatican's secret archives. My curiosity is scientific, not religious, and the marches and protests don't affect me much. If whatever God exists, I doubt that he would be overly concerned what man writes about him."

After managing to get a parking spot on the street, they walked toward the East Coast Grill restaurant. Inside the cool, rustic interior, they snagged a table by the tall glass window overlooking the roadway. Still relatively early, they had the place pretty much to themselves. Three individuals sat beside the bar deep in conversation, nursing drinks. Chandler ordered oysters and Krafter opted for the Gulf white shrimp, accompanied by a crisp Gruner Veltliner from Austria. The service quick and efficient, both had the Uncle Butt's Tri Platter of barbequed pork and beef, washed down with a smooth Californian merlot. By the time they got to the brandy stage, Krafter felt pleasantly full and mellow, enjoying the buzz in his ears.

Chandler skillfully steered the conversation away from topics that might rile the stomach. Krafter learned about Boston and its attractions, and he gave Chandler an opportunity to know a bit about Laramie. When Krafter got back to the motel, both walked away enriched.

A refreshing shower perked him up and Krafter sprawled across the bed to go over his notes. He picked up Reed's recorder and pressed the playback button, trying to pick up nuances from Chandler he might have missed. When the tape finished, still feeling ridiculous using it, he placed the recorder on the night table and turned off the lights.

Buttery sunshine streamed through gauzy curtains when he woke. He glanced at the bedside electronic alarm clock, only 7:20, plenty of time to make it to his scheduled 9:30 meeting. He preferred to view it as a meeting rather than a confrontation, but ready to have it either way. Chandler seemed to be sympathetic, but would that count for anything when they confronted Bollinger? After all, Chandler worked for the poisonous turd. Hands locked behind his head, he stared at the ceiling. After a while, he switched on the wall-mounted TV and skipped through the news channels, allowing his mind to wander.

Refreshed after a warm shower, he changed and went down for breakfast. An elderly couple and two business types were already there. None of them bothered to give him a look. The place had a cozy atmosphere: layered stone brick walls, white floor tiles, glass-topped square tables with gray and white checkered tablecloth. He walked to the wooden buffet bench, poured himself coffee and orange juice, and carried them to a corner table. Loading a large plate with scrambled eggs, little fried sausages, heaped hash browns, he dug in with gusto. A little ketchup on the eggs added zest. The second cup of coffee settled things down nicely and he lingered before going back to his room. At nine o'clock, he checked out and with bag in hand, made his way toward Cambridge Street.

As he walked up Divinity Avenue, the Peabody Museum that housed Harvard's Anthropology Department loomed in front of him. From the street, the two buildings facing each other looked regal and imposing, befitting the institution to which they belonged. Lots of students were heading the same way, singly and in pairs. Krafter asked a pimply young student for directions to the main entrance and walked into the spacious interior of an echoing foyer. At the reception desk, he asked for Professor Chandler and was told to wait.

The foyer was crowded enough to keep him from being lonely, but Chandler's appearance made him smile, glad to see a familiar face. After shaking hands, Chandler steered him toward the elevators.

"We're meeting in one of the tutorial rooms," Chandler announced briskly as they entered the elevator, sounding very much a professor. "Afterward, I'll show you around the Paleoanthropological Lab and some equipment we're using. You'll have lunch with Dr. Van Neuman. He extends his apologies for not being able to attend the meeting, but lunch should make up for it."

Krafter was wary when somebody started fussing around him, and he felt like a piece of meat about to be dropped into a pool of piranhas.

"I am sure he had his reasons," he said lightly and Chandler frowned.

"This is a serious matter, Larry, and Van Neuman wanted to make sure you received a fair hearing. Sorry, that's not what I meant. He wants—"

"Don't apologize, Mike. I know what you meant."

Getting off at the second floor, they walked down a wide corridor covered with gray linoleum. The doors on either side were numbered, the familiar atmosphere reminding Krafter of UW. Universities everywhere had the same look and smell. Fingering the digital recorder in his pocket, he switched it on.

Chandler paused before Room 2.11 and peered at his visitor. "Are you ready for this?"

Krafter had pondered that very question all morning. He told himself that the men on the other side of the door had nothing, except years of academic standing and professional authority. He could not help being slightly intimidated by that. But he had hard evidence that no amount of bullying could remove. Then why did his insides churn as if he were about to take a final?

He took a deep breath and nodded. "Let's get this done."

Chandler opened the door and strode in.

The conversation inside the large room stopped when Krafter walked in and the two men sitting at the front desk stood up. He recognized Bollinger immediately, at least six-foot-two, heavyset, dressed in a dark gray double-breasted suit, jowls sagging, white hair cut short, the man was everyone's image of a distinguished academic. Originally from the University of California, Berkeley, before moving to Boston, Bollinger's initial works on Native American cultures were widely acclaimed and his books thoroughly researched. Fame and prominence seems to have turned him into a politician and a conservative critic, supremely suspicious of emerging technologies as tools of choice, preferring dusty references from past masters as definitive guides. Part of the problem, he hadn't published an original piece of research in years, something painfully noticed among his peers.

Beside him, Maddson was equally imposing, but thinner and a couple of inches shorter. Bald, wearing thick-rimmed glasses, a poised velociraptor ready to pounce. At fifty-two, Maddson was one of those academics caught between established methodologies and new thinking that sought answers through genetics and molecular biology to unravel anthropological mysteries. Not finding enlightenment from accepted theories, and suspicious of embracing new ones suggested by hard science, he now channeled his analytical talents into being a dogmatic reviewer of someone else's creative output.

Both men wore what could charitably be called smiles that didn't fool Krafter at all. This was an Inquisition and the torture rack waited below as soon as he confessed.

"My dear Krafter, so good of you to come," Bollinger said in his best lecture room voice and overwhelming influence that allowed no dissent, and held out a meaty hand.

Krafter was not sidetracked at all. All his life, Bollinger had slaved across the Americas searching for that major find which would have established him in the pantheon of anthropology luminaries, and Krafter, barely out of his egg, from Bollinger's point of view, had the gods smiled on him. Bollinger simply couldn't accept that his find was authentic. To do so would mean abandoning everything he had worked for all his life, and his theories shown to be worthless.

Well, that was just tough crap.

"I wouldn't have missed it for anything, Professor." Krafter put his bag down, grasped the offered hand and squeezed firmly, sensing the big man trying for a knuckle crusher. Young and in top shape, Krafter smiled as he countered with mounting pressure.

Before his discomfort became obvious to everyone, Bollinger backed off and nodded to his colleague.

"And this, of course, is Professor Karl Maddson."

"Nice to see you, young man," Maddson said in a clipped voice and they briefly shook hands.

Krafter suppressed a smile. The venerated personality condescending to mix it with an underling, expecting Krafter to show suitable restraint and respect in his presence. Krafter wasn't a raw PhD. He had grown up fast lately and wasn't overawed at all.

"How was your trip down?" Bollinger queried absently as they pushed chairs around.

"Comfortable enough," Krafter said, taking a chair on the opposite side of the desk, facing the two men.

Chandler seated himself at the head. Behind him, a large blackboard smeared with duster marks covered most of the front wall. Apart from three rows of plain white desks, the room was unfurnished. Morning shadows lay thick around the corners.

Bollinger leaned back, held the tips of his fingers in an inverted V, and cleared his throat.

"All right, we might as well get on with it. Professor Krafter, let's get down to cases. Picking over the details of your fanciful claim is distasteful, and frankly, a waste of everybody's time. Including mine. However, I was asked to organize this and here we are. Nobody actually disputes that you found something. Your films provide clear enough evidence, despite what Karl might have said in a moment of boyish enthusiasm."

"I don't happen to agree with Ryan's assessment at all, young man," Maddson declared stiffly, pushing back glasses that had slid down his nose, clearly irritated that Bollinger would choose to play dominance games. "Your films show an overburden wall and what is presumably part of a cast blast bench where you claim the bones were found. Although you carefully show how the bones were extracted, that is far from being conclusive of *in situ* burial. The ridiculous claim of age is an inference only. Your singular evidence are samples taken from the overburden wall and lignite seam. I don't dispute the dating data you obtained from independent labs, but those dates came from the surrounding strata! I most definitely dispute that the hand bone you claim to have found is of the same period."

"You're rejecting dating data of the bone itself, Professor?"

"Hopelessly contaminated," Maddson declared flatly. "Everyone knows that the Powder River Basin has extensive uranium beds. Your bone would have absorbed heavy concentrations of U-238, making the bone appear to be of the same period as the surrounding strata."

"The independent labs I used corrected for any possible U-238 bias, minimal anyway in the Karringa Mine area. You're suggesting intrusive burial as an alternative theory?" Krafter asked softly, relieved to have the matter in the open without any pretense at cordiality. Although somewhat nervous and tense, he felt ready to defend himself with total mastery of his subject.

"Definitely. Your films show lengthy extraction sequences, all faultlessly done, I'll grant you that, but there are significant gaps, young man. Gaps that don't show everything."

"How do you account for the fact that the samples I extracted had to be cut from solid coal? That would mean someone had to embed them in fine coal dust beforehand, somehow bake it to achieve the observed solidity, then planted the bones in the seam so perfectly that I couldn't detect it from the surrounding layer. Is that what you're saying?"

"That is exactly what I believe *did* happen!"

"Discounting that my films refute such an improbable suggestion, what about the eye-witness accounts from the miner who discovered the protruding bone and the mine engineer who secured it? Are you saying *they* might have put it there?"

"We checked with Ferguson, the mine manager," Bollinger said ponderously. "There was a time difference of almost two hours between the cast blast and when the push dozers moved in to start clearing the bench, more than sufficient for somebody to insert the bones."

Krafter smiled. Under a veil of respectability, his opponents were not here to present scientifically verifiable evidence to back up their assertions, or any evidence at all, but simply bully him with hollow accusations and overwhelming power of their positions. Indulging them with an emotional response would only drag him down to their level and achieve nothing. That did not mean he liked what was going on.

"Even if somehow the bone and bracelet could have been inserted into the coal seam as you suggest, where would this perpetrator come from?" he asked seriously, striving to appear as if he earnestly sought an explanation.

Maddson waved a hand in dismissal. "It doesn't matter. It could have been any one of the miners at the site."

"Why would somebody do that, even if he had the necessary skill to prepare the fake bones beforehand? He certainly couldn't have expected monetary or other gain, seeing that a dozer driver found the hand bone. Besides, it was only a fortunate accident the dozer driver noticed the bone at all."

"Why do it? To dupe someone like you, young man, and spark an unfounded controversy! And you were blind enough to fall for it."

"That's an interesting supposition, Professor Maddson, but inconsistent not only with physical evidence and Professor Chandler's own findings, but Professor Bollinger's claim of accidental

119

burial. Which is it?"

"A mineshaft *could* have been sunk through the overburden," Bollinger countered gamely, casting a dark look in Maddson's direction.

Krafter caught it and knew what Bollinger was thinking. The intrusive burial assumption was thin and Maddson was foolish to have suggested it without presenting compelling evidence.

"It makes more sense than accepting the idea of humans walking the earth forty million years ago. Bah!" Maddson snarled.

"Tell me, Professor," Krafter said, enjoying seeing a split among his opponents. "Why would a native American dig a shaft ninety feet into the ground to reach a coal seam when he had no surface evidence the seam was there to begin with? That would entail a lot of labor on an unfounded assumption. If a coal seam actually protruded from a cliff face, your supposition would have some credence. But then, why would they bother sinking a shaft? They would simply pick the coal off the face. Moreover, how would a skeleton be encased in coal so completely as shown in my films? If there were a cave-in, I would expect to see the skeleton covered by a layer of material consistent with the makeup of the shaft overburden. My examination of the site and films I took show no such detritus."

"Your own films show a nine-foot layer of rock and soil above the lignite seam!" Bollinger declared, looking triumphant.

"But undisturbed, and consistent with the surrounding strata! If a shaft were sunk into the lignite, there would be evidence of tool marks and digging. I found none."

"Your examination technique was flawed, as is your interpretation of what you saw," Bollinger said simply, smiling broadly. "Not surprising, given your inexperience."

"Professor Hartman made the same interpretation I did when he examined the bones first hand," Krafter said evenly. "Is his experience also to be dismissed?"

"The fool didn't know what he was doing!" Bollinger cried

angrily.

Krafter understood the slight undercurrent of enmity between the two personalities, which stemmed from the fact that Hartman had a Nobel Prize and Bollinger didn't.

"And Professor Walsh? Is he also a fool?"

"My dear Krafter, he only saw the films and observed the bones in a brief video link. He was misguided at reaching an erroneous conclusion without examining the specimens first hand. None of that matters, as I had the bone C-14 dated. The test reveals an age of 386 years, plus or minus forty," he announced triumphantly, head held high, daring anyone to challenge him.

Chandler sat up and Krafter gaped. Even Maddson gave him a startled look, pushing back his glasses.

"Where was that done, Ryan?" Chandler demanded. "It certainly wasn't in *my* lab!"

"I had it done independently by the Geochronology Laboratories at Melno Park after I got the hand bone from you," Bollinger said offhandedly.

"Independently? Analysis was supposed to be *my* job!"

"No damage done."

"You have the lab report?" Krafter prompted, stunned, unable to believe it. It simply wasn't possible. Bollinger *couldn't* have gotten that date reading.

"I'll give you a copy before you leave."

"Have you accounted for carbon contamination? I don't care what you say, but that bone was encased in solid coal, not mineshaft detritus! It would have absorbed carbon from the lignite layer, hopelessly throwing off any C-14 reading, even if one was possible."

"There is an error factor, I admit, but the test still proves my point," Bollinger countered coolly. "Even if the reading were off by fifty percent, it would only show that the bone is younger than it actually is. Either way, it's certainly not forty million years as you allege."

"I examined that bone in detail, Ryan," Chandler announced hotly. "It was almost completely mineralized. There is no way a C-14 test could be made off it, and the encasing coal layer showed no presence of C-14, normal for a coal strata millions of years old. I have films of *my* examination to prove it."

"You can read the test report if you want," Bollinger said, apparently unconcerned. "Whatever you saw, you clearly misinterpreted."

"I'll read it, all right, but I didn't misinterpret anything. A mineralized bone isn't something you can miss easily. I want that sample returned to my lab and I'll do my own tests."

Bollinger sat up and glared. "Are you questioning me, Professor Chandler?"

"I am questioning your methodology and the validity of your test. I simply want to corroborate your claim by doing my own tests."

"We'll talk about this later, Mike," Bollinger said softly and turned to Krafter. "Your dating data proves that the Powder River Basin Roland and Smith seams are thirty-five to sixty million years old. You needn't have bothered conducting independent tests to find that out. As we all know, the U.S. Geological Survey would have given you the same numbers. What you were careful not to do, and which totally invalidates your announcement paper, you never bothered to test the bone itself, the crucial piece of evidence that would have proven your claim!"

"I *have* tested the bone, Professor, although not with AMS spectroscopy," Krafter said with a smile, feeling more confident. "You must have missed that paragraph in *Nature*, the potassium-argon test from the sample I sent to the Geochron Labs at Billericia and the fission track test done by the New York's Union College lab on the same sample? Like Professor Chandler said, the bone was fully mineralized, which by itself indicated extreme age. Far older than the four hundred years you claim. Surely, you could not have overlooked the indicative mineralization shown in my films at UW when I cleaned the samples. A C-14 test would be out of the question. With acceptable variations, the K-Ar test returned an average age of thirty-six-point-four million years from both labs, in line with the early Oligocene period, which is almost the same date as the surrounding lignite seam," Krafter stated forcefully and turned to Chandler. "You observed the one centimeter cavity where the test sample was removed?"

Chandler nodded heavily. "The footage you took during the extraction showed a cavity."

"Meaningless!" Bollinger snarled. "Your films show something being extracted, granted, but that doesn't prove what the labs received was the same thing!"

Krafter tried to look unconcerned. "The lab reports say different. Professor Chandler, as part of your analysis, did you do a K-Ar or fission track test on the bone itself?"

Clearly uncomfortable, Chandler shifted in his seat and shook his head. "Ah, I only tested the enclosing coal, which supports your dating results. I planned on doing the other tests, but Professor Bollinger asked me to turn the sample over to him before I got around to doing them."

"What is this?" Maddson snapped. "Are we questioning Ryan's integrity? He is not on trial here!"

No, I am on trial here, Krafter agreed. A kangaroo court!

"Not at all," he said smoothly, liking how things had developed. In his rush to discredit him, it looked very much like Bollinger was careless with his procedures, or worse still, guilty of fabricating evidence, a charge he leveled at him. "As far as I can see, the whole question of age, and thereby the validity of my discovery, can be resolved very easily. We'll ask Professor Chandler to repeat my tests and I'll abide by whatever result he comes up with. If that piece of bone can indeed be C-14 dated and shows an age of four hundred years, I will publicly state that I was deceived by an elaborate fraud."

Somewhat mollified, Maddson nodded. "That's a very magnanimous gesture on your part, young man. Although I am still skeptical that this will clear you, your suggestion has merit. What about it, Ryan?"

Bollinger pursed his lips and braced himself. "I no longer have the sample."

"You don't have the sample?" Chandler stared at him in astonishment. "But I haven't finished my analysis!"

"What did you do with it?" Maddson demanded bleakly, giving his friend a very hard look.

"Having got what I wanted, I asked our mailroom to FedEx it back to UW."

Krafter had to smile. "That's very convenient, isn't it, Professor? What you're saying, the only proof we have of your alleged test is your word."

Bollinger stood up, placed both hands on the desk and leaned forward. "You insufferable little pipsqueak! Are you accusing me of something underhanded? You, who perpetrated a fraud on the entire anthropological community?"

"Ignoring your slur on me, sir, I'm not accusing you of anything. All I asked for is independent corroborative testing by Professor Chandler under controlled conditions. It seems somewhat convenient that the sample in question is no longer available. That's all."

"There is still the skull," Chandler said quietly and Maddson hissed in surprise. Bollinger blanched and suddenly looked very uncomfortable.

"Indeed." Maddson nodded and turned his eyes to Krafter. "You reported in *Nature* finding a skull, young man. Why wasn't it sent to Professor Chandler with the other sample?"

"I was working on it," Krafter said innocently. "I thought the hand bone and bracelet would have provided ample material for any test you wanted done. Clearly not."

Bollinger composed himself, sat down, and straightened his

jacket. "This is nonsense! But if you ship me the skull, we'll carry out the tests you suggested."

Krafter chuckled with genuine amusement. "With all due respect, given what's happened, if you think I would risk parting with the only remaining piece of evidence that backs up my claim, you're sadly mistaken. If that FedEx package ever arrives, I'll send it directly to Professor Chandler. In the meantime, I am more than happy for any of you gentlemen to come to Laramie with a representative from an accredited independent lab of your choice, take a skull sample and have it tested using whatever method you want. I'll also have a representative from a lab of my choice as a control, subject to your approval, of course."

Maddson gave Krafter a thoughtful look and slowly turned to Bollinger. "I hate to say it, but his proposal makes a lot of sense," he declared firmly and looked at Chandler. "Professor?"

"It should settle things one way or another."

"Then it's agreed. Ryan?"

"Who is to say he won't tamper with the skull?"

Even Maddson looked startled. "Don't be ridiculous. He knows what is at stake here. I don't understand your attitude."

"Instead of dismissing the whole thing as a joke, you're lending credibility to his so-called discovery if you agree to this outlandish proposal."

"I for one am not lending credibility to anything," Maddson announced in a chilly voice. "I am prepared to confront Krafter and his spurious find, but I won't be tainted by any hint of impropriety on your part. I am after evidence, pure and simple. To get it, we need the skull rigorously tested, observing every step in the process. That's why we had Chandler ask for the samples to begin with, remember?"

"This is a complete waste of time," Bollinger growled. "If that's the way you want it, we'll get it done."

"It's not the way I want it. It's the way it must be."

"I can make the skull available at your convenience," Krafter said smoothly, wanting to hug Maddson.

The old fossil was a pain and a professional enemy, but at least he still believed in the scientific method. Maddson might not acknowledge the test results, but was something he could face later.

"All right. Today is Wednesday," Bollinger mused. "I can have things organized with the Geochronology Lab at Melno Park. They do thermoluminescence, fission track and K-Ar dating. If that's acceptable to Professor Krafter?"

Krafter ignored Bollinger's sarcasm and nodded, not concerned that he used the same lab for his supposed C-14 dating. "I propose to use the Luminescence Geochronology Lab at Reno, Nevada. To remove any hint of collusion on my part, I would prefer that you make the arrangements."

Maddson and Bollinger exchanged glances. "Satisfactory," Maddson said with a nod. "When do we do this?"

"Is next Wednesday okay with everybody?" Bollinger asked and everyone looked at each other. "Agreed then."

"There is one more matter to settle," Krafter said. "Harvard pays all expenses."

"Impossible!" Bollinger snapped. "You have a case to prove, Krafter. You pay for the tests."

"I have already proven my case and paid for my tests. If you wish to repudiate those findings, you do it at your own cost. I will not pay for additional tests that you might refute later or use against me because you don't want to acknowledge what they tell you."

Maddson ginned, pushed back his glasses and looked at Bollinger fuming beside him. "I hate to say it, but he has a point. The ball is in our court. Anyway, you've got a bigger budget. Hell, Stanford will split the costs with you to see this scam exposed."

Bollinger glared at Maddson, then looked at Krafter. "Very well. I'll email you once the arrangements are in place."

"One last matter," Krafter said, suddenly very tense. This

could derail everything. Bollinger turned his predatory look fully on him.

"What is it this time?"

"Both labs must send their results to the four of us, Dr. Van Neuman and Dr. Larson."

"Out of the question!" Bollinger raged and Maddson scowled deeply.

"Young man, this is preposterous! You get your results and we get ours."

"I'm not afraid to have you or anyone else see the Reno results. Why should you be concerned if I see the Melno Park data? We agreed to use independent labs for transparency. This is merely a small step in the same direction. If we're all seeking to ascertain the truth, I cannot see why you should object."

"You're impinging on the veracity of both our institutions to independently announce the findings!" Maddson declared hotly. "I for one won't stand for it."

"Tell me, Professor. What difference does it make if I receive a report directly from Melno Park instead of waiting for you to make the announcement?" *Apart from giving you a chance to doctor it*, he added to himself.

Maddson made a guttural noise, clearly not comfortable with the idea, glanced at Bollinger, then jerked his head once in a nod.

"Very well. For the sake of getting this over with, I agree, but I'll remember this, young man."

Bollinger stood up and pulled down the lapels of his jacket. "If that's all, Krafter, I think we're done."

Krafter looked his enemy in the eye, not bothering to hide his disdain. "When we're through, I hope you'll be satisfied with the authenticity of my claim, however uncomfortable the implication for you personally or professionally."

He regretted the words even as he said them, but there was no going back. Anyway, he was only saying the bare truth. There was no love lost in this bleak room.

Bollinger made as if to say something, then his features smoothed into a bleak smile. "We shall see. I'm not done with you yet."

The meeting clearly over, Krafter stood up and nodded to Maddson. "Professor, I hope to see you in Laramie."

"You will indeed, young man. You will."

No one bothered to shake hands.

* * *

Krafter sat in the crowded, noisy departure lounge sipping a flat white coffee, waiting for his 3:15 p.m. flight out of Logan. He watched arriving passengers hurry toward baggage collection, or those about to depart, anxiously checking gate numbers as they wandered past the small café. According to the electronic domestic departures board, United flight 779 was on time, and that made him happy. He'd had enough of Boston, and Harvard in particular. Although Bollinger appeared to have tied himself into a knot and the meeting ended up other than a whitewash he expected, Krafter was not deceived. His opponents were still determined to tear him down any way they could, especially Bollinger. The man had been humiliated, which now made him doubly dangerous. The hiatus until next Wednesday merely gave everybody time to gather more ammunition. What boosted his confidence, the two men had revealed themselves as very human, not towers of unshakeable learning they projected. Reduced to that dimension, he felt he could handle them and others like them.

And Van Neuman's pathetic offer at lunch? He could not believe that Harvard—

The cellular went off and he dug the phone out of his pocket. "Professor Krafter."

"It's Neil Reed, doc. I heard you were in Boston and decided to see how things were going."

"How in hell did you know I was in Boston?"

"I'm a reporter. I know everything."

"Oh, yeah? If you know everything, tell me how to get myself out of this mess."

Reed laughed. "Simple. You hire a hitman and kill off your opposition."

"You know any good ones?"

"You wouldn't be able to afford one. Not on your salary."

"Well, that's it, then. Not a bad idea, though."

"Anyway, Dr. Larson's secretary told me where you were."

"Laura? Take it from me, she's not your type."

"I haven't even seen her," Reed protested. "I merely fished for information."

"And?"

"Didn't catch anything much. From the background noises there, I'd say you were at an airport. Logan?"

"Waiting to board my flight."

"So, you survived the interrogation?"

"It went better than I had any right to expect. They're still out to discredit me, but Bollinger threw me a lifeline."

"Oh?"

"He claims to have done a C-14 test on the hand bone and backed it up with a report from the U.S. Geological Survey Melno Park lab."

"What? I thought you told me a C-14 test was impossible."

"It is. All the bone mass has been replaced with leeched minerals. You saw it."

"Then how—"

"Obvious. He gave the lab a substitute specimen. Easy enough to do and he has a museum full of the stuff."

"He cannot hope to get away with it, can he? All you need to do is run another test with everybody watching."

"I can't. He no longer has the bone. Claims to have FedEx'ed it back to me."

"That's convenient. Especially if the thing gets lost in the mail."

"Yeah. Even Maddson thought so."

"You still have the skull."

"Everybody will be in Laramie next Wednesday hovering over me while I extract two samples to be tested by labs of our choice."

"You know that not everyone accepts fission track and potassium-argon testing as conclusive."

"That was true when the techniques first emerged, but the technology has advanced. They won't give me precise year readings, no test does in the longer time ranges. Even AMS spectroscopy and PIXE analysis have a margin of error. Given the age of my sample, I don't need a precise value. As long as I get a reading older than Bollinger's four hundred years."

"Not good enough and you know it. If that reading isn't close to your original thirty-six million years, you're dead."

"Oh, I'm not worried about the tests. With everyone using independent labs, no one can cry foul or attempt a fudge."

"You hope, but it appears like you're making progress to counter them."

"It's an encouraging step, but I'm not cleared yet. You won't believe what Harvard tried to do."

"Sounds juicy. Tell me."

"After our meeting, Professor Chandler showed me around his lab. I wish UW had such facilities. It's nice what you can do when you've got lots of money. Anyway, after the tour, I had lunch with Dr. Van Neuman. He's—"

"I know who he is, Larry."

"He offered me a tenured position as Associate Professor in his department. I told him I would consider it."

"You're kidding. And will you?"

"Sell my soul to Bollinger? Because that's what I'd be doing if I accepted the offer. They would slap a non-disclosure agreement on my find and Bollinger would have won. Six months later, I'd be out on my ass on some trumped-up charge of administrative or professional misconduct. Score an easy one for the other side."

Reed laughed. "For someone so young, you sound remarkably cynical, Professor Krafter, and very disrespectful of a world eminent institution."

"Sounds like it, doesn't it? But I've been taking a crash course on the subject, and you provided a lecture or two."

"I'm glad to hear that you paid attention. Van Neuman's offer implies that he's in on the smear campaign."

"Perhaps. Or maybe, he simply recognized talent when he saw it."

"Sure. Talking of lectures, you didn't happen to make use of a certain gadget I gave you, by any chance?"

"I got every word."

"Good man. And Larry? Make copies, hear me? Things have a way of disappearing."

"Now who's being cynical?"

"Always, my boy. You wouldn't care to share? I could write an article on the impending Laramie shootout. How about, 'Harvard agrees to independently test Professor Krafter's find', or something along those lines."

"Provided I proofread the copy first."

"Agreed."

"Of course, Bollinger will go critical. He'll know I talked to you."

"So? He talked to reporters himself about you. Why should he resent if you do the same thing to him? But don't be fooled by their apparent cooperation. Like you said, they're still out to eat your heart."

"I know. Bollinger made a mistake and has to regroup. He's not finished with me yet, but after seeing him revealed as nothing more than a jealous old man, he doesn't intimidate me anymore."

"Good for you. What are you going to do now?"

"Although he saw the bones over a video link, Professor Walsh asked me if he could come to see them personally, the skull at least. He'll be in the States next week visiting Yale, and the timing would suit him. Columbia U has also made a request. The University of Paris and AFA, the French association of ethnologists and anthropologists, are making similar noises. Now that the initial hurrah has died down somewhat, it appears that some rationality is being injected into the argument. I somehow neglected to mention this to Bollinger at our meeting."

"I don't believe you need more lectures on cynicism, but let me know if I can help further."

"As a matter of fact, there is something you could do for me, Neil."

"And that would be…"

"Come to Laramie next Wednesday."

After a moment of silence, Reed chuckled. "Wow. It would be worth being there to see Bollinger and Maddson's faces fall apart when they see the skull. I'll let you know if I can make it."

"Thanks for everything. I mean it."

"I love a fight and you've got a good cause. Talk to you soon."

Krafter switched off, stared at the cellphone for a moment, then smiled. When he took a sip, the coffee had cooled, but he didn't mind.

Although his visit had not been entirely unsuccessful, it *had* ended on a thoughtful note. After seeing the yellowed John the Baptist Scroll encased behind bulletproof glass, lit with non-emitting UV or infrared lamps to reduce damaging the precious papyrus, it left a profound impression on him. Surrounded by subdued visitors and tourists, he did not notice them as he stared at the Sahidic text. As he read the translation posted beneath the tractate, the words moved him more than he cared to admit. History from 2000 years ago spoke loudly from the scroll. The words, whether true or not, did not matter as much as the connection with that time.

The Church had a lot to answer for.

Chapter Four

At the corner of 12th Street, Krafter turned left toward the Anthropology Building. Two white Chevrolet Impalas stood parked beside the entrance with 'Laramie Police' painted in large black letters on their sides. Blue and red roof lights cycled lazily from side to side. Not overly concerned, he walked up the wide steps and the glass panels slid out of his way. Like any large campus, there was always some minor trouble from time to time.

He followed a routine coming to UW. Mondays were his must-walk-in day. He left other days of the week open between walking and cycling, not wanting to sink into a rut and become predictable. When bad weather prevented him taking either option, he used his little Ford Focus. There were limits to being green or worrying about reducing his carbon emission footprint. He came in during weekends purely on a whim, or when compelled by pressure of work.

On the third floor next to the elevators, Krafter paused beside two rows of locked pigeonholes and picked up his official mail. Down the corridor, he saw Dr. Perkins talking to a police sergeant and nodded to both.

"A moment, Larry!" Perkins shouted and hurried toward him as Krafter approached his office. Reaching for the keys, he was surprised to see the door open. He stood in the doorway and waited.

"We had a break-in last night," Perkins said gravely. "So far, it doesn't appear that anything much was taken, although some items are missing from the Lab Three storeroom. We're still checking. Go over the stuff in your office and whatever you may have in the labs."

Krafter blanched. "My specimens!"

"Don't worry, the skull is safe. Whoever ransacked the place didn't touch the basement strongroom, or couldn't crack the lock."

Krafter felt a wave of physical relief. Perkins told Larson what they did with the skull; they could not very well hush it up. Instead of receiving a blast, the department director said nothing, at least not to Krafter. He wasn't about to question his luck.

"There are still the finger bones and the vertebrae."

"Check the Lab Three storeroom, unless you stashed the stuff someplace else?"

"No, they're there." With the hand bone and bracelet almost certainly disposed of, FedEx having denied receiving any shipping request from a Professor Bollinger, losing the finger and vertebrae bones would be serious, but nothing compared to the disaster Krafter faced if the skull vanished.

"No one saw anything, I suppose?" he asked and Perkins shrugged, his features severe.

"This is an open university, Doctor, and people can come and go as they please."

Krafter had mixed feelings regarding campus security. Valuable items were firmly stored and beyond access to casual thievery. He didn't know how other departments handled things, but apart from an access pad to Lab Three and ordinary Yale locks on faculty and Admin offices, the building was wide open as Perkins said. Uniformed and plainclothes guards of the UW Police Department wandered about, but Larson did not believe in having CCT cameras installed everywhere. Not only a question of cost in additional staff and equipment, but he abhorred the idea of an armed campus. Krafter largely agreed with him. This was a center of advanced learning, not a military school. Bad enough having to live with campus police on the grounds. But as last night's break-in showed, openness also made them vulnerable.

"I'll check the storeroom," he said, dumped his mail on the

desk and hurried off, leaving the door to his office open. If some-one wanted to steal student records or boxes of professional pub-lications, they were welcome to it.

Lab Three was open, but looking around quickly, all the dis-play cases seemed intact. Perkins would undoubtedly have al-ready checked. He unlocked the storeroom and stepped toward metal lockers arrayed along the back wall. This time, he did not need a key; his locker ajar like several others, including a number of ripped cardboard boxes. He peered into the empty locker cav-ity and slowly nodded. The burglar may have been after valuable specimens, there were certainly enough to choose from if one knew what to look for, and Krafter's bones could have been merely part of a bigger haul, but his cynical part didn't believe it. He had been deliberately targeted, and finding the skull probably the objective. Whether true or not, he didn't care, thankful that he took steps to safeguard it.

He only had one question, theoretical now. Was it Bollinger or the International Anthropological Society? Perhaps knowing which did not matter, as the two could be one and the same. Or it could have been anybody. Back in his office, apart from some papers and books moved around, everything appeared in its usual messy order. He considered advising Perkins of his suspicion, but saw little point. Although he had no doubt what had happened, he couldn't prove anything. Besides, even if he did tell Perkins, what could he do? The bones were gone.

Krafter reached across his desk to power up the computer and noticed a plain white envelope beside the keyboard. He picked it up and turned it over. There was no writing on either side. Intrigued, he opened the flap and pulled out a folded A5 sheet of paper. Reading, it wasn't so much the note, although clear enough, that sent his skin crawling. The sheer audacity of the messenger, in his mind obviously the same person who bur-gled Lab Three, gave him the chills.

The note also revived old anxieties and fears brought on

when his house was picketed, which he thought were safely buried. A flush spread over his body when he realized he was scared. Despite Reed's sound advice and Larson's patronizing words, they were not the ones under attack.

No matter what, this was definitely no longer merely an intellectual game.

Clutching the sheet, he jumped up and ran down the corridor to Perkins' office. The lab head looked up in surprise when he burst in.

"Larry—"

"Are the police still here?" Krafter demanded breathlessly.

"Downstairs, I think. Why, what's the matter?"

Krafter slid the note across the desk. "Read that."

Perkins picked up the paper after giving Krafter a searching look.

"Walk away. You have been warned." Perkins sat back and nodded thoughtfully. "So, maybe you were the target after all. Or more accurately, your specimens."

"Or both," Krafter agreed.

"The finger bones and the vertebrae?"

"Gone. Adam, we're not talking about a case of professional difference anymore, but intimidation, plain and simple."

"Perhaps, but you should also consider a more logical and likely explanation."

"There is a more logical explanation?"

"Certainly. You've been keeping a file of hate letters and emails?"

"Sure, as required by university policy. So?"

"You told me that you received a number of hate letters since your article in *Nature* came out, and I read some of the chucklers."

"That nonsense has forced me to change my home phone and cell number to stop crank calls."

Perkins shrugged. "We all get crank calls and hate mail. This

137

could simply be another one for your collection."

"This one wasn't mailed. Someone delivered it personally. It has to be tied in with the burglary," Krafter protested, not willing to give up his theory, although Perkins' explanation made a lot of sense.

"Coincidence. It could be, you know."

"Then we do nothing?"

"What do you want me to do? Give the note to the police? They'll take down your story, a wild flight of imagination as far as they're concerned, check for prints and tell you to wait until something comes up. What you have is a tenuous link between your discovery, the hate mail in your drawer and this note."

"It isn't tenuous to me."

"Only because you're filling in the missing pieces from un-substantiated inference. Apply the scientific method, Doctor, and see what you come up with."

"Damn it, Adam! You cannot apply formal methodology to something like a gut instinct, and you know it. If the police applied that method to all their cases, they would never solve any-thing."

"They hardly solve anything now," Perkins growled wryly. "Look, unless somebody takes a shot at you or something, I would ride this out."

"I won't be riding at all if that shot doesn't miss," Krafter said darkly, acknowledging that he spun a fragile web of circum-stantial evidence.

Perkins chuckled. "I doubt the situation is that grave. If you're right and the break-in was designed to remove your sam-ples, all you need to do is sit tight until Wednesday. The lab reps will get their bit of bone, Bollinger and Maddson will have their films of the procedure, and everyone will be chewing their fingers as they wait for the results. By the way, that was a very smart move having the labs send their report to everybody. I would never have thought of it."

"Don't think there wasn't bitching when I brought it up," Krafter said, recalling the exchange with relish. "All right. I'll file the note for now, but if something else happens, all bets are off."

"Go tidy up your office, Larry. I've got work to do."

Good advice and Krafter tried to follow it, but he could not stop speculating whether reaction to his find had taken on a more sinister aspect. What if he didn't walk away? Not that he would. If he admitted defeat, it would give Bollinger an easy victory, all on account of one unsigned note. He wanted the writer of that note to stand before him and tell him to his face to walk away.

Krafter stood six-foot even and most of it hard muscle. He did not walk to the university and maintain an exercise and martial arts program simply because he liked fresh air and sweat. The idea of turning into a sagging, paunchy, eccentric professor revolted him. Besides, the girls preferred someone who looked after himself. He did not consider his relationship with Elena decided, but he wouldn't mind developing what they had into something more than casual dating. At least she hadn't rebuffed him, and the few times they went out together were enjoyable for both.

Of course, he could be spinning himself up over nothing. Perkins could be right that this might all be a coincidence, and probably was. His imagination had taken over and he now chased shadows.

A sudden thought made him sit up with a jerk. If somebody *had* been looking for the skull and didn't find it here, where else could it be? He switched off the computer, locked the office and hurried toward the stairs. He had a tutorial, but that wasn't until one, plenty of time to check his house.

He arranged for a cab to pick him up. Walking home would take too much time, and with the idea planted firmly in his mind, he was in a rush. At the corner of E. Sanders Drive the cab turned right from S. 15th Street into a green avenue. The narrow nature strips between the sidewalk and road were mostly covered with lush lawns and shrubs. Almost every house had tall trees in front and back. The cab stopped opposite number fourteen, a modern, stone-clad single-story dwelling covered with dark green tiles. Krafter told the cabbie to wait and half ran toward the main door.

While a lot of homes had an entrance alcove and corridor that serviced the rooms, Krafter bought this place because it was open plan, spacious and airy. Large double-glazed windows allowed plenty of natural light to come in and provided protection against long, biting winters. It didn't take much oil to heat the place and keep it warm. It would be a while before he paid it off, but at least he had a place of his own. He had lived in an apartment block while working on his PhD and did not fancy doing it on a full-time basis. He hurried from room to room, checking for signs of disturbance. Nothing seemed to be missing, but there were several items not quite in their right place, something not normally noticed until the familiar balance was disturbed.

He climbed up from the basement and stood in the middle of the kitchen, thinking deeply. Whoever broke in this morning must have watched, waiting for him to leave. He had deadlocks on his front and back doors, and a monitored security system, but like most people, he never bothered to set them. There simply were no home break-ins in the neighborhood. He sometimes walked to a nearby corner store for a carton of milk or something without taking the trouble to lock up. Well, this settled it. If Perkins believed the burglary at the university was a coincidence, Krafter's ransacked house made that very unlikely, although his place was not actually torn up or anything.

One thing was clear. Somebody did not want the meeting on Wednesday to take place, or more accurately, wanted it to fail.

He locked up, set the alarm and climbed into the waiting cab. The irony of doing that after his house had been broken into did not escape him. As he drove back to the campus, he went over his options. Tell Perkins? Then what? Notify the police? Yeah, with nothing stolen, both were dead ends. Perhaps Perkins was right. All he needed to do was sit tight until Wednesday and he would be home free. Or would he? Could the tests by Reno and Melno Park be compromised somehow? He could not see how, not unless somebody was prepared to pay off the lab technicians. Even if that somebody managed to pull it off, Krafter only needed to insist on another test. Reno and Melno Park might be embarrassed and a subsequent investigation would probably identify the technicians responsible, but by then the negative publicity would likely have killed him, and no independent lab would touch him. Besides, it was too complicated. No, he could not see how the tests could be compromised. What then?

He built an elaborate case of conspiracy and worked himself into a state over a remote possibility at best. For Chrissake! It's not as if he stole government secrets or anything and the Feds were after him. He had a forty-million-year-old skull, that's all. His cynical part pulled him up, then. He had an ancient skull, all right, but that was definitely not all, far from it. If it were, his critics would not be trying so vehemently to tear him down.

Still undecided what to do when he returned to his cubicle office on the third floor, he picked up his mail and quickly sorted through the envelopes. One was from Admin, his refund for the excess baggage charge. The last caught his attention, a letter from the International Anthropological Society in their trademark hard yellow envelope. He tore it open and extracted an embossed cream paper.

Dear Professor Krafter,

Given the controversy surrounding your alleged discovery at the Karringa Mine and the unsubstantiated claim of its extreme age, contrary to all established evolutionary theory, which has brought disrepute not only on this body, but your professional colleagues worldwide, the IAS Executive Committee has no choice but to advise you that you are no longer eligible for membership or accreditation. Should you agree to publish a retraction of your position, the

Society might reconsider your application standing.

   Sincerely,
   Brenda Beudeswan
   Executive Committee Secretary
   For the LAS President

Krafter read the note again, smiled and filed it in the drawer with other hate mail, as if the letter would make him lose sleep. Still smiling, he picked up the phone and punched in numbers. A familiar voice answered after two rings.

"What can I do for you, doc?" Reed queried pleasantly.

Krafter could hear snatches of rushed conversation in the background filled with newspaper parlance.

"How did you know it was me?"

"I have call line identification on."

"Hah! Have you decided to show up on Wednesday?"

"Still working on it."

"This may help you decide. We've been burgled last night and my specimens from Lab Three are gone. Someone also went through my house this morning."

"Shit! Did they get the skull?"

"It's still safe, thank God."

"You make sure it stays that way, or come next Wednesday, you're toast."

"Tell me about it."

"You told the police about the house?"

"Not yet, but since nothing was stolen…"

"I hear you. They will listen, file and forget, but telling them will establish a chain of events."

"Perhaps you're right."

"Larry, I hate to say it, but somebody doesn't like you."

Krafter gave a sour laugh. "As if that's a revelation. Anyway, I thought I'd give you this juicy tidbit to rev up your dull Monday morning."

"It's no longer morning over here."

"Whatever. I hope you can make it on Wednesday."

"I'll let you know," Reed said and cut contact.

Krafter slowly replaced the phone and stared absently at the PowerPoint slide on the computer screen.

* * *

UNIVERSITY BRIBES LABS TO FAKE RESULTS

$150,000 PAID TO HUSH UP 40-MILLION-YEAR-OLD SKULL FRAUD!

GOD DID CREATE EARTH 6,000 YEARS AGO!

PROFESSOR KRAFTER SUBJECT OF A SMEAR CAMPAIGN

PROFESSOR BOLLINGER URGES KRAFTER TO COME CLEAN

Dr. Larson slowly folded a copy of the *Laramie Boomerang* and carefully placed the paper on the left corner of his desk. He took out a small square of white cloth from his jacket pocket and proceeded to thoroughly clean his glasses. Done, he folded his hands over the desk and peered at the visitors sitting before him.

"Doctor Perkins? Do *you* have anything further to add that might enlighten me and somehow make me believe this isn't happening?" His voice slow and deliberate, always a bad sign.

Perkins crossed his legs and shrugged, not looking concerned at all. "Doesn't look good, I admit, but we don't have a case to answer, Rick."

"No case to answer? The Wyoming State Bank records show a transfer of fifty thousand dollars to the Luminescence Geochronology Lab at Reno, and another transfer for the same amount to the Geochronology Lab at Melno Park, both made from the Department of Anthropology's working account. They also show a deposit of fifty thousand to Dr. Krafter's personal checking account at his Wells Fargo branch. This university's accounting department categorically denies making any such transfers, one that I am inclined to believe. Yet the transfers *were* made. Our records show the transactions. This was way out of Sheriff Ramanof's depth and he called the Denver FBI Division for help, given that a criminal act occurred across a State line. You're saying that we have no case to answer?"

"Someone is obviously out to discredit Professor Krafter and embarrass this university," Perkins said evenly.

"And they've done it!" Larson roared and slammed a fist against the desk.

"We issued notices to the papers denying the allegations."

"And they printed them…buried at the bottom of page four. We cannot sue them for libel because they printed facts as given to them. As to who gave them those facts, although erroneous, is also the subject of an FBI investigation. Do you two have any idea what damage has been caused to UW by this…slander? The board of Trustees are looking to scale down the activities of this department and I have given them a perfect excuse to do so." Larson sighed and shifted his gaze.

"Professor Krafter, you and your enemies have placed me in a most awkward position. Despite the urging of the University President, I am not removing my support, but let's not have any misunderstanding. That support will vanish if the lab tests don't corroborate your initial dating data. Do I make myself perfectly clear?"

"Quite clear, Doctor," Krafter said tightly, feeling awfully naked hanging on a thin thread fast unraveling.

He didn't blame Larson for anything. The department director had priorities and Krafter was not one of them, regardless of any academic principles that might be sacrificed along the way. No use being bitter. That's how the shitty things were.

Who would have thought of planting bribe money? The

move brilliant as it was devastating, just when he figured his prospects were looking up. Under different circumstances, the whole thing could even be amusing.

On Wednesday, everything was congeniality and polite laughter. Larson himself made sure that his two distinguished guests were looked after, lacking for nothing. Always a fly in the cream, Wethermans insinuated himself into Lab One to watch the proceedings, but Krafter had no time for him, ignoring him completely. The smiles slipped a little when Maddson recognized Reed sporting an intimidating grin and a camera draped around his neck. He shot a dark look in Krafter's direction, which he returned with indifference. He didn't mind the light of publicity or the scathing article Reed had written in *The New York Times* about the proposed tests in Laramie to settle the controversy, and Harvard's machinations to block them. Bollinger must have complained to Larson, saying that Krafter had divulged confidential information, because the department director took him aside and in a fatherly voice advised him to be careful of possible legal reprisal from Harvard if he crossed the line.

In full view of everyone, campus police brought in the Pyrex case and Spiro made sure everything was filmed. The two independent lab reps observed closely as Krafter carefully removed two slivers of mineralized bone from under the skull, which caused minimal damage and outward disfiguration. He scrupulously invited everybody to examine the skull to see for themselves that the bone was indeed mineralized. There was reluctant agreement all around, which definitely put paid to the silly four-hundred-year-old assertion.

Grim, Bollinger hovered over him, literally breathing down his neck, but said nothing, his eyes glittering as he studied the skull. The samples were placed in glass flasks, labeled with narrow barcode stickers and given to the reps. They made Krafter sign receipts and the flasks were sealed in small padded bags, the flaps taped with more barcode stickers. Satisfied that everything was done correctly, Larson took charge of his guests and ushered them away.

"Do the police know how the fund transfers were made?" Krafter asked out of sheer curiosity, his mind occupied on his future standing at UW, if he had one.

"The FBI Computer Analysis and Response Team in Denver is looking into it, as are our IT people," Larson said after a moment. "Obviously, somebody hacked into our network. Once past the firewall, the accounting software package would be easy to crack."

"They had to know how to run it."

"That's not important. What is important is that I dissociate this department and the university from the negative publicity the incident has generated. Young man, I have requests from CNN, NBC, and several papers to interview you. I was tempted to hand the whole thing to Professor Wethermans—"

"Sir!"

Larson raised a hand. "He has his faults, but he does know how to manipulate the system. Don't worry, it hasn't come to that, yet. You will make yourself available to answer any questions the media might have. Laura will give you the details. Sort this out, Dr. Krafter, and sort it out quickly. That's all." Larson's eyes shifted and his mouth tightened. "Adam, a moment, if you please."

Dismissed like an undergrad, Krafter stood up and walked out.

In the suddenly gloomy confines of his office, he sat down and pushed aside a copy of the *Branding Iron*. The student paper was outraged at the vitriolic publicity Krafter's find attracted and urged Student Union bodies around the country to protest. Comforting, but apart from boosting his ego, the move would have little substantive value.

He stared aimlessly at the green Orion Nebula desktop image

on the computer screen, wishing he could fly there, see the towering columns and canyons of superheated gas lit by furiously burning young stars and stars not quite born. Measured against the flicker of galactic time when man first lifted a club with a gleam of emerging intelligence in his eyes and then loosed a nuclear mushroom, the stars in that nebula had hardly changed.

For all its apparent speed, light crawled across the deeps. Since the first proto-human stood erect, the Milky Way had barely moved twenty degrees of arc, and rotated only sixty times since its formation. Would the stars notice man's passing? Would they care? Did Earth? In 250 million years or so the continents would again merge into a single super landmass, erasing whatever might have remained of man's structures and of man himself. Nothing that anyone did mattered. Nature moved its hand across the Earth regardless of his puny efforts. Why struggle then, why strive, claw, destroy, and in moments of ecstatic creation, dare reach for the flickering lights in the sky?

I think, therefore I am, and I will shape creation in my image.

Perhaps that was the difference. The stars merely moved, but man shaped. From the first chipped stone axe to the intelligent computer, man shaped, refusing to be dictated to by forces outside his cave. At least that's how it appeared, and perhaps brought a measure of comfort and a sense of destiny to what otherwise would be a meaningless existence and equally pointless procreation.

Krafter stared at the beautiful swirls of color on the screen.

He had reached a tipping point. From an amusing academic exercise of daring to challenge established thinking, a sophisticated game he played with relish, he now confronted not a scientific discovery to be embraced and eagerly examined, but base human emotions and drives. A simple question of primordial territory. The Bollingers and Maddsons of this world have fought and clawed to stake out their field and were prepared to do whatever it took to defend it, from anyone. Expressed in basic anthropological terms, Krafter understood the drivers motivating his opponents. The thing was, he never anticipated that their opposition would be conducted outside the lecture halls or scientific journals, not really. Rationally, he knew differently, but such behavior was something he expected to read in history books. People were more civilized now, weren't they?

His cynical self laughed. Scratch a crabby professor and you uncover a primitive wielding a knobby club.

It looked very much like he needed a club of his own.

Elementary, my dear Watson.

A loud knock pulled him out of his reverie. He stood up and opened the door. Surprised, he stepped back.

"Adam, come on in."

Perkins gave Krafter a searching look and took the single visitor chair. "I just finished with Dr. Larson. You mustn't judge him too harshly, Larry. This thing has come at a bad time and he's being squeezed from too many places."

"I could tell," Krafter growled unsympathetically as he sat down. "Never mind the science, look after the department and his own ass."

"There are so many ways I could respond to that, but I won't dignify your crass remark by doing so. I shouldn't tell you this, but you need to realize something before you start blaming everybody who is trying to help you."

"What are you talking about?"

"Dr. McBride told Larson to fire you and he refused."

Krafter gaped, not believing. "The President—"

"Is a first rate administrator whose only concern is the welfare of this university, and you're an infection he wanted cut out."

"So, that's how the wind blows, eh?" Krafter shot back, angry and disillusioned. "Be politically correct at all times. Don't rock the establishment boat. Most of all, don't jeopardize those federal grants. Smile and sweep the new and the awkward under the rug. Right?"

"Now listen to me, *son*!" Perkins snarled. "You're partially correct, but you're also wildly wrong. You got your PhD at twenty-three, eyes shining at the prospect of showing the old fuds how things were going to be done, ready to rewrite history according to Dr. Krafter. Still wet behind the ears, you got an assistant professorship and figured it vindicated the image you had of yourself. You *had* to be right! You don't care how things get done around here, expecting them to simply get done. You and others complain and whine at lack of equipment and facilities, regardless of how much it costs, as long as Perkins and Larson made it happen. Don't bother me with tiresome administration, politics, fundraisers or grant applications. Just let me get on with my heady research. The rest is beneath me. Well, *Doctor*, those same old fuds are not only protecting their own asses, but yours as well, because without us, you wouldn't even exist. Instead of considering yourself used, climb off that high moral pedestal of yours and be part of the solution, not the problem."

Taken aback by this unexpected tongue-lashing, Krafter swallowed his resentment and reluctantly admitted that much of what Perkins said was true. A bit tough having to grow up all the way at twenty-six and face a nasty world that lay out there, but that's how the cards were dealt. Either play or fold, and his mentor had always played fair with him. He remembered fondly the jam sessions Perkins held at his Grand Avenue apartment with other doctoral candidates. Serious work did get done sometimes, but the meetings were designed to blow off steam and debate outrageous propositions without having to be always politically correct. Krafter missed those sessions.

He looked at Perkins and slowly nodded.

"You're right. Everything you said is true and I was guilty of stargazing. I've got to tell you, though, this has been rough on me. I believed I could handle anything, defeat any challenge, and do it alone. I'm smart and I have a PhD to prove it. I'm a scientist, not a politician or publicity manipulator. This is twisting me up." Krafter gave a bitter laugh and shook his head. "I should have listened to your warning."

Perkins looked hard at Krafter. "Okay, I guess you do understand it all and you're merely venting spleen. Perhaps everyone is doing a bit of steam venting today. What you need to do is balance your rational and emotional accounts before you can move forward. Besides, you had to find out the hard way."

Krafter bit his lower lip and smiled wanly. "I'm beginning to see that. When you were my thesis advisor, why didn't you tell me that when I got my degree, I would be opening a door to hell, not an academic heaven?"

"Because you wouldn't have believed me," Perkins said flatly.

The words struck Krafter like bullets.

"Nobody ever does," Perkins added.

"I certainly wouldn't have. When I looked at you, I figured the man was over the hill, what does he know? When all the time, you and Larson knew everything, because you've been through it yourselves."

"More or less. Larry, it's unfair to be forced to face something like this so early in your career, but life isn't about fairness. It's about survival. Anthropology 101."

"In other words, if I let them roll me, no one will care if some human bones truly are forty million years old. There won't be anyone there to shout it. To survive, you and Larson must also survive. This university must survive."

"You got it in one."

Krafter studied his mentor's serious features and made a hard decision. "I can't do this, Adam. Not alone."

Perkins nodded. "I know what it cost you to make that admission and the courage it took to say it." He reached across the space between them and patted Krafter's knee. "You've been taking it on the chin, confident that science and truth would win out.

You made a critical tactical error, though. Not that you could have avoided it. The man on the street doesn't care about truth. He wants to hear about scandal, controversy, dirty politics and conspiracies, because they reinforce his image of a rotten world. That's where Bollinger and Maddson stole the march on you. You cannot rely on a single article in *Nature* or one favorable newspaper report to carry you. To win this, you must wage war on the same ground your enemies are using if you can't pick your own. You must use the same weapons, only more destructive.

"They print an article in *The Boston Globe* or the *Los Angeles Times*, you print in every paper across the country. They smear your character, you expose their underhanded dealings. Instead of waiting for TV networks and papers to ask for an interview, you tell Laura to call everybody and book you. You have facts on your side, always convenient when rebuffing innuendo, but you need to tell that to the guy on the street, and keep telling him until he takes notice. Sitting here, staring at that pretty nebula on the screen, won't get the job done, Doctor. So, what's it going to be?"

Standing on an emotional crossroad, Krafter took it all in, considering which path to take. He lifted his head and stared hard at his friend.

"I guess I better go and see Laura," Krafter said with a broad grin, relieved that he had a way out, although a rocky road with an uncertain ending.

"You got that right." Perkins stood and held out his hand. "See me after lunch and we'll talk tactics."

Krafter grasped the hand and felt a rush of affection for the older man. Perkins could be difficult and a pain, but he came by his lumps the hard way. Somewhat in shock, he realized it was the only way to get them. Talk about being naïve!

"I'll do that. And thanks, Adam."

Alone again, before seeing Laura, he needed to make a call first. Tactics, eh? He picked up the phone and dialed.

"I thought you'd ring me sooner or later, Larry," Reed said comfortably.

"I wanted to say thanks for the article you wrote about me being the subject of a smear campaign."

"Don't mention it. It was an easy one to write because it's true. If I can believe what I read in other papers this morning, someone has put a real squeeze on you, doc."

"And I'm getting it from all sides. I didn't call you to cry on your shoulder. I've had that session already. Remember the tape I sent you of my Boston meeting?"

"What about it?"

"If I'm being smeared, I want to do a bit of it back, but politely. Walk softly and all that, but leave an impression. My critics have had an easy ride so far and it just ended. If you're still willing to go that extra mile for me, I want you to write an expose on Bollinger and Maddson. Use the Boston tape and anything else you can dig up. They've been around a while. There must be some dirt. I don't want you to fabricate anything or open yourself or your paper to a libel suit, but a creative writer of your caliber should be able to generate a suitable slant on the proceedings. I also want the article plastered across every paper in the country prepared to carry it. Can you do that?"

"Okay, put the real Dr. Krafter on the line, because you're not him."

"I'm afraid I can't do that, Neil. That guy's been buried."

"I see. Well, doc, I hope you're prepared to wade in and slug it out, because that's what it will take, I'm happy to hand you the gloves. What triggered the metamorphosis?"

"A dose of harsh reality."

"Always cold stuff, but sobering."

"There is something else. I would like you to check if my two erstwhile colleagues have sandbagged anybody else. I cannot believe that I am the only one they've ever targeted. There must be other professional corpses lying about whom you could revive. It might make for some interesting reading, don't you think?"

"Man, you don't want gloves. You want a tank!"

"That's right. I want to roll right over them without even feeling the bumps."

"I'll see what I can do. It might take a little time to gather all the dope, you know."

"As you pointed out, time is one thing that I don't have. Make it a series of articles, then, but I want to keep the pot boiling. Instead of everyone dismissing me as a fraud and a nut, I want to show the guy on the street how murky the hallowed halls of academia can really be. Rather than handle this as a dry scientific curiosity, we'll turn this story into a vendetta drama. Bollinger wants to discredit me, fine. If planting money in my account is the best he could do, I want to expose that for the fabrication it is."

"Whoa! I'd be careful saying that, Larry. You don't know he did it."

"I know, and I won't be mentioning it in polite circles. I believe I know who *did* do it."

"Oh? Let me guess. Not the International Anthropological Society, by any chance?"

"That's my best bet, albeit a suspicion only. They're the only ones with the resources necessary to run such a prolonged campaign against me, but it could also be somebody just like them. Which brings me to ask for yet another favor."

"I'm not sure you have enough credit to pay for them all," Reed said and laughed.

"Send the bill to Dr. Larson. What I want—"

"Is an expose on the IAS?"

"That's it. Those bastards need to be taken down a notch or a whole bunch."

"You could be opening yourself to some serious shit, you know."

"I'm already in serious shit. Time to throw some back."

"You know what they say when you step on a rattler? You've got about two seconds to kill the damned thing before it turns on you."

"Only one thing wrong with that, Neil. Their rattler has already struck."

"I'll send you the galleys before I publish. We're gonna have a fight on our hands, but you've got a good cause."

"Neil, you've been a real friend here. I won't forget."

"You're doing *me* a favor, Larry. *The New York Times* circulation will go ballistic. My editor cannot complain about that, now can he?"

Krafter laughed, wanting to hug Reed. "I guess not. Watch CNN and NBC today. I've got a few things to say."

"Knock 'em dead, doc, and hang in there. We'll ratchet up our campaign on Tuesday when the test results come in."

Krafter replaced the receiver and gave a satisfied nod. This felt right. He got up, locked the office and made his way toward the stairs.

* * *

"Professor Krafter, there is no possibility that the independent testing labs you used could somehow be wrong?" Jae Leno demanded in his deep voice and beguiling smile, square jaw thrust out. "After all, the science is still new and many anthropologists and geologists dispute its validity."

Hooked to *The Tonight Show with Jae Leno* through Laramie's KCWC-TV studio link, Krafter felt uncomfortably hot under the overhead lights, but there wasn't much help for it except take a hurried gulp of water when the scene switched to his host. He gazed directly at the active camera and nodded.

"That might have been true some years ago, Mr. Leno, but the technology has advanced. Granted, there is still a wide variation in results from fission track and potassium-argon tests I used, no technique is accurate to a year, but given the geological age of my discovery, or more accurately, discovery made by the Karringa Mine, the results are well within the range of tests performed by the U.S. Geological Survey and other government and private bodies that used purely stratigraphy techniques."

"Without getting too deeply into the technical terminology, Professor, can you enlighten us as to what these tests are?"

"Certainly. When uranium atoms decay, break down into less complex elements, they release energy in a form of charged particles, which burn tracks or tunnels in the sample material. The number of fission tracks is proportional to the amount of time the sample cooled from its original state. The potassium-argon test is based on the fact that potassium decays into argon and calcium at a known rate. Measurement of the amount of argon in a sample determines its age.

"Stratigraphy is simply aging material based on an assumption that deeper strata should be older. That's not always true, of course, given that landmasses can fold due to continental shifting, but it's a good rule of thumb. Generally, if fossils from one layer resemble fossils from another locality with a similar layer, the two can be roughly correlated to have the same age. By using what are called index fossils, markers that occur in the same strata in many localities, we can give an approximate age to a sample found in that strata."

"Excellent clarification, Professor," Leno said and the audience applauded. "Although the tests you had done are more suited to dating rock, you had bone matter tested. How can that be?"

"Although the hand and skull were indeed bone when buried, over millions of years the original bone material was replaced with leeched minerals from the surrounding strata, leaving behind a composite crystal, similarly to what happens to petrified wood. Although an involved procedure, fission track and K-Ar dating can certainly be done on such material."

"Your critics vehemently deny the forty million years age of the bones, and offered proof that they are much younger; in fact, only some four hundred years. How do you respond to that?"

"Professor Bollinger from Harvard's Anthropology Department claims to have conducted a C-14 test on the hand bone that gave him that age. Your viewers saw a short movie clip of my dig earlier. The footage I took at the University of Wyoming lab where I examined the hand and skull, and which independent observers confirmed, including Professor Hartman from Texas State University, a Nobel laureate, the bones were indeed completely mineralized. It would be impossible to extract a sample with any organic content, unless done by scraping the coal-contaminated surface. Dating coal using a C-14 test is meaningless. The half-life of C-14 is 5,730 years. That means all radioactive carbon would have decayed within 30,000 years. As everyone knows, it takes nature millions of years to produce coal."

Gray-haired, distinguished, completely in charge of the situation, Leno placed his elbow on the desk and leaned forward.

"Let me get this straight. You're saying that Professor Bollinger, one of this country's eminent anthropologists, falsified his test because he couldn't believe modern humans existed millions years ago?"

"You've seen his report, Mr. Leno, provided by the independent lab he used. I'm not questioning the accuracy of that report or the lab's integrity, but it's curious that Professor Bollinger couldn't produce the bone for testing by Harvard's own Paleoanthropological Laboratory, claiming that he returned the sample to me. Another curiosity is that FedEx has no record of ever receiving any shipment order from the professor. I leave you to draw your own conclusions."

A ripple of laughter came from the studio audience, which Leno did nothing to discourage.

"Professor Maddson from Stanford University suggested that the bones were deliberately buried."

"A convenient claim to make when one has difficulty explaining awkward facts. The films I took at the Karringa Mine show without any doubt the impossibility of intrusive burial. My critics have tried everything possible to discredit my find, discredit me personally, and tarnish the reputation of the University of Wyoming. Having failed to do so with demonstrable science, they have now resorted doing it through crime."

"You're referring to money transfers made by the Wyoming State Bank?"

"And the break-in at UW where some of my samples were stolen. The university never made those transfers. Someone clearly hacked into our computer system, something that has already been confirmed by the FBI."

"Can you suggest who might be responsible?"

"I have my suspicions, Mr. Leno, but that's all they are. The matter is under investigation and I hope the FBI will manage to identify the perpetrator."

"You said you have suspicions, Professor. Can you at least speculate?"

Krafter allowed himself a small smile. "I cannot say anything categorical without proof, and I definitely don't want to insinuate in any way that professional bodies in this country or organizations such as the International Anthropological Society had anything to do with those transfers."

Jae Leno grinned broadly at his guest as a round of titters and applause rippled through the audience. "I understand completely." He turned and looked directly at another camera. "Please stay tuned for this short break and we'll be right back to talk to Professor Larry Krafter about his astonishing discovery." When the red active light faded, he again looked at his visitor.

"You've done well, Professor. You handled my last question with diplomatic skill. Everyone watching the show will be in no doubt that IAS was behind the whole thing."

"That is an inference only, Mr. Leno," Krafter said with a

disarming grin. "I didn't want to be responsible for a lawsuit against the NBC."

"Or yourself," Leno added knowingly. "After appearing on David Letterman's *The Late Show*, I wasn't surprised you were willing to tackle me."

"I'm interested in presenting to the world a genuine scientific discovery, Mr. Leno. The fact of its existence might be uncomfortable to some of my professional colleagues, and you've seen what they're prepared to do to dismiss it and me, but the existence of my find cannot be dismissed. The skull exists. It's tangible. I don't know what happened to the hand bone and bracelet, that is something you will have to ask Professor Bollinger, but its loss is a loss for all mankind, as are the stolen finger bones and vertebrae."

"Oh, I'll ask him, all right. He'll be my guest on the next show," Leno said and someone behind him pointed at his wristwatch. "We're back in five, Professor," the producer interrupted, then folded each finger of his upraised hand in countdown. At one second, he lifted his hand.

Leno paused and smiled his trademark grin into the active camera. "This is Jae Leno at *The Tonight Show* with Professor Larry Krafter. Professor, the Harvard Paleoanthropological Laboratory only tested the hand bone, but we all know that you also found a skull at the Karringa Mine. Why didn't you send everything to them if you weren't afraid of an independent examination?"

"As reported in my article in *Nature*, Mr. Leno, I did send samples to independent labs. Sending the hand bone to Harvard was a courtesy to forestall any question of a cover-up or tampering on my part. In view of what happened to that bone, perhaps it's fortunate that I didn't send Harvard the skull. The explanation why I did not is quite simple. Instead of hiding or doctoring it as some have suggested, I and my colleagues at UW were still in the process of carrying out our own examination, not anticipating that Professor Bollinger would be so careless as to misplace my irreplaceable sample."

More laughter and clapping came from the audience.

"I understand that last Wednesday, Professors Bollinger and Maddson were present in Laramie where samples were extracted from the skull and given to representatives of two labs for validation of your original dating tests."

"That is correct, and this Tuesday, everyone will receive the results of those tests from the labs, which will categorically prove that my find is indeed millions of years old."

"If the results do not substantiate that?"

"I will publicly state that I was duped by an extremely sophisticated fraud."

"Well, there doesn't seem to be much one can add to that. Thank you Professor Krafter for appearing on the show."

"My pleasure, and I want to thank you for having me."

Leno waved a hand at the large 52" LED screen mounted beside his desk. "Professor Krafter, ladies and gentlemen."

Krafter nodded as the NBC studio audience clapped, waited for the red light on the active camera to fade, then sighed.

"Professor Krafter, any time you wish to provide further information, you only need to call," Leno said warmly.

"Thank you. I appreciate that very much."

When the studio link camera died, Krafter unclipped the mike from the lapel of his jacket and stood up. Perkins walked up to him wreathed in smiles and grabbed his hand.

"That dished it out to them, Larry. You made Bollinger and Maddson look like fools, but I'm not sure it was wise to mention the IAS."

"Oh, hell. They're in on it. I just can't prove it. Besides, I was most respectful."

"Sure you were, while driving in the knife. Well done, my boy. Who is next?"

"The *Colbert Report*, and that's also being prerecorded."

Krafter glanced at the studio clock hanging on the wall. "In twenty minutes, to be exact. Barely enough time to grab a coffee."

"You seem to have made a firm friend in Neil Reed. That article he wrote yesterday in *The New York Times* wouldn't have made your two favorite detractors very happy."

"Whatever makes them unhappy works for me. I only followed your advice, Adam."

"A somewhat extreme application, I would say. Anyway, we'll find out tomorrow when we get the lab results."

"We certainly shall. And thanks for standing by me on this."

"Even Larson cracked a smile the last time I saw him. You used the weekend well and raised your public profile considerably, not to mention giving UW a much-needed boost. I've got to go. Good luck with Colbert."

They shook hands and Krafter watched Perkins leave. After three TV interviews and half a dozen sessions with newspaper reporters, he was getting the hang of it. That had not been the case with the first canned interview for CNN. He thought he handled the technical side well, but a touch of stage fright almost messed it up. Fortunately, the reporter was a pro and assured him that the takes would be edited to remove any embarrassing moments. On Saturday night, he did see the CNN clip and edited to show his more favorable side. After that, he took it all in stride.

It was not until two in the afternoon that he managed to get away from the studio and take a cab back to UW. Walking toward the Anthropology Building entrance, several students recognized him and cheered him on. Pumped up, he got to his office buoyed.

* * *

Kessler finished reading the article by Neil Reed, and with a look of disgust, threw the folded copy of *The New York Times* into the bin. Of *course* IAS was out to discredit Krafter! What did the man expect, give him the Nobel Prize? Press or no press, Reed had become an impediment and a serious nuisance. Perhaps something should be done to discredit *him*—permanently!

With business, Kessler never allowed personal feelings to interfere with his professional judgment. That invariably led to getting emotionally involved, losing perspective and detachment. In the long run, it always turned out to be counterproductive, but in Reed's case, he was tempted to break his rule. Calling IAS an anthropological Inquisition had cut too close to the bone. Reed had written that article some time back, but Kessler had never forgotten or forgiven the reporter. The two latest pieces almost pushed him over the edge. Not that Reed published anything slanderous or untrue, and that was the sticking point. His articles were entirely too factual to be dismissed as mere tabloid mud raking. It simply was not the exposure the organization needed, especially now with a number of universities having cancelled their quarterly contributions. Presumably, that was why Reed wrote them, and to make everybody reconsider their position on Krafter's discovery. Where the hell was Reed getting his information? A leak from within the office?

Under different circumstances, Kessler could almost admire the man. There had to be a handle to make the irritating reporter more tractable. He would need to put somebody on it.

He stood up, stepped to the window, and gazed down at the streaming traffic along the Avenue of the Americas, the sounds of cars barely audible through the thick glass. Some skyscrapers and lesser buildings were already lit, ready to face the creeping night. In the west, the sky was streaked orange and yellow. He should go home, but home was an empty apartment and cold walls. Stella had loved him with feverish passion and unflagging devotion, and he returned that love, believing it would never end. A burst brain aneurysm nine months ago did end it, and part of him died with her. He still had not gotten over her, and perhaps he never would. After two days of headaches and Nurefen tablets, he woke one morning and she was there beside him, a small smile on her cold, angelic face.

He didn't know if he would ever love like that again, or wanted to.

Krafter...the young man had proven to be more resilient and resourceful than expected. Kessler had to give the kid credit, and whoever must have coached him. His TV appearances and newspaper articles had started too many in the paleoanthropology community questioning Bollinger and Maddson's hardline views, and IAS's own position, a far more dangerous development. Despite its apparent impossibility, the discovery had generated a certain growing fascination with the public, which in turn created unwanted sympathy for Krafter, rather than branding him a fraud.

Kessler retaliated immediately by sending follow-up notices to all members and affiliated institutions, warning of negative endorsement and cancellation of accreditation if support continued to be extended to Krafter.

Perhaps he had gone in a bit heavy, as many ignored the directive and some actually cancelled their membership, which only provided more fuel for Reed. With Hartman's endorsement, and having Columbia U publicly announce that Krafter's discovery was authentic, after conducting its own examination of the skull, was a body blow. Ted Horowitz carpeted him about the whole mess, the first time he had shown any dissatisfaction, and the censure cut deep. Perhaps Horowitz and some of his more prickly academic colleagues could use a dose of professional detachment themselves.

He knew what had to be done, of course. Krafter would need to have the matter explained in terms even he could understand. Since coming into the organization, Kessler himself had the nuances of paleoanthropological infighting explained to him in succinct detail, present and historical. The arcane scientific reasoning behind accepted human evolutionary theories left him bemused, the basic concepts were simple and clear enough for him to understand perfectly what Krafter's find implied…and threatened. He needed to be careful not to overreach himself. The disinformation campaign waged against the young scientist was like compound interest. No matter how professional or careful Striker might be, an accumulation of small, seemingly random clues, could undo everything.

Nevertheless, this had to be ended promptly. Things were already getting out of hand.

Returning to his desk, he pulled out his HTC phone and dialed. He didn't have to wait long.

"Identify," the electronic voice demanded.

"Raven."

"Proceed."

"Activate supplementary measures."

A click and the line went dead. Kessler stared at the phone, hoping he had not left it too late. If the scientific community accepts Krafter's find, the IAS's reputation would be irreparably damaged.

* * *

A strong gust made a hollow booming sound and rain beat against the window. 'Striker' opened his eyes and glanced at the electronic alarm clock beside the bed: 4:50 a.m. He had woken ten minutes early. Slipping his arms from under the covers, he locked his fingers behind his head and gazed vacantly at the fathomless blackness of the ceiling. The wind continued to sigh outside.

Thinking about nothing in particular, his thoughts wandered. The time for serious thinking was done. Some bridges along the road of his life, he had burned. Others were merely singed a little. Life was a tapestry in which one could not make too many large holes without falling through. Hemingway or somebody said that no man was an island. Perhaps, but he could be a peninsula and still do business.

Things could have turned out worse.

Ever since that slime worm Zardwovsky scuttled his performance evaluation as an international operative, his CIA career effectively ended. Everybody pretended that his desk job at Langley was a routine rotation, but after eight months of mind-numbing paper shuffling and doing intelligence reviews on Colombian drug cartels, he stopped pretending and tendered his resignation. Sorely tempted to waylay the National Clandestine Service Director, he refrained. Although deserving a bullet, Striker knew that doing something so foolish, the CIA would never rest until they caught up with him. The shit simply wasn't worth it.

Mark Price had also been on the receiving end of Zardwovsky's attention, admittedly with some help from the director, Raymond Grant. Price was now with the Department of Homeland Security as Director, National Operations Center, with perhaps a better career than he'd had with the CIA. If Price could reinvent himself, Striker figured he could also. And he did.

Being a strategic consultant with TriCon Security paid him a large six-figure salary, far more than he ever hoped to get on a public payroll, and his expertise valued. The organization was primarily a private think tank made up of former government and military people, and TriCon used their talents to give corporations, government and military agencies its view of the world. It never ceased to amaze him how a report from an external consultancy firm was readily accepted, and which most of the time said exactly the same thing as a company's own internal study, usually ignored. Then again, that's how all consultants made their money. They were 'experts' and therefore utterly credible. If clients wanted to go along with the fiction, TriCon was not about to disabuse them. It helped pay for the corporate Lear jet and the Fifth Avenue offices.

Striker had done moderately well since leaving the CIA, and although he enjoyed his new job, he was still an operations man at heart and liked to keep his hand in. With his credentials and special skills, there was enough demand for his time on 'personal' assignments that he seldom got bored. TriCon didn't mind, as long as his distractions did not interfere with their own assignments. Ironically, the CIA was one of his best customers, perhaps because it involved work in the continental United States, or because deep down they knew he was good. He never tried to figure it out. Some things were beyond rational understanding.

The alarm went off with a sharp trilling and he reached across the bed to shut it off. He snapped on the master light switch and the comfortable Hampton Inn room burst into light. He squinted and blinked, then swung his legs out of the bed and pushed back the covers. Standing on the hard gray carpet, he executed his usual deep breathing exercises, did his neck stretching moves, hearing the vertebrae crackle, and went into the calisthenics routine. Pleasantly warmed, he stretched on the floor and did sixty quick pushups.

After a shower and shave, he dressed and slipped into a dark brown corduroy jacket. Opening a slim black leather valise, he removed two small narrow plastic cases. He opened one and put on a pair of black-framed non-prescription glasses. From the other case, he removed a thin peppery mustache, walked into the bathroom and, standing before the mirror, carefully peeled back the adhesive tape cover. He pulled down his upper lip and fixed on the mustache. Eyeing himself critically, he decided it would do. If anyone saw him, they would remember his glasses and mustache, but they would not be able to recall his face, something to do with how the brain did pattern recognition, or so his CIA trainers told him when he went through the Farm indoctrination course.

A loud knock on the door caused him to turn his head.

"Breakfast, sir," a muffled voice announced.

He walked to the door and opened it. The young man standing in the corridor beamed at him, wearing the hotel attire of black trousers and vest.

"Morning, sir. Bad day to be up."

Striker didn't say anything as he stepped aside. The boy wheeled in his little trolley and made straight for the low square table tucked against the window. Humming cheerfully, he unloaded a covered tray, a carafe of juice, a steel container of coffee, and a basket of mixed rolls.

"Enjoy."

Striker nodded and held out a five-dollar note. The young man smiled broadly as he pocketed the note.

"*Thank* you, sir."

Striker sat down, poured himself a cup of coffee and mixed in one sugar. He took a thirsty sip and uncovered the tray: bacon strips not overdone, grilled sausages, two eggs over easy, and a pile of hash browns. He took an appreciative sniff, poured a glass of juice and quickly drained it. Not hurrying, but not dawdling either, he demolished everything in sight. It took fuel to power his large frame. The third cup of coffee settled things down nicely. After brushing his teeth, he walked out of the room and hung a 'Do Not Disturb' sign on the handle.

Outside the hotel, the wind cut through his jacket and he pulled back his lips in a frown. The kid had it right, a bad day to be up, but his job didn't allow him to pick his hours. He walked quickly across the small parking lot and got into the low slung dark Chevy. He wanted to do this without hassles, get back to the hotel and work on his Denver intelligence job.

The drive to the University of Wyoming campus only took a few minutes, one of the advantages of being in a small town. An odd lone vehicle made a whispering swish as it went past him going the other way, the headlights glittering against the wet windscreen. Rounding the corner of 12th and Lewis, he drove into the faculty parking lot beside the Anthropology Building. He locked the car and hurried toward the entrance, pursued by slanting rain. Inside, without breaking stride, he headed for the stairs. He knew that the UW Police Department had officers prowling about, but they were usually called only after something happened. Like any open university, anybody could come and go pretty much anywhere, and it wasn't likely that they would be moving around in the rain.

On the third floor, he walked down the deserted corridor and stopped before Krafter's office. Pulling on surgical gloves, he took out a special lockpick, something he had inherited from the CIA, slipped it into the keyhole, twisted up and right, and the lock clicked. He pocketed his glasses and dragged out a thin black cotton balaclava from his pocket. Slipping it on, he entered the office, the layout now familiar. He reached inside his jacket, slid out a plain white envelope, and placed it on the computer keyboard. Staring at the dark screen, he smiled as he remembered hacking into the accounting system, which caused a satisfactory amount of running around by everybody. Although that had been child's play, his job did have an odd pleasant moment.

Tempted to search for surveillance cameras, Krafter having almost certainly spoken to the cops and the FBI, he didn't bother, and didn't have the time. If there was a planted camera, whoever put it there wouldn't get much. Opening the door, he pressed the locking latch, dragged off the balaclava and gloves, and walked out.

Back in his car, Striker started the motor and swung out of the parking lot. He paused at the 12th Street intersection and turned right. The dashboard digital clock said 6:43. The air-conditioning made a soft background whisper as he drove down S. 15th Street, a gray dawn breaking over a cloudy sky. At the corner of E. Sanders Drive, he turned right and slowed as he approached number fourteen. Lights burned in the front window. He drove past, did a U-turn and parked a couple of houses up from Krafter's place.

He sat back and turned on the radio, not listening. It was merely to fill the emptiness and the silence. He didn't know at what time Krafter usually went to the university, but his surveillance showed that if he walked in, he would be out by 7:40. If he drove, which was likely on a day such as this, and something Striker counted on, it would be a bit later. Then again, the professor could have something special going and might go early. He didn't want to miss him and there might not be another opportunity within the timeframe he operated, the job being a sideline to his main assignment in Denver, doing a bit of friendly industrial espionage. The term 'friendly' being relative, of course.

He crossed his arms across his chest and waited.

* * *

Rain fell steadily, a soft dreamy drizzle that blurred outlines and made the headlights of oncoming cars glitter and sparkle. After days of unremitting heat, everyone reveled in the crisp sharpness, and Krafter fancied the trees and shrubs were expanding as they reached out thirstily to catch every drop. The morning news said the front would pass by noon as a new high-pressure system moved in, bringing with it warm southerly winds and clear skies.

Motoring along S. 15th Street, wipers making a steady swish across the windscreen, he crossed Russell Street, making his way up toward Lewis Street. Tall trees crowded the lots on either side, providing welcome shade on sunny days, and created magic as branches groaned under a load of winter snow. He preferred fall the best. The days were usually clear and although cool, he enjoyed the changing colors as aspen, birch, oak, and maple, took on hues that blazed from yellow to orange, then flaming red, the fallen leaves carpeting roads and sidewalks with a brown blanket. A few more weeks, he told himself.

Krafter slowly tapped the steering wheel to Ravel's *Bolero* and its haunting, building rhythm. He slowed as he approached Garfield Street, mulling about today's classes and nothing in particular. Not showing any lights, a black sedan ran up and pulled up behind him, hugging his bumper. It flashed on its high beam and Krafter squinted at the sudden glare reflected in the rearview mirror. He muttered something uncharitable about idiot drivers.

The black car crept forward, looming large. He stopped at the intersection and looked back. The car nudged his rear and he could feel the Ford Focus being pushed forward. Startled, he slammed on the brakes and heard the throaty growl of a powerful engine. The Focus shuddered beneath him, then slued right as the black car swung left. With a screech of tearing metal, the Focus hit the curb hard and the sedan accelerated past him, tires squealing. Krafter glanced left as it roared by, but could see nothing through its tinted windows. Catching a few letters and numbers off the registration plate, he hurriedly opened the glove box and took out a pen and pad, mouthing the numbers to himself. Writing down everything, he let out a loud breath and felt his mouth go dry as reaction set in. Taking a few deep breaths to steady himself, he climbed out of the car, wincing at the bite of cold rain.

The left bumper and part of the paneling were crushed where the sedan had rammed him. Touching the wet panel, he could clearly see black paint streaks, either from the other car's panel or bumper. Although hard against the curb, the Focus did not otherwise appear damaged, but looking at the mess, he figure it would cost at least two thousand to fix. Damn, an added complication he didn't need right now. A couple of cars sped past him and one tooted its horn, probably cursing him for presumably parking at an intersection. He got back into the car, brushed raindrops off his jacket and wondered what the hell just happened.

A crazy driver? Replaying the incident in his mind, he decided not. He was deliberately rammed and forced off the road.

Another warning, or a promise of more serious reprisals if he kept up with his publicity campaign? At least he got a partial on the registration.

Shaken and more than a little angry, he drove to UW, parked in his reserved slot next to the Anthropology Building. He wouldn't mind if somebody actually confronted him over his discovery and they had it out, man to man, like two jousting knights. This filing down at arms-length was infinitely worse. He was a mouse and a big cat out there played with him, biding its time before deciding to bite.

Rain hissed softly as he climbed out of the car. Huddled figures hurried along glistening sidewalks. Those with umbrellas took it more sedately.

On the third floor, he walked down the long corridor toward Perkins' office. He leaned his umbrella against the wall, knocked once, and stepped in. Perkins looked up from his desk, but made no comment on his wet appearance.

"Someone forced me off the road on my way in," Krafter said without any preliminaries and placed a page torn off his notepad on the desk. "That's a partial make on him."

Perkins sat there for a moment, then glanced at the page. "You're sure it was deliberate?"

"My rear end isn't crumpled because the guy skidded past me."

"Mmm. Well, I guess that note you got isn't a coincidence after all. Okay, I'll call Sheriff Ramanof. The LPD might be able to get a full ID and nab the guy. The FBI may also be interested."

"Agent Briggs is going to be annoyed that we haven't told him about the note I got."

"He'll live through it, but this is getting serious, Larry."

"By noon today or earlier, we'll get the lab reports. That should put a plug in it. I better go and call my insurance."

"You want the page back?"

"I've got the original."

Krafter unlocked his office and walked in. After snapping on the lights and hanging up his black blazer in the tiny corner cupboard, he pulled back his chair and sat down. Reaching across the desk to power up the computer, he saw a white envelope placed across the keyboard. He slowly picked it up and opened the flap. Frowning, he peered inside and pulled out two newspaper clippings. He read them and felt his mouth go dry as blood drained from his face. He swallowed hard, stood up, and walked out.

"Twice in five minutes," Perkins commented mildly, then noted Krafter's pallor. "What is it? You look like you've seen a ghost."

"Two, actually. Our burglar seems to have been back," Krafter said tightly and held out the clippings.

Perkins took them and began to read. "Gene Hartman, a professor at Texas State U, was seriously injured after his car mysteriously ran off the road…" He glanced at the second clipping. "Professor Dennison Walsh suffered a broken arm after his car…" Perkins didn't have to go on. He got the idea. "It seems you're not the only one being targeted. Your supporters have attracted some unwanted attention of their own."

"I wonder if they received a warning letter like me," Krafter mused, the shock slowly wearing off, but not the implication.

"Something for Briggs to look at," Perkins muttered, then sighed, looking disgusted. "And I was going to enjoy a nice, uneventful day. You sure know how to spoil things, Professor Krafter. It might have been better if Karringa never found that damned bone. Running people off the road is not how science is done!"

"What if this doesn't stop, Adam, regardless of what the lab reports say?"

"You can't put the genie back into its bottle. You'll simply have to face it as it comes."

"Freshman psychology, Doctor, but easier said than done."

"Perhaps, but you must do it anyway. You're no good to anybody if you turn yourself into a basket case."

"Okay, but you won't mind if I worry a little?"

Perkins grinned, but without humor. "We'll all worry a little."

Back in his office, Krafter logged on and checked his email list. His eyes widened when he saw messages from Reno and Melno Park. He clicked on the first one and eagerly scanned the text. After the usual dry preliminaries and references to attached details, Krafter stared at the prominent number, an average of thirty-nine-point-eight million years from the fission track and potassium-argon tests. A warm surge of exultation rushed through him. He pumped his right arm and tilted back his head.

"Yes!"

Leaving the message open, he returned to the list and clicked on the Melno Park line. He hurriedly read through the intro and focused on the number: thirty-five point seven million years.

His throat suddenly tight, he blinked rapidly and muttered a silent thanks.

Eat your liver, Bollinger.

Noting the send times, Bollinger must have read the emails already. Krafter would have loved to be a fly on the wall of his office right now. He hoped the son of a bitch burst an ulcer.

He typed brief, but cordial expressions of thanks to both labs and sent them off. His next email was to Reed and he smiled all the way through the composition. The reporter deserved to hear the good news. The least he could do in return for Reed's articles and unflagging loyalty. He attached copies of the two emails, pressed the Send icon, sat back and exhaled loudly. His detractors may run him off the road and mangle his colleagues, but science and truth would win out, he promised himself, but he crossed fingers anyway.

Absorbed in another email, the phone rang and he groped for the receiver. "Professor Krafter."

"The headline in the afternoon edition will be all yours,"

Reed gushed warmly. "I'll bet you're relived."

"And then some," Krafter said forcefully. "It's not over yet." He told Reed about the car mishap and the clippings.

"I told you before, Larry, somebody doesn't like you. Is the FBI on it?"

"Doctor Perkins is handling that end."

"I want to use that in my column. It's too much of a coincidence for the three of you to have the same accident."

"I would rather that you held off for a while, Neil. You could be muddying the waters for the FBI."

"I hear you. Okay, but I'll be wanting to run a full story on that later."

"You got it."

"You planning on sending Bollinger and Maddson some broken glass to chew on?"

Krafter laughed with genuine pleasure. "You have a nasty sense of humor, did you know?"

"It's been mentioned, but I'm not the one being nasty here."

"Yeah, I hear you. I'll simply have to sit it out."

"My draft piece on the IAS is ready and it would be better if I could run it and the lab article together. I'll shoot it through to you."

"Say, that's great, thanks."

"It's more detailed than the piece I did a week ago and you'll find it interesting reading. Catch you later."

More kindly disposed at the world, Krafter printed the lab emails and attachments. He closed the office and walked lighthearted down the corridor.

"Jesus, Larry! Why don't you simply move in?" Perkins complained sourly as Krafter stepped in.

Wearing a beatific smile, Krafter laid the printouts on his desk. "The lab results, and both confirm my initial tests."

"Ah, I see now why the broad grin. Well, that takes the stale taste out of my mouth. I guess congratulations are in order, although I never had any doubts. Write a couple of short paragraphs summarizing the results and give them to Laura. She'll want to wire it to the papers, the networks and radio stations."

"I spoke to Neil Reed a minute ago. He'll have a front page spread in *The New York Times* later today," Krafter announced.

"We can sure use the positive publicity. By the way, Briggs *was* a bit upset that we held back on your note, but not too much so, and he'll follow up with the Houston Division and Scotland Yard on the other two incidents."

"At least the FBI is taking this seriously."

"I hope so, but apart from a partial ID you got of the car, they don't have much to go on."

"They're the detectives," Krafter said indifferently.

"Let's hope they detect something." Perkins stood up and gathered the printouts. "I'm off to see Larson and tell him the good news."

"He's probably got it already. The emails were CCd to him."

"I've got to see him anyway. You want to tag along?"

"Thanks, but he's all yours. If he wants me, he knows where I am."

Perkins gave Krafter a searching look. "Any other junior Assistant Professor would ordinarily be eager to bask in the limelight with the Department Director, but it seems you're happy to have results speak for you. You've matured in these past weeks, Larry, but I secretly bemoan your loss of innocence."

Chapter Five

INDEPENDENT LABS CONFIRM AGE OF PROFESSOR KRAFTER'S FIND!

PROFESSOR BOLLINGER CLAIMS TESTS WERE CONTAMINATED

THE INTERNATIONAL PALEOANHROPOLOGICAL SOCIETY SEEKS TO DISCREDIT PROFESSOR KRAFTER

ANTHROPOLOGISTS INCLINED TO GIVE KRAFTER'S DISCOVERY CREDIBILITY

40-MILLION-YEAR-OLD BONES SPARK A RETHINK OF MAN'S EVOLUTION

Krafter hummed something he heard on the radio recently, and spooned a rich pork casserole onto a plate and took it to a small table beside the kitchen serving as his casual dining area. He uncovered a woven reed basket and sniffed the freshly warmed rolls. Sitting down, he slid a dark green cloth napkin across his knees and lifted an opened bottle of mature claret. Ready to pour, the front doorbell chimed. Frowning at the interruption, he wondered who could want something on a Sunday evening. One of his neighbors short of sugar? There weren't any pretty ones around, at least he hadn't seen any, so he kind of doubted it.

Last night, he took Elena to the Library Restaurant on Grand Avenue, followed by a short walk and sweet indulgence at the Cherries Ice Cream eatery. Warm and intimate, the night had everything going for him. They mostly talked about her job at Bartlett & Strong, and how the law firm wanted to move her to their Denver office. If she agreed, it wouldn't happen until next February. It would mean promotion, more money and a chance to run court cases as a junior counsel—if she agreed to go. The problem was, she liked Laramie and its easy lifestyle, and hated the idea of leaving her parents and friends, but…

Suddenly coltish and shy, she revealed that she also liked him, her eyes enormous over the rim of her wine glass. It planted the ball firmly in his court and he was caught flat-footed. Trying to appear unconcerned, although her revelation caused his heart to flutter, he patted her slim hand and told her she was right to consider her career first. She had recently passed her Bar exam, and Laramie was not replete with career opportunities, not to someone with ambition, which she clearly had. What about him, she asked. Will he be staying at UW? She knew what he was going through right now, and seeing his scowl, was immediately contrite, regretting scratching a fresh wound.

Nothing was settled as they walked hand in hand to his car, but Krafter knew that another variable had been added to his life's equation, and he wasn't sure that the two sides balanced. More than merely fond of her, but committing to a stable relationship she hinted at? Too many things occupied his mind already without having to add another complication.

After driving to her apartment on N. 6th Street, they lingered at the main entrance and exchanged pleasantries. As she turned to punch her access code into the security pad, he took her in his arms and kissed her. Her soft mouth melted against his and their tongues danced around each other as her long silken hair enveloped his shoulders. Breathless moments later, feeling suddenly warm, he wished her good night and stepped to his car. Opening the door, he turned and looked at her. Smiling secretly, she fluttered her fingers at him.

That equation definitely needed work.

He gave the steaming casserole a sniff, pulled off the napkin and stood up. The doorbell chimed again.

"Okay, keep your socks on," he muttered, walking toward the entrance.

He opened the heavy door and saw a tall man, perhaps six-foot-three, dressed in black, wearing tinted glasses over a brown balaclava. Even as he tensed, the man shot out a stiff right arm at his middle. Krafter's training took over and he blocked instinctively with his left, countering immediately with a right elbow to the stranger's face. It never connected. The man leaned back far enough to avoid a blow that would have smashed his nose, and his left fist slammed into Krafter's solar plexus. Pain exploded in Krafter's chest as air rushed out of his lungs, and he doubled over. The man kneed him in the groin and Krafter screamed as his genitals suddenly turned to molten lead and his body tingled like he had been electrocuted. The next second, he was on the floor gasping, clutching himself.

The man in black stood over him, flexing his fingers.

"I was told not to hurt you," he rasped in a deep voice that could not hide his desire to do exactly that, "but your counter made that somewhat hard. In case you want to know, it wasn't a bad move either, but I've been doing this shit a whole lot longer than you. Keep practicing, though. Anyway, I'm not here to give you self-defense freebies. You ignored two of my warnings, Professor Krafter. I figured that maybe they might have gotten lost in the shuffle or something, so I thought I would deliver this one personally. You're upsetting some very nice people and that's no way to treat such people. Walk away, doc, before I'm forced to see you again and bad things happen. Trust me, you won't enjoy it."

The man patted Krafter on the shoulder, turned around and softly closed the door after him.

It took a while, but the pain in his groin subsided sufficiently for Krafter to sit up. He wiped his eyes and breathed deeply, then forced himself to stand up. After some exercises his *sensei* had shown him, he felt better, although still tender. He slowly walked into the dining area, sat down and poured himself a glass of claret. He took two deep swallows, leaned back against the chair and let out a loud sigh. Whoever the man was, he had a fist of stone.

If the man in black wanted to make sure he got the message, he got it, all right. A repeat reminder was not necessary. At least the visible face of his enemies was revealed and the mouse game over. Shaken, he drained the glass and topped up. His opponents were clearly not satisfied with evidence from the independent labs, however conclusive. It appeared that nothing less than his total silence would do

The problem was, he didn't know who wanted him muzzled. Sure, Bollinger and Maddson were on top of his bad guys list, but they didn't look the type to resort to something physical. They *could* have arranged for someone else to do the dirty. Then again, it could be anybody. He had annoyed enough far-right religious groups and conservative professional bodies who saw his find as a direct assault on everything they stood for, and dangerous enough to warrant shutting him up. Perhaps the faceless men who controlled the International Anthropological Society arranged for this latest visit? It didn't matter. The fight now conducted on a different level, and the previous incidents were too professional, too well organized, to be random hits from a nut group.

Despite positive dating results and favorable media exposure, what if he did walk away now? Would that be so bad? Sure, he had been over the arguments already and made his decision. The world now knew his discovery was not a fraud, and whether they liked it or not, his critics would have to come to terms with its existence. They would *have* to look at man's evolution in a new light, wouldn't they?

He recalled what he told Reed about discovery of ancient artifacts millions of years old and shook his head. Others before him had made finds that could not be explained by the establishment. Instead of sparking off a methodical analysis and re-evaluation of man's history, the finds were treated as curiosities and dismissed by most anthropologists, citing contamination, lost corroborative evidence, and plain amateur forgeries. It was an old argument. Unless the artifact was found by a reputable scientist and recovered under perfectly controlled conditions, the thing was a mere oddity, not worthy of serious study. After a few headlines, the papers turned to current scandals and controversies, and people forgot. History was forgotten. Truth was forgotten, something the venerated towers of learning claimed to strive for and uphold, all the while holding it up as a convenient shield to protect wedded ideas, reputations and positions.

Perhaps Wethermans had it right. Being a pure scientist did not count for much if he couldn't hold his own in the rough and tumble of academic politics. But *this* rough was getting a tad too much.

Having his nose rubbed in it, Krafter thought he knew how the game was played, but the man in black reminded him that he still had a way to go. If he walked away now, it would mean embracing the establishment, accept what his detractors stood for and become one of them for the sake of his own reputation and position. Could he look himself in the mirror every morning if he did that? Did he want to be another Wethermans? But if he didn't walk away, the man in black would be back, and like he said, he would be delivering more than merely a white envelope.

Was he afraid of getting hurt physically, and that's why he dithered? Startled by the notion, he dismissed it immediately. A broken arm could not be any worse than being kicked in the balls, and he doubted that he would be killed over his discovery. His detractors were out to murder him professionally, not for real. Still, Hartman and Walsh weren't in a hospital having a rest. The bottom line, he didn't know how far he would be pushed, but at least the waiting was over.

In the end, there was nothing to decide. He either fought for truth and acceptance of his discovery, or crawled into a cave and slammed the door shut after him. Although a charming notion, being a hermit had never appealed to him. So…

He stood up, walked to the wall-mounted kitchen phone and lifted the portable receiver. At the table, he poured himself another glass and took a mouthful of casserole. It had cooled slightly, but he didn't mind. After punching in numbers, he pressed the dial button and sat back.

"Hi, Larry. Feeling lonely?" Reed answered cheerfully.

"I had nothing to do and I thought I would bother you," Krafter said with a smile. "I'm not interrupting anything, am I?"

"A reporter's life is never his own."

Krafter glanced at the kitchen clock and winced. "Sorry to be calling this late. I forgot the damned time difference."

"Not a problem. What's up?"

"I contemplated having a quiet evening when a gentleman in black decided to come over and ruin it. He left me with a couple of bruises and a reminder that publicizing my discovery would not be conducive to prolonging my good health."

"You were attacked?"

"Whatever I believed I knew about martial arts, I might as well forget it. The man was a pro."

"Are you okay?"

"I'll live. And no, I didn't call the police, but I'll have a long talk with Dr. Perkins in the morning. The FBI will also want to know about this."

"I wonder how much they can do?" Reed mused. "I suppose you want me to write an article on this? It wouldn't be a front page item, even if you're today's news."

"I don't mind, but that's not why I called. Two prominent people who stood by me suddenly had a mysterious accident and you definitely stood by me."

"The connection had already occurred to me, Larry, and thanks for the heads up, but I wouldn't worry. Shutting down the press has never worked in this country."

"It's not shutting down the press that worries me. It's shutting you down."

"That's been tried before, and I doubt things are that desperate."

"They will be if my man in black decides to call on you. Maybe you better email me a couple of names in case I have to talk to another reporter."

Reed laughed. "Bastard, and I haven't even been buried yet."

"Seriously, Neil, I would watch those swinging doors."

"I'll keep it in mind. Don't let them rattle you, doc. This action against you only goes to prove the weakness of their position."

"I'll remember that the next time I get a visit."

Smiling, Krafter switched off and placed the receiver on the table. Taking another mouthful of casserole, he reached for a bread roll.

* * *

"Professor Krafter, I would prefer getting my information from you personally, rather than reading about it in the papers," Special Agent Julian Briggs complained aggrievedly.

Outside, heavy clouds hung low, making no move to leave. Over breakfast, the TV weatherman assured everybody that the overcast would burn off by mid-morning. Krafter hoped so and took a chance on walking in, not wishing to break his Monday routine.

"I apologize for that," he said evenly, not sounding at all apologetic, "but I didn't seek publicity, Mr. Briggs. I wanted people to know what my detractors are prepared to do to silence me."

"I am aware that you're engaged in a battle of professional warfare, Professor, but I cannot help you if you don't cooperate."

"Rest assured, Mr. Briggs," Larson interjected smoothly, shooting Krafter a peremptory look. "He'll extend the FBI his full cooperation without the repeat of this embarrassment."

"I am gratified to hear that, sir."

Krafter took Larson's veiled threat in stride. If he waited cap in hand for the FBI to act, he might as well give up now. They were fumbling around, merely going through the motions to give him a false sense of security. He had taken the initiative and meant to keep it. Sitting back would mean that everything up to now had been for nothing.

"Have you managed to find out anything of substance, Mr. Briggs?" he asked and glanced at Perkins sitting beside him, but his mentor showed no reaction.

"We already know that your accounting system was hacked, done through a terminal in your IT student lab. As a matter of fact, by you, Professor."

"What!" Krafter sat up in shock, then heard a laugh.

"To be more precise, the perpetrator used your logon ID. It's clear what happened. When he broke into Lab One and dropped off the envelope, he must have planted a keyboard stroke clicker, retrieved it at some stage and analyzed your access profile. You probably use your accounting system fairly regularly?"

"All the time."

"There you are. The rest was simple."

"As is your warped sense of humor, Mr. Briggs," Krafter said crossly, more than a little annoyed.

"Sorry about that. I trust, Dr. Larson, that UW has taken appropriate security updates?"

"Our IT department is working the problem."

"Good. As for the envelopes, Professor Krafter, we've drawn a blank. No fingerprints, apart from yours, but you probably suspected that already. We're clearly dealing with a professional here, which is bad news for you. Sheriff Ramanof's people traced the Chevy that rammed you to a local rental, Enterprise Rent-a-car. It appears that our man returned the car the next day and disappeared without reporting the damage. Checking it, my forensic team found nothing, which is not surprising. Our man had cleaned off any evidence of paint scraped from your car, but we'll continue to follow up on the identity he used."

"Which is almost certainly false," Krafter added grimly.

"Probably, but right now, any detail, no matter how small, helps. The rental agency description of him doesn't tell us much either. Apart from having a similar height to the man you said attacked you, it could be anybody. That's why your attacker wore a balaclava when he saw you. Like I said, we're dealing with a professional."

"What about his threat?"

"That's a complicated one. Short of providing you with twenty-four/seven protection, which the Bureau is not prepared to authorize, there isn't much we can do. If he does take further action against you, my assessment is that it won't be physical."

"That's very reassuring," Krafter mused dryly. "I trust the FBI will be prepared to authorize some action once you scrape me out of my car after I'm forced off the road for real."

"I understand your frustration, but the Bureau simply doesn't have that kind of manpower. At least the Denver Division doesn't. I reported this case to Washington—"

"Washington?"

"Contrary to what you might think, Professor, I take my responsibility seriously. Once the people who are after you began targeting others, this case was no longer mere financial fraud or assault, but terrorism, and Washington has the resources to do something about it. As you yourself pointed out, the attacker intended to frighten you, not harm you. You're being subjected to psychological harassment rather than deliberate physical violence."

Krafter squirmed in his seat, his groin giving a protesting twinge. "I hope my attacker keeps that in mind, Mr. Briggs. Anything further on Professor Hartman?"

"A broken left wrist and collarbone. The contusions looked

worse than they actually were. The Houston PD went over his car a second time when we suggested foul play and found a nut missing on the left steering rod connection. Without our warning, the entire incident would have been dismissed as an unfortunate accident. Incidentally, Professor Walsh had a similar mishap. According to Scotland Yard, it was loose front right wheel nuts. The wheel simply came off the car. Walsh had his car serviced the day before. If it weren't for those newspaper clippings our man left you, nobody would have thought twice about either incident. Whoever is out to silence you doesn't care if their intimidation is known."

"Perhaps they wanted it that way," Krafter added softly.

"As a warning to others who might consider taking your side? We haven't discounted that possibility. In case you were wondering, both of them received a letter before their accident."

"Are we talking about one man here?"

"The incidents were two days apart, plenty of time for one man to be in London and back to Houston. If this is an organized campaign, which it looks like it might be, I doubt that whoever is running our man would risk compromising himself by engaging another party. That's only a supposition, of course."

"What are you going to do now?"

"The message he gave you last night suggests he is still in Laramie, waiting to see what you will do."

"Knowing that the FBI is involved, he might decide that psychological harassment isn't working."

"I know this doesn't help, but if he's still in Laramie, we can make use of that fact. He has to be staying somewhere, and there are only so many motels and hotels there. I wish I could say more, but without a photo or a reliable description, I don't fancy our chances of catching this guy."

"Then I'm on my own," Krafter said and snorted with derision.

"I am sure the FBI is doing everything possible, Agent

Briggs," Larson added diplomatically, "and Professor Krafter didn't mean to imply otherwise."

"He did, but I'm not offended. This is frustrating for everybody. Next time you have an incident, Professor Krafter, be so good as to call me first, okay?"

"I will try and remember that," Krafter said coldly, not at all impressed, wondering why Larson even bothered to call the FBI. So they managed to confirm the UW computer was hacked. Big deal.

"Gentlemen, I'll be in touch," Briggs said and the line went dead.

Larson reached across the desk and pressed the phone speaker button. Sitting back, he took off his glasses, cleaned them, then leveled his eyes on Krafter.

"You didn't have to go out of your way to be antagonistic, young man."

"Antagonistic? What was I supposed to do? Thank him for sitting on his hands? They're quick to slap you with a speeding fine and throw the book at you for having a milligram of coke, but when it comes to something serious, there are always excuses for not doing something."

"They don't have much to work with here, you know."

Krafter sighed and nodded. "You're right, sir. It's only…"

"I know. You want to hit back, except there is no one there to hit. But you *have* hit back. Your TV appearances and newspaper columns are undermining your critics, and your discovery is gaining a measure of acceptance from many of your colleagues. I might as well tell you now, after reading about your latest round of dating results, Arizona U is sending Professor Allbright to take a look at your skull."

Krafter sat up, his eyes wide. "Allbright? When?"

"Next Thursday."

Allbright was a noted anthropologist, but with limited experience in paleoanthropology. Nevertheless, impressing the old fossil would go a long way toward muzzling his critics.

"I'll be ready."

"There is something else. Professor Piere Lacroe also made an application to come over."

Krafter was impressed. Lacroe was a bonafide paleoanthropologist and a senior figure at the University of Paris. Although a skeptic, he had not dismissed outright the possibility that the find could be genuine. Whether his detractors liked it or not, the latest dating data ruled out blatant fraud, and the outlandish claims made by Bollinger and Maddson were being viewed much more critically.

"That's all very good, Doctor, but it won't help me if my visitor attempts something more drastic."

Larson waved his hand in dismissal. "You can also be run over. You cannot worry about it." He touched the phone speaker button and typed in an extension. "Laura? You can make that connection now."

"Yes, sir."

After some moments, a familiar voice answered and Krafter frowned.

"Doctor Van Neuman."

"Good afternoon, Doctor. This is Dr. Larson."

"Ah, so good of you to call. Is everybody there?"

"Professor Krafter and Dr. Perkins are both with me, Doctor."

"Splendid. Professor Krafter, I wanted everybody to hear what I have to say. Following Dr. Chandler's complaint against Professor Bollinger's unorthodox article and subsequent investigation into the missing FedEx package, I discussed the matter with him. He has been censured for breach of professional ethics. It might not sound like much to you, but the censure severely compromises his position with Harvard and curtails any ambitions he might have had for advancement within the Anthropology Department. We cannot ascertain what happened to your sample after Dr. Chandler handed it over to Bollinger, but it's possible that our mailroom could have mislaid the package. We're still looking into it. As for any professional disagreement you might have with Professor Bollinger regarding your discovery, that's something you'll have to resolve yourself. However, speaking personally, the latest dating data has done much to discredit his position. Nevertheless, you face other critics, Professor."

Krafter listened hard, weighed everything Van Neuman had said, and didn't care for the taste it left him. Bollinger censured? A slap on the wrist and it was business as usual. Bollinger was a powerful figure in the anthropological field and a big draw card for Harvard as a magnet for prospective students entering the field. Van Neuman would not go out of his way to antagonize him too much.

"What about blatant falsification of the sample he sent to the Melno Park lab that gave him the date of four hundred years? Where does Harvard's ethics committee stand on that, Doctor?"

"Well now, without the original sample, we cannot repeat that test. Your allegation that he falsified the test is only an allegation. However, dating results from the skull does suggest a major irregularity."

A major irregularity? That covered it nicely, Krafter thought, but he did not see any value pursuing the point. Besides, the skull dating data had nullified Bollinger's test very nicely anyway.

"Sir, will Harvard stand by Professor Chandler's paper that supports my find, despite negative endorsement by the International Anthropological Society?"

"Professor Krafter, contrary to popular opinion, the IAS doesn't speak for Harvard or for me. Dr. Chandler will be free to publish his findings as he sees fit, with the full backing of this university."

Krafter wondered in Van Neuman genuinely believed what he was saying. If he dismissed the IAS so casually, why was he still a member?

"Dr. Perkins here. Tell me, Dr. Van Neuman, will *you* publish a supportive article?"

Krafter glanced sharply at his mentor. Publishing such an article would definitely put Bollinger on that breezy limb, but would Harvard have the political will to do it, risking not only Bollinger's wrath, but also raising the IAS ire? Still, if he could get Harvard's endorsement, he would be laughing.

Van Neuman cleared his throat, probably considering his options and the impact of each.

"I shall give it serious consideration, Dr. Perkins, but given the circumstances, it's not a decision I can make alone."

Krafter smiled at the nice evade. Harvard was prepared to hang Bollinger and Chandler out on that limb, but Van Neuman did not want to be sitting on it himself. Not counting reaction from the IAS, there were probably internal considerations to resolve. Politics...the whole thing stank like a plagiarized assignment.

"I believe that Harvard will do the right thing in the end, Dr. Van Neuman," Larson said tactfully. "And I want to thank you for the call."

"Not at all, and good luck, Professor Krafter."

"Thank you, sir."

When the line went dead, Larson took off his glasses and gave them a quick clean. Finished, he put them on and peered at Krafter.

"Satisfied, young man?"

"It's a start, Doctor, but I doubt that I've heard the last from Bollinger or the IAS."

"I dare say. That will be all, gentlemen."

After the meeting, Krafter brooded through his ten o'clock tutorial, unsettled not only by his attack, but attacks on Hartman and Walsh. Everything that happened so far had not been over a difference of opinion, but overt intimidation with a single purpose to silence his opinion. Despite FBI's assurance that this was as far as his opponents were likely to go, he wasn't reassured at all. What if next time the man in black turned his attention on Elena, or worse still, his parents? Unlikely as that might be, he couldn't get the awful possibility out of his mind. With Allbright coming, perhaps the skeptics would realize the futility of their vendetta and hopefully call the whole thing off. Yeah, and he also believed in fairies.

At least his lectures were more popular and the large auditorium now had standing room only. Clearly, not everyone was an attending course student, some probably wanting to rub shoulders with a celebrity, but his notoriety did have an unexpected side benefit for UW. Enrolments into anthropology undergraduate programs had risen markedly. If nothing else, he demonstrated that a lot remained out there still to be discovered. What attracted them, of course, was the scandal surrounding his discovery and the unexpected vitriolic reaction from his peers. This naked insight into anthropology, divided into schools of thought, or camps, dominated by powerful figures, each seeking to destroy the other's evolutionary theory by whatever means possible, ethical or otherwise, was not academia they understood and hoped to join, but they enjoyed the show nonetheless.

Tuesday enabled him to dabble a little into his side project, poking into the mystery why the Powder River Basin held so much coal. After pouring over dry geophysics articles and several teasing Internet publications without getting anywhere, he gave up in disgust. His heart simply wasn't in it, which demonstrated how badly he had been distracted. He wondered absently why the burglar or the man in black had not attempted to break into the department's vault and steal the skull. When he reasoned it through, the answer obvious. Although an attempt was still possible, with independent dating data now in the public domain, there wasn't much point in spiriting away the skull, for now. Nevertheless, it might be wise to consider moving the thing to a more secure location. After all, it was his only remaining piece of evidence.

It rained most of Wednesday, the heavy clouds matching his mood. By late afternoon the weather lifted, for which he was grateful, as he biked in. He had an umbrella, but with a brisk northerly pushing against his back, had it rained, he would've been soaked going home.

Krafter finished sending emails to his students with pointed reminders that tutorials cannot be missed if they wanted to avoid incurring his wrath, he packed up and went home. Bright sunshine broke through the overcast as he cycled down S. 15th Street and his spirits lifted. October was pleasant, and there were obvious signs of nature getting ready to hunker down for a long winter. He toyed with the notion of getting away for a few days to regain his perspective, but however attractive the idea, he could only dream about it. Until the next semester break, he would remain chained to UW.

Not in the mood to cook, he settled for a thick grilled cheese and pastrami sandwich accompanied by a dark ale. Not normally a beer drinker, this time his body craved it and it felt good pouring the rich brew down his throat. After cleaning up, he settled in the living room to watch an old Robert Mitchum movie, *The Yakuza*, allowing his mind to get caught up in the story. Like Sean Connery, Mitchum had matured with age as an actor and Krafter enjoyed the subtle nuances of motion and expressions Mitchum used to portray his character, producing a powerful effect. Krafter had seen the movie before, but it still managed to enthrall him every time he watched it.

The doorbell chimed and he frowned. He pressed the stop button on the DVD remote, got up and padded toward the front door. Opening it, he faced two uniformed police officers wearing leather jackets over tan shirts and dark green trousers. One was freckled and looked awfully young compared to his more seasoned and taller black partner. Both had an edgy look in their eyes like they were expecting trouble. A cruiser behind them had its roof lights going. What the hell did they want with him?

"Can I help you?"

"Excuse me for bothering you, sir," the black cop said, his eyes roving over what he could see from the entrance, "but we've had a report of gunshots coming from this house."

Krafter looked blank, completely thrown off the track, his mind still on the movie he'd been watching.

"Gunshots? I haven't heard anything, officer. The only gunshots in this house came from Robert Mitchum shooting it out against some bad guys. Besides, I don't even own a firearm."

"The report we received was definite, sir. Mind if we come in and look around?"

Krafter stepped aside and extended a hand. "Be my guest."

Wary, but less tense, the two officers walked in. Krafter left them to it, wondering what was going on, and went into the kitchen to boil water for a coffee. This was ridiculous, but he guessed the busybodies had to go through the motions.

"Parker!" he heard one of the cops call out, sounding as if it came from the garage. A few moments later, both cops strode into the kitchen. The black officer held a handgun by its trigger guard.

"You told us that you didn't own a firearm, sir. We found this in your bedroom. It's a Bersa Thunder .380 ACP, but I guess you knew that already. What's more, there's a body under a plastic sheet in your garage, and it's still warm. It also has a bullet hole in its chest."

Mesmerized by the gun, his thoughts in disarray, Krafter gaped at them. "A body?"

"I think you've got some explaining to do, Mister."

Catching his breath, Krafter spread his hands. "I don't know anything about any of this."

"I must ask you to accompany us to the station, sir."

"Am I under arrest?"

"This will likely take some time and it would be better if we do it downtown."

Stunned, Krafter could not believe this was happening. He had been set up, the only thing he could come up with. The man in black? It mattered little now. His priority was to get himself out of this mess. His mind whirled in confusion before he started thinking clearly.

"I want to make a call first."

The two officers exchanged glances. "You can do that downtown," the black cop declared.

"Look, if I'm not under arrest, I can call anyone I damn well please, okay? And if you're going to arrest me, I'm still entitled to make a call. So, what's it going to be?"

"Make it brief."

Angry and bewildered, he walked into his study with both cops tagging after him. He yanked open a drawer in his desk and took out a note with a scrawled number string. Not believing this was happening, he sat down heavily and reached for the phone. He dialed quickly and placed the receiver against his ear.

"Special Agent Julian Briggs," the familiar voice answered and Krafter sagged with relief, not sure he would catch the FBI agent, not relishing the idea of having to explain everything to someone else.

"This is Professor Krafter, Mr. Briggs."

"What can I do for you, doc?"

"My apologies for the late call, but I might be in some trouble. I have two Laramie police officers in my house. They found a handgun in my bedroom and claim there's a body in the garage. They're taking me downtown for questioning."

There was a moment of silence, then Krafter heard a long sigh. "I'd say you were in some trouble, but I'm glad that you heeded my advice about calling me. You said they conducted a search of your house?"

"They said someone reported gunshots and I let them look

around."

"Without a warrant, that still constitutes an illegal search. Never mind. Let me speak to the senior officer."

Krafter held out the phone to the black cop. "If you're in charge, this is for you."

Still holding the gun, looking uncertain, the cop reached for the phone. "Wayne Parker, Laramie PD."

Krafter watched with interest as Parker stiffened. He couldn't hear what Briggs said, but it seemed to take some steam out of Parker's enthusiasm.

"Yes, sir…I understand…Yes, sir." Parker pursed his lips, held out the phone and Krafter took it.

"Krafter."

"Let them take you downtown, but I've taken charge. One of my men will fly up and see you in the morning. I'll call Sheriff Ramanof and get him squared away. Tell him what you know and don't hold anything back."

"That's easy. I don't know anything."

"You're beginning to be a problem for me, doc. Sit tight and we'll get to the bottom of this."

"I'm sorry as hell for dumping this in your lap—"

"We'll talk tomorrow," Briggs said and hung up.

Vastly relieved, Krafter replaced the receiver, pocketed his wallet and cellphone, and stood up. He walked into the living room and switched things off. Facing the two officers, he slid his hands into his pockets.

"Okay, let's go."

Parker's mouth twitched and glanced at his partner. "Give forensics a call, Norris, and wait for them."

He reached into his jacket, took out a plastic bag and popped the handgun into it. He sealed the bag, nodded, and extended a hand at the front door. Outside, Krafter walked to the police cruiser and climbed into the front seat. Parker got in, started the engine, and with a throaty growl, the car pulled away from the curb.

Light poles cast milky pools on black asphalt as the squad car made its way up Russell Street. Several houses along the deserted road had their front porch lit; many did not. Parker's radio crackled and hissed as the dispatcher made routine requests to patrolling cars. With the initial shock wearing off, Krafter had time to consider what a body in his garage meant for him. It certainly wasn't anything good. If they could pin a murder on him, it would definitely put him out of action as far as his discovery was concerned; also end of a promising career. He pictured the ensuing headlines and shuddered. At least Briggs seemed to give him the benefit of the doubt. He wondered if the sheriff would be as understanding, remembering that they were both police. There was one definite thing he could do to improve his chances, and he should have thought of it sooner, although it might not make him too popular with the sheriff.

He took the cellular out of his trouser pocket, flipped open the lid, and dialed a familiar number. Parker glanced at him, but said nothing. It took four rings before she answered.

"Hello?"

"Hi, Elena. It's Larry. Can you talk?"

"Sure. I'm running water for a bath. If you want to go out, it'll have to be a rain check."

He had a fleeting image of her naked, stepping into a hot tub, wishing he were with her in case she needed her back soaped…or front.

"Sorry to spoil it for you, but I need your professional help."

"Oh? You want to fight a parking fine?"

He held back a smile. "It's a bit more involved, I'm afraid. Can you come to Plaza Court? The police found a body in my garage and want to chat."

"A body! Larry, tell me you haven't killed somebody?"

"It's a setup."

"What've you told the cops?"

"I haven't told them anything. There is nothing to tell."

"Keep it that way. I'll be right down."

"Thanks. Sorry to spoil your bath. I owe you big time."

"And I'll be collecting," she told him primly and hung up.

Krafter leaned back against the seat and felt better. Although serious, the whole thing was silly, but cops had their own way of looking at things and were always eager to make a quick arrest. With a warm body and a gun, to them, it looked like an open-and-shut, even if they did get the wrong man. Argue about it later, they would figure. With Elena's legal mind in his corner, he felt reasonably confident that he would not make a major gaffe.

The cruiser turned left into S. 3rd Street, cleared the I-80 overpass and slowed to pull into E. Skyline Road. On his left the Plaza complex stood brightly lit. Enough cars and pedestrians moved about to keep it from looking deserted. Parker stopped beside the two-story Laramie Police Department building and killed the engine. Powerful motorbikes and Chevy Impalas crowded the small parking lot. Two uniformed officers walked out of the double-glass entrance and hurried toward one of the squad cars.

Krafter followed Parker into a spacious foyer that opened to a deserted floor and workstations cluttered with computer screens, files and piles of paperwork. Although the place seemed empty, there had to be cops somewhere. The desk sergeant never looked up as they walked by, the hard gray linoleum floor echoing their footsteps. They walked past glassed cubicles toward a back wall crowded with announcement boards and posters. Parker paused before a ceiling-high brown door, knocked once and walked in.

Krafter had never seen the sheriff and didn't particularly care to do so now. Under different circumstances, he would not have given Ramanof a second look had they met on the street. Dressed in a tan shirt and green trousers, a star on the collars, looking young for his position, the man had a hard face and severe expression. He figured that his job probably didn't involve much humor.

Ramanof looked up from behind his cluttered desk and motioned with his hand at the visitor chairs.

"Make yourselves comfortable," he growled in a surprisingly deep voice. "This will take a while, I imagine." When everybody settled in, he smoothed back black hair above his right ear with a swipe of his hand and turned his full attention on Parker. "Okay, tell me what you've got."

Parker glanced at Krafter and cleared his throat. "Well, sir, we received a dispatch call around seven-twenty, advising of a shooting at fourteen East Sanders Drive. On checking the premises—"

"You had permission?"

"Yes, sir. Professor Krafter told us we could look around."

"Go on."

"Going through the master bedroom, I found a Bersa .380 and Norris discovered a body in the garage. The Professor denied owning a firearm or any knowledge of the body." He dug out the plastic bag out of his jacket and placed the gun on Ramanof's desk.

The sheriff barely glanced at it. "Yeah, that's what Norris reported while you were on your way over. Anything else?"

"That's it, sir."

"Okay. Take the gun to ballistics and check it for prints. I also want to know if its been fired recently. Check if the Professor here has a gun license."

"Yes, sir." Parker stood up, grabbed the bag and walked out.

"We'll want your prints as well, Professor," Ramanof declared darkly, giving Krafter a cold stare. "I just came off a call from Special Agent Briggs in Denver, informing me that he's taken jurisdiction. FBI or not, son, you've got some explaining to do."

"Like I told your officers, Sheriff, I don't know anything. Somebody is trying to frame me and you know it."

A knock interrupted whatever Ramanof was about to say. The door opened and a cop in mufti jerked his head at a woman standing beside him.

"This is Miss Elena Spiteri, sir. She's from Bartlett & Strong."

Dressed in a smart beige business suit and a light green silk neck scarf, hair rolled up in a bun, Elena nodded to the cop and walked in.

"Sheriff…" She gave Krafter a small smile and sat down.

Ramanof shot her a hard look. "How the hell did *you* get here?"

"I drove."

"I don't care for flippant answers, Miss Spiteri!"

"Professor Krafter is my client, Sheriff."

"I see, and you just happened to be in the neighborhood?"

"Has my client been charged with anything?" she demanded, ignoring his sarcasm.

"This is still a preliminary investigation, Miss Spiteri, and the Professor is cooperating with our inquiries. A murder has been committed, you know."

Elena turned to Krafter. "What have you told him?"

"Nothing, because I don't know anything."

"In that case—"

"In that case, Miss Spiteri—"

"My client is free to go, unless you're charging him with something."

Controlling his temper with a visible effort, Ramanof took a deep breath and squared his shoulders.

"There is no need for us to be hostile, Miss Spiteri. I have a murder on my hands and Professor Krafter is a natural suspect. Granted, there might be extenuating circumstances, given that his car was rammed and he was personally assaulted recently, but until I have all the evidence, I want to hear his side of it."

"I don't have a side, Sheriff, and this isn't your case anymore," Krafter pointed out and turned to Elena. "Special Agent Briggs has taken charge. He's sending up one of his men."

She gave Ramanof a searching look. "Is that true?"

Ramanof gave a weary nod. "That's right."

"Then you have no business questioning my client at all," she declared in a frosty voice. "Has the FBI asked you to detain my client?"

"No, they haven't."

Elena stood up. "Then we're done. Come on, Larry. We're leaving."

"I need a set of prints off him first."

"Once he's charged."

"His house is a crime scene, damn it!" Ramanof declared in a last ditch effort to retain control. "He cannot go back there."

"Fine, and I expect all evidence to be made available to me under the terms of the search warrant. I would like a copy now, if you don't mind."

Clearly embarrassed and looking uncomfortable, Ramanof pulled at his chin. "Ah, we haven't issued a warrant."

Elena stared at him. "You're searching a citizen's home without a warrant? And presumably you've gotten forensics trampling all over the place?"

"We were responding to a call! And besides, Professor Krafter gave the two police officers on site permission to look around."

"That doesn't constitute permission to search and it's certainly not a substitute for a warrant, which you know very well. That means anything you come up with is inadmissible. Moreover, you've opened your department to a possible lawsuit."

"Look, lady! I've got a body in his house and I want to find out how it got there!"

"Then I suggest you find out, Sheriff, but not by taking advantage of my client's innocent cooperation. Let's get out of here, Larry. You have nothing more to say to this gentleman."

Ramanof glared at her. "You've got your way for now, Miss Spiteri. Just make sure he doesn't leave town!"

"When my client gets home, your people better not be there. With the exception of the body, I wouldn't even think of removing anything. If you want to look around, get a warrant. Come on, Larry."

Krafter got up, flashed Ramanof a grin and shrugged. He followed Elena out and closed the door after him. Both heard a short, sharp expletive coming from inside and chuckled. Grabbing her by the shoulders, he planted a grateful kiss on her inviting lips.

"Wow, some performance. I would hate having you mad at *me!*"

She giggled and sagged against him. "I operated on raw nerve, expecting him to throw us both in the pen."

"You had the man floored, beautiful. You're a tiger when you put your professional face on. I understand now why Bartlett & Strong want you in Denver. You're going to make a terrific trial lawyer."

When they climbed into her red Honda Civic, she gave him a searching look. "What's going on, Larry? Car accident, assault, and now this?"

He didn't pretend not to understand and gave a small sigh. They had talked about this before, but then, it had all been a game. It wasn't a game anymore.

"Somebody is out to shut me up for good to keep my discovery from being recognized as genuine."

"But murdering to do it?"

"It's either that or I murder some powerful reputations. If I'm behind bars, I'm not causing trouble over some forty-million-year-old bones, and they won't have to rewrite man's history."

"This is unreal. It's gangster warfare. I never expected that this kind of thing goes on in the academic community."

Krafter sympathized fully. "It's certainly not the reaction I expected either. When I first saw the hand bone and the gold bracelet stuck in a wall of coal, some of its dazzle must have gone to my head. I had this vision of standing on a podium, holding it up and hearing the applause of admiring colleagues. There would be awards, lecture tours, television. I was going to be famous."

"You *are* famous, but clearly not the way you thought. What are you going to do now?"

"I won't be giving up, and my detractors haven't had it all their way."

"Because they haven't, they tried to pin a murder on you!"

"Looks like it. How bad is it?"

"If the cops had a warrant, you would have been in trouble, at least for a little while, but they were too eager. You were lucky the FBI was already on your case, or that clown Ramanof would have had you in the pen."

"Yeah, I've had a lot of luck lately." He gave her a tender smile and brushed her cheek with his fingers. "Sorry, I didn't mean to be gloomy, and thanks for getting me out of his clutches."

"We're not clear yet." She touched his shoulder and started the car. He turned to look at her, grasped her right hand, and she tensed. It felt warm and comforting. Emotions churned inside him, feelings he didn't know he had…or was afraid to face them before.

"This past month has been hard on me. When I believed that the whole world was against me, you were there. When I needed to talk to someone, you listened, and I appreciated that in my clumsy, thickheaded way. I'm not much good around women and it always amazed me that you wanted to be with me, not that I'm complaining. In my lab, surrounded by fossils and skeletons, I am in my element. I know what I'm doing and no one can challenge me. With you, I'm lost, torn with conflicting emotions."

Elena remained rigid, watching him intently.

"One moment, I want to tear your clothes off and make love to you. The next, I simply want to be close to you, to hold you and protect you. Intellectually, I understand what's going on, but emotionally, I'm floundering." He searched her eyes and smiled ruefully. "I'm not making any sense, am I? What I'm trying to tell you, this is getting serious. What if they come after you? If you got hurt, I would never forgive myself."

She flashed him a smile, withdrew her hand and reached for the gear bar. "You're sweet, but you can be such a dope sometimes."

He stared at her. "Because I care what happens to you?"

"Don't you see?" She gave him a searching look, then shook her head. "You don't get it, do you?"

"Get what?"

"I don't want you pushing me away. I want to be a part of your life, an important part, if you will let me. Sometimes, I wouldn't mind if you tore my clothes off." She flashed him an impish smile, then turned serious. "If you got troubles, I want to share them with you and help you get through them."

"That's my point! Whoever is after me doesn't want to hurt me, or they would have done it already, but there is nothing to stop them from hurting you, if that's what it takes to make me back off. Since I won't, you could be a target."

"What are you getting at?"

"I want you to go away for a while, at least until this mess is cleared up."

"Larry Krafter, you don't run my life and I can take care of myself. If you think that I would run out on you…" Her eyes sparkled as tears welled, threatening to spill. He grabbed her hand.

"Look, I know you want to share my problems and I love

you for it, but you haven't considered my side of it. At home or at the university, every time I'm not with you, I would worry what might be happening to you. Be sensible about this, Elena."

"You big lug! I'd worry about *you* if I left. I am not your kept woman and I also have a job and a life, just like you."

"I know that, but neither of us will have anything if this gets messy. You could go to Denver. Bartlett & Strong would love it. They've been pressuring you to go and the FBI has an office there. They can protect you, certainly better than they can here. My parents are there and you could stay with them."

"I'll think about it," she declared, but he knew that she wouldn't.

In many ways, she could be irritatingly stubborn. Was he overreacting emotionally, looking for a casual romp one moment, then trying to control her, *make* her into a kept woman? An image of a fur-clad primitive standing in front of his cave, a club in one hand, holding his woman by her wrist with another, flashed through his mind and he held back a smile. He loved her, if he knew what that meant, but he didn't own her, and he certainly had no claim on her, yet.

She put the car into gear and pulled out of the parking lot.

As they turned into S. 3rd Street, Krafter brushed her thigh. "When we get home, can you stay a while? We can talk, and maybe have that bath together?"

He couldn't see her large almond eyes in the gloom, but her look told him what he wanted to know. Perhaps that equation he had been worrying about may have a solution after all.

Chapter Six

"A straight swap, Garry. You get Greenfield and I get Johnston. It's not like I'm trying to steal him, damn it."

"The hell you're not. I'll be giving up one of my best men and I get a lemon in return."

"Christ! The kid is a good investigator. He is simply not cut out for intelligence work. I would transfer him to another section, but it wouldn't look good and everyone would know why I did it. This way, he gets a clean break."

"You sound like a used car salesman," Garry Strand said. Even over the phone, Tom sensed amusement.

"You want to deal or give me a hard time?"

"Both. Okay, I'll bite. Send me the kid's file. You're sure you want Johnston? With his promotion to Special Agent, he might not want to move and I've got cases to handle."

"I want him. He's a cold, constipated fish as we both know, but he knows how to do his work. He's a self-starter and I trust his instincts. A stint in Washington won't hurt his career at all."

"If he lives long enough to enjoy it," Strand said dryly. "The way you operate, I wouldn't give much for his chances."

The Boston Division Special Agent in Charge had a point and Tom smiled. After Israel sabotaged the Valero Texas City Refinery and almost got America to bomb Iran for it, he was transferred to Washington where he expected to be buried in dull counterterrorism analysis work. Just settling in, the John the Baptist Scroll case, as it became known, got dumped in his lap. The case not only cost two prominent cardinals in Vatican their jobs, but also got his former boss, Bruce Wellard, axed when he conspired to get Tom killed. All three cases were still to go to trial.

"There is nothing exciting on my plate these days except boring analysis briefs, and maybe some visits to see the Brits at MI5 and MI6. Johnston will love it."

"You haven't talked to him about this, have you?"

"I know better than that. This is strictly by the book."

"Sure, but it's one that you have written yourself," Strand added darkly and Tom laughed.

"I may have pulled a few fast ones now and then, but getting you mad at me wasn't even on the page…sir."

"Like I said. You're a used car salesman, Meecham. I'll talk to Johnston. Why the hell a man would want to move from Boston's quiet sanity to DC's nuthouse, I can't imagine. Never mind. I heard that Peroni is going to trial in November."

"The fourteenth, I think. At the committal hearing, his bigshot lawyer went for a dismissal of all charges due to lack of sufficient evidence, but the judge didn't even let him finish his opening statement. Trimble then wanted a continuance, claiming the defense didn't have enough time to prepare. The judge merely banged his gavel and that was that. See you in court."

"Trimble is one of Lambert Associates' heaviest hitters, and our case is far from solid, you know," Strand pointed out.

"Tell me about it. We *do* have Cardinal Belconi's confession going for us. Anyway, we'll just have to see how our DA plays it out."

"You worried about testifying?"

"It's only another murder case."

"Not with the Vatican involved it's not and you know it. I'll get back to you on Johnston. Pop into the office when you're around," Strand said and rang off.

Tom replaced the receiver, leaned back against the chair, and propped his legs on the edge of his desk.

What happened to Peroni now was definitely up to the District Attorney. As far as Tom was concerned, he did his bit for justice. He got his man out of Italy and delivered him. If Trimble gets him off, Peroni might decide to look him up and even the score. He killed six men in an attempt to recover the John the Baptist papyrus. One more body wouldn't faze him at all. Then again, the man was a professional and his mission was a scrub. There would be no percentage in pushing a failed mission. At least Tom hoped so. At any rate, there weren't any calories in it worth worrying about. Like Mark Price said, maybe the CIA would have him. The three of them could get together for a beer and rake over old times.

That might be an amusing thing to do in some future scenario, but right now, he had more pressing problems to deal with. When Wellard self-destructed, the FBI Director appointed Drake Hancock as Assistant Director of the Counterterrorism Division. A balding man of forty-five, at only five-foot-ten, Tom never recalled seeing him in the building. Then again, he himself had not been in Washington long enough to know all the fast-track movers in the Bureau. What he picked up on the grapevine, though, Hancock had been Deputy Director of DC's Security Division for three years. He served time as Assistant Special Agent in Charge of the Chicago Division before being promoted as SAC of the New York Field Office Criminal Division. Clearly, the man knew what he was doing. He had not interfered with Tom's Counterterrorism Analysis section, probably because he was coming up to speed with Division issues. The two interviews Tom had with him were friendly and Hancock seemed genuinely pleased to have him on board. If he harbored any resentment that Tom was the cause of Wellard's demise, he hadn't shown it. From what Tom heard, the two of them had been buddies.

He dropped his legs to the floor and reached for the coffee mug. What was left in there had gone cold and he didn't want to get himself a refill right then. If he could get rid of Greenfield, his section would be humming. While he was at it, why not get rid of his client units at the same time? One of his section's prime responsibilities was to provide analysis service for Operations I who dealt with international terrorism, and Operations II who looked at weapons of mass destruction and domestic terrorism. With those sections gone, his life would be perfect, but enjoying it was not part of his job description.

Well, you can't have everything.

The one thing he *did* have was Melissa, recalling a dinner they had last Saturday, followed by a nightcap at his apartment, it rounded off a very pleasant day. He hadn't even taken advantage of her when she got a bit giggly. He wanted a relationship that would last, not a series of grab-and-run. Having her slim arms wrapped around his neck, her long straw hair cascading over her shoulders, deep blue eyes staring into his, soft lips aching to be kissed…

He pulled himself out of his reverie and came down to earth. Melissa was a woman to be cultivated and courted, not abused, but he wondered if he could afford the courting. An FBI salary didn't stretch to dinners at Sea Catch or the 1789 Restaurant every weekend. Never mind, he had not reached bottom yet. Being with her was also educational. After visiting the Smithsonian and a couple of other museums, and even attending a play, his intellectual horizons had expanded and he found that he liked it. In turn, she got to learn more about the pointy end of FBI work. It balanced out.

He turned to the computer screen and quickly scanned his email Inbox. Tuesdays were a drag. Not long enough into the week to look forward to the weekend, and too early to have forgotten the weekend. He had the list cleared this morning, but the number of new messages demanding his attention made his shoulders sag. A quick scan when he opened a few showed that most were CC copies for his information only. Definitely time for another fatherly pep talk with his unit leaders. Unless someone wanted him to do something, he didn't care to know the nuts and bolts of what the guys were doing or how they were doing it, or to whom. Did they think that by sending him their decisions would in some way grease him up? This clutter had to stop.

An email from Hancock caught his eye and he clicked on it. His boss didn't waste any time on explanations. The message heading simply said, 'Deal with it'.

Okay, he would deal with it, whatever 'it' was.

'It' turned out to be a request from Vince Saxon, Denver Division SAC, for manpower to properly investigate the Professor Krafter case. The name and the associated headlines were immediately familiar, as was the controversy the professor's discovery generated. As he read through Special Agent Briggs' background notes, Tom wondered why Hancock had handballed the thing to him. Briggs had a simple murder case on his hands. What the hell did that have to do with counterterrorism? When he finished reading the write-up on the IAS and articles from Neil Reed, he began to understand.

Terrorism was not simply blowing up trains and buildings, or sending a brainwashed kid into a crowd to blast himself to bits in the name of Allah, or whatever those extremists believed in. His job description defined it fairly well.

Unlawful use or threatened use of violence committed against persons or property to intimidate or coerce a government, the civilian population, or segment thereof, in furtherance of political or social objectives.

Like bureaucracies everywhere, the Bureau tended to get carried away with its language.

If this IAS crowd targeted Krafter to suppress a scientific discovery, their actions definitely fell within that definition. Reading the papers when the story first broke, he found it hard to wrap his mind around all the fuss the ancient bones appeared to have stirred up. The further he dug behind the one-line second-guessers, he came to understand more fully what Krafter's find implied. To rewrite history meant not only reprinting whole libraries of old books, it also meant wounding or killing influential academic reputations. It was like telling the pope that Christ never existed, which was a controversy of another kind, and still running.

Finishing the email, he summed it up: bank fraud, Krafter assaulted, two professors run off the road, and a body, which turned out to be a local electricity meter reader. That in itself could have been enough reason to shoot him, he mused. So far, both Laramie PD and Denver forensics have drawn a blank. Well, given their basic facilities, that wasn't totally unexpected. Briggs had asked for manpower, to do what?

He shook his head, sighed, and reached for the phone. Checking the number attached to the email, he dialed. When he got through, he spent a frustrating minute punching option prompts from an annoyingly sweet female voice.

"For emergencies, press one. For general inquiries, press two. For—"

Tom pressed zero to cut through the crap.

"I am sorry. You have not made a valid selection. Please press nine to hear the menu options again."

Christ! Teeth grinding, he pressed zero again.

"I am sorry. You have not made a valid selection. Please wait while you are being transferred to the first available consultant."

As he listened to mind-numbing music, tempted to hang up, the line eventually clicked.

"FBI Denver Division, Carry speaking. How can I help you?"

"You can help me by dismantling your automated answering system and offer real service," Tom snapped.

"I am sorry, sir—"

"Never mind. This is Thomas Meecham, Supervising Special Agent, Counterterrorism Analysis section, Washington. Please connect me to Special Agent Julian Briggs."

"Just a moment, sir. I have to check if he's in."

After more music, a strong male voice answered. "Mr. Meecham? Julian Briggs."

"You should have added your direct line to that email, Julian. It would have saved me a small war with your phone system."

Julian laughed. "I am sorry, Mr. Meecham—"

"Just, Tom."

"I believe they set it up that way to discourage the public from calling us."

"And it's working."

"I'm glad to hear from you, Tom. When Vince Saxon sent my request, I thought it was swallowed by the system."

"The wheels may turn slowly, but they do turn. I've read the email and I understand the general background, but what exactly do you want us to do?"

"Carry told me you were in Counterterrorism. I'm a little fuzzy why you're involved."

Tom wondered how Briggs rated his job if he hadn't figured that out. "Your email outlined a succession of retaliatory acts against a number of individuals, presumably in an attempt to suppress Professor Krafter's discovery. That reads like domestic terrorism to me, with possible international connotations."

"I understand all that. My request was for manpower, not analysis."

"Now you're going to get both. With my umbrella covering your case, and it's still your case, you won't be hassled by jurisdictional protocol. You and I will work out our to do list and I'll assign resources as required to get the job done. Does that answer your question?"

"I read about you in the papers. They say you're a go-getter. I hope that's true, because I certainly can't get this job done with what I've got. But don't try muscling in on my turf."

Tom chuckled, getting the measure of the man. "Sorry if I stepped on your toes. It wasn't intentional. How about you send me everything you got, including all forensic data and original samples from your lab and Laramie PD, including the Bersa they found. If Sheriff Ramanof baulks, cut him off at the knees. With you in charge, this is a federal case now. By the way, where's the body?"

"Laramie PD have it at the local morgue."

"I'll have a word with our lab and send someone over to check it out and go over Krafter's house at the same time."

"I don't know what you're expecting to find. The house was clean. As for the body, a straightforward shot through the heart. We didn't find any powder burns."

That immediately rang an alarm bell for Tom. An amateur like Krafter would probably hit a man somewhere in the chest area if standing at fairly close range, but a direct heart shot from a handgun at a distance took skill, and lack of powder burns suggested a distance shot. From the way Briggs reacted, Tom had another suspicion.

"Did you go to Laramie yourself to see Krafter?"

"I spoke to him a number of times over the phone. Why?"

Tom bit his lip. As far as he could see, Briggs was running this case without a plan, reacting to events rather than taking the initiative, but he would get nowhere by criticizing how somebody else worked. To be fair, Briggs might not have had the time to personally do the legwork on the case, regardless how controversial. Hence his request for manpower. The quicker Tom put an action plan into place the better.

"Do you need any men on the ground right away?"

"I could use somebody to run down Laramie hotels and motels. The killer had to have stayed somewhere, but with only a vague description of height, weight, and voice, getting an ID will be tough."

"I'll send someone to help you out. That Bersa they found, any prints?"

"The forensic specialist I sent up on Thursday confirmed

that Laramie PD lifted off a set, but Krafter's lawyer refused permission for us to print him. She's worried that if we can't find anybody to blame for the murder, we'll end up blaming her client."

"Can't say I blame her."

"Very funny. From what my guy told me, Miss Elena Spiteri is one fiery lady and not to be messed with. She's also Krafter's girlfriend."

"A professor and a lawyer? That's some combination."

"I think I can talk her into getting Krafter to cooperate, but it doesn't matter. Despite the fact that Laramie PD carried out an illegal search, I don't believe the kid did it. There is no motive, no real opportunity, even though he appears to have had the means."

"The Bersa…I believe it when you said in your email the thing was planted. Still, he *could* have done it and is using his current problems as a smoke screen."

"It's a possibility, but I don't buy it. No motive, and from what we've dug up so far, Krafter has never even met the victim, and I don't see him as the type who's into random shootings."

"Send me what you've got and I'll kick it around. Once I have a team together, I'll keep you advised on what they're doing. Any right-now things you want done?"

"He hasn't said so, but Krafter is worried that the attacker might pay him another visit. He's also nervous about his girlfriend and family getting hurt if this turns ugly."

"A lever to keep Krafter quiet? I don't buy it," Tom said bluntly. "All he would need to do is shout it to the world and the ensuing hue and cry would silence his critics for keeps."

"Perhaps, but do we want to take that chance?"

"If you're going down that path, what about protecting Krafter?"

"You mean an attempt to kidnap him?"

"Or kill him. His discovery has caused a small revolution and has apparently upset a lot of powerful people."

"The pattern of action against him suggests psychological intimidation. Whoever is after him wants him quiet, not dead."

"He'll be quiet if he's dead. This is more than a mere spat between squabbling professors. Leave it with me. So far, everything we have tells me that we might be dealing with a professional."

"That's the way it stacks up with me."

"And is probably the reason why you need more men."

"There is one other thing I'd like to do."

"Oh?"

"I want to search the Peabody Museum for that hand bone Professor Bollinger so conveniently misplaced, but I can't talk Saxon into authorizing it. His position is that even if Bollinger did spirit it away, it's petty theft and not part of the case."

Tom thought about that for a moment. "Saxon is wrong, and you should have just gone ahead and did it. Everything to do with Krafter is part of your case. Call Garry Strand in Boston, let him know what's going on and get things set up." About to ring off, he had an idea flash. "Have you considered the possibility that we may have two attackers here?"

"I have, actually, but I don't consider that likely," Briggs said. "Unless evidence turns up to the contrary, I'm assuming we're dealing with one man only. The case is messy enough as it is."

"You got that right. Okay, I'll be in touch." Tom rang off and frowned.

If they had a professional on their hands, was he dealing with another Peroni? That would really make his day. If true, somebody seriously wanted Krafter out of the way. Using a trained operative took money, which an individual probably wouldn't have. Not always the case, but a specialist doesn't come cheap. That implied an organization, a university or a professional body. Professional associations everywhere were not independent bodies, but voluntary unions of people they represented. In Krafter's case, these were anthropologists and paleoanthropologists. They were not professional bruisers, but academics.

In every association he knew, there were layers of membership, but those who actually ran things were usually the most prominent people in their field. They might hire business experts to manage the society's administrative affairs, but they were the ones who gave the orders. That meant an individual *could* be responsible for trying to silence Krafter, and given the furor, probably a select group of individuals. He remembered reading a couple of articles on the IAS, revealing its history and laundered some of the more unsavory deeds. He would need to go over them again and brush up on its organizational structure, and the structure of other domestic and international societies who may have a vested interest in making Krafter go away.

The tangled web we weave…

Feeling happier, he went over his conversation with Briggs, leaving him with a strong impression that the man was carrying a chip on his shoulder. Then again, working in a backwater like Denver, responsible for a huge geographical area, frustrated by lack of adequate equipment and agents, Tom figured he would carry a chip of his own. Whatever Briggs might think, he wasn't running the case anymore and probably knew it. The minute he had Saxon yelling to Washington for help, that had been it. Tom didn't mind letting Briggs believe that he was still in charge, as long he didn't interfere too much.

Until the forensic stuff came through, there wasn't much to be done, but he wasn't going to hang back on things that could be done. He reached for the phone and dialed an extension.

"Greenfield."

"It's Meecham. Can you come to my office, please?"

"You got it."

Tom hung up and smiled. At least one of his problems would get solved, if only temporarily.

A knock on his door and Greenfield walked in. A profusion

of freckles covered his nose and cheeks, and his carroty hair refused to behave, standing out in its usual disarray. The young agent had a solid build that was often mistaken for flab, but was all muscle. At five-foot-eleven, he made a formidable impression, even if he did look like a dressed up juvenile.

"Come in, Will," Tom said pleasantly and waved at a visitor chair. "Take a seat."

Greenfield sat down and waited.

"I've got a new job for you. Pack a bag, enough for three days or so. Get yourself to Denver and report to Special Agent Julian Briggs. You'll be working under his direction."

"Denver?"

"There was a murder in Laramie last Wednesday, and Denver needs help in tracking down the killer's whereabouts and making an ID. You'll probably be spending most of your time there, so pack accordingly. I'll forward you an email, which will explain what's going on and what we have so far. Briggs will fill you in on the details. Clear so far?"

"Yes, sir."

"Good. When you're nosing around Laramie, ask for security surveillance tapes from hotels and supermarkets, if they have them. We'll need them. While you're at it, get tapes from Laramie Regional Airport and all airports servicing the city. Positive reports only, Will. I don't have time to read that you haven't found anything. If you get a lead or run into a problem, talk it over with Briggs. If he can't help you, call me. You got all that?"

Greenfield's face had turned into a blank mask long before Tom finished. He stirred and cleared his throat.

"What about my current case load? Slats…I mean, Mr. Slater—"

"That'll keep, and don't worry about Slats. This has priority. Besides, a trip to Laramie will clear up your sinuses."

Greenfield sniffed and rubbed his nose. He always sniffed and blew into tissues.

"When do I leave?"

"I want you in Denver today. Get Marsha to arrange flights and accommodation for you. While you're getting yourself organized, I'll let Briggs know that you're coming. Study the email and the attachments. If you have questions, save them for Briggs. That's all, Will."

Somewhat uncertain, Greenfield stood up. When he closed the door after him, Tom shook his head and typed an extension into the phone.

"Brian Peters."

"Hi, doc. It's Meecham." That news was rewarded with a long groan.

"You're not going to ruin my day, are you?"

"That's hardly fair, Brian. I haven't even said anything yet."

"You don't have to. Just calling me told me enough."

Tom grinned, enjoying needling the forensic specialist. A top mind, the Bureau was lucky to have him. Any number of universities and private corporations would love to poach him and everybody knew it. The Bureau gave Brian something those places could not. It added zest to his work, not to mention the leggy Patricia Riley he was sweet on, boss or no boss. Tom wondered how long that zest would last. Probably until some megacorp offered him a salary with more zeros at the end than the FBI did. After all, zest didn't pay the bills.

"You got a minute to chat?"

"A short minute."

"Want me to come down to your office?"

"I've got coffee going on a burner. Give me a minute so I can poison it. They'll never trace it."

"See you down there," Tom said with a grin and hung up.

He didn't mind going to the lab, and it gave him an excuse to get the blood circulating through his legs. Besides, when asking for a favor, it was only polite to do it in person, and he didn't believe in issuing unnecessary orders.

On the second floor where all the forensic work was done, he made his way toward a corner office, past open benches cluttered with equipment, glass tubing twisted into odd shapes, machinery making noises, chemical smells, technicians chatting or doing whatever they were doing. As head of the special investigative analysis section, Peters rated an office. Nobody seemed to notice Tom as he walked by. The theory being, if he was here, it had to be for a reason. He knocked on a plain gray door and walked in.

Peters looked up and waved in greeting. "Coffee's over there," he said, nodding at a percolator burbling on a corner bench. Wearing a neat navy blue pinstripe suit and dark orange tie, thick black hair neatly combed back, the tall skeletal scientist looked imposing.

Tom made his black, one sugar, using a mug with far too many brown tree rings inside, and sat down. He took a sip and nodded. At least Peters served good coffee, poisoned or not. It couldn't have been Bureau issue.

The scientist leaned back and regarded his six-foot-one visitor across the cluttered expanse of his desk.

"Okay, Tom. Let's have it, while I'm still in a good mood."

"You've been reading about Professor Krafter and his bones?"

"Who hasn't? The discovery has anthropologists all over the world tearing their hair out or smiling with satisfaction. The man has certainly caused a stir."

"Not altogether a welcome one."

"He's getting some flak, but that's nothing unusual when you kick over a beehive."

"What's your view?"

"His dating data and footage are pretty conclusive," Peters acknowledged, then frowned suspiciously and wagged an index finger. "You're not going to involve me in forensic paleoanthropology, if that's what you had in mind. I'm still getting over the fake John the Baptist papyrus I did for you. And you haven't signed off for that overtime yet!"

Tom lifted his palm. "Peace! Talk to Marsha about the damn overtime."

"Hah!"

"What I want is straight forensics to give Denver a hand. The news hasn't come out yet, and I wouldn't talk about it, but it turns out that Krafter's detractors took enough dislike to his discovery to try and pin a murder on him. Someone planted a body in his garage and left a Bersa .380 ACP in his bedroom to make sure the local cops made the right connection."

Peters laughed. "I know we have a rough world out there, but this is stepping over the line a bit."

"More than a bit. This is where you come in. Denver is sending us all their forensic data, including the gun. I would like you to assign somebody good to go over everything. We also need him in Laramie to check the body. Whatever equipment and expertise Denver might have, it can't be as good as ours, and they could have missed something."

"Mmm. Denver has a pretty good basic forensic lab, you know. They wouldn't have missed much."

"Have your man talk to them. Lab reports are fine, but they're not a substitute for an on-site examination."

"You don't seem to have much going for you."

"That'll be right."

"I've got a master's graduate who knows her stuff," Peters mused. "She'll enjoy a field trip. What else you got?"

"I want to trace that gun."

Peters exhaled and shook his head. "No way the killer would have left prints or used an off-the-shelf piece."

"Not his prints anyway, but there are other ways of going about it."

"Well, if he hasn't filed off the serial number, something an amateur like Krafter wasn't likely to do if he is the murderer, that should help. No guarantees, though."

"Any lead would be good," Tom said and sipped his coffee. "So far, we've got squat. While your genius is in Laramie, she can also check out Krafter's office at the university and go over his house."

"There won't be any clues left, not after all this time, but we'll go through the motions. What else?"

"I can't think of anything right now. Get Marsha to arrange things for your genius. Charge it to my expense code."

"Don't worry, I will," Peters said and grinned broadly.

Tom finished his coffee and stood up. "Thanks, Brian. I owe you."

"Get that overtime signed!"

"Christ! Enter it against my code!" Tom flared, waved at him and walked out. The bureaucracy side of his job was slowly killing him.

Upstairs, making his way past Marsha's desk toward his office, she motioned at him. In her fifties, peppery hair, unassuming and very competent, she was the Division's gofer. Anything that needed done or unclogged, she did it. Her smiling, motherly attitude made everyone feel good when things got bleak.

"Mr. Hancock wants to see you."

Frowning, Tom nodded to her. "Okay, thanks."

He marched to Wellard's old office, knocked and walked in. "You wanted to see me, boss?"

"Ah, Meecham. Take a seat, will you?"

Tom made himself comfortable and waited until Hancock finished pushing papers around. His boss finally looked up, brown eyes hidden beneath prominent brows and bushy eyebrows.

"You got my memo on the Krafter case?"

"Yes, sir. Already working on it."

"Good, good. Ordinarily, we wouldn't be bothered with an academic squabble, but resorting to bank fraud and murder to drive home an argument makes it our problem. Especially when we also have an international dimension. The thing to keep in mind is that we're not only dealing with high-powered prickly academics, but also the universities behind them. A lot is at stake behind this seemingly innocent discovery, and prominent reputations could be broken here."

"I got that, boss."

"I thought you would. This is one of those nasty little cases where if everything goes right, nobody will notice, but if we screw up, we could get everybody mad at us. Bear one thing in mind, Meecham. Don't tread too heavily."

Was this a warning or sage advice? Tom was not sure and couldn't be bothered. If Hancock objected to what he was doing, he can have the whole mess back.

"I hear you."

Hancock twitched a smile and nodded. "Well, keep me posted. Let me know if you run into problems or need help."

Back in his office, Tom sat down and cracked his knuckles, Hancock's veiled message still ringing in his ears. Perhaps the Assistant Director was settling into his new job and did not want anything upsetting him. Tom had just gotten comfortable with Wellard's political setup, and now, he would have to go through the whole dreary rigmarole with Hancock. Well, he would keep working the best way he knew how until told otherwise.

Going over things he should do first, he mulled over the possibility that Briggs could be right and the killer might turn his attention to people close to Krafter. He didn't have anything like the resources needed to babysit Krafter's girlfriend or his parents, but the OPS II domestic terrorism section did. The catch? Would they let him have the men even if he managed to convince them that he had a genuine threat? There was only one way to find out. He picked up the phone and dialed.

"Dennis Sawko," a hard voice answered.

"It's Tom. I need bodies."

"Go to the morgue, pal."

"Warm bodies. A protection detail."

"Ah, shit. You know how many men I'd need if we deployed them in shifts?"

"Your guys aren't doing anything anyway. This job will give them exercise and fresh air."

"My boys didn't join the FBI for the exercise. Besides, isn't your section supposed to be serving *us*, not the other way around? I seem to remember reading something along those lines."

"Details, Dennis. How about it?"

"Okay, give me the beef."

The Special Agent in Charge of the Domestic Terrorism section always bitched and moaned, but he usually came through. There would be a price to pay later, but Tom could always cash it on Hancock's check. They both worked for the same boss.

He quickly sketched out the situation and his problem. It made things easier that Dennis was aware of the controversy surrounding Krafter. When he finished, he waited for the senior agent to chew it over.

"I don't believe they've got anything to worry about," Sawko said. "A professional wouldn't be bothered."

"That's what I think, but there is still that possibility, and it's more than a mere possibility where Krafter is concerned."

"Okay, I'll humor you. If you want to give everybody coverage, you're looking at three teams of two. A lot of manpower, you know. Even if I concede the threat might be real, I'm not sure I can convince my boss."

"Hancock is already convinced," Tom told him.

"This is coming from the Assistant Director?"

"It's coming from me, but he has a special interest."

"Okay, how come you rate all the good cases?" Sawko complained petulantly and Tom chuckled.

"If you want it, it's yours."

"Hah! And then carry the blame? No, thanks. If I do this, it's gonna cost, you know. Hancock might be brimming with enthusiasm now, but that could evaporate once you hand him the bill and Accounting gets involved."

"I'm running a likely terrorism case, not a profit center, Dennis. Anyway, what's a few more lousy thousand on Uncle Sam's already voluminous debt?"

"He could be saving them by firing your ass, that's what," Sawko said and laughed.

"Never happen. I know this will cost, but if you got a better idea, I'm listening."

"Okay. Hide them. That way, it will hardly cost us anything. Not as much anyway."

Tom raised his eyebrows and nodded in appreciation. It could just work. "You know, that's almost inspirational."

"It is, isn't it. We would need to talk to them, of course, and they might not want to go anywhere. Spiteri is a lawyer with a job. I don't know about the Krafters, but it's probable that they also have commitments."

"They won't have any commitments if they're kidnapped or shot," Tom pointed out. "I'll talk it over with Briggs and he can raise it with Krafter. We might not be able to do anything with him, given his university job, but we should be able to ease his worries about his parents and girlfriend. Anyway, see what you can do about getting me those men, in case he cooperates."

"Have you considered a threat to Neil Reed?"

"It has crossed my mind, but I doubt our guy would be dumb enough to go after the press."

"He's going after Krafter."

"That's slightly different."

"Okay, if you say so. I'll be in touch," Sawko said and rang off.

Tom pressed the disconnect button, then dialed another extension. "Slats? Can you come over for a minute…good."

When he took over the Counterterrorism Analysis section,

Albert Slater got moved into his old job to run the Strategic Assessment and Analysis Unit. Slats was a good agent who always delivered.

There was a knock on his door and a lanky individual, looking like a banker or accountant, walked in. He sat down without waiting for an invitation.

"We have a situation, Slats," Tom said and quickly went over the salient points of the case. Slater did not need everything explained in detail, unlike some.

"Is that why Greenfield is looking so worried?" Slater asked with a grin, his voice precise and measured.

"My fault," Tom said. "I should have cleared this with you before stealing one of your men, but I needed to have him moving. He's not exactly a vital cog in your machinery."

"That's okay. The swap we discussed, how's that going?"

"Nothing definite, but it looks promising. In case it doesn't work out, I still want options what to do with him."

"Got it. Getting back to this Krafter deal, Hancock may have handed you a no-win potato. Especially if our man is a professional."

"I'll do the pessimistic bits here, Slats. Your unit is overstaffed and underworked. This is an ideal case to get them warmed up."

Slater rolled his eyes and shook his head. Tom knew how short of people they were. Slater bit his lower lip and went into a trance, working the angles. When he focused again, he gave a small shrug.

"I can see why you want my unit to run with this. It's mostly analysis. If Greenfield gets us those surveillance tapes, we'll be flooded with data. There is an obvious catch here, you know."

"We don't have a face to match against, I know. Having those tapes will be good, but they're a backup at best."

"You want to bug Krafter's house?"

"And his university office: sound and vision, including IR

cameras while you're at it. If our man shows up at either place, even with a mask, I want to make sure we get his best side. Set it up with Briggs. Greenfield can do the legwork. That's only a starter."

"I thought it might be," Slater said dryly and waited.

"The next part is going to take some sharp research," Tom said, warming up. "Check newspapers and stuff, and find out who has the most to gain with Krafter discredited. We need an organizational structure breakdown of the International Anthropological Society and professional bodies such as the American Anthropological Association and the World Council of Anthropological Associations. I want to know who's in charge of each and if Krafter is on their hate list. I also want to know if any of them have offshore accounts."

"Cayman Islands, for instance?" Slater said with a raised eyebrow.

"Or a Swiss bank. They could be using it to finance a bruiser or something. We already know the motive. Without an ID on our man, the other two factors don't matter, and our guy doesn't have a motive anyway."

"Except for the money."

Tom winced. Money was a powerful driver. That's why mercenaries, economic and political spies, went into the freelance business. He had Peroni as a case example.

"An ideological motive, if you want to be picky. For our man, it's simply a job, which he'll prosecute out of professional pride and an assumption that there is no one better out there."

"If he silences Krafter, he'll be right."

"That was the other thing. I want your guys to study everything Krafter's written in journals or papers, and I want them to see every appearance he made on television. I already have a pretty good picture in my mind of the type of man he is, but I need psychological validation. What we want to do is spread all the pieces on the table, throw away the clutter and build a scenario we can work with from what's left."

"Right now, clutter is all you got."

"Hence the legwork. While that's bubbling away, request records from the NSA, CIA, DEA, NCIS, and any other agency you can think of who specialize in dirty tricks—"

"They all do."

"—and anybody they may have let go who was deemed a security risk or violated operational procedures and has turned freelance."

Slater stared at him. "You're kidding, right? Even if they were willing to give us the information, by no means a done deal, we'll be buried in names."

"Let me know if you run into a wall, but we won't be buried. We can only run a mug compare if we get a snapshot of our man. In the meantime, we'll simply sit on the stuff."

"Why not ask for an ID once we do get his picture? Less work for everybody and we're likely to have a better chance of getting a response."

Tom gave him a nasty grin. "Because our boy could still have contacts with his *alma mater* and they might tip him off."

"You've got a morbid mind, Tom."

"Not me. Everybody else."

"It could be an ex-cop, you know. Or even an FBI man."

"It could, but I'll give our sister services the first benefit of the doubt."

"Like I said, a morbid mind."

"Once we establish a link with Krafter's most vocal detractors or a professional body, we'll ask NSA to provide us with phone and email records made between all the parties. Something might surface."

"Man, we'll be hip deep in data CDs."

"Details. What I also want your guys to do, and get expert help here, is to draw me a profile of the man behind our killer. I want to get an idea what he's thinking and likely to do next. When he does it, I want to know how Krafter will react."

"You're dreaming. With the body plant gone sour, the killer has probably gone to ground. I would."

"But you're not him. Our man is acting under orders. If he's a professional, he'll not care for the reasons why he's doing this. His concern will be risk factors. He knows that we're alerted. He also knows we have nothing. That means he's still operating in a low risk environment. Believe me. He'll move again."

"Unless whoever is pulling his strings tells him to lay off."

"There is always that and we'll be screwed."

"What about that professor in Houston and the one in England?"

"We're looking at a big net there with large holes. Until we get something definite on our guy, we can't do much." Tom gave Slater a searching look. "You okay with this?"

"How about we just swap jobs?" Slater offered with a grin.

"Christ!"

Chapter Seven

PROFESSOR KRAFTER FRAMED FOR MURDER
FBI INVESTIGATING CASE OF DOMESTIC TERRORISM
REPORTER WOUNDED IN A HIT-AND-RUN
BOLLINGER PROTESTS HIS INNOCENCE
ARIZONA U SCIENTIST AUTHENTICATES KRAFTER'S SKULL

"Tell me you had nothing to do with it. That's all I want to know," Ted Horowitz demanded coldly.

Kessler sighed and pursed his lips. Academics…in many ways they were no different from the obfuscating, ass-covering military weasels he got to know while at BioChip. They always sought to ram down functionality not included in the specs, dropping veiled hints that cooperation would be suitably rewarded with future contracts, then baulked when the costing came through. What did they expect? Changes in circuit design took time and money, as did simulations, prototyping, and breadboard testing. Sometimes it took millions to simulate a major functional upgrade. Too many military project officers, once it was pointed out that a change would delay the planned production rollout, cancelled the upgrade, leaving BioChip to absorb the cost.

Kessler put a stop to such nonsense soon after he took over as COO. From now on, he told the board, if a client wanted a change or additional functionality, the work would only be done under a signed contract variation. If they simply wanted to tinker with the specs, BioChip would play on a time-and-materials basis. There was always a degree of give and take, the board had argued, unwilling to annoy powerful generals. They caved in when he showed them a chart of bottom line write-offs the company had absorbed over the past four years. If the military had a problem with this policy, they could take their business elsewhere, knowing they wouldn't. Even if they did, BioChip had plenty of work subcontracting to Intel, IBM, Sony and other civilian chipmakers.

Horowitz reminded him of those project officers. The IAS president was smart, Kessler had to acknowledge that, but in many respects, naïve and wanted everything without considering the consequences. Sheltered in his ivory tower of learning, head stuck in a cloud of theory, or buried in moldy ancient texts, the academic had a distorted view of how the real world operated. IAS had a problem with Professor Krafter and Horowitz wanted Kessler to take care of it, unwilling to be involved in the messy details as long as the thing was done. Like sausages, knowing how they were made could interfere with his enjoyment while eating them.

"What do you want me to say, Ted? At the last meeting, you told me that Krafter had to be crushed."

"Discredited, yes, but not like this! And now we're waging war on reporters!"

"If Krafter is behind bars, he's neutralized; end of story. Regardless of the legitimacy of his discovery, no one will listen to a convicted murderer. You'll be able to retire to your drawing rooms, sip fine brandy and indulge in contraband Cuban cigars. As for Neil Reed, whoever did it, he had it coming."

"I will not tolerate impertinence from you!" Horowitz snapped. "You forget yourself, Kessler. This organization will not be turned into an academic Gestapo, not while I'm in charge."

"Not a bad description, you know, but it's a bit late to parade your shield of righteousness, you know. Do you want me to run down the list of careers we trampled and discoveries we buried to maintain not only your reputation, but the reputations of your academic brothers?"

"Some lines we don't cross!" Horowitz thundered.

"What did you expect me to do, Ted? Send Krafter a polite letter asking him to keep quiet because his discovery is an embarrassment to everything Bollinger, Maddson and others have lied, cheated and covered up all these years? You brought me into IAS to make the organization a world force within the anthropological community. I have done that and more, but when things get a little ugly, you cry foul."

"You pushed too hard. Instead of hurting Krafter, your actions are hurting us! Professor Fuijuma has resigned and taken UCLA with him. Walsh is gone and so has Oxford's funding. When such prominent institutions leave, people take notice. They're not the only universities we've lost."

"They'll come around once Krafter is taken care of," Kessler said comfortably. "The Europeans were always twitchy and quick to react. They've never forgiven you for headquartering the IAS in New York rather than Paris. Once they get over their pique and remember what we're all about, they'll be back. As for the Brits, they think they invented archaeology."

"But it's not the kind of publicity we need!"

"We're going to get far worse publicity if we don't deal with Krafter."

"I'll expose you! I'll go to the FBI and tell them everything."

"Tell them what? Your insinuation that I had somebody killed and tried to frame it on Krafter? Where is your evidence? I certainly never said that I did anything of the sort."

"You ordered it done!"

"Did I? You're using a grand leap of imagination. For all I know, it could have been Bollinger. His vocal opposition to Krafter's find is on public record. I have no interest or motive to harm him."

"You as much admitted that you had that meter reader murdered."

"I said no such thing. Ted, this isn't getting us anywhere and you still have a problem that needs to be dealt with. Now, are we going to argue like children, or deal with it? It's your call. As far as I'm concerned, Krafter can do and say whatever he wants. He's your problem, not mine. So, what's it going to be?"

"I never expected you would push it this far," Horowitz said after a while, his voice subdued.

"You didn't mind creating the mess, but you're too squeamish to clean it up yourself. Well, this particular mess is being cleaned up and you'll just have to swallow your indignation."

"I'll call a special executive meeting and have you removed."

"That's your privilege, but I still have two years on my contract. Can you afford to pay out the severance clause?"

"I don't care what it costs as long as you're gone. After this, you won't be able to get a job as a janitor, not with my reference."

Kessler smiled, amused at the working of an academic mind. "That would not be wise. I hate having to step down to your level, but if you try anything against me, I would naturally have to defend myself."

"Oh? And how would you do that?"

"Remember that little database of, shall we say, compromising information the Executive Committee asked me to compile on our members? It has lots of interesting stuff in it on a lot of people. You'd be surprised, and it's proven to be very useful. I believe there might even be a file on you. Something about plagiarized papers while you were at Berkeley, I believe. There could be more. I'll have to check."

From the prolonged silence at the other end, Kessler figured he had made his point. People usually comprehended even complicated things once they were explained in simple terms. Horowitz didn't need a lot of explaining. After all, the man held two PhDs. Nothing personal in this, merely business.

"Very well," Horowitz said glumly. "We shall say no more about this. I was upset and said things best forgotten. As you pointed out, Krafter is still a problem. Deal with him, but I don't want to hear about any more murders. Is that clear? It's not how

I want IAS to operate."

Ted might pretend to be upset, but Kessler knew that neither of them would forget what was said. The Society president an enemy now, and Kessler knew his position as CEO was on a short fuse. The Committee would not act until he took care of Krafter, but it would act. Perhaps it was time to dust off his resume and contact some people.

"Tell me, Ted. How badly do you want Krafter silenced?"

"You know the answer to that," Horowitz said gruffly.

"Then let me deal with him without you crying on my shoulder. If I were you, I'd start thinking real hard about reconsidering the Committee's position."

"What do you mean?"

"I advised you against this course of action. Professor Krafter's discovery has developed a certain inertia, which can no longer be dismissed or neutralized by simply issuing notices to our members. The Society is ignoring verifiable evidence and our position is becoming increasingly radical, and we're getting marginalized. Although I don't see it as a major problem for now, UCLA and Oxford leaving is nevertheless symptomatic of growing unease. The Committee needs to deal with the core issue of Krafter's discovery, not bury him. Give it some thought."

"We have thought about it and we have made our decision. The young upstart must be silenced!"

"Not smart, but it's your call." Kessler rang off and replaced the handset. He reached into his pocket and dragged out the HTC smartphone.

"Identify," the electronic voice prompted.

"Raven."

"Proceed."

"You bungled it," Kessler said without a trace of emotion.

"Acknowledged. Fee waived."

Kessler clutched the PDA tighter. The damned fee did not make up for the ensuing complications. With the FBI on the case, it made life difficult at many levels. Still, the situation was retrievable.

"This is what I want you to do."

* * *

Still early, the floor was almost deserted. Tom unlocked his office, hung up his jacket and powered up the PC. He picked up his empty mug, strolled to the small kitchenette, and filled up with fuel. Someone had left a box of sticky buns on the bench and he eyed the glistening assortment with a tug of interest. Summoning courage, he refrained from taking one and went back to his office. His gym sessions were starting to deliver results and his muscles no longer protested like they used to, not as much anyway. He patted his stomach. There was a thin layer of flab there, but that too had begun to melt off. Besides, he had a workout session in the afternoon and a sweet bun would mean that he would have to put in an extra effort to get rid of it. It wasn't worth the sweat.

Feeling virtuous, he settled his cup beside the computer and brought up Outlook. By coming in early, it was about the only quiet time in his day where he could catch up on administration without being disturbed. Once everyone started arriving, that would be it—bedlam. One message from Greenfield with yesterday's date perked him up and he clicked on it.

Running down the text, he nodded. The report clear, concise and factual, and he wondered why the kid couldn't apply the same approach to his analysis work. One of the mysteries of life. It was good to hear that the cameras were in place at Krafter's house and his office at UW. A receptionist at the Hilton Garden Inn recalled that a tall, heavyset man stayed there for two days. He looked distinguished: peppery hair, rimless glasses, a pencil mustache, and a trim little beard. She said he was a professor visiting the university. She had those coming through all the time and thought nothing of it. The University of Wyoming generated a lot of business for Laramie. What she did remember were the man's penetrating blue eyes. They were lifeless and made her shiver. The man was big; probably six-foot-four. When Greenfield checked the dates, they coincided with the break-in at the university. The hotel didn't have surveillance cameras.

Although unfortunate, Tom accepted the fact that small town places would not bother with expensive security. Too bad the university didn't believe in surveillance, at least the Anthropology Department didn't, despite urging from the campus police. That was something Briggs had already checked. Tom shook his head ruefully. Where security was concerned, if people would only heed advice from experts, life would be so much easier all around. He took a sip of coffee and had to smile. If everybody listened to a good, paranoid security type, every house and street corner would be bugged—George Orwell's *1984* come true. The world far too close to that scenario right now.

At the Holiday Inn, they also remembered a heavy man staying there two days, shorter, perhaps six-foot-one, and had a limp in his right leg, which made him stoop a little. Tom wondered if it was a ploy to make him appear shorter. The man was bald and always wore dark sunglasses. He had yellow skin and looked Asian. What was strange, Greenfield reported, the man never had any meals at the hotel diner. He either had them delivered or ate out. Probably didn't want to be remembered by the hotel staff, Tom mused. According to Greenfield, the man's stay coincided with the infamous bank account transfers affair.

By talking to the concierge at the Hampton Inn, Greenfield had established that a tall man stayed there two days, exactly the time when Krafter's car was rammed, and the man in black paid him a visit. The staffer said the man had peppery hair, severe features, and wore a thin mustache. What was unusual, the concierge reported that on the second day of his stay, the man had an order for a 5:30 breakfast. The concierge remembered because there was an extra charge for the service. And no, the place didn't have surveillance cameras. They might not be out of luck completely, Tom noted. Safeway and Albertsons-Osco were large stores and had cameras. Perhaps their guy stepped in for a Milky Way. The tapes were being sent to Denver and would probably be forwarded on to Washington within days.

Smiling, Tom took another sip. If the same man stayed at all three hotels, he was clearly wearing makeup and disguises. Perhaps not something he might ordinarily use, but it would be a wise precaution when having to stay repeatedly at one location. If this was indeed his man, he was dealing with a pro, all right.

Greenfield could not establish whether a heavyset man stayed anywhere in Laramie at the date of the murder. Tom wasn't altogether surprised. The killer probably used his time during previous visits to select his victim and establish a movement pattern. On the day of the murder, he might have driven in, did his business, and driven out. It was interesting that Greenfield said that no one could recall a heavy man being at any of the few motels along I-80. Talking over his findings with Briggs, Greenfield had arranged for an artist to come to Laramie and get drawings of the man at each of the hotels he visited. That was using initiative and Tom nodded with approval. The boy had a clear head and was running down every possible lead, not skipping anything.

He had to chuckle when he got to the part about getting airport surveillance tapes across all the dates they were interested in, and could almost hear Greenfield groan. There was not only Laramie to consider, but also Gillette, Denver and other hubs who had direct flights into Laramie Regional Airport. He sympathized. Instead of flying in directly, to cover his tracks, their man could have flown into an intermediate airport and driven to Laramie. When the tapes started coming into Washington, he was certain to get an acerbic call or two from the photo lab, but that was a problem still comfortably in the future.

Almost as an afterthought, Greenfield said that he was off to Boston, and Tom grinned. The boy had done well to canvas over a dozen motels and hotels in Laramie, and Briggs had already called to thank him. An idea bubble burst then. If Strand didn't want to swap Johnston, perhaps Greenfield might fancy a stint in Denver?

Happy that the boy had things humming, he picked up the phone and dialed a private number. He sat back and waited for the connection. Just shy of eight o'clock, he hoped she was in.

"Dr. Norginson."

"Good morning, doc. This is Tom Meecham."

"Ah, Mr. Meecham. Why do I get the impression that you're about to darken what has so far been a nice start to my day?"

"That's hardly fair, and this could be a social call."

Sidris Norginson laughed. "Coming from you, I hardly think so."

He could clearly picture the tall, five-foot-nine slim woman smiling at him, her large gray eyes sparkling with amusement. In her spacious office, decorated with diplomas, awards, and crowded bookshelves, her brown hair held up in a curl, she would lean back against her black leather chair, cross her long legs, and play with a small gold pen she always carried. He had seen her doing it. Although she had invited him to call her by her first name, he felt uncomfortable crossing the invisible line of formality that surrounded the president of Harvard University.

"How goes the exhibit?" There was only one item he could be referring to, and she undoubtedly knew it.

"We're drawing them in, Tom," Norginson said crisply. "We did have a bit of excitement the other day when someone tried to smash the reinforced case housing the papyrus. Even as security dragged him away, he kept shouting that the John the Baptist Scroll was an abomination and everyone who saw it was damned to burn in hell. As it turned out, he was a member of the New Lambs of God, an ultraconservative, right-wing evangelical cult based in Georgia."

"Why do they always seem to come from Georgia?" Tom reflected, not expecting an answer. "What did he use to try and break the case?"

"A steel-reinforced boot. He didn't know the glass could withstand a shot from a .45 Magnum. After all the trouble it took to get it, we wanted to make sure it was properly protected."

"Well, it gave the other visitors something to talk about," Tom said comfortably and Norginson laughed.

"You have a morbid sense of humor, Mr. Meecham."

"So I've been told. I read in the papers that Vatican has dropped its lawsuit against Harvard. It must have come as a relief."

After failing to convince Tom to return the real papyrus, true to his word, Karpeli, Cardinal Secretariat of State, launched a fifty million dollar action against Harvard, claiming the tractate rightfully belonged to the Church, which was a load of crock, of course. When the news broke, the outcry could be heard around the world. It wasn't enough that the Vatican sent an assassin to recover the priceless artifact, but now they were resorting to bully tactics? Already facing a backlash, the pope quietly quashed the action.

"We would have weathered it, but it saved us considerable resources not having to fight it. Now, what can I do for the FBI? You want to give me another papyrus?"

Tom grinned, vastly amused. With all the ongoing controversy surrounding the tractate, he doubted that he could top his last effort. Unless…

"I have something else in mind. What's been the reaction from the learned community?"

"The Christian theologians wish the thing would go away, citing writings from early apologists that the papyrus is a fake. Everybody else is holding it up as proof of Christian fathers doctoring or burying early writings that contradicted their version of

Christ and his life."

"That's nothing new."

"It will be once NBC get done with it. They want to do a documentary on the whole affair. Don't be surprised if they come knocking."

"Christ! That's all I need. Any more publicity over that thing and the Bureau will put *me* in a glass case!"

Norginson laughed. "You have my advance sympathies, but it's the price you pay for notoriety."

"Not if it costs me my career. Anyway, I'll come up with something to get out of it, but I didn't call you about the tractate."

"It wouldn't have something to do with Professor Krafter's discovery?"

Tom nodded in appreciation. The doc was one smart woman who always cut right to the point. "What do you know about it?"

"Mostly what I read in the papers. I had a briefing from Dr. Van Neuman about Professor Bollinger's role in the missing FedEx package. He got censured over that, by the way. Contrary to popular opinion, Tom, the learned community is not a united body of dedicated and selfless scientists. Clashing over new theories and discoveries is not unlike a gladiator arena. Those who are left standing, win."

"I always did believe that might was right, but I'm glad to have it confirmed academically."

"What did you expect, flowers and handshakes? Nobody likes to see a lifetime of work discredited, even when it's backed with supposedly irrefutable evidence. Add an overbearing, prickly personality or two, and you have sparks."

"Do you believe that Professor Krafter's discovery is genuine?"

"The jury is still out, but he has some convincing data behind him. It's hard to argue against facts. Personally, what he has is the equivalent of the John the Baptist Scroll and the paleoanthropological church has assassins out to kill it."

"You might be more correct than you think," Tom said soberly.

"I thought I was speaking allegorically."

"We could be dealing with a genuine assassin, Doctor. A professional at least, who either alone, or under somebody's direction, is trying to intimidate Krafter to quietly go away and take his bones with him."

"You can't be serious."

"This isn't the first time someone wanted to bury a new discovery and ridicule the discoverer. I checked."

"Yes, but—"

"You must have read about the body planted in his garage."

"Hardly evidence that some anthropologist did it."

"Granted, but someone almost succeeded in having the professor put away for a very long time. That would definitely have shut him up and made his find go away. At the very least, the issue would be comfortably shunted to back room musings."

"You've been put on the case to clear Krafter's name?"

"His name is already cleared. Whoever murdered the meter reader was either careless or impatient. We established that the body was moved from the murder scene, something to do with the rate of blood clotting in certain positions when at rest. To delay the onset of rigor mortis, the killer must have used an electric blanket or thermal cover to keep the body warm. That's where he slipped up. The warming wasn't uniform. At the time we calculated the murder took place, Krafter was conducting a lecture and he spent the whole day at the university with lots of witnesses who say so. Although the killer took care to leave blood under the body, a lot more should have leaked out if the victim was shot in the garage. Anyway, I don't think Krafter would be so dumb to leave the body there and keep the murder weapon in his bedroom, waiting for Laramie police to find them."

"Even clever people sometimes make the most foolish mistakes."

"I can't argue with you there, but the most likely hypothesis is that someone in the academic community feels sufficiently threatened by Krafter's discovery to want to do something permanent about it and him."

"You believe Professor Bollinger could have been that someone?"

"It's possible, but his name isn't the only one on my list. Add professional associations who have a grievance, and you've got lots of people with a clear motive. They would not be worried about means or opportunity. They left those to our killer."

"Why are you telling me all this, Tom? If what you're suggesting is true, Harvard has a vested interest to discredit Professor Krafter. At least the Anthropology Department does. The Peabody Museum is a bastion of orthodox human evolutionary theory."

"I think Bollinger definitely has an interest, but it's a personal one, and I doubt that Harvard as an institution would do this. What Harvard has, or more precisely, what you have, Doctor, is contacts…contacts with other universities and professional bodies. You know all the powerful people in the paleoanthropological community. You're therefore in a position to deliver a warning. I might not be able to catch our killer, that's still an ongoing game, but what I am able to do is put every prominent anthropologist who has voiced extreme opposition to Krafter's find under a microscope. That includes anyone outside the United States. Sooner or later, I'll find out who's been giving our killer his orders. When I do, it's not going to be pleasant for that individual."

"I resent the implication that somehow Harvard is involved."

"I don't know about Dr. Van Neuman, but Bollinger certainly is. From what we managed to find, it looks very much like he appropriated the hand bone and bracelet, and attempted to blame it on your mailroom staff and FedEx. I might as well tell you now, Dr. Norginson, the FBI is executing a warrant at this moment to search the Peabody Museum, all Anthropology Department premises and faculty offices, for the bone. I'm working on an assumption that although Bollinger might detest what the bone represents, it's still a unique and priceless anthropological artifact. Although possible, I doubt that he destroyed the thing simply because it sticks in his craw. I'm betting he kept it to either gloat or cry over it."

"If he in fact took it."

"Of course."

"Well, you don't do things by halves, do you? But knowing something about you, I'm not altogether surprised. Stipulated that Bollinger might have taken the bone and falsified his dating test, it's hardly proof that he had anything to do with intimidating Krafter or being involved in murder."

"Agreed. I'm trying to build a chain of evidence which will hopefully lead me to whoever is involved with that murder, and Bollinger could be implicated in another way."

Norginson was silent for a moment. "I'm beginning to see what you're up to. Very clever, Tom."

"I didn't know I was so transparent."

"You are to me. If you do find the hand bone, it won't do much to catch your killer, but it will take the heat off Professor Krafter. Publicizing what is technically a theft would discredit Bollinger, embarrass Harvard, and go a long way toward silencing Krafter's critics. We would have to formally announce Krafter's discovery to be genuine, or join the detractor's camp. I didn't know you had that level of sneakiness in you."

Tom chuckled, admiring how her mind worked. "You give me far too much credit, doc. I only want to establish whether Professor Bollinger still has the bone. I hadn't worked through the implications if we do find it. Not all of them anyway."

"Very well, I'll accept that you're not sneaky. You mentioned delivering a warning."

"We established that Bollinger is a member of the International Anthropological Society's Executive Committee. He's a member of several other associations, but they're not important to my investigation. We also know that Professor Maddson is a Committee member."

"Both have vehemently opposed Krafter's discovery."

"As has Dr. Ted Horowitz, although less vocally, and he happens to be—"

"The IAS President. I see what you're getting at."

"This is still pure speculation on my part. I have nothing concrete to suggest that IAS or any of its members had anything to do with personal attacks on Krafter or that murder."

"But you have a connection and a lead."

"One that I am following diligently."

"What do you want me to do?"

"That's obvious."

"Mmm. I know Ted. I'll talk to him, but if you believe he had anything to do—"

"I am simply following one of several possibilities. He might be pure as the driven snow. Then again, he might be wearing muddy boots."

"Like I said, I don't quite understand why you're telling me all this. If Ted or the IAS, and I also know its CEO, Raymond Kessler, are involved, and I tell them that the FBI is looking their way, it will only drive them underground. It would do nothing to catch your killer, if they're the ones controlling him."

"It will hopefully prevent another attack on Krafter, and more importantly, another murder. Right now, that's all that matters to me. For the rest of it, I don't give a toss over any cerebral disagreement he might have with his academic colleagues, but breaking the law to quash a discovery is a no-no."

"What if your killer strikes again?"

"That would make me very unhappy, doc."

Norginson laughed. "Forgive me, there is nothing humorous

about this, far from it. I shall talk to people, Tom, and we shall see. Do let me know what your agents find at Peabody."

"I dare say Dr. Van Neuman will do that, if he hasn't tried to reach you already. I appreciate the time, doc."

"You haven't exactly made my day, but I guess you're only doing your job. What do you intend doing with that hand bone if you do find it?"

"That was the something else I had in mind."

After a moment of stunned silence, Norginson hissed. "You want us to exhibit it!"

"With your seal of approval, this whole mess would go away, at least as far as Krafter was concerned. You did say his find was genuine."

"I take it all back, Mr. Meecham. You *are* sneaky. Still, it's an intriguing concept."

"Consider what an attraction it would make. You could put it next to the papyrus. Everybody would be talking paleoanthropology and falling over themselves to see it."

"They certainly would," Norginson said dryly. "And I would probably have more pickets and marches on the campus. Before we get carried away with our vision, all this would depend on you finding the hand bone."

"Even if we don't, there is still the skull," Tom pointed out, confident he had her hooked.

She might be a high-powered administrator now, but she was still a scientist at heart, and Harvard would have scored another major coup. Her Trustees could not very well complain about that.

"Mmm. I would have to talk to a few people, including Professor Krafter. Leave it with me and I'll get back to you."

When she rang off, he smiled, replaced the receiver and leaned back into the chair, then started whistling the opening bars from *Chariots of the Gods*. If Greenfield does find the hand bone, his case parameters would be simplified enormously, as would

Krafter's problem with his academic detractors.

* * *

With cold rain sleeting across the slick roadway, and gusty wind stirring the branches, sending stripped leaves fluttering into a gray sky, Krafter decided to drive to UW, despite the fact it was Monday. Pushing macho had its limits. He pulled on his overcoat and walked into the garage, shuddering at the sudden chill inside, and hurriedly opened the door to his Focus. Although he had scrubbed the concrete where the body lay, a dark patch still lingered that no amount of detergent or solvent appeared able to remove. It looked like it would remain a ghost haunting his nights. He backed the car, paused when he turned into the street, and pressed the remote to close the garage door. His mind in neutral, thinking about nothing in particular, he pulled the gearshift bar into drive and stepped on the gas.

Last Thursday, Professor Allbright fronted up as promised, escorted by Larson and Perkins. The introduction cordial if somewhat stilted, and Krafter wondered if he faced another Bollinger. Without wasting time, he took his distinguished guest to Lab One where an armed campus cop stood guard over the skull. Pulling thoughtfully on his goatee, left hand behind his back, leaning forward like a pecking crane, Allbright gave the impression of being an inquisitor searching for sins. His frown quickly faded as he keenly examined the skull under a large mounted magnifying lens. Putting on white cotton gloves that Krafter held out, he gingerly picked up the skull and peered at it from several angles, with Larson and Perkins hovering anxiously in the background. Finally done, he pulled off the gloves, stroked his goatee and slowly nodded. After a moment, he turned to Krafter and smiled, revealing stained teeth.

"It's genuine, all right. I can hardly believe it. I must confess, Professor, even with all the independent dating data, I was still not completely convinced. The only way to be certain, of course, was to see it for myself." He glanced at the skull. "It's looking at me, daring me to deny it. And I want to deny it, badly, because its existence mocks everything we thought we know about human evolution. I'm not surprised that many of our revered colleagues find it impossible to accept what that skull represents."

"You will state your finding publicly?" Krafter asked, fearing the old codger would play politics and cover his ass.

"Professor Hartman has supported your discovery from the beginning, young man, and he carries far more authority than I do. For what it's worth, Arizona U will stand behind you, even at the risk of being run over for my trouble," Allbright said lightly, clearly aware of incidents that had befallen two of his contemporaries.

To give the old fossil credit, he made a media announcement right in front of the Anthropology Building, Perkins having tipped off the reporters. Krafter had not been too happy at first, but realized that Allbright would talk to the media eventually, whether favorably or not, and given the minimal risk of something negative, the quicker an affirmative declaration was made, the better. Most networks carried the segment that night, which did Bollinger and Maddson's positions little good.

They also carried a soundbite of Neil Reed involved in a hit-and-run as he walked out of *The New York Times* building, which spoiled Krafter's day somewhat when he figured the worst was now behind him. As it turned out, Reed was lucky to get away with only a bruised elbow and hip. A coincidence, perhaps? Possible, but Krafter didn't believe it, certain it was a pointed warning from the man in black. Reed's articles had hit the IAS and his detractors hard, and they decided to hit back just as hard, if it was the IAS.

Despite the inclement weather, the UW campus was busy with students hurrying along sidewalks between buildings to catch classes, tutorials, put in lab time, or finish off a last bit of research in one of the three libraries. He parked the car, took his large black umbrella out of the trunk and snapped it open, the biting rain making a loud staccato beat against it. Slanting it against the wind, he made his way toward the Anthropology Building.

Inside, he gave a small sigh of relief and folded the umbrella, tapping the steel point against the tiles to get rid of the clinging water. Satisfied, he walked quickly toward the stairs. On the third floor, he extracted mail from his little box and ambled toward his office. Several students greeted him as they headed for one of the labs. He opened the door and stepped in, grateful that the air-conditioning maintained a comfortable seventy degrees.

He hung his overcoat, still thinking this was utterly ridiculous, took a slim gray box out of his jacket pocket and switched on the scanner. Moving slowly around the room, he swept the office, watching the little yellow display. He swung it around the computer and phone, and nodded when the device remained silent. Greenfield had left the thing with him when he planted little bug cameras in the office and his house. Although unlikely that the man in black would snoop on his calls, and why would he want to, better be safe, Greenfield argued cheerfully. Krafter suspected that the young agent enjoyed the theatrical side of his job, but he could not fault the FBI's caution. No need to give their man any more freebies. He pocketed the scanner, sat down, and turned to the computer. With a nine o'clock lecture, he couldn't afford much time on administration.

A plain white envelope lying across the keyboard caught his eye and he froze, the fun draining out of his day. As he stared at the envelope, he had to accept the glum fact that the witch-hunt was far from over. He pursed his lips, picked it up, and slowly opened it. Inside were two small photographs, both of Elena. One showed her getting out of the Bartlett & Strong office on 3rd Street, and the other of her going to her apartment on N. 6th

Street. Studying the images, he didn't need to have them explained, the warning unambiguously clear.

After an initial stab of fear and gnawing worry whether she could be hurt because of his stance, he felt a hot surge of anger and outrage wash through him. Wasn't any plain old decency left in the world? The photos answered that for him unequivocally. Whether it was the IAS or an individual wanting to silence him, instead of confronting him in open debate with science as an impartial judge, like cowards, they hid behind a masked thug. He could understand the man in black, and even admire his professionalism, but he only had utter contempt for whoever gave him his orders.

Krafter slammed his fist against the desk, making the loose paperwork jump.

"Show yourself, you sons of bitches!"

He wanted to rip out somebody's throat right then, but that did not diminish his concern for Elena. This time, she would have to listen or he would drag her to that plane himself. Taking out the stiff FBI card out of his wallet, he sat down and dialed a cellular number. The two photos seemed to mock him.

"Special Agent Julian Briggs."

"Mr. Briggs, I'm afraid I have more troubles."

"Another body, doc?"

Krafter smiled, although there was little to smile about. "Nothing that simple, unfortunately. I found two photos of Elena Spiteri in an envelope on my desk when I walked in." He didn't say anything further, figuring the man would understand.

"This is not entirely unexpected, Professor," Briggs said after a moment. "However, the move did come sooner than we anticipated."

"So, what do I do?" Krafter demanded irritably.

"We could take her into protective custody."

"She would never agree to that."

"No, I didn't think she would. We'll make her disappear instead. We'll send her overseas somewhere until this blows over, which should place her out of our man's reach. I want to do the same thing with your parents."

Krafter sat back and frowned in concentration, liking the idea. With two major concerns out of the way, the problem would be reduced to a single dimension—him.

"You'd be wise to consider a similar option, Professor," Briggs added gently.

"I wouldn't mind a nice cruise somewhere, but I simply can't do it. I'm needed here, and if I disappear for a while, I would be running away and my detractors would win by default."

"No one is indispensable, but you can best judge your situation."

"There is something else you need to consider. I am your magnet," Krafter said, hoping the agent would get his meaning.

"With you in town, it definitely gives our man a reason to linger, which is good for us," Briggs admitted. "Although I don't like leaving you exposed. I'd hate to find *your* body in some garage."

Krafter chuckled, appreciating his point. "The idea doesn't exactly enhance my cool either, Mr. Briggs, but I won't be running away."

"I didn't figure you would, doc. Okay, we'll arrange for somebody to watch over you."

"I thought you said you didn't have the men to do that."

"Washington will provide the men. Now, this is what I want you to do. Call Miss Spiteri and ask her to come and see you. Explain to her what's going on, then tell her to take a cab to the airport. I'll book a flight to Denver and she can pick up the ticket at the service desk. If I remember correctly, Great Lakes have a flight at eleven twenty-six every morning. Make sure she's on it. She'll be met when she gets here. Tell her not to go home or pack, we'll provide everything she'll need. If she is being watched, we don't want to give our man any warning. You go that?"

"What do I do if she won't go?" Krafter said, not a rhetorical question at all. Elena had amply demonstrated that she was her own girl and didn't care for anyone running her life.

"It's up to you to convince her."

Nice of Briggs to leave him holding the bag, but he had to admit the agent was right. Still, the idea of not being able to drag suitcases of favorite things with her could sink him. What about money and a passport if they planned to send her overseas? But Briggs did say that they would provide everything.

"Okay, I'll call her."

"We'll sort out Bartlett & Strong for her and make sure her bills get paid. I also want you to call your parents. Even if our man hasn't thought of it yet, with your girlfriend gone, he may get around to them, and we might as well do this properly right now. I don't want you getting a picture of *them* in an envelope. We'll send a car for your mother and pick up your old man at the Resolute Energy Corporation. You won't know where they're going, but at least you'll know that they're safe. Anyway, they'll be able to call you, as will Miss Spiteri."

"Sounds like a good plan, Mr. Briggs."

"It should work if everybody plays their part. In a way, this may have given us a break we've been waiting for. Our man has made his first mistake, and if we're lucky, we've got a clear shot of him in your office."

"How will you retrieve the camera images?"

"The server Greenfield installed in Lab One has a wireless Internet facility. We've been downloading the data from here. Before I go, some good news. We found your missing hand bone and bracelet."

"I heard. Dr. Larson told me yesterday after getting it from Dr. Van Neuman."

"You don't sound excited."

"I am glad to hear that Professor Bollinger is under investigation by Harvard's ethics committee, and I'm sure Dr. Chandler will keep the bone safe, but I've got other worries right now."

"Make those calls, Professor, and we'll take care of your girlfriend. I'll be in touch," Briggs said and hung up.

Krafter listened to the dial tone and sat back. If everything worked out as Briggs hoped, it would relieve him of a major headache, and he saw no reason why this should not work. He glanced at his wristwatch: 8:40. She should be at the office by now. Not looking forward to this, he leaned across the desk and dialed her private number.

"Bartlett & Strong, Elena Spiteri speaking."

"Hi, beautiful," he said, trying to sound cheerful, although his stomach churned.

"Well, if it isn't my favorite client. Someone found another body?"

Krafter smiled at the stale joke. "As a matter of fact, somebody found you. Take a cab and come to the university."

"Now?"

"Now."

"Without a word of explanation? You're being very mysterious, Larry. My boss will think I'm goofing off."

"This is serious, Elena. Please do as I say and take that cab."

For several seconds, he only heard her soft breathing, and the waiting tore him apart.

"This better not be merely an excuse to have a coffee with me, Professor Krafter! I have work to do too, you know," she declared stiffly and broke the connection.

He quickly dialed the KCWC-TV news desk, hoping Laura wouldn't give him a hard time over making private calls on university time. He explained the situation to the day producer and was told a crew would be at the university at ten. At least he was still newsworthy enough for the station to be interested. All he needed to do now was square away Perkins before Elena showed up.

Quickly scrolling through the email list, he shot off several replies, got up and walked out of the office.

His mentor looked up when Krafter entered and motioned with his hand for him to come in.

"Don't you have a lecture at nine?" Perkins declared, glancing at his watch.

"That's what I came to talk to you about," Krafter said and took a chair without being invited. "I need to ask if you can find somebody to take it for me. It's late notice, I know, but I found another envelope on my desk and I need to take care of a few things."

Perkins bit his lower lip, nodded and turned to his computer. After a moment, he picked up the phone.

"Wethermans? I need to you take Dr. Krafter's nine o'clock lecture...No, I'm not kidding...Just do it, okay?" he grated and replaced the receiver.

Krafter winced at the prospect of his next encounter with Wethermans, but right now, he had bigger problems to deal with.

"Did he leave a note?" Perkins asked.

"He left two pictures of Elena."

"Bound to happen sooner or later, since you insist on doing things the hard way."

"The hard way? *They're* the ones doing it the hard way. After Allbright's announcement, I expected a measure of sanity to prevail."

"Having Allbight in your corner is good, but he's merely a speed bump on the road. You must have realized by now, Larry, that nothing short of an open declaration from you saying that the bones are an elaborate fraud and you played along with it, will satisfy whoever is after you."

"Well, they can go and screw themselves, and I'll never make such a statement. They'll have to shoot me first."

"I don't believe they'll go that far," Perkins said, then

frowned. "They're doing the next best thing by targeting Elena. Wouldn't that shut you up?"

"Ordinarily, it might, but Briggs has a plan to relieve me of that worry."

"Oh?"

"The FBI will make her disappear."

Perkins nodded in appreciation. "Good move."

"At ten o'clock, I'm going on local television and give my detractors an earful."

"Might not be such a good idea, you know. You could be preempting an attack on her."

"She'll be safely out of here by then."

"I hope you know what you're doing."

"I'm doing exactly what you told me to do, Adam. If I back off now, I might as well make that declaration you suggested."

A knock on the door caused both to turn their heads.

"Come in!" Perkins barked.

Elena walked in, gave Krafter a dark look and flashed Perkins a bright smile. "And how are you, Doctor?"

"I've had better days, thanks," Perkins said wryly and waved a hand at a chair. "Please, have a seat."

She sat down and folded her hands in her lap, looking smart in her tan business jacket and trousers. "Terrible day outside," she declared.

Krafter took a deep breath and turned to face her fully, hoping this wouldn't get difficult. She had not been exactly brimming with enthusiasm last time the subject came up.

"Remember that chat we had about you going away for a while? Well, it's time to make a decision. This morning, I found two photos of you on my desk. I hope I don't have to explain what that means."

She was silent for a moment. "I understand what it means, Larry," she said in a small voice and waited.

"I spoke to Briggs and he arranged a flight for you to Denver.

You'll be met."

Bright red spots appeared on her cheeks. "Just like that, eh? Well, I don't care what arrangements you two made, but I'm not going anywhere. I told you before. I've also got a life and I won't be intimidated."

Krafter sagged, afraid that this would happen. He glanced at Perkins, but his mentor merely looked back at him. This was something he would have to deal with by himself.

"Don't you see? It's not merely a question of intimidation anymore. God knows what the man is capable of."

She stood up slowly and glared at him. "You could have said this over the phone and saved me a trip in the rain."

Krafter rose and grasped her hands, his face tragic. His heart hammered and he swallowed hard.

"Will you listen to me…please? I cannot protect you if you walk out that door, and I can't be with you every minute. I don't know what else to do," he said softly and spread his hands in helpless resignation.

"You're staying here to face this alone?" she demanded, her eyes misty.

"I won't be alone. I have Adam and the FBI."

"But you don't need me, is that it?"

He stared at her, his throat suddenly tight. He blinked rapidly to take the sting out of his eyes, then lifted her hand to his lips and kissed it.

"I'm doing this because I do need you, and because I love you…and because I'm nothing if you're not with me. I don't know how to do this any other way, Elena," he said brokenly and let go of her hand.

He wanted to take her in his arms and crush her against him, make her part of him and be one. She wouldn't have to go away then, and he would be able to face everything this crummy world wanted to throw at him.

Her mouth curved down and a tear slid down her cheek. She

251

brushed it away with a finger, then slowly reached into her jacket pocket and held out a picture. Krafter hesitated before taking it, fearing it would burn him. It was a picture of him walking out of the Anthropology Building with a hole where his chest was supposed to be. The man in black was not playing with his mind alone.

"I found it in an envelope in my office last Friday," she whispered. "I *couldn't* abandon you now, Larry! You see that, don't you?"

He showed the picture to Perkins and sighed. After a moment, he reached for her and pulled her against him.

"I know, beautiful," he said gruffly and swallowed a lump in his throat. It went down hard. "We'll do this together. It also means that you must let me make you safe. By going away, you won't be abandoning me. You'll be helping me. The faceless men who are after me want me humiliated and ruined professionally, not dead. If you get hurt because of me, I *will* be dead…inside." He placed a finger under her chin and lifted her head, then gently kissed her cheek.

"You're a dope, Larry Krafter," she mumbled and sniffed. "I'll need to think about this."

Not expecting this, he looked at her in alarm. "What's there to think? Everything is arranged!"

She stepped back and regarded him with cold dignity. "You expect me to leave now? Without any warning or preparation?"

"The FBI—"

"I don't care what you and the FBI have cooked up. You will simply have to give me time to think about this, okay? I can't just up and go!"

"Yes, you can! They'll provide everything."

She shook her head and set her mouth. He clenched his fists against his temples in anguish.

"You're killing me, Elena!"

Startled, she brushed his cheek with soft fingers and smiled.

"I don't want to do that, but you'll have to give me time, okay? You can't spring this on a girl and expect her to just waltz out of here laughing. There are arrangements to be made."

"I understand, but the thing is, the man in black might not give you the time to make them," he said helplessly, all his fears returning with crushing weight.

"Twenty-four hours," she said firmly, turned to Perkins and nodded. "Is he always this difficult?"

"Only where you're concerned," Perkins said quietly.

She gave him a small smile and turned to Krafter. "I'll call you tonight." She fluttered her fingers at them and walked out.

When the door closed, Krafter stood there, then sagged into his chair. "What do I do now, Adam?" His heart was breaking and he felt betrayed. Why couldn't she understand and do the sensible thing?

"You give the lady time to make up her mind. You cannot push a woman around, any woman, for that matter. She has to decide to do this on her own. She knows you're right and your plan is sensible, and she'll come around. She just doesn't want to be controlled. There *are* practical considerations to take care of. She was right about that."

"But I wasn't controlling her!"

"You weren't?"

Startled by the notion, Krafter mulled it over. He and Briggs had everything sorted out, but neither of them had bothered to consult the one person most affected. Best of intentions? He would not make the same mistake with his parents.

"I *am* a dope, aren't I?"

"No, you're simply a young man who has to learn that it's people who matter in this crummy world, not science, discoveries, or professional glory, but people. Elena has merely given you a reminder."

"Too bad there isn't a course in how to deal with people," Krafter said ruefully. He had followed a rational, logical plan, and despite his PhD and understanding of social anthropology, the emotional dimension had defeated him.

"There is only one, and it's called life," Perkins said gently. "It's all practical, with no exams at the end, but you'll know when you have failed."

"And I've failed this one, haven't I?"

"You've been given a chance to do it over, which is more than most people get."

Krafter grinned and stood up. "Thanks for the psychology lesson, Dr. Perkins. Don't be surprised if you hear some yelling coming from my office. That'll be Briggs going terminal."

"Don't be too hard on him, he's doing his best. You still want to do your ten o'clock interview?"

"Definitely, and I could be damned either way, but I won't sit back and simply take it."

"Good luck, my boy."

Back in his office, Krafter made two lengthy calls to Denver. When he finished, he sat back, vastly relieved. His parents understood his position, having followed events in the media, and promised to cooperate. With winter approaching, the idea of getting away somewhere warm appealed to them. Besides, his old man was due to take his vacation anyway.

With that chore done, he dialed again, not relishing this one.

"Special Agent Julian Briggs."

"Mr. Briggs, it's Krafter, and I have a development."

"Miss Spiteri is on her way to the airport?"

"Not exactly. She asked for twenty-four hours to think things over."

"Shit, Krafter! What the hell is there to think about? You just get her ass on that flight. This isn't the time to be dicking around."

Krafter gently replaced the receiver, sat back and waited. It didn't take long. When the call came, he let it ring four times before picking up.

"I'm sorry, Professor. I was out of line and I apologize," Briggs said contritely. "This couldn't have been easy for either of you."

"You're right, it wasn't. I would love nothing more than to haul her bodily to the airport, but it wouldn't solve anything."

Briggs gave a heavy sigh. "I know. Women! There's a flight leaving at eight oh-two in the morning. Try hard and get her on it, okay?"

"I'll do that," Krafter said and smiled at the thought of holding a squirming Elena in his arms, marching through the terminal. "If it's any consolation, my parents were more agreeable. My old man has vacation time coming and there is no problem with him leaving right away."

"That's something. I'll get things moving here."

"Mr. Briggs? Thanks for everything."

"Thank me when this is done, doc," Briggs growled and hung up.

Things were happening, although not entirely to plan. Satisfied or not, Krafter figured he would just have to lump it.

He finished going over his correspondence and emails, and it was time to face the cameras. Twitching his jacket into place, he walked down the corridor after locking the office. As he went down the stairs, he wondered mildly how Wethermans was handling his lecture, certain he would have a visit from the starched associate professor before the day was out.

Still short of ten o'clock, the film crew were already down in the foyer. Krafter recognized the reporter and held out his hand.

"Hi, Phil. Thanks for coming out."

A cheerful individual, Phil grinned as they shook hands. "You're big news these days, Larry, and things seem to happen around you. Anyway, it makes a break from covering fender-benders and funerals. How do you want to handle this?"

"It'll be a statement. When I finish, you decide if you want to ask me questions."

Several students made a group in the background, waiting to see what the big deal was about. Phil turned to his cameraman, who lifted the bulky device to his shoulder and nodded.

"You're on."

Phil stood next to Krafter and brought a black snout mike to his mouth. "This is Phil Stevens for KCWC-TV, Laramie. I have Professor Larry Krafter with me. We all know of his recent discovery and problems with his detractors, who still refuse to believe that the find is authentic, despite overwhelming scientific evidence and support from a number of reputable universities. Professor, I understand that there has been another development," Phil said and shoved the mike toward Krafter.

After numerous live interviews and press conferences, Krafter had the confidence of an old hand at handling the media. Although this was going to be a canned take, he didn't want to waste Phil's time by being sloppy or indecisive. He straightened and looked directly at the camera, fire burning in his belly.

"My critics have tried hard to prove my discovery is a forgery or a misrepresentation. I countered their criticism with impartial scientific data. Despite growing acceptance from the paleoanthropological community and eminent scholars such as Professors Hartman, Walsh, and Allbright, my detractors continue to maintain their vendetta against me. Not satisfied with trying to besmirch the reputation of this university, and having failed to silence me by a murder frame-up, they have now turned their attention to those around me.

"This morning, I found pictures on my desk of someone I love. I don't know who left them, but I know why they were left. They're a warning. If I don't denounce my discovery, the person I love will be harmed." Krafter paused and swallowed.

"I will not bow to intimidation or threats. My detractors have crossed the line when they resorted to standover tactics. Instead of denouncing my discovery, I denounce them, and I look forward to the day when they stand exposed before the law for their acts."

After a moment of silence, applause rippled through his impromptu audience. Phil smiled and pulled the mike toward him.

"Professor Krafter, have you spoken to the police about this latest incident?"

"I informed the FBI. They are handling the general investigation."

"Do you know if they have any leads?"

"They haven't confided in me on the success of their efforts."

"What will you do now, Professor?"

Krafter glanced at his watch. "I have a tutorial at one and a lecture at three. Somewhere before then, I hope to squeeze in lunch."

There was spontaneous laughter and more applause.

"Thank you, Professor Krafter," Phil said and made a cutting motion to the cameraman.

"Way to go, doc!" someone shouted as the students slowly dispersed.

"Not bad at all, Larry," Phil said. "I am sure the networks back East will carry it on tonight's news."

"My thanks to your producer, Phil." They shook hands and Krafter made his way toward the stairs.

The interview might not stop the man in black, but he hoped it would give whoever ran him seconds thoughts. If they meant to go on and Elena got hurt, it would all be his fault. Although Biggs was trying, Krafter doubted that the FBI were getting anywhere.

Why did she have to be so stubborn?

If she decided not to leave, he *would* carry her bodily to the airport in the morning.

The rest of the day remained uneventful, and Wethermans didn't show up to berate him. After his three o'clock lecture, he spent time going over assignments, but he was too stirred up to concentrate and left at five. The rain had turned into a thin drizzle and he squinted at the glare of oncoming headlights as he drove home. Reaching his house, he opened the garage and parked the Focus.

Krafter placed a piece of fried crumbed veal on a plate and heaped assorted vegetables around it, then took the plate to the table and switched on the television to catch the six-thirty news. On the local front, they showed clips of flash flooding and several fender-benders. This was followed by his interview, uncut. Watching himself, Krafter decided it was a good performance, but hoped it wasn't a futile gesture. After a lengthy commercial break, there were the usual sound bites of national and international events, mayhem and gunfire, with little substantive content. He switched off when it came to the sports segment. Looking at hobnailed gorillas jumping on each other under the pretext of chasing an oddly shaped ball was not his idea of amusement or sport.

He was finishing the washing up when the wall phone went off.

"Hello?" he said after picking up.

"You know what I told you would happen if I had to come back?" the heavy, rasping voice said softly. Krafter felt himself go pale and his mouth turned to ash.

"I heard you," he said after a moment.

"But you didn't believe I meant it, right? Well, you've gone and upset me, and we need to talk. I'm outside in my car and we're going for a little drive. If you're worried about getting hurt, don't be. It's not part of the deal. I've got something else in mind for you. Do come out, Professor, because you don't want to do this the hard way."

The line went dead and Krafter stared at the handset, dreading what was to come. He knew what the man in black would do. He simply knew. Tempted to call Ramanof, he chuckled at the absurdity of the idea. How the man in black managed to find his new unlisted number didn't even cross his mind. Letting out a loud breath, he picked up his keys and slowly walked toward the front door.

Activated by his movement, the porch light flickered on. A dark car stood parked on the street. He locked the front door and walked steadily toward the waiting sedan. Streetlights cast milky pools on the slick roadway. The drizzle had stopped, but a biting wind cut through his sweater. He got into the front passenger seat and turned to the large man beside him.

"Lousy night to be out," the man rasped amiably and started the engine. "Some things just have to be done."

Krafter could not make anything behind the balaclava, dark jeans and a heavy brown leather jacket. The man didn't wear glasses, and they weren't necessary. In the poor light, Krafter couldn't make out his eyes if he were a foot from him.

"No hard feelings I hope about the body I left in your garage?" the man remarked casually as the car turned left into S. 15th Street, then left again into E. Garfield.

Krafter didn't bother answering. The man glanced at him and chuckled.

"A dirty trick to pull on you, I know. Unfortunately, it didn't work out, otherwise I'd be sunning my ass somewhere warm. Never mind, this next move will interest you."

When they turned right into N. 6th Street, Krafter knew where they were going, but he had known it all along. As they approached the two-story tenement block, the man in black slowed the car, then stopped. He switched off the engine and shifted to look at Krafter.

"I don't have to tell you where we are. There is no pleasant way to say this, Professor, so I'll just go ahead and say it. Tomorrow morning, you will call KCWC-TV and tell them your discovery is a fake and you were the victim of an elaborate fraud. You can pretty it up by saying that you just found out, but that's what you're going to tell them. And this is the good part. If you don't, by tomorrow night, your girlfriend will be dead. I'll also be paying you a visit, but it won't be for a chat and a drink. I hope you believe me, Professor, because we're not having any more drives."

Listening to the man's cold words, devoid of any emotion, Krafter believed him implicitly. They had reached the end game and he held the ball. He wanted to smash his fist into the masked face, but refrained from doing anything so stupid. He would not only end up breaking his wrist, but the man in black might give him a demonstration of what Elena could look forward to tomorrow. He didn't fear for himself. They needed him healthy to make his announcement. Afterward, he would be a nobody; disgraced, ridiculed, and reviled. He might as well be dead.

"I'll make the announcement," he said woodenly.

"I thought you would," the man in black said cheerfully and started the car. "See how things can be pleasant when we all act reasonably? By the way, if you're thinking of calling the cops or the FBI, go right ahead. If you do, remember this. You'll be putting a bullet in her head, because wherever you take her, I'll find her. Now that we've got this sorted out, I'll take you home and you can sleep on it. Oh, I saw the interview you made this morning. Very stirring and noble, but not very smart, just when I was starting to think you were a clever man." He exhaled loudly and shook his head. "I guess some people simply don't know when to quit."

The drive back to his house done in silence, and Krafter didn't particularly want to chat. When the car stopped, he got out without saying anything. With a surge of power, the dark saloon pulled away from the curb and he noted the registration. Not that it was likely to help, probably another rental. He watched it turn into S. 15th Street and disappear. As he stood in the empty street, the cold wind stirred his hair. He expected to feel something: shock, outrage, anything, but he felt unnaturally calm. He wasn't even afraid for Elena anymore, for he knew what he had to do.

He walked into the house, jotted down the registration and picked up the wall phone.

"Briggs." The agent sounded tired and Krafter knew how he felt.

"It's Krafter. I know it's late, but I just had a visit from our man. He took me to Elena's apartment to drive home his point and told me that if I didn't denounce my discovery, by tomorrow night, she'll be dead. He also said that it wouldn't make any difference if I told the FBI."

"Did he come to the house?"

"I had to go to his car."

"Okay, we don't have any pictures of him, then. Never mind. Our man might be a professional, but so am I. You've run out of time, Professor, and so has Miss Spiteri. I'll call Ramanof and have him send men to guard her and take her to the airport in the morning, under arrest if necessary. I'd suggest you go and see her, doc, and talk to her. This time, there is nothing to think about. As for his threat to find her, he won't."

"I feel like shit," Krafter said miserably. "If she had listened to me—"

"That's history. We have to deal with the here and now. Go talk to your girlfriend and straighten her out. I'll call you in the morning."

"What if he tails me to her apartment?"

"It doesn't matter. He won't do anything until he sees whether you'll make the announcement or not."

"With Elena gone, he might turn on me."

"I haven't discounted that possibility, but I wouldn't worry about it. Like I told you, we'll get somebody to watch you," Briggs said briskly and hung up.

Holding the phone, Krafter shrugged. Don't worry about it, the man said. Sure, as if that was going make everything okay. Briggs was right about Elena. Mouth set, he dialed her number and waited.

"Hello?"

"It's me. I'm coming over."

"Why, Larry! Are you going to sweep me off my feet? I'm still going over what you told me this morning."

"Time for thinking is over, Elena. Five minutes," he said and hung up.

He drove quickly, but the streets were mostly empty. He parked in front of her building and hurried in. Outside the main entrance, he paused, took a deep breath and pressed the numbered button for her apartment. After a moment the speaker crackled.

"Larry?"

"It's me."

The door clicked and he hurried upstairs. When he knocked, she opened the door and stood there, dressed in a loose navy blue track pants and black track top. He walked in and she closed the door. Seeing his expression, her smile faded and she turned serious.

"What is it?"

Standing there, looking innocent, vulnerable and beautiful, his heart ached for her. He steeled himself, determined to remain unmoved by whatever she had to say.

"The man in black dropped by my place and drove me here not fifteen minutes ago. He left me a message. If I don't denounce my discovery, by this time tomorrow, you'll be dead."

She stared at him for several seconds, then smiled and tilted her head. "You mean it, or do you? This isn't some plot you and Briggs hatched—"

"Elena! We're past that! Ramanof will send men to guard you tonight. Tomorrow at eight, you're taking a flight for Denver."

"Even if I don't want to?"

"I'll drag you there in handcuffs if that's what it takes," he told her bluntly, in no mood for banter. She grinned and her features softened.

"That won't be necessary, Professor Krafter," she whispered and came close. She leaned against him and her soft lips touched his. His arms went around her and he held her tight. When the kiss broke, he brushed back a strand of hair from her forehead.

"I'm sorry for being a dope," he murmured, relieved that she was at last being reasonable.

She smiled and her eyes glittered. "Sometimes, you make me so mad…"

"I was just thinking the same thing," he said and they both laughed, lightening some of the tension. She pulled back and straightened her track top. "I guess, I better start packing," she said, then froze. "I don't have any money!"

"The FBI will cover everything," he assured her.

"Where are they sending me?"

"Briggs didn't say."

"Not even to you? What if I'm going overseas? I'll need my passport, and it's at the bank." She lifted her hand. "Don't tell me. The FBI will provide everything."

"That's the deal."

"I take it they made the same deal with your parents?"

"Except they weren't so hard to convince."

She set her mouth and lifted a finger, when a loud knock on the door cut off her rejoinder.

"Miss Spiteri? This is Laramie PD."

Her eyes opened wide. "You *were* serious."

Two uniformed officers stood outside when she opened the door.

"Glad to see you again, Officer Parker," Krafter said amicably. The black cop smiled briefly and nodded.

"Professor."

"Come in, gentlemen," Elena said and stepped aside. The two cops walked in. Parker stopped in front of her when she closed the door.

"I guess Professor Krafter told you what's going on,

ma'am?"

"In general."

"My partner and I will be your first watch. We'll change during the night. In the morning, the last team will take you to the airport. There'll also be a squad car outside all night."

"I guess you're determined to keep me safe."

"Yes, ma'am. Now, is it all right for us to stay in here?"

"Of course. I'll show you to the living room and kitchen. Watch TV if you want to."

"Thank you, ma'am. We'll try not to be too much trouble."

"I should be thanking *you*."

Krafter cleared his throat. "I'll drop by tomorrow before you leave," he said and turned to Parker. "What time are you going to the airport?"

"I understand it's seven-fifteen, sir."

"You're not staying?" she queried with an impish smile.

Krafter was tempted to take her across his knee and spank her. He glanced at the two cops and had to grin at being frustrated out of a diverting evening.

"That wouldn't be convenient."

She leaned against him and pecked him on the cheek. "In the morning, then."

Driving home, Krafter felt better. Elena would be safe, and that was all that mattered. She'll be safe.

Chapter Eight

"Did you see Krafter's interview on the news last night?" Slater asked casually as he walked into Tom's office, holding a brown envelope under his arm. He pulled out a chair and shook his head. "The man prefers to live on the edge."

"It's always nice to hear a professional assessment," Tom said with a broad grin, regarding the agent with amusement. Almost eight o'clock, it looked like he wasn't the only early riser here. "And, yes, I did see the interview, which, by the way, precipitated a predictable reaction from Professor Krafter, and an equally predictable response from our killer."

"What response?"

"Last night, our man threatened to kill Miss Spiteri, which prompted Briggs to arrange a hasty disappearance for her."

"The shrinks missed that one," Slater said softly and frowned.

"It wouldn't be the first time. What do you want? I've got work to do."

"My, eating raw bran this morning, have we?"

"I'll be eating you in a minute."

"Before you start chewing, bite on this." With a flourish, Slater slid the envelope across Tom's desk.

Tom peered at it suspiciously, opened the flap and extracted four, six-by-nine glossies. One showed a color shot of a large man wearing a black balaclava. Another was an infrared of a broad face, distorted by red and orange shading, but the features were clearly visible through the balaclava. The remaining two were computer-generated renditions of a fully restored face. Beneath a full growth of hair, the face strong without being chiseled. The eyes were large, sunk deep under prominent eyebrows. A square chin jutted below fleshy lips. The last print was a fully rendered black-and-white portrait.

"Not a bad looking guy, is he?" Tom said, staring at the image.

"All devils are handsome," Slater agreed comfortably. "We caught this one in Krafter's office."

"Presumably when he left his last calling card? Too bad we didn't have a pickup in the corridor. It would have saved everybody a lot of time. The fact that he is wearing a balaclava suggests he probably suspected we planted cameras."

"He took the bait anyway. FACE is still processing the IR shot and we should get a better likeness later today. We don't know for certain the color of his hair or eyes, but we'll infer that from statements Greenfield got at Laramie hotels."

The Facial Analysis, Comparison, and Evaluation Services Unit of the Biometric Services Section provides investigative lead support to FBI field offices, operational divisions, and legal attachés by comparing facial images of persons associated with open assessments and investigations against facial images available in state and federal face recognition systems. In limited instances, the FACE Services Unit provides face recognition support for closed FBI cases and to federal partners.

"If he didn't disguise himself or wear contacts," Tom added. "When you get the prints, you know what to do."

"Greenfield isn't going to enjoy canvassing all those hotels again, photos dangling in his hand."

"The fresh air will do him good," Tom said indifferently. "What's happening with the supermarket and airport surveillance tapes?"

"We got 'em, but we're still waiting on Denver. That's a big airport, you know, and these things take time."

"Christ! How long does it take to copy a few DVDs? Talk to Briggs and have Vince Saxon lean on them, because if I call them,

I'll be upset, which isn't going to make their day."

"Right, but if you decide to call them, let me know first. I want to watch a master at work."

"Asshole!" Tom growled, then laughed. "Anyway, now that we've got a possible mug shot, it's time the photo lab started processing the tapes we do have."

"I've already alerted them to be ready."

"Any bitching?"

"You don't want to know," Slater said glumly.

"I won't pry. What's happening with our request to NSA, *et al*?"

"I hoped you wouldn't ask," Slater said ruefully. "The bottom line? Deep silence. And I'm not going to tell you I told you so."

"I heard you the first time. Send me copies of your requests. I'll have a word with Hancock and see what we can do. What else you got for me?"

Slater sat back and crossed his arms. "The profile you wanted of our man? Going over the incidents with Krafter, Hartman and Walsh, the pattern seems pretty clear. The shrinks tell me, he probably received instructions on what to do, but not how to do it."

"That's a revelation," Tom muttered sourly. "What about that reporter, Reed?"

"Part of the same picture. Leaving everybody letters before taking action was a nice psychological touch, guaranteed to make his victims nervy. When he did act, it was with controlled violence. That implies a superior stalking mentality."

"A cat playing with a mouse before the jaws close, is that it?"

"You got it. He bungled the murder frame-up, which was almost certainly a blow to his ego. To salvage his pride, his next move is likely to be terminal."

"By threatening to kill Miss Spiteri. I know, he's done that."

"It's not what I meant. He'll go after Krafter," Slater said

267

formally. "Having tried everything else—"

"Killing the professor would wrap up his mission. End of an embarrassment."

"For our man and for those pulling his strings."

Tom scowled and tapped his fingers against the desk. "I don't like that kind of thinking. What if he has orders not to kill?"

"The shrinks say that our man might do it anyway. His masters might baulk, but their problem would have been taken care of."

"What would we do without shrinks to do our thinking for us, eh?"

"With Krafter's girlfriend out of the way, they could be right about him being a real target now."

"Mmm. Briggs told me the same thing last night. According to your report, Krafter is smart and knows it. He's determined and headstrong like young people everywhere. Nobody's going to make him knuckle under. Short of being shot or run over, given his declaration yesterday, which fits his behavioral pattern, he won't be backing down. I guess we'll just have to put a detail on him."

"If we're dealing with a professional, I wouldn't give Krafter much for his chances, detail or not."

"There you go again, Slats! More pessimism. From everything we know so far, our man prefers to work up close and personal. Having a bodyguard hovering around Krafter should cramp his style. Of course, if he tries for long distance termination, everybody'll have a bad day. Leave that one with me. Anything else?"

"Krafter's fan list. Although prominent, Professors Bollinger and Maddson don't appear to be the type to resort to organized violence."

"You can pretty much scratch Bollinger off the list. After Greenfield found the hand bone in his office, our professor has more pressing problems on his mind than going after Krafter."

"I still can't believe he had the thing in a box sitting on a shelf," Slater said and chuckled.

"Goes to show you that having a PhD doesn't necessarily make you brilliant. About Krafter, you were going to say that our killer is being run by one of the Society bodies?"

"A number of them would prefer him to quietly fade out of sight, but the International Anthropological Society stands out above all of them by a long neck, and not only because our two professors are on its Executive Committee."

Tom waited, then raised an eyebrow. "You going to tell me why, or what?"

Slater grinned. "Testy, aren't we? The search you wanted done for offshore accounts? It turns out the IAS doesn't have such an account, but they did make several deposits to a Cayman Islands bank."

"Payoffs for services rendered?"

"Likely, and this could prove it." Slater reached into his jacket pocket and extracted a sheaf of folded pages. "Transcript of a teleconference at IAS just before all those bad things started happening to Krafter."

"My man!" Quickly scanning the pages, Tom looked up. "Makes for entertaining reading, but we've got nothing. It's all circumstantial."

"It's suggestive."

"Agreed, but it doesn't prove that Kessler is running our killer or paying him off."

Slater beamed from ear to ear as he produced another sheaf of papers. "I thought I would save the best for last. A chat between Dr. Ted Horowitz and Raymond Kessler last Thursday, the day after they found that body."

"Christ! Are you going to be drip feeding me?"

"It's my way of saying thanks for giving me this job."

"Asshole!" Tom picked up the pages and spent a minute going over them. When he finished, he bit his lower lip. "So tantalizingly close, but it's still circumstantial. Kessler hasn't said anything that could possibly implicate him or the IAS."

"But…"

"It's worth crap without solid proof. The only thing we have is that IAS is pissed off at Krafter and they issued notices to all and sundry expressing their displeasure. It might not be nice, but none of that is against the law."

"What about the Cayman Islands payment?"

"Without a good look at the transaction, which none of their banks will let us do, we're driving on empty."

"You're being deliberately difficult here, Tom," Slater complained, his enthusiasm deflated.

"Nope, just realistic. I'm not raining on your work. You've done well here, and we may have reached first base, but we're still a long way from home plate. The thing is, and you know this as well as I do, if we cannot positively tie Kessler with our man, we've got squat. Does NSA have anything on calls he might have made to our man?"

"Not even a hi."

Tom thought about it for a minute. "'Curiouser and curiouser', said Alice. In your report, you said that Kessler is a highflyer, specializing at straightening out ailing companies. Makes me wonder. His last job at BioChip dealt with some heavy customers, including NASA and the Defense Department."

"Most everything they do is classified, and their commercial work is all hush-hush," Slater agreed. "What are you getting at?"

"Everybody working there probably has a high security clearance. Especially their Chief Operating Officer, right?"

Slater stared, then slowly smiled. "They could be using encrypted phones!"

"If Kessler had such a cellphone—"

"And took it with him when he joined IAS—"

"It would explain why NSA came up blank on his calls to

our man, if he is in fact the one controlling him," Tom finished.

"That would mean our man must also be using such a cell-phone."

"Especially if he previously worked for somebody like the NSA or the CIA."

"In that case, it still leaves us at that first base you so color-fully described."

"Maybe a step in front of it. We now have a plausible expla-nation why NSA has no record of Kessler's calls. At least calls he might have made to our man."

"We could get a warrant and find out if he has such a cell-phone."

"Which would do nothing for us. And NSA might have given him the thing. Apart from violating several telecommuni-cations regulations, the most we could do is take the phone off him. Big deal."

Slater stared and his shoulders sagged. "Which means we'll have to do this the hard way: get our man and have him implicate Kessler."

"Not necessarily. Call your contact at NSA and find out if they've issued Kessler a special encryption cellphone. Another thing. Don't get fixated on him," Tom warned him. "We could still be dealing with somebody else."

"That hasn't been lost on me," Slater said dryly. "If they did give him the cellphone, maybe we should ask them to deactivate whatever call number he's using."

Tom immediately wagged a finger. "No, we don't want to do that. I want Kessler to believe he's secure. If he's running our man, his connection might come in handy somewhere down the track."

Slater looked skeptical. "It'll come in handy, all right, espe-cially if he orders Krafter killed."

"If he wants Krafter dead, he can order it done any number of ways. He doesn't need a phone. We do have one thing working

271

for us. There is now a rift between the IAS academic and administrative arms. Something we might be able to exploit."

"If we start messing with Horowitz, he's going to go screaming to Kessler and everybody'll take cover."

"Perhaps, but don't forget what we're about here. We want to keep Krafter alive. Catching our killer will simply be a big bonus."

"If you say so. I'll email you the final photo when it comes through. Other than that, I've got nothing else for the moment."

"Get Greenfield packing. I want him out of here soonest. In the meantime, I'll have a chat with Hancock. Good work, Slats, and give my thanks to your team."

When the special agent left, Tom planted his feet on the desk and went into his thoughtful mode.

So, what did he have? A lot of things had happened around Krafter and his girlfriend, but when boiled down, the only tangible thing he had was a computer image of the killer. Correction, he had an image of a man who walked into Krafter's UW office. It might be the only thing, but it was invaluable. It enabled the investigation to move forward. All good, but there was something he needed done first. He picked up the phone and dialed.

"Dennis Sawko."

"It's Tom. A quick heads up. Krafter's family are safe and his girlfriend should be out of Laramie this morning their time. I'll confirm with Briggs once he crawls out of bed. We're up against a two-hour time difference with Denver, remember?"

"His girlfriend's taken care of, but I gather Krafter isn't going anywhere, right?" Sawko finished for him.

"I'm afraid so, but we always figured that would be the case. About the protection detail we talked about—"

"After seeing his broadcast last night, I knew you'd be calling. I've sent the men off already and they'll be in Laramie around one p.m. their time."

"You used one of our own aircraft?"

"A Gulfstream V out of Andrews. A commercial flight would have taken too long and I figured you'd want them there in a hurry."

"You're right. Thanks, Dennis. I owe you."

"I'll hold you to that. Any idea how long they're likely to be on the ground?"

"It's hard to say."

"I hear you. You will either nail your man or Krafter will be dead."

"Stark, but real."

"Have fun," Sawko said and rang off.

Tom held the receiver and smiled. Dennis was all right when he got activated. Still smiling, he dialed Marsha's number.

"It's Meecham," he said when she picked up. "Please check if the boss is in and if he can see me for a few minutes."

"Hold on, Tom." There was a click and background music filled the silence. "He can see you now," she said when she came back on.

Another early riser…

"Thanks."

"By the way, a reminder that you have an NBC producer coming to see you at eleven."

Tom groaned, still trying to come up with a dodge not to see the guy. Norginson was right and the NBC were doing a documentary on the John the Baptist Scroll. Naturally, he was going to feature prominently in it. They'll blow it all out of proportion and make him look like Captain America! His colleagues would laugh their heads off behind his back or harbor resentment for being a publicity grabber.

He made his way to Hancock's office and knocked. Getting a muffled 'Come in', he opened the door. Hancock looked up from his desk and waved at a chair. Tom made himself comfortable and waited for the assistant director to finish shuffling papers.

273

"What did you want to see me about?"

The man sounded grumpy, but Tom had problems of his own.

"It's the Krafter case, boss. His parents and girlfriend have taken a sudden holiday. Health reasons. We managed to secure a surveillance camera shot of our man and can now move into high gear to locate him. We've hit a roadblock and I need your help to remove it."

"I'm glad to hear that you're making progress. From what I've seen, Krafter has run a very effective publicity campaign, and whoever is after him could get desperate."

"That's what we were thinking, boss," Tom said.

"What do you need?"

"Two things. I asked Special Agent Slater to request information from the CIA, NSA and a few others, and they've clammed up. Without their input, it makes our job that much more difficult."

"Send me Slater's requests and I'll take care of it. And the other thing?"

"I would like permission to plant a bug on the International Anthropological Society's current CEO. The man worked for a specialty chip design and manufacturing outfit down in Silicone Valley doing a lot of development for the military."

"They're probably covered by a security blanket," Hancock said and snorted. "You're interested because…"

"It's possible that the IAS are running our killer."

"I'll get back to you. Anything else?"

"Not right now, boss."

"How close are you to closing this?"

Tom stood up and shrugged. "Hard to say. If we get the breaks…"

"That's always the case. Anyway, it's only been a week." Hancock nodded, then smiled. "Has Marsha reminded you about the NBC meeting?"

"Christ, boss! Isn't there some way of getting me out of this?"

"The publicity will do the Bureau good."

Walking back to his office, resigned to the inevitable, Tom saw Brian Peters waiting for him.

"Hi, doc. You must have hot news to ambush me this early," he said easily and held the door open for his visitor.

Peters smiled ruefully and walked in. "It's not all good, I'm afraid."

"Take a seat and tell me," Tom invited, pulling back his chair. "If I haven't mentioned it, good job by your genius on the body they found in Professor Krafter's house. It's got him off murder one."

"You have, and I've passed it on to her. About that Bersa you asked me to trace. We've hit a wall."

Tom smiled without humor. "It's the day for it. Why should you be any different?"

"I'll take that as being rhetorical. The serial number hasn't been filed off, which helped a lot. According to the supplier, the gun was part of a shipment bought by The Weapons Works in Phoenix about two years ago, and sold to a guy working for a private security firm. The gun shop was kind enough to give us his details. I asked one of my guys to call him and the man confirmed that he bought the gun. He wanted it for his wife, but she picked something else. After having it sit in his drawer for better part of a year, he sold it to Mo Money Pawn, also in Phoenix. When my guy contacted them, he got the usual polite runaround."

"It's likely the shop owner couldn't be bothered checking his records," Tom growled. "If he's got them."

"Anyway, I called the local FBI office and asked them to send somebody to the gun shop."

"And?"

"They will...one of these days."

"Christ! We're not asking them for money or something. What about getting Phoenix PD on it?"

"Already tried."

"Don't tell me. It's not their case, right?"

"Pretty much."

"With friends like that…"

"Unless we can trace who bought the Bersa from the pawn-shop, you're stuck," Peters said.

"It's at times like these that I wish we had a national gun registry law," Tom mused and sat back. "Leave it with me. I'll think of something, and thanks for dropping by."

Peters stood up and smiled. "Glad it's your problem, not mine," he said and walked out, leaving Tom scowling after him.

After a moment, he shrugged. It *was* his problem and Brian had done all he could. He picked up his coffee mug, stood up, then froze. He put the mug down and reached for the phone.

"Albert Slater."

"It's Tom. Has Greenfield gone?"

"Marsha's getting his flight organized, but he's gone home to pack a bag."

"Tell her he's going to Phoenix first. If she can get him a morning flight, ring him and tell him to go straight to the airport. He can pick up his ticket there. I need him to do a follow-up on that Bersa they found. He can fly to Laramie tomorrow."

"You believe our killer bought the gun in Phoenix?"

"It's possible. At least the trail ends there. With Arizona gun laws, it's easy as buying a carton of milk."

"Seems a roundabout way of going about it. If I were the killer, I'd buy the thing in Laramie. It's simpler and I wouldn't have to worry about airport security."

"Wyoming has a mandatory FBI and National Instant Check System search for all firearms transactions. Our man already has a trail in Laramie and I doubt he would want to broaden it by buying a gun there. Besides, he could have driven with it to

Laramie. We've got to follow the leads we have and Greenfield is going to be in the neighborhood anyway. I'll tell Dr. Peters to email you the details and you can forward them to Greenfield."

"He won't mind a day in Phoenix," Slater said comfortably. "I'll tell Marsha to book him a hotel."

"He can enjoy it all he wants as long as he gets there today," Tom said briskly and pressed the disconnect pin on the phone's cradle. Holding the receiver in his hand, he smiled. Slats was right. Greenfield wouldn't mind the trip at all, not when the alternative was being in Washington, fumbling through his analysis work.

But he had a different problem now. Like he told Slater, he didn't want to spook the killer into making a preemptive strike against Krafter, but that didn't mean the man controlling him couldn't be rattled. The problem was, he could also be rattled into ordering the very action Tom did not want. Still, Krafter would be protected, as far as possible against a professional, and he figured the advantages outweighed the risks. Of course, he wasn't the one taking the risk.

He set his mouth and dialed. Marsha answered almost immediately.

"It's Tom. I need you to track down a number for me, please: Dr. Ted Horowitz, Chair of Archaeology at Princeton University."

When Marsha rang back, Tom jotted down the details and made the call.

"Department of Arts and Archaeology, Sally speaking."

"Good morning, Sally. This is Thomas Meecham, Supervising Special Agent, FBI. I would like to talk to Dr. Horowitz, if he's available."

"Ah, just a moment, sir."

Tom could imagine her reaction, wondering what the FBI wanted with the department chair. The good doctor must also have wondered, for it took almost a minute for Sally to come back.

"Putting you through now."

"Thank you…Dr. Horowitz?"

"Mr. Meecham, I can hardly imagine what the FBI would want with me."

The voice strong and confident, and Tom visualized Horowitz wearing a puzzled expression, but still in command of the situation. He was dealing with a powerful personality and could not afford to make a mistake.

"Merely a routine inquiry, Doctor. The FBI is investigating the incidents surrounding Professor Larry Krafter and the attempt to frame him for murder. You must have heard about it. His discovery has generated considerable controversy in the paleoanthropological field, and as the IAS President, your organization has been particularly vocal in denouncing his find."

"You're suggesting that we're behind those incidents?"

"Not at all, Doctor. Some of your members have expressed strong opposition to Professor Krafter, personally and professionally. I wanted to ask whether you might have heard something said in a heated moment, which could suggest that someone was prepared to do more than simply denounce Professor Krafter publicly."

After a few moments of silence, Horowitz cleared his throat. "I had a call from Dr. Norginson about your investigation, Mr. Meecham. If you're looking for a confession or a revelation, I cannot help you. I won't deny that the IAS views Professor Krafter's discovery as a sham. At best, the young man was duped, but that hardly translates into murder."

"Perhaps, but your CEO, Raymond Kessler, might not have been so squeamish."

"Are you insinuating—"

"I am merely saying, Doctor, you might not know everything that goes on within your organization."

"We want to discredit Professor Krafter, and still seek to do so, but I resent your allegation that it was anything more than that."

"I want to give you some informal advice, if I may. In the course of our investigation, if we discover that IAS was instrumental in organized murder, even though you may not have been involved personally, you could be facing a charge as an accessory after the fact. I would talk to a lawyer, if I were you, Doctor."

"You dare…you dare suggest that I, or the organization I built from nothing, and which is now recognized as an authority on anthropology world over, would stoop to something so monstrous?"

"I'm not suggesting anything. The FBI is investigating a murder case and IAS has a motive. I can understand professional rivalry and jealousy, but when it descends to threatening someone's life and the life of those around him, that's clearly stepping over the line."

"What are you talking about?"

"Krafter was warned that if he didn't denounce his discovery, his girlfriend would be killed."

"It's a lie!"

"I'm telling you this to emphasize what someone is willing to do to silence Professor Krafter. Thanks for your time, Doctor."

Pleased with himself, Tom picked up his mug and headed for the kitchenette, confident that Horowitz and Kessler were going to have a lot to talk about. When he got back to the office, he checked the time: 8:52. That would be 6:52 in Denver and Briggs should be up by now. If not, this would wake him up. He reached for the phone and dialed.

"Special Agent Julian Briggs," the agent answered promptly.

"It's Meecham. Sorry for the early call—"

"Don't worry about it. I was just about to head for the office."

"What's the latest with Miss Spiteri?"

"She's due to take the eight-o-two flight for Denver and we'll meet her when she gets here. Arrangements are done for Krafter's parents and they'll be on their way later today. I can't tell you where they're going, but they'll see a lot of ocean and tropical islands."

"I'm sure they'll enjoy themselves," Tom said, wishing he were going.

"With Uncle Sam footing the bill, I hope so. Miss Spiteri should be out of Denver tomorrow and on her little junket within a couple of days."

"More tropical islands?"

"And coconuts. I wouldn't mind being with her. I've seen her picture."

"Set your hormones into neutral, Agent Briggs. The FBI is supposed to be a professional organization."

"Can't shoot a man for fantasizing a little."

"They haven't passed a law against it yet. That's not why I called. Krafter's protection team are on their way to Laramie and should arrive around one this afternoon. I'll forward you the details as soon as I get 'em."

"Thanks. They probably won't be needed, but right now, I don't know what our man will do."

"Perhaps Krafter's detractors still only want to disgrace him, but events have moved against them, and the tide of public and professional opinion has turned. If Krafter won't denounce his discovery, they might as well get rid of him. That's what I would do."

"Well, it can't hurt to have your guys there. You want me to call him?"

"As soon as I send you the details. Until they get there, call Sheriff Ramanof and ask him to put a plainclothes detective on Krafter. I'd hate to have our man get in a quick one. Of course, we could be spinning our wheels here and overreacting, but we don't want to risk losing him, not when we're so close to getting our man."

"You got something usable off the cameras?"

"FACE says they'll have the final image for us later today. You'll get a copy."

"I'll pass it on to Ramanof and he can issue an all-points."

"I'm tempted, but better not do that. It could spook our man and drive him underground."

"So what? He's got to know we're hunting him."

"Sure, but he doesn't know that we have a mug shot, and I would prefer to keep him ignorant of that fact. Greenfield is flying out to Phoenix to try and track down the Bersa, and he'll be in Laramie tomorrow to canvas the hotels. With a photo, we've at last got a chance now that someone will positively identify our man."

"You're dreaming. If he's a professional, no way that he'd have stayed at the same hotel twice," Briggs said.

"Agreed, but he's got to be staying at one of them. It's unlikely he slept in his car. Roughing it wouldn't be this man's style."

"Well, it'll keep Greenfield busy. Incidentally, that's a good man you've got. I wouldn't mind having him."

"I'll talk to him about it," Tom promised, not overly surprised by the praise. He had always known that Greenfield was a good field investigator, reminding himself to call Garry Strand on what's happening with the Johnston swap. "Fast work on Miss Spiteri and the Krafters, by the way."

"It reduces the problem by having them out of the way," Briggs said simply and sighed. "All this over some lousy bones. Hardly seems real."

"I know what you mean, but it's real enough for somebody to kill for." Tom hung up and nodded. Perhaps he had been wrong about Briggs. The man moved when it mattered.

* * *

Kessler dashed off his signature on the last letter and slipped it on a pile in his Out tray. He dropped the pen on the desk, sat back and nodded. Administration was one aspect of his job he never liked much—in any of his past jobs. It was important and necessary, but on some days, it got to be a bit too much. This morning, he had an additional incentive to clear the backlog, a lunch meeting with an Intel vice president responsible for all integrated circuit production. Having met the man at BioChip, he respected his hard sense of professionalism and ruthlessness. They were a kindred spirit. To succeed in today's cutthroat marketplace against the likes of Japan, South Korea and the looming Chinese monolith who didn't give a damn about intellectual property or patent infringements, one had to be totally ruthless.

In most companies when it reaches a certain size and inertia, the bean counters and bureaucratic procedures tended to stifle innovation and vigor that made the firm initially prosperous. The paper shufflers wanted security and stability, not risky originality. This was happening to Intel and the VP wanted Kessler on board to help sort it out and prune dead wood. It would mean moving to Santa Clara in California, but the hinted multi-million dollar salary, bonus and options package would make up for any inconvenience. The climate would also be better there.

He was under no illusion regarding the tenability of his current position. Fun while it lasted, he could read the writing. As soon as the Krafter mess was resolved, Horowitz would orchestrate a move by the Executive Committee to demand his resignation. Kessler didn't hold a grudge. It was merely a difference of opinion on how business should be done. Nothing personal, at least not from him.

The phone rang and he pressed the speaker button. "Yes, Brenda?"

"Dr. Ted Horowitz on line two."

Speaking of his nemesis…

"Thanks." Perhaps the call for his resignation might be coming sooner than expected. He pressed a glowing yellow button on the phone pad. "Morning, Ted."

"I'll get right down to the point, Raymond. I just finished talking to the FBI. They know everything!"

Momentarily taken aback, Kessler realized that Horowitz had to be exaggerating. At least a little. The FBI must have asked NSA to provide transcripts of IAS phone records and were rattling his cage. He had done the same thing against competitors. Without solid evidence, he had nothing to worry about.

"Take it easy, Ted. You're jumping at shadows. What exactly did they say?"

"They know about the smear campaign against Professor Krafter, and they as much told me that we tried to pin a murder on him."

"They're fishing, trying to get us unnerved. It won't work because we've got nothing to hide. If they knew something, they would have acted," Kessler said easily.

This was as much for Horowitz's benefit as for the FBI should they try to retrieve this conversation, all part of the price of doing business.

"I wish I could be sure," Horowitz said uncertainly, clearly unsettled. "They also told me that Krafter's girlfriend was threatened. I don't know what's going on, but I'll tell you this one the last time. If you had anything to do with any of it, I want you to stop everything right now. This is not the reputation I want IAS to have. Do I make myself clear?"

Kessler had seen Krafter's announcement on CNN and admired the youngster's pluck.

"Ted, you're upset and overreacting. We're not the only ones who want Krafter out of the way. Our problem is that we've been more vocal about it and the FBI are looking for someone to blame."

"You better be right, because I'll cooperate with them in

every way. I'm not going to be dragged down with you!" Horowitz declared and abruptly cut contact.

After listening to the disconnected line for a few seconds, Kessler switched off. He wasn't worried about Horowitz's threat. A hollow reed as the man knew nothing. He wasn't overly concerned about the FBI either, and any phone transcripts they had were circumstantial evidence at best. The value of his security precautions and keeping aspects of IAS operations undisclosed was now paying dividends.

Although he felt himself beyond the FBI's reach, he had a serious decision to make. He had treated the operation against Krafter like any other the IAS had successfully orchestrated before. Young, inexperienced, idealistic, Krafter would be easily manipulated. At least that's what he believed. Unfortunately, the scientist had shown himself to be unusually resilient and resourceful. The whole thing could have been mopped up nicely had Striker's murder gambit worked. But it didn't, and it was no use hashing over the whys. The thing was, should he keep going?

From what he read and seen on TV, the optimum moment to discredit Krafter and his discovery had passed. There was simply too much credible scientific evidence and professional support behind him to be dismissed out of hand. Even he could see that as a layman. After the announcement Krafter made yesterday, he now also had public sympathy on his side. Although nobody had any proof the IAS was involved, people were talking, none of which did the Society any good. Horowitz was right to be concerned.

Which brought him back to a decision he had to make. He hated to leave a job half done, but his hard business acumen told him that he had reached, and passed, the point of diminishing returns. Besides, it wasn't his fight. Horowitz and the rest of the fuds would have to clean up the mess they had created in the first place. Ruining Krafter at the cost of destroying the IAS wouldn't be smart.

He reached into his jacket pocket, dragged out the HTC PDA, selected the Secure icon from the main menu and dialed. It didn't take long.

"Identify."

"Raven."

"Proceed."

"Report status."

"Krafter's girlfriend took a flight to Denver this morning, accompanied by Laramie PD. I'm assuming that she is now under FBI protection. I'm waiting to see if Krafter will denounce his discovery before taking further action."

Kessler bit his lower lip. He knew that Krafter's parents lived in Denver, and it was possible she would go there to be with them, believing she would be safe. If the FBI were now looking after her, she might not be visiting them at all. What if they spirited her away somewhere, placing her out of Striker's reach?

Diminishing returns...

"Cancel operation," he ordered abruptly.

There was a moment of silence. "Acknowledged."

Kessler cut contact and nodded. He disliked admitting failure, and he didn't blame Striker. Sometimes things simply happen and one had to cut losses.

* * *

Striker scowled deeply as he stared at the silent cellphone. After a moment, he pocketed the device and let out a sigh.

"Crap!"

Just when he was about to close the assignment, 'Raven' had gotten cold feet and bailed out. Professionally, he understood his client's position. With successive setbacks, small in themselves, the risk factors had accumulated to a point where everybody was now potentially vulnerable. That was the key, *potentially* vulnerable.

Despite the hiccups, and some of them were of his own making, he had to admit, in all respects the operation was still doable, but not for much longer, not with the FBI now on the scene. He didn't know what resources were pitted against him, minimal if only the Denver Division was involved, but if Washington was on the case, he had a limited window of opportunity before inertia tipped the balance in their favor. Anyway, it was a moot point now. The smart thing to do would be to text Raven the bill and walk away. He'll definitely text the bill, but walking away?

Every professional instinct told him the job was over and he *should* move on. With his Denver assignment done successfully, he was due back at TriCon. It would be a mug's game to take failure personally, especially for such a small job. Random factors had not favored him and it was useless hashing over the circumstances. The bottom line? He had screwed up by being careless and underestimating his opposition, always fatal in his line of work, although in this case, not terminally so. Shit happens.

Unfortunately, he did take this failure personally, and there was still time to retrieve the situation, provided he took prompt and decisive action. He was dealing with an amateur, but one who so far had enjoyed all the breaks. This time, no more freebies. Once done, he would fly to New York and reenter his public persona, the trail swept clean after him.

It was simple. He hated being sloppy, and he hated the idea that his client believed he had been sloppy. That kind of thing tended to filter through the select community of underground operatives, marking him a leper. And that would never do. However, by continuing, he *would* be stepping outside the understood rules. Without perfection and pride in his work, he was nothing.

One final hit on Krafter and he would be out of Laramie and its squabbling academics.

As he stared down from the first floor of his hotel at traffic moving steadily along 3rd Street, despite his psychoanalysis, his professional part warned him that what he contemplated was dumb. Emotion had no place in his work. Should he walk down that path once, his judgment would become forever suspect. Besides, it went against everything he had been trained. Training or not, he was more than a mere killing machine. He had emotions and feelings.

The traffic whispered below him.

He would assess the situation and make his decision on site, conceding that much to his professional alter ego. With his girlfriend safely out of the way, it made little sense now waiting for Krafter to make a media announcement. The professor had reacted quickly to his threat, or been advised what to do, prepared for Striker to make the next move. He had been ready to kill Miss Spiteri, but he wasn't quite so keen to pursue her all over Denver, not with Krafter around representing a much softer and preferred target.

Getting to him was merely choosing from a variety of options, depending on how quickly he wanted to get this done. With the decision made, Striker moved. Glancing at his watch, he nodded: 11:10. By the time he walked to the university, Krafter would be thinking about having lunch at Turtle Rock Coffee, his usual haunt. With lots of people milling about, he shouldn't have any difficulty getting close to his target. Even if he missed him this time, he was sure to find the troublesome academic at home tonight.

He checked his peppery hair and goatee add-ons, slipped into a bulky black leather jacket, and retrieved a Glock 17, 9mm semiautomatic from his carry bag. He screwed on the silencer, chambered a round and slid the now ungainly weapon into a special holster under his armpit. It would be more convenient to carry the thing without a silencer, but when it came to the business end, there might not be time to fumble about trying to attach it.

He closed the door to his room and walked down the faded gray carpet toward the stairs, ignoring the elevator that served the basic Travelodge. Although used to more luxurious accommodation, he had no complaints, having experienced far worse. Outside, the wind had cleared yesterday's clouds and feeble sunshine cast sharp shadows. Ignoring the garish blue hotel sign mounted on two poles beside the road, he started walking toward the intersection. At University Avenue, he turned left.

By the time he got to 9th Street with its cafés and the university sprawl on his left, he was pleasantly warm. Only 11:23, he decided to meet Krafter as he came out of the Anthropology Building. He turned left and headed toward E. Lewis Street. Three blocks up, he walked right onto Lewis. Being a nice day, lots of students wandered up and down, singly or chatting in small groups. At 12th Street, the modern Anthropology Building on his right shone in noon light. Still early, Striker continued to stroll down Lewis.

By the time he got back, it was 11:55. He slowly strolled around, keeping the glass entrance under observation, and waited for his target to emerge. Shortly after twelve, a steady stream of students made their way out. When Krafter appeared, a large man in a dark blue suit at his elbow, Striker slowly nodded, reconsidering his position. He had no doubts about taking out the professor, but he would also have to deal with the plainclothes detective or FBI man, for that's what the shadow had to be. His bearing, carefully searching eyes and attentive manner, stamped him in the mold. Striker could kill him, but he had little desire to do that. Krafter was the target, and collecting more collateral damage along the way would be a beginner's move, and messy.

He discreetly followed the two as they headed up Lewis Street. At 9th, they both turned left and he smiled. They seemed to be heading for Turtle Rock Coffee, all right. They reached the popular eatery and went in. Striker walked past the crowded restaurant and glanced through the high plate glass window. The serving counter was busy and the available small square tables scattered around the floor were full. With nowhere to sit, people would have to take their meal and scram. Krafter stood beside the counter waiting for his order. Striker turned and slowly checked his surroundings. The sidewalk was taken up by students hanging about, talking, eating sandwiches and hot tidbits, and others trying to get through the crush.

He reached for the Glock, keeping it hidden behind his jacket, and flipped off the safety. Positioning himself close to the entrance, he waited as teenagers walked in or tried to push out. Some of them gave him indifferent glances, but nobody paid him any attention. After a couple of minutes, the suited man came out and held the door open for Krafter. Two slim girls, talking hurriedly, immediately pushed through just as Krafter emerged. He paused and smiled at them.

Surrounded by bodies, Striker didn't hesitate. He squeezed past the suited man, lowered the handgun under his jacket and pressed the silencer against Krafter's side. Someone jostled his arm just as he pulled the trigger, the sound of the shot a muffled *thuft*. He saw Krafter stagger, but did not wait to watch him fall. He pushed the gun into the holster and strode past the suited man still looking at the two girls, oblivious to what had happened. Someone screamed then, but Striker kept walking, the sidewalk full enough for him not to stand out. At E. Clark Street, he turned left, the commotion safely behind him. He didn't know whether his shot had been fatal, and there was nothing he could do about it now. Fatal or not, he was definitely done here. Lingering now to make sure of his target would not be wise.

Striker hurried up the relatively quiet avenue toward 3rd Street and the Travelodge, wondering if he could catch the 1:54 p.m. Great Lakes Airlines flight to Denver.

He would not charge Raven for this hit.

* * *

With the Phoenix downtown skyline looming over trees and

buildings almost within touching distance, standing outside the noisy Sky Harbor Airport domestic terminal, waiting for the complimentary hotel van to arrive, Greenfield nodded stoically. He didn't mind the flying part, it was the dull hanging around in between that wore him down. Although the four-hour-forty-minute flight from Washington was pleasant enough, and the business class seat made it even more so, he would be cramped to catch the US Airways 10:50 a.m. departure time. On the ground now, he wanted to get on with it.

He reminded himself that he could be back in his office, bull-pen actually, shuffling papers and not liking it much. He had done a fair bit of legwork in Laramie and enjoyed the little interlude in Boston. Briggs thought his performance deserved a 'well done' and said so. He must have told Meecham, for the boss trusted him enough to send him out again. His intelligence thinker-upper skills might not be on par with Slater's, but as an investigator, Greenfield knew he was as good as anybody. Besides, how hard can it be to find a gun?

So why had he accepted a post with the Strategic Assessment and Analysis Unit in the first place, especially since it was only an in between assignments thing? The mystique of counterterrorism work? He had no ready answer and it bothered him. By sending him into the field, was Meecham trying to get rid of him? Probably, as he certainly wasn't doing anything worthwhile in Washington.

The air smelled of jet fuel, oily car exhaust and dry sand. Somewhere behind him, an aircraft was taking off and the air shook with its roar. People waited patiently in the taxi queue for their turn at a Yellow or Allstate cab to take them to wherever they were going. A Sheraton Phoenix white van pulled in beside the hotel pickup sign and a waiting gaggle surged in as soon as the driver slid open the door, then spent a minute piling in luggage. A cop waved angrily at a black limo double-parked beside a bus. Greenfield watched the people around him, most of them wearing the same vacant expressions, not looking forward to lining up at a check-in queue for their flight out or too weary to be glad they made it to solid ground.

A light blue minivan, painted with a beige SpringHill Suites Marriott logo, squealed to a stop in front of him. Taking his time, the driver slowly got out, walked around and opened the door, not minding the cars and cabs streaming past. Greenfield threw his bag across the seat, climbed in and the driver pulled the door shut with a clang, cutting the outside noises. The van jerked and moved out, mindful of pedestrians crossing where they had no business crossing. The driver got into E. Buckeye Road and, after about a mile, turned right into S. 7th Street.

Despite the skyscrapers and the sprawl, Phoenix had an unfinished frontier look so different from the dense unorganized crush of cities back East. Greenfield didn't philosophize about it, accepting it as simply another fact.

The ride slowed as they hit downtown proper and the traffic could have been anywhere. Turning right into Van Buren Street, the van cut across the road almost immediately and pulled into a side driveway under the hotel's heavy red brick portico. The entire ground floor was red brick and the remaining five floors rose into a clear sky, the solid façade painted dull beige.

This time, the driver hurried to open the door. Greenfield handed him a fiver and got out. With a nod, the driver climbed back into the van. Indicator flashing, he roared down the driveway into the street. Greenfield smiled, wondering if he had to go back to the airport. It was a hell of a way to make a living. Lugging his bulky bag, he walked into the lobby. Like the rest of the hotel, it gave the impression of solidity and permanence, unlike the slick modernism of a Hilton or Sheraton. He didn't care. He was sleeping over, not buying the place.

He strode across the hard olive-green carpet and made his way to the heavy Reservations counter, fronted by dark red wood paneling. The walls were beige, the large fireplace was beige and even the ceiling had an off-white look. It looked like beige was the color of the day here.

A slim young woman dressed in a black business suit looked up from her computer and smiled.

"Welcome to SpringHill Suites, sir."

"Thank you," Greenfield said, eased the bag to the floor and produced his booking reservation printout.

The girl took the page, flashed him another smile and bent over her keyboard. Satisfied, she walked toward him and held out a small cardboard folder.

"Your key, sir. Room 104. Do you need help with your bag?"

Greenfield took the card. "No, thanks." He glanced at the round wall clock behind her. Even though it was only 1:26 here, his body told him it was much later than that, having gained three hours jumping time zones, and he was hungry. "Say, is this place open for lunch?"

"Sorry, sir. Breakfast and dinner only, but there is a nice English pub restaurant just around the corner on 7th Street, Rose & Crown. Turn right as you exit the hotel, then left into 7th. It's only a couple of hundred yards."

"Thanks, I'll try it."

"Enjoy your stay."

He nodded and headed for the stairs. The olive-green carpeting along the long corridor on the first floor muffled his footsteps. His room, like all the décor, had a worn beige look. Everything had a beige tinge, even the bed sheets. He dropped his bag next to a small round table tucked into a corner, washed his hands and face, and walked out.

Van Buren Street was busy with traffic and pedestrians. He found the little pub restaurant without trouble and the dark interior indeed had an old English atmosphere, including a Union Jack on the wall. He took a corner table and ordered Aunty Shirley's sausage rolls and a St. Mary's pale ale. He sipped his beer and glanced around at his fellow connoisseurs. Most were business types. A few leaned against the bar for moral support, nursing drinks. After about ten minutes, the waitress impartially slid a large plate in front of him, including the bill. He nodded to her, added ketchup, and got stuck into tender sausages wrapped in puff pastry. It was a great meal, if plain, made better with his hunger providing added sauce. He finished his now cool beer, picked up the bill, left notes on the table and walked out. Time for some paid work.

Outside, ready to tackle the world, not feeling at all tired, it took only a moment to flag down a passing Yellow Cab. He took the front seat and buckled in as the driver waited patiently.

"Where you headed?" the cabbie demanded in a clipped voice like he didn't give a damn, and probably didn't.

"Mo Money Pawn on East Indian School Road," Greenfield told him and the driver's eyes lit up.

"Hey, if you're after some serious hardware, Arizona Tactical is the place to go."

"Mo Money," Greenfield said. The driver shrugged and eased the cab from the curb.

Traffic, buildings, shops; Greenfield didn't pay attention. He had seen cities, and apart from a specific attraction or two, they were all the same: noisy, smelly and crowded. As they turned right into N. 16th Street, a white Phoenix PD Holden Caprice roared by, its lights flickering. Other cars obediently made room for it.

After what seemed a long time, the cab turned left into East Indian School Road, the neighborhood looking used and seedy. The driver stopped in front of a single-story brick building and fiddled with the meter. A heavy steel grill protected tall windows on either side of the entrance. Greenfield could see all types of weapons displayed inside. He undid the seatbelt and opened the door.

"Wait for me."

"You got it," the driver said and switched off the engine.

Inside the large shop, smelling of leather and gun oil, the walls were festooned with rifles, handguns and military-type hardware. A kid in loose black jeans, baseball cap turned backward, black T-shirt sporting a white skull and crossbones on the back, looked up from a glass display case of handguns and resumed his inspection. Greenfield walked to the counter where a bald elderly man sat reading a *Soldier of Fortune* magazine. A dripping red heart with a knife stuck through it shifted on the man's left bicep as he flipped a page. He glanced up, his dark brown eyes expressionless.

"Yeah?"

Greenfield reached into his jacket and pulled out his ID. "FBI. I have a few questions for you."

The kid's head jerked, and with a sidewise glance at Greenfield, he hurried out. The man behind the counter slowly stood up. He looked only about five-foot-nine, but his solid build and wary stance showed he could take care of himself. A semi-automatic protruded from a holster on his hip. Well, it was a frontier town, Greenfield figured.

"What can I do for you? You aren't from the local office, are ya? I know most of the guys there."

"I'm from DC. We're trying to trace a gun you bought from one Toni Andrini about four months ago. A Bersa Thunder .380 ACP. I want to know who you sold it to."

"A Bersa, eh?" The man scratched his head and grinned. "Hey, I remember one of your guys calling me about it the other day."

"And you brushed him off."

"Is that why you're here? To lean on me?"

"This is a murder investigation, and unless you want to be charged with obstruction, or maybe even conspiracy to commit, I would suggest that you cooperate. Simple enough for you?"

The man scowled. "Pushy, aren't ya? But, look, I don't remember every piece I sell or whom I sell it to. A guy walks in and wants to buy a gun. As long as he's got an ID, he's got a gun. All legal."

"But you're required to take down the details of his driver's license, or whatever ID the customer used. You're also required to record the type of weapon he bought, serial number and the date you sold it." Greenfield glanced at the LED screen behind the counter. "If you simply told us what we wanted when we called, you'd have saved me a trip. Since I had to come here, and my ass is still asleep from sitting on a concrete airplane seat, I don't care if I'm pushy, okay?"

"Hey! Take it easy! No sweat, man. I'll check it out, but sometimes, well, not everything gets written down, if you know what I mean."

"I sure do. I hope you have this particular transaction written down. Otherwise, I'd have to take a closer look at how you run this shop. All kinds of people might be interested, like the IRS, for instance."

The man eyed Greenfield's muscled form, then smiled. "No need to get riled, Mister. I'll do what I can, but I'll need more than a make to find the thing for you."

Greenfield reached into his pocket and held out a Post-It note. "Serial number."

Frowning, the man took the note and slid down behind the computer. After some keyboard clicking, he smiled and looked up.

"Guess this is your lucky day. Got the details right here. Want a printout?"

"If you wouldn't mind."

A moment later the man stood up and held out a sheet of paper. Greenfield glanced at it, folded it and slipped it into his jacket.

"Thanks, I appreciate it. You perhaps happen to remember what the guy who bought the gun looked like?

The man stared at him. "After four months? You're kidding.

Say, you wouldn't be interested in a gun yourself, would you? I've got some nice hardware here, a Glock for instance? Since you guys are into that kind of thing these days. I can give it to you cheap. If you're after real penetration power, I've got that too."

Greenfield smiled and shook his head. "I've got a piece already, but I'll keep your offer in mind if I'm this way again. Catch you later."

He walked out, still smiling, and got into the cab.

"All done?" the driver asked indifferently, starting the engine.

"All done. Take me to the FBI building on East Indianola Avenue."

"Trouble?"

"Merely poking at things," Greenfield told him and sat back. The driver nodded and eased the cab into the street.

"We're not far from there. It's practically around the corner."

The cab crossed N. Central Avenue and turned right into N. 2nd Street, and they were there. It stopped in front of a blocky building, tall palms swaying along the sidewalk. Greenfield again told the driver to wait.

"It's your money," the man said comfortably.

Inside the air-conditioned foyer, Greenfield walked to the reception window built into the wall. The plainclothes youngster shuffling papers inside looked up.

"Can I help you, sir?"

Greenfield showed him his badge and the youngster stood up. "This shouldn't take long. I need a photo ID and current address on a driver's license."

The kid looked at him. "You came all the way from Washington for a photo ID?"

Greenfield chuckled. "Sounds strange when you say it like that, doesn't it? But if I had the ID when I was there, I certainly wouldn't have bothered coming to your charming town."

Not sure if Greenfield was pulling his leg, the kid shrugged.

"Well, I can bring everything up on my terminal. You got the details?"

Greenfield gave him the gun shop printout and waited. After a few minutes the youngster looked up.

"Karl Brenner, sixty-two, but the man's dead. Died over a year ago."

"You got a mug shot of the license?"

"Sure." A second later the kid held out the printout.

The man in the photo had peppery hair and a neat goatee. His eyebrows were thick and black, and the eyes stared from beneath prominent ridges. The face strong and determined, it looked exactly like one of the computer images Slats gave him this morning. He certainly wasn't sixty-two.

He had his man, confirmation at least that he bought the Bersa and planted it on Professor Krafter. The guy appeared to be walking around behind a stolen identity, but it didn't matter. He had their first real break. Well, second if he counted the computer photos. Meecham would be pleased.

Having got what he came for, there wasn't much point hanging around Phoenix. If he stayed, he would be wasting a better part of tomorrow simply getting to Laramie when he might be able to get there tonight. It would definitely make for a long day, but that came with the territory. He lowered the printout and stared at the youngster.

"Can you check available flights to Laramie for me, please? Either direct or via Denver."

"There aren't any direct flights, but there are lots of connections to Denver, every ten or twenty minutes," the young agent told him as he sat behind the computer. After a few moments, he looked up. "The last Great Lakes Airlines leaves Denver at 7:15 p.m. local time, but you'd have to catch a flight out of here by four."

Greenfield glanced at his watch: 3:28 p.m. There was no way he could get back to the hotel, check out and reach the airport in time. He sighed and his shoulders sagged, resigned at the prospect of spending the night in Phoenix after all. Perhaps he could do half the trip.

"What's the first flight from Denver to Laramie?"

"Let's see…ten-thirty in the morning."

"Okay, book me a seat. Also, I need a flight to Denver for tonight."

"The closest available one is at four-fifty with Southwest and gets there at seven-fifty. The other one is with Frontier, but it doesn't leave until six."

"I'll take the four-fifty." If he took the later one, he would really be beat by the time he got to Denver.

"I'll need an expense code," the youngster said apologetically.

Greenfield reached into his back pocket and pulled out his wallet. He extracted a card Meecham gave him and held it out. The youngster copied down the number and nodded.

"I'll notify Southwest that you'll pick up the ticket at the airport. You'll be able to do the same thing with Great Lakes tomorrow."

"That's great, and thanks."

"Not a problem."

Knowing he had done a good job, Greenfield walked out, hurried to the cab and got in.

"Take me to the SpringHill Suites hotel, please."

"You got it!"

Chapter Nine

PROFESSOR KRAFTER WOUNDED AND INNOCENT GIRL DEAD

VENDETTA AGAINST KRAFTER TURNS DEADLY

FBI SETS A CORDON AROUND KRAFTER

IAS DENIES INVOLVEMENT IN KRAFTER SHOOTING

BOLLINGER ACCUSED OF STEALING ANCIENT HAND BONE

AAA TO REVIEW MAN'S EVOLUTION

Krafter shifted and winced as the bandages pulled at his wounds. They had loaded him with painkiller and his side didn't hurt much. The drawback was that he would have to sleep on his back or left side, which he hated. He wasn't complaining, considering himself lucky. Luckier than he realized, the surgeon told him, but as a walking wounded, he wouldn't mind a bit of gratuitous sympathy.

Feeble sunshine slanted through gauzy curtains, brightening an otherwise depressing room. Apart from the hospital smells, he could be in a hotel. The décor was the same. There was one cheery side to his predicament. Now that he had been shot, he could lay back and relax. With grim Laramie PD hovering in the corridor, he doubted the man in black would be back anytime soon. No guarantees, but whoever gave the orders was not likely to push this further; not after this latest incident hits the media. At least he hoped so. He might have been shot, but the fundamentals of his position had not changed. They have now become merely more serious.

The scene kept replaying in his mind: students pressing around him, the sudden searing fire in his side, and a moment later, someone screaming and he felt himself sagging to the ground. Although his side burned, he did not feel pain anywhere else, probably shock. He wondered how long it would take him to die. A gut shot was always bad news. There was so much he still wanted to do and say, especially to Elena. At least she was safe. She was safe…

Despite what he heard and read, life did not flash before him, and there were bits he wouldn't care to repeat. Clutching his side, warm blood oozing between his fingers, Krafter slowly realized that he wasn't going to die, and felt a flood of relief. He had been given a reprieve and a chance to fix some things. Then he saw the glazed expression of the girl beside him and whatever color was left in his face drained. Another girl was kneeling beside her, sobbing quietly. Others stood frozen, gaping at the suddenness of it all.

His plainclothes minder bent over him, checked his side and gripped his shoulder, looking a bit pale himself.

"Take it easy, it doesn't look bad. I'll call an ambulance."

"What about her?" Krafter gasped, indicating with his head.

The detective shrugged and Krafter felt nauseous. It should have been him, not an innocent bystander. Although he regretted what happened to the girl, he was also thankful it wasn't him. It was plain bad luck that she got caught up in this. He knew he shouldn't feel guilty, but he did, at least a little.

The ambulance came wailing and the bystanders made way. A paramedic slapped pressure bandages on his entry and exit wounds, while another jabbed him in the arm with a ridiculously long needle. Then he was lifted onto a gurney and wheeled in. The drive to Ivinson Memorial took minutes, and the last thing he remembered was a green-robed nurse putting a black mask over his face.

It seemed like a lifetime ago.

He reached for a glass of water on the small bedside cabinet and took a long drink. The surgeon told him he would be thirsty.

They gave him whole blood to replace what had leaked out, but he needed to build up his plasma. Beside the pitcher of water lay his wallet, watch and cellphone. Looking at the cellphone, leaving it was either a mistake or they figured he was well enough to use it.

He glanced out the window, but could not tell what time it was. Judging by the light, it appeared to be late afternoon. A knock on the door made him look up. He frowned when a dark suited man peered in.

"Professor Krafter? I'm Frank Ross, FBI. We'll be looking after you from now on. There is a Dr. Perkins outside wanting to see you."

"Please show him in."

Perkins appeared in the doorway, hesitated, and Krafter broke into a wide smile.

"Adam!"

Perkins grinned and closed the door. He checked out the room with a sweeping glance, dragged up a chair and sat down.

"If this isn't the lousiest reason for skipping lectures, I don't know what is."

Krafter made a face and patted the bed. "I'd be happy to swap places with you anytime."

"How's the side?"

"They tell me I'll live. The bullet got me above the kidney and below the ribs. It's a shallow wound and nothing vital was touched. In surgery, they basically just stitched up the holes."

"You were fortunate."

"A couple of inches farther in and I'd be feeling somewhat different."

"I can imagine. How long will you be laid up?"

"Hopefully not too long, but they tell me it'll be at least ten days before I'll be able to get back to light work."

"I wouldn't worry about it."

"You got Wethermans taking my classes?"

Perkins smiled. "He came bitching, but I squelched him. By the way, Dr. Larson sends his best."

Krafter raised an eyebrow. "Thanks. Tell him I appreciate it. I also appreciate you coming over."

"I almost didn't get in, what with reporters and cops hovering outside. You're big news again, Larry."

"Shit! I don't want to be big news. Not like this."

"You'll simply have to tough it. Are you in a lot of pain?"

"It's not bad. They've got me doped up, but it hurts when I think about it."

"Psychosomatic reaction," Perkins said sagely and nodded. He glanced at his watch and stood up. "They told me five minutes only. It's good to see you're not badly hurt."

Krafter didn't mention the girl, and from his mentor's look, Perkins didn't want to either.

"I'll see you later," Perkins said and walked out.

"Thanks for coming, Adam. Bring me a book next time!" Krafter called after him.

He leaned back against the pillows. Did the man in black go after him because Elena was out of reach? Or did he tired of the game and decided to finish it? It didn't matter, not now. He closed his eyes and listened to the silence.

His cellphone trilled and his eyes snapped open. He reached with his left hand and groped for the device.

"Krafter."

"So the rumors are true. You *are* alive," Reed said lightly and Krafter smiled.

"It's all true, including the bad parts."

"How are you?"

"Better than the girl standing behind me."

"I heard. Tough break, but don't beat yourself up over it. It wasn't your fault."

"I know what you're saying, Neil, but right now, it doesn't help. My mind is churning over 'what if' like I'm on a treadmill."

"Talk to a trauma counselor. It sounds corny, but they can help."

"I'll think about it. Say, isn't it rather late where you are?"

"A reporter's day never ends. You okay to talk? I don't want to tire you out or anything."

"I'm fine, and thanks for the call."

"I have to admit to a dual motive, doc. I was genuinely concerned about you, but I am also after a story. A lot of stuff is flying around the airways, and I suspect most of it is made up, like you were shot in the spine and paralyzed. I thought you might want to give me an exclusive."

Krafter laughed, then gasped as pain lanced through his side. Reed had turned into a real friend and stuck by him when many would not have, but he had to keep reminding himself the man was also a hardnosed reporter, and getting a story by whatever means probably came first.

"I'll tell you what I know. You'll have to fill in the blanks yourself."

"Deal."

Krafter went over his story, reliving every savage moment. Finished, he realized that both had been silent for several seconds.

"I appreciate the human angle, Larry," Reed said softly. "It'll make good copy. I'm also hoping it will make the people behind this sit up and reconsider."

"I'm hoping the FBI will nail the sons of bitches and string them up," Krafter hissed, venting emotion and frustration.

"I'll talk to Briggs and see what's going on at his end. Have you heard from him?"

"Not yet, but I'm sure he'll be calling. He's got an FBI man outside my door, so it appears they're serious about looking after me."

"Too bad they hadn't thought of doing that before you were shot."

"Yeah, it would have helped."

"Well, don't do anything strenuous and I'll talk to you later."

When Reed hung up, Krafter sipped more water. He closed his eyes and began to pleasantly drift, thinking about having something to eat, when the phone rang again. Tempted to dump it in the pitcher, he picked up.

"Krafter."

"Larry! Are you okay? I've been going out of my mind here!" Elena gushed and Krafter could hear the raw emotion in her voice. He saw her face swim before him and his features softened.

"I'm fine, beautiful, truly."

"Briggs just called and I thought I would simply die. You stay put and I'll see you tomorrow."

"Elena! You're not doing any such thing. Do you want to end up beside me, or worse?"

After a few tense seconds, he heard her sigh.

"Do you think I care?" she asked softly and sniffed.

"I care, and you know it. The worst is over."

"How do you know? How do you know anything?"

"I don't, but the man in black has slipped up badly by not getting me. I'm not complaining, mind you. He won't be trying again. At least I'm hoping he won't. Anyway, I'm surrounded by cops and there's an FBI agent hovering outside my room. What can happen?"

"How badly are you hurt? Briggs only said that you were shot through the side."

"It's a flesh wound, except it's under the skin. The CT scan is clean and there is no organ damage."

"Thank God!"

"Enjoying the sun, sand and surf?" Krafter asked, trying to lift the atmosphere, and imagined he could see her smile.

"I'm still in Denver packing. They won't tell me where they're sending me. I'm scheduled to leave this evening."

"I wouldn't mind joining you."

"If only you could," she whispered and his throat tightened.

"When this is over," he promised. "Love you."

"You're a dope, Larry Krafter," she said gruffly and hung up.

Krafter placed the cellphone on the side cabinet and smiled.

* * *

Kessler closed the email screen, sat back and nodded. Yale had canceled its membership, and that made it four major universities this week. He didn't worry about the small fry, but losing the likes of Cornell and Caltech hurt. Those were influential institutions, trendsetters that others followed and took their cues off. They were also important financial pillars for the Society, something Prowse had pointed out a number of times in his severe, irritating manner. As though that was a revelation, Kessler thought. Pushing a point of ideology was one thing, but the IAS wouldn't be able to push anything if its reputation was trashed, never mind becoming insolvent.

Fluffy clouds outside had taken on a faint orange hue as the sun rose above the Manhattan skyline. Right then, he didn't want to worry about the Society's diminishing membership base or its potentially shaky financial position. The situation wasn't that dire yet. Prowse couldn't see it and Horowitz was stuck in a mental rut to accept the futility of what he and the others were doing. And it was so easy to fix.

All it would take is a simple announcement saying that the Society would objectively review Professor Krafter's discovery and present its findings in due course, which meant comfortably in the future. The glare of public focus would shift to something else and Krafter would be forgotten. Plenty of time then to quietly bury him and his bones. But like an author wedded to his work, unwilling to cut out a bad piece of writing, the Executive Committee were obtusely blind to the self-destructive nature of their position. The aim was to hang on and survive. Kessler only had to look at what that idiot Bollinger did to himself to prove his point.

So far, the Committee had not cared to listen. Well, if the situation came to a confrontation, the Intel job was his if he wanted it. Horowitz wouldn't have to ask for his resignation. Kessler had reached a point where he would be happy to leave right now. As somebody said, a change was as good as a holiday.

A knock on the door made him look up. Brenda walked in carrying newspapers. She placed them on his desk and picked up the empty coffee mug.

"These just came in." Without saying anything else, she slipped out.

Kessler glanced at the bold headlines, then stared in dismay. He grabbed the *New York Post* and unfolded the paper.

Krafter shot and a bystander killed?

He quickly skimmed the column and threw the paper onto the desk in disgust. Reed's article in *The New York Times* provided more information, but no new revelations. No, this couldn't be happening.

He reached for the HTC phone and pressed Secure, then dialed.

"Identify."

"Raven."

"Proceed," Striker's electronic voice answered.

Kessler gripped the PDA and forced himself to relax. Perhaps it was simply a random campus shooting...

"Did you attempt to terminate Krafter?"

"That was outside my terms of reference and none of your concern. There is no associated fee."

Kessler ground his teeth. "I ordered you to stop all action."

"As far as you were involved, I did that."

"This was personal? You were recommended because you never got personally involved."

"I didn't go after the target for personal reasons, but professional considerations."

"Because you failed with the body plant? You've compromised the entire operation!"

Striker didn't say anything.

Kessler took a deep breath and let it out slowly. "Your services are terminated. No further action is to be taken against Krafter under any circumstances, professional or otherwise. Are we clear?"

"Understood."

Kessler cut contact, tempted to throw the PDA against the wall. Instead, he placed it on the desk and sent his fist crashing against the polished surface. Fists clenched, he stood up and paced, wanting to lash out at anything that came within reach.

A knock on the door stopped him. Brenda came in holding his mug. "Is everything all right?"

"No, everything is not all right," Kessler told her, "but I wouldn't worry about it."

"Maybe this will help." She walked toward him, stopped and held out the mug.

He grinned, took it and sipped. It did help. "Thanks. No interruptions for a while, okay? I've got some things to do."

"Very good." She nodded and softly closed the door after her.

He glanced at the closed door and nodded. Good girl, that. He reminded himself to ask if she would care to work for Intel. An efficient personal assistant was worth her weight in emeralds, and Brenda was the best he'd had.

Kessler stood before the wide window and gazed at the morning traffic moving along the Avenue of the Americas. Many of the cars still had their headlights on as they made their way down the dark concrete canyon. The jutting skyscrapers glowed from internal lighting and gave the skyline a dreamy quality, almost unreal, removed from the harsh truths they contained.

What Striker did was unexpected and disappointing, especially since he failed. He even understood why it was done, but he paid for a straightforward job, devoid of any emotional element. That Striker would allow a personal consideration to override his professional judgment revealed him to be a flawed tool, regardless how highly recommended.

"Idiot," he said softly and sipped his coffee.

The damage done, it was useless hashing over it now. Time to pick up the pieces and move on. The phone rang and he looked at his desk, a frown creasing his brow. He walked to the desk and pressed the speaker button.

"What is it, Brenda?"

"I'm sorry for the interruption, but Dr. Horowitz is on line two."

"Thank you."

Well, not entirely unexpected. He moved around the desk, sat down, and pressed a glowing yellow button.

"I imagine you saw the headlines, Ted."

"What the hell is going on, Raymond?" Horowitz demanded, his anger palpable. "Were you responsible for this fiasco?"

"I had nothing to do with it," Kessler said truthfully.

"But you ordered it done."

"I haven't ordered anything, and I'm just as shocked as you are."

"I don't believe you."

"Right now, I frankly don't give a damn. We're faced with a much more pressing problem, and this incident could have given us a way out."

"What are you talking about?"

"You've missed your window to nail Professor Krafter, and I again urge you to rethink your stance. The Executive Committee's position has become untenable and is endangering the Society."

"That's your professional opinion, I suppose?"

"You don't want to throw away what's been achieved to date on an arguable point of ideology."

"Ideology? Let me put it in terms that even you will understand. What if you told everybody that Stonehenge was built by the Egyptians? You would be a laughing stock. Krafter's discovery is equally ridiculous."

"He has science behind him, Ted," Kessler pointed out gently.

"Bah! A matter of interpretation. You're a layman and don't understand. You don't dictate policy for the Society," Horowitz shot back.

"No, I don't. But you're forgetting the reason why you brought me in. I turned your gentleman's club into a real force, which you're now destroying."

"We just sit back and simply accept Krafter's discovery, is that what you're recommending?"

"Not accept, but influence its impact on the Society and the paleoanthropological community at large. Our hardline stance has become counterproductive and it's time for new tactics."

"I shall take your suggestion under advisement. Getting back to the matter at hand, I cannot prove that you ordered this unwarranted level of retaliation against Krafter, but I don't need proof. You've done this thing before and we all closed our eyes while you did it. That was a mistake on everybody's part. This time, you've gone way beyond what the Committee authorized. I'm calling a special Executive session where I'll demand your resignation."

"Your privilege, but you're making a grave mistake. Despite what I told you about fighting back, I don't mind going, but it won't fix the problem you're faced with."

"A problem that you created!"

"Indeed?" Kessler said slowly. The man simply couldn't see it. "Have it your way. Was there anything else?"

"The Committee will handle Professor Krafter. You're out

of it," Horowitz snarled and hung up.

With a grim smile, Kessler pressed the glowing speaker button.

"I don't mind it at all."

* * *

"That's the story, Mr. Saul," Tom said, eyeing the headlines in *The Washington Post* with distaste. "I can't say that Kessler is running our killer, but he's the best lead we've got."

"I'd say he was the only lead you've got," Werner Saul, Special Agent in Charge of New York's Intelligence Division, said dryly. "Email me the authorization and I'll get somebody on it."

"Thanks, I appreciate it."

"We'll email you daily audio files every morning."

"I do have one more request."

"And what would that be?"

"I need you to put a tail on Kessler. I'd hate for him to get away when we're so close to getting him."

"Very well. I'll see to it."

When Saul hung up, Tom took Hancock's wiretap authorization and covering letter, and went to see Marsha, asking her to email the things. Back in his office, he picked up his coffee mug and took a sip. The stuff had cooled and lost much of its appeal. Glancing at the newspaper, he scowled.

Krafter shot in broad daylight and nobody saw a thing, including the Laramie detective standing next to him. Thankfully, the bullet passed clean through Krafter's side without damaging any organs, but the freshman behind him had not been as lucky, striking her in the stomach. According to the report, she died on the scene. The paper didn't tell him anything more than what Briggs said yesterday.

The detective shepherding Krafter *thought* he saw a large man squeeze past him a moment before the professor got shot, but he couldn't swear to it. There were a lot of people moving around the front of the eatery. The guy obviously felt bad about the whole thing, especially the girl, but there wasn't anything he could have done. Oh, in hindsight, there were a number of things everybody could have done, but that was little consolation now, and scant comfort to the girl's family.

Two murders on his hands…

If he didn't have enough reasons to catch his killer before, Tom definitely had another one now. Catching him was only half the job. He wanted the man behind the killer. He wanted to face him when the cuffs went on.

Once New York bugged Kessler's office, he might be a step closer to getting both men. If Kessler turned out to be a dry hole, he could be facing a dead end, and that was something he didn't want to contemplate. In that respect, he wasn't very different from the killer. Both of them hated to fail.

Well, he did not face a dead end yet, Tom reflected. Greenfield had managed to confirm that their man had bought the meter reader murder weapon in Phoenix and they now had a driver's license mug shot. Although probably a disguise, the boys at the Facial Analysis, Comparison, and Evaluation (FACE) Services Unit of the Biometric Services Section, should be able to strip it away and try matching the underlying image with the surveillance shot they already had. If Hancock could cut through the CIA and NSA red tape, it would help get things moving.

He was tempted to take up Slater's suggestion and send the mug shot to the agencies, and discarded it. It would speed up the search, but there was still a real possibility that someone could tip off his killer, something he did not want to risk. Anyway, sending them the shot wouldn't speed up the search very much. Once the FBI had the tapes, FACE computers should be able to make a match fairly quickly.

Someone knocked on the door and Tom looked up. "Come."

Slater walked in, grinned when he saw the newspaper, and sat down. "I see bad news travels quickly."

"It's bad enough," Tom growled.

"Talking about bad news, I heard NBC is doing a documentary on you."

"Christ! Are you here to bend my ear about that?"

Before Slater could respond, Tom's phone went off and he picked up. "Meecham!"

"It's all sorted out with the agencies," Hancock said. "You should start getting stuff tomorrow."

"Say, that's great news, boss. Thanks."

"How's Professor Krafter?"

"They've patched him up and he should be out Ivinson Memorial by the weekend. They want to keep an eye on him for a while to make sure infection doesn't set in."

"He was lucky."

"I'll say. Sawko's men will now be with him twenty-four/seven."

"Too bad your man managed to get in his shot, but there is no way to counter it. Keep me in the loop."

"You got it." Hancock hung up and Tom looked at Slater. "At least something has broken our way. The agencies are sending in their stuff, but don't wait for them. If everybody hasn't responded by Friday, jump on their bones."

Slater nodded. "I'll let FACE know. Something else occurred to me the last time we talked and I forgot to mention it."

"About the NBC?"

Slater grinned. "Not exactly. Just because CIA and the others agreed to send us the data, doesn't necessarily mean that they'll send all of it."

Tom frowned, not liking where that was leading. "No, it doesn't, and you're an asshole for bringing it up."

"So how do we check if we in fact have everything?"

"We can't, but before we start rushing around, let's wait and see what we do get. Remember, they don't know who we're after. If we draw a blank, then we'll get excited. Good point, though. Now, what else have you got?"

"A little present from the NSA. They confirmed giving Kessler a specially modified HTC PDA smartphone when he was at BioChip. Nobody can say whether the thing was ever returned. I got the impression they're handing them out like candy and no one's keeping track."

"That'll be right," Tom growled.

"They offered to deactivate Kessler's call number, but I told them to hold off like you wanted."

"The New York office should have Kessler's office bugged today. Then we'll see what happens."

"How are they going to get in?"

"Probably use the old janitor trick or something. Their problem. With Krafter shot, we can only hope that Kessler or our man make a call."

"Hopefully after we get the place bugged," Slater said brightly.

"That would help," Tom agreed. "We might be too late already, though. Never mind. Have you identified anybody else who has Krafter on their hate list?"

"My boys have pretty much gone over everybody. Nobody stands out, or they've covered themselves too well."

Tom bit his lower lip. "Yeah. That means we'll have to get our killer and work backward to identify his controller. Well, we never expected this to be easy."

"By the way, have you talked to Ted Horowitz?"

"Yes, yesterday morning. Why?"

Slater reached into his pocket and dragged out a folded paper. "This came in the mail, copy of a conversation between Horowitz and Kessler, courtesy of NSA. They recorded more calls since and promised to send me the transcripts as soon as they're ready."

Tom read through the note and nodded. "Another tantalizing link in a nebulous chain of suppositions."

"I'd say those links are firming up. Greenfield has done well getting us the driver's license," Slater added.

"He used his head by flying on to Denver instead of hanging around Phoenix," Tom agreed, reminding himself to call Garry Strand about the swap with Johnston.

"You still want to get rid of him? If we're going to get more of these screwy assignments, he'd be handy to have around."

"In the meantime, we hang him in the closet?"

Slater's mouth twitched. "He wouldn't be doing much good in there, would he?"

"No, he wouldn't. What he's done so far proves my point. Greenfield is a good investigator who should be allowed to develop his skills, and it's not going to happen if he stays here. Damned if I know why my predecessor took him in the first place."

Slater shrugged and stood up. "I'll let you know if we strike it lucky with the agency tapes." He turned toward the door, then raised his hand. "Oh, I almost forgot. We got a match on our man from Denver airport and Laramie Regional. I'll email you some shots. One's almost a dead ringer with the computer-generated image FACE came up with."

Tom stared at him. "All this time you've been busting my chops chitchatting?"

"You got told, didn't you?" Slater smiled and waved his arm. "Later."

When Slater shut the door after him, Tom sat back and shook his head. Everybody was going stir crazy.

Going over what Slats said, it might not be a bad idea if he took out some insurance. It couldn't hurt. He reached for the phone and dialed. After two rings, a firm voice answered.

"Mark Price."

"Hi, it's Tom."

"Well, crap! If it isn't my favorite FBI agent. You still too chicken to play golf?"

Ever since he and Mark nailed the Israelis for sabotaging the Valero Texas City Refinery and prevented America from bombing Iran over it, they had kept in touch and developed a useful friendship. Tom had a call to collect on that friendship, asking Mark if his CIA buddies could find Peroni's Rome residence, which contributed to bringing down two Vatican cardinals.

Over a whiskey once, Mark invited him to a game of golf, and was surprised when Tom told him he didn't play. What was more, he had no desire to chase a little white ball simply for the dubious privilege of tapping it into a small hole. Ignoring the alleged virtues of the game, which Mark extolled at every opportunity, Tom remained unmoved. Besides, his spare moments were taken up with Melissa. A man had to have priorities, and being with her was much more enjoyable than slamming a ball around that wouldn't do what he wanted.

"Ask me once I'm retired."

"Coward," Price declared. "I'll just have to kidnap you and drag you to a game. Anyway, what's up?"

"You still okay for Saturday night?"

"You bet. It will give me a chance to show your girl some real bachelor cooking."

"That's a good reason not to bring her," Tom said dryly. After talking about Mark, Melissa insisted that she wanted to meet him, and Tom was secretly glad. He had wanted to show her off to his friend, and this made it easier.

"That irreverent attitude won't get you very far in this town, you know," Price said darkly.

"I'll manage," Tom said. "The reason I called, I've got a favor to ask you."

"You're rubbishing my cooking and you've got the nerve asking me for a favor?"

"It's an unjust world. You're following what's been going on with Professor Krafter?"

"I've seen some of the stories. You're involved?"

"I'm afraid so. I believe we're close to catching our killer, but I've got a small problem."

"Don't tell me. You've asked the CIA for help and you're not sure if they'll come across, right?"

"Pretty much." Tom wasn't amazed that Mark had it figured out. The man ex-CIA and knew how the place operated. "If I send you a couple of mug shots, I wondered if you still had enough pull inside to do a match analysis. I want to know if our man is one of their former operatives."

"Mmm. I know somebody good at the Office of Advanced Analytics who might be willing to do this. What do I get out of it?"

"Asshole! I'll buy you a bottle of twenty-one-year-old Chivas Regal."

"Deal!" Price hooted with glee. "Send me the shots and I'll see what I can do."

"Thanks, Mark."

"Well, crap! Somebody's got to do your job around here."

"On Saturday, then," Tom said with a smile and hung up. He picked up his mug and nodded. Now they were cooking.

* * *

"A positive match," Slater said as he spread the three glossies on Tom's desk, then lowered himself into a chair. "Professor Krafter's office, the Phoenix driver's license and Laramie Regional Airport. Greenfield also got a confirmation from Travel Lodge, Hampton Inn and Enterprise Rent-a-car. I think we've got our man."

Tom nodded, reached into his desk drawer, pulled out a printout and held it out. Slater took it and did a quick read.

"Sean Foreman, thirty-four, six-foot-three—that matches—

discharged eighteen months ago, but still listed as a part-time operative. Code word 'Striker', currently working for TriCon Security." Slater looked up and frowned. "Where did you get this?"

"A friend," Tom said. "This nails it. Our man's ex-CIA, a field operative, and right now, into industrial espionage."

"Is that what TriCon does for fun?"

"Among other things."

"Given that we've now got him, you want me to tell FACE to stop processing further tapes?"

"Everybody except the CIA. I'm curious to see if they've been honest. If Foreman is still on their active list, they might want to keep him under wraps."

Slater grinned in wonder. "They don't care what he does in his spare time as long as they can keep using him."

"They could be playing straight with us for once."

"Sure. What now?"

"The last phone transcript you got from the NSA yesterday pretty much does it for Kessler as far as I'm concerned. I don't know what Dr. Horowitz intends doing with Krafter, but we know it won't be lethal. The problem is, Kessler still hasn't said anything to implicate himself or the IAS, and he hasn't made any calls to Foreman."

"You mean, he hasn't made any calls since we planted the bug," Slater said dryly and Tom sighed.

"That's it. We probably closed the door one day too late. Which leaves us having to make a connection between the two the hard way. If we can't, they both walk. We got nothing on either of them."

Slater sat up in alarm. "You can't mean that. What about the gun, the murdered meter reader and the girl? Then there's the car rental and the hotels Foreman stayed at."

"What about them?" Tom said, enjoying the wash of confusion on Slater's face.

"It's evidence."

"It's not evidence, Slats. They're merely alleged facts. So Foreman stayed at the Holiday Inn. Big deal. He rented a car, but we can't prove that he ran Krafter off the road. Anybody renting the car after him could have scraped against the curb or something. Remember, forensics found no trace of paint on the bumper."

"Foreman probably cleaned up after himself," Slater mused.

"Probably. As for the Bersa, he might have purchased it, but it doesn't prove he killed the meter reader or the girl, or left the gun in Krafter's bedroom. Everything we've got is circumstantial, even though it all hangs together, but we don't have a single piece of hard evidence for anything. If you took this to the DA, he would laugh you out of court."

"We have his mug shot when he broke into Krafter's office."

"What we have is a computer processed infrared image. You think a jury would take that at face value, even if we could get it to trial? Any defense lawyer fresh out of law school would have it thrown out. Computers can fake anything these days, he would say, and he'd be right."

"You're a hard man, Tom."

"You got it, and you better become hard if you want to succeed in this game. It doesn't matter how narrow the chasm between what you know and what you can prove, as long as it exists, you're defeated."

"Okay, mister know-it-all, what do we do?"

Smiling, Tom threw the ball right back. "Suppose you tell me. You've got all the information I have."

Glaring, Slater went into his thinking trance. When he looked up, it was with respect.

"You had this figured out all along, didn't you?"

"Figured out what?"

"The Cayman Islands account. We need to find out if Foreman owns it. Even if he's using a phony name, we can break through it."

"What if TriCon owns that account?" Tom said softly. "Have you thought of that? Foreman could have been doing a job for the IAS."

"He *was* doing a job for the IAS, but I know what you mean, and I'll find out, but I'm not hinging the whole thing on Cayman. What we need is a transcript of a conversation between Kessler and Foreman where Krafter is mentioned."

Tom pointed his finger at Slater and nodded. "My man! That's exactly what we need."

Pleased at the compliment, Slater's face suddenly clouded. "How do we get them to talk to each other? Kessler could have called off the whole thing and wouldn't have a reason to call Foreman."

"Then we give him a reason," Tom said patiently.

Slater opened his mouth, then shut it with a snap. "The HTC smartphone! If NSA gave one to Kessler, they might also have given one to Foreman."

"Or the CIA did. They would have as much incentive to keep some of their conversations secret as anybody else."

"Sure, but the NSA would, or should, have a record of each phone's encryption calling number. Now that we've got names to go with the faces, they might be willing to tell us what those numbers are."

"And give us a HTC to do a bit of calling ourselves, eh?" Tom said, wearing a broad smile. He knew Slats would figure it out sooner or later.

"In the confusion, one of them might call the other and the bug in Kessler's office will have it all on tape. Provided, of course, the conversation happens in Kessler's office. Shit, it's too complicated. Too many things have to fall our way."

"That's how it works out sometimes. We'll follow this through and hope for a lucky break."

"What if Foreman disappears and doesn't go back to Tri-Con?"

"Why would he do that? Sure, he must know we're after him, but he also knows that we don't have anything on him. No, he'll reenter his normal life, and once he's in New York, our office there will keep an eye on him. I'll make sure."

"If this doesn't work?"

"There you go. More pessimism."

Slater chuckled. "Okay, we'll do this first and see. I'll get Greenfield on the Cayman Islands account and I'll talk to the NSA." He frowned and bit his lip. "You think Foreman would still be using his old CIA code word to identify himself to Kessler?"

"If the CIA are using him, we have a good chance he might."

"Well, let's hope NSA can confirm it. If not…"

"Tell me about it," Tom said. "While Greenfield is having fun with the Cayman thing, get him to check out TriCon as well…discreetly."

"You got it. This is beginning to look as if it might actually work."

"We'll take it step by step. While we're talking about Greenfield, I had a call from Garry Strand last night. He's willing to do a swap. Did I tell you that Briggs is also interested?"

"No, you didn't."

"I'll have a chat with Greenfield. Send him in if he's at his desk."

Slater got the hint and stood up. "If he's willing to go, you want him out of here right away?"

"Once he's done with Cayman and TriCon."

Alone, Tom stretched his arms and grunted. Slats was right and they might be closing in on their targets. There were a lot of things that could still go wrong, but they now had positive leads to follow. He picked up his mug to get a refill when a knock on the door stopped him.

"Come in."

Greenfield entered, closed the door and stopped beside

Tom's desk. "You wanted to see me?"

"Sit down, Will," Tom said and waited for the junior agent to make himself comfortable. "I'll come straight to the point. You and I both know that you haven't been exactly burning the program since you've been here. The plain fact is that you're not cut out for counterintelligence. You're an excellent field investigator and your work in Laramie and Phoenix was first rate. I wish I could take advantage of what you have to offer, but the bottom line is, you don't have a career in my Section."

Greenfield's face sagged. "You're kicking me out of the Bureau?"

"Why would you think that?"

"You said—"

"That you don't belong in counterintelligence. Nobody's looking to kick you out of the Bureau. You've got good career options, and I'll name a few of them. You don't have to make up your mind right now, just consider them. You can let me know tomorrow what you decide."

"What are the options?"

"Briggs liked what you did and he's offering you a slot in the Denver Division. They cover a huge area and you'll have a lot of responsibility. Far more than you have here. You've been there and saw how his people do business. The other option is a position in the Boston Division. They're running major operations and I think with your background, you'd be an asset. Garry Strand is a first rate SAC and could certainly use you."

"And my third choice, if there is one?"

"A transfer to wherever I say," Tom told him bluntly. "Frankly, with your background, I don't know why you accepted this posting to begin with."

"That's just it. I didn't. I was supposed to be doing white-collar crime. They stuck me here while they shuffled bodies around. This was to be a temp job only."

Tom stared at him. "Why the hell didn't you say something?"

"I did. I talked to Mr. Young, and he said he'd take care of it. Then you came…"

"Yeah. Well, I'm glad you told me. I didn't want you to think I was shafting you."

"I never did, sir, and I appreciate you giving me a choice."

"Not a problem. Think about it and let me know."

Greenfield stood up, nodded and walked out. Tom sat back and shook his head. His predecessor had screwed up. Wellard probably knew what was going on, but his sudden departure only served to pour more sand into the machinery. In the meantime, Greenfield was left wondering if the Bureau even remembered that he existed.

Tom shook his head at the muddy internal workings, picked up his mug and heaved himself out of the chair. With fresh coffee in hand and ready to face the world, he grabbed the phone and dialed.

"Julian Briggs."

"Hi, it's Tom. Got a minute?"

"Sure, what's up?"

"I wanted to give you a quick update on the latest goings on."

"I could use some good news. With you running the pointy end, I feel like a fifth wheel around here."

Tom sympathized, but that's the price Briggs paid for lack of manpower to do the job himself. He quickly ran through the points discussed with Slater.

"You believe the phone entrapment will work?" Briggs asked.

"No way to tell. We'll just have to try it and see. By the way, I spoke to Greenfield about your job offer. He'll think about it and let me know."

"He'll find it interesting here, that's for sure. Thanks for the call."

"No problem." Tom hung up and sipped his coffee.

* * *

"Ouch!" Krafter cried out as the nurse extracted the drainage tube. His whole side felt like it was being ripped open.

"Sorry about that," she said briskly, not looking sorry at all as she dabbed antiseptic on the spot. Her top-sergeant manner clearly held little sympathy for a patient's minor discomforts, especially one in his grave condition. She fixed on a patch and patted his shoulder.

"Sit up."

Krafter propped himself up with accompanying grunts and groans, and watched with interest as she wrapped a fresh bandage around his torso. Leaning over him, her short brown hair smelled of lilacs, or it could have been her perfume. He hoped she wasn't as stern with her boyfriend and wondered what she would look like out of uniform, then dispelled the thought. He wasn't *that* well! Done, she pushed him back against the pillows and pulled the double blanket over his chest.

"If you don't give me any more trouble, I'll let you have some coffee."

"Gee, what possible trouble could I have caused *you*?" he complained crossly, his side smarting from the impersonal handling.

She flashed him a smile and walked out. Annoyed at being treated like a side of beef, he had his fill of hospitals and wanted out. Not about to leap tall buildings or anything, but a change of scenery would be refreshing. Perkins brought him a couple of books, but reading in bed had lost its appeal after the first day. It was the forced inactivity that wore him down. He hated to admit it, but he was bored. The room had a TV, but the stuff they showed drove him to distraction. Always active physically and mentally, this enforced idleness wasn't nearly as refreshing as he had anticipated.

The door opened and his surgeon walked in. "Morning, Professor. How are you today?" he asked indifferently, glanced at the chart, then clipped it back to the foot of the bed.

"I'd be better if I was out of here," Krafter told him firmly.

"Mmm." The surgeon pulled back the blanket and probed with his fingers around the wounds. Krafter winced when one prod became a bit too aggressive.

"Still tender?"

"Not as much, but it's a little uncomfortable when I move around."

"It's only natural. There is no inflammation and the wounds are healing nicely. I would prefer to keep you here over the weekend, but if you promise not to do anything strenuous that could tear the stitches, I'll let you go this afternoon. How does that sound?"

Krafter immediately brightened. "It's a deal."

"I want you back on Monday for a checkup, though. The way you're healing, we should have the sutures out by next Friday. I'm serious about not straining yourself. You suffered significant transverse abdomis trauma, that's the muscle group above the hip, and it'll take time for everything to get back to normal, which it will."

"How long before I can start exercising?"

"Give yourself two weeks, then light stuff only to start off with. Merely moving about the house will exercise your side enough for now. I also want you to keep the torso bandaged, at least until we get the sutures out. It will remind you not to make any sudden movements."

"It will be good simply not being here," Krafter said with feeling.

"Hospitals can be depressing," the surgeon agreed, scribbled something on the chart and smiled. "I'll tell the front desk that you'll be out at three."

"Thanks, doc."

When the surgeon left, Krafter eased himself against the pillows and smiled. The prospect of getting out of here had cheered him up. All he needed was a cup of coffee to celebrate. On cue, the door opened and his favorite nurse stepped in with a tray bearing a steel carafe, two rolls and other sundries.

"You see, I didn't forget you, Professor."

"Sorry for being grumpy earlier," he said and she smiled.

"You're okay. You should see some. I have to peel them off the wall." She gave him another smile and walked out.

He grinned at the conjured image and fixed himself a cup. After a thirsty sip, he allowed himself to sink into the pillows. Life wasn't bad after all. His cellphone went off and he picked up.

"Krafter."

"Professor, this is Dr. Norginson. Do you have a moment to talk?"

Krafter raised an eyebrow, wondering what Harvard's president wanted with him. "Certainly, Doctor. How can I help you?"

"Actually, I might be able to help you."

"Oh?"

"Before I go on, I read what happened and I sincerely hope that you were not hurt too badly."

"Thank you for your concern. I'm doing well enough for them to let me go home this afternoon."

"That's good news. To think something like this could happen…never mind. The reason I'm calling, Dr. Van Neuman told me of his offer to you and I want to renew it."

The lady doesn't waste time, apparently. UW might not be the best university in America, and Wethermans cast a gloom around him wherever he walked, but Krafter knew the people and understood the political setup. He had no desire to exchange that by allowing Harvard to grind him up.

"I appreciate your offer, Doctor. Under different circumstances, jumping into an Associate Professorship would be a dream posting, but I simply cannot see how I would fit into your Anthropology Department."

"I understand your concern and the reason behind it, but it's unwarranted. Harvard needs bright, inquiring minds and you certainly qualify. I hope you will forgive me if I stepped over the line, but I discussed your situation with Dr. Perkins. He regards you pretty highly and would hate to lose you, but on this, the two of us are of the same opinion. Harvard will open a lot of doors to you which are currently closed."

"Dr. Norginson, Harvard has tried hard to close doors I already had open," Krafter said with a trace of bitterness.

"Ah, you're referring to Professor Bollinger. I should have mentioned this earlier. His activities have discredited this university and he has been disciplined."

"I know. Dr. Van Neuman told me of his censure."

"I would hardly call it a censure, Professor. With the discovery of the hand bone and bracelet in his office, his positions as Director of the Peabody Museum and Deputy Director of the Anthropology Department have been suspended. Dr. Chandler was appointed to take both posts."

"Chandler?" Krafter was stunned. If true, the development definitely cast a more favorable light on Norginson's offer, and he would enjoy working with someone like Chandler, even if they did not agree on everything. The important difference being is that any disagreement would be professional, not personal.

"The appointments will be *Gazetted* on Monday."

"What about Bollinger?"

"He has been told. His research program and teaching position is unchanged, but he will be retained as a senior lecturer only. Of course, if he finds these arrangements unsatisfactory, he is free to seek other opportunities. In view of what I told you, I trust you will reconsider my offer."

"I'm flattered, Doctor, and I shall certainly consider it. When do you need a response?"

"Take your time, but not too much time."

"There is one thing I want to make sure you understand," Krafter said. "If I accept the position, I hope you realize what it might mean for Harvard."

Norginson laughed, a pleasant and rich sound. "Rest assured, I am fully aware of your discovery and its impact on modern paleoanthropology. As a progressive and freethinking institution, I can confidently say that with Harvard behind you, your discovery will be treated with all the serious diligence it deserves. I cannot say that your Pacific migration theory will receive the same acceptance, but you'll have some sophisticated tools and resources to conduct further research to promote it."

"I wouldn't want it any other way, Doctor," Krafter said earnestly, already seeing himself planning field trips and issuing papers, welcomed or not.

"Good! Which brings me to another point, one that might be mutually beneficial; the status of your hand bone. Now that it's been found, what do you propose doing with it?"

"I was going to ask to have it returned to the University of Wyoming. After all, it is our property."

"Yes, that's what I thought. After speaking to Dr. Perkins, he is open to another arrangement. Basically, I want Harvard to exhibit it."

"What?"

"I am sure you heard me," Norginson said dryly. "It would make a terrific attraction, and I'm not above exploiting that. It would also demonstrate Harvard's unequivocal support for your discovery. I want to do this regardless of whether you accept a position with us or not."

"That's very generous of you," Krafter said soberly. "Given the derision with which I have been treated, I admit to being surprised that Harvard would even consider making me an offer, let alone exhibit my find."

"Dr. Van Neuman explained to me his initial offer to you,

suggested by Professor Bollinger, by the way. On reflection, I know why it was made, and why you may have been skeptical at accepting, but I can tell you that there is no ulterior motive on my part. Every cupboard needs airing from time to time, and your discovery, however unsettling for some, has caused a reluctant airing of paleoanthropology. I'm not saying that you will have an easy time of it simply because of your position here, but you will not be dismissed either, regardless of what the IAS might say. Isn't that what universities are supposed to be?"

"They certainly are. Sadly, a lot of them are not."

"Then help us change that mindset. Accept my offer."

"If Dr. Perkins hasn't raised an objection, I agree to Harvard displaying the hand bone. But only that. The skull belongs to UW."

"Dr. Perkins made the same point, and I am quite happy to have it that way. However, he is amenable to loaning us the skull for a time."

Krafter thought about that and saw the potential for everybody. Exhibiting the bones would be a tremendous crowd drawcard, rivaling the John the Baptist Scroll itself.

"I wouldn't object to that. As for your offer of a position, I'll have to get back to you."

"I understand. It will mean a major change to your lifestyle, but I am confident that you can rise to the challenge."

"You've given me a lot to think about, Doctor, and I want to thank you for everything, regardless of my decision."

"Get well, and I hope to hear from you soon, Professor," Norginson said and switched off.

Krafter placed the cellphone on the bedside cabinet and smiled. Despite being shot, he had come out of it wreathed in glory and Bollinger got shafted, which wasn't going to make him shed tears for the man. The bastard deserved what he got. That was all good, but did he want to move to Harvard? And what about Maddson? With his front line ally discredited, would he continue the vendetta? Right now, Krafter didn't actually care. He needed to sort out in his mind what *he* wanted out of life, which wasn't as easy as he first thought.

Norginson was right about the move being a major change in many ways. Professionally, it would be a significant achievement to be an Associate Professor at twenty-six. Most postdocs have to wait until their mid-thirties to get that far. And it would be a tenured position! It meant recognition and security, not having to suck up to the department head all the time, at least not as much.

The other change was more personal and Krafter wondered if he was up to the challenge. The prospect of committing scared him, as it meant sharing everything with someone else, and he wasn't sure he could do that. Unfortunately, in a relationship there were no training wheels. He would be on his own as soon as he took off. That was the scary part. Intellectually, he understood the gulf that existed between casual dating, an occasional stolen kiss, and having the other person around all the time. Well, not all the time. Both would be working, but he was dancing around a technicality.

Didn't somebody say it was better to have loved and lost, or some tripe thing?

He wanted the nice things a relationship delivered. He wasn't sure how he would cope with the bad bits in between. His inner self sneered at him for being a coward. For better or for worse, eh? Well, if somebody else left another body in his garage, he would have someone to bail him out. That had to count for something.

Lunchtime came quickly, but the afternoon wore on with glacial slowness. At two o'clock, his nurse came in and handed him two plastic bottles of white pills with detailed instructions when to take them. She also left a walking stick.

As she was leaving, she flashed him a smile. "Good luck, Professor."

Krafter got the hint and scrambled out of bed. His clothes were in the cupboard, neatly laundered and pressed. He held up the jacket against the window and gazed at the two holes in the right side. His shirt had similar holes. He wondered vaguely if this was covered by his health insurance.

At the front desk, his FBI shadow hovering beside him, he signed papers and was free to go.

Outside, he squinted at bright sunshine and took a deep breath, the fresh air tasting wonderful after the hospital's canned air-conditioning. A Yellow Checker taxicab pulled up in front of him and he glanced at Ross.

"I took the liberty of calling one for us."

"Good thinking," Krafter said and carefully got into the back seat, wincing only once as his side protested. The cab moved out of the driveway and entered N. 30th Street.

It felt strange sitting there, listening to the car engine, watching the traffic and people moving around, not having to worry about lectures, tutorials or assignments. It was like being on vacation, but not exactly. It felt more as if he were stealing time off and he took perverse pleasure at not caring about anything, at least for a while.

The cab turned into E. Sanders Drive, slowed and stopped opposite his house. Before Krafter could reach for his wallet, Ross was already settling the fare. Standing on the sidewalk, looking at his house, it felt good being home. Beside him, Ross cast watchful glances up and down the street. Krafter took out his keys, walking stick under his arm, and hobbled toward the front door. Before he could unlock it, it opened and he gaped at the figure framed in the entrance.

"Is that all you can do, stare?" Elena said primly with a mischievous glint in her almond eyes, knowing she had pulled a fast one on him.

"My God! What are *you* doing here?" Krafter managed to gasp, drinking her in.

"Some welcome after all the trouble I had to go through to come."

Krafter reached for her and she slid into his arms. Her lips were soft and eager and he forgot all about his side. He pulled back and stroked her hair.

"I missed you," he whispered.

"Me, too," she said gruffly.

He turned and extended his arm. "Meet Frank Ross, FBI. He's one of my three minders. Frank, this is Elena Spiteri."

Ross smiled and offered his hand. "Glad to meet you, Miss Spiteri."

Elena shook hands. "One of your colleagues is inside, Daron Kovach."

"I know him. He's a good man," Ross said politely.

"You've got a detail on you?" Krafter demanded.

"Briggs wouldn't let me leave Denver without Kovach," she told him. "Let's get inside and I'll tell you all about it." She noticed the hole on the front of his jacket and took a sharp breath. "How are you feeling?"

"Coffee and bedroom slippers for a while."

"It's what they told me," Elena said. "That's why I'm here. Somebody's got to look after you."

Krafter turned and glared at Ross. "You ratted on me?"

The FBI man glanced at Elena and lifted both arms. "I merely gave Mr. Briggs my usual daily report."

"Sure you did," Krafter growled and took Elena's hand. Inside, she steered him into the living room and introduced a slim, tough looking individual.

"Mr. Kovach."

"Glad to see you, Professor. How you doing, Frank?"

"I think the two of us need to take some fresh air," Ross said pointedly. Kovach grinned and nodded.

"We'll be outside, Miss Spiteri."

When the two FBI men left, Krafter eased himself on the

couch and Elena slipped in beside him, her expression serious.

"Don't be mad at me, Larry."

"I was, but I'm also glad to have you here," Krafter said, still sorting out his emotions. She was here and no use hashing over the possible consequences. Anyway, with the FBI hovering over them, they should be safe.

"When did you get in?"

"My flight landed at eleven-fifteen, but I had a layover in Denver yesterday after flying in from Honolulu."

"Is that where they had you stashed?"

"I was on Malakai. You should see the place, Larry. I only had a couple of days there, but it's a true paradise."

"All right, how did you do it?"

"Briggs knew you were being discharged today. The FBI talked to the surgeon. I told him you wouldn't be able to look after yourself and that was it. He didn't like the idea of me coming back, but I shut him up before he could argue. I can be very determined, you know."

Krafter sighed. "I do know." He reached for her and gave her a brief hug. "This wasn't smart, but we'll face this together," he said, searching her eyes.

"That's all I want," she said softly.

After a timeless second, he kissed her. "Let's go to Malakai."

"Oh, Larry, if only we could!"

Chapter Ten

Slater lifted the PDA phone out of the foam-lined box and held it up. Tom took it and flipped open the cover. For multi-tasking work, it was a large device, but also top of the line stuff. Nokia, Apple and others thought they made cool smartphones, but HTC beat them all for sophistication.

Slater sat down and crossed his legs. "Select the Secure icon from the main menu and you're ready to go. Dial as you would normally. For an incoming call, you'll see a little red square flashing on the bottom right of the screen. Press Secure to initiate the encryption sequence and complete the connection. You disconnect as usual."

"Neat," Tom mused, studying the comfortably sized keyboard. "Okay, what else you got?"

"You want the good news or the bad news?"

"Bad," Tom said immediately, following his policy to always get the bad stuff out of the way first.

"NSA couldn't give us Foreman's number or code word, but we do have Kessler's. It's on a note in the box. If they *are* using a code word, this makes calling them difficult."

"Mmm. Awkward, I agree, but I'll come up with something. Anything more?"

"We've got the thing on loan only and NSA wants it back as soon as we're done with it, or someone will be knocking on my door."

Tom chuckled. "Don't worry. I'm not going to steal it."

"What now?"

"We go after our guys, but I'll have to do it in New York."

"You?"

"Remember what you said about the master's touch?"

"You remember what I said about being around when you did your thing?"

"I'm sorry, Slats. I've got to have Briggs. It's his case, sort of."

"And three's a crowd. Oh, well. They also serve those who stand and wait," Slater said glumly.

"And you served well," Tom told him. "I can't delegate this to the New York office. They don't know the situation, not in detail, and it would take too long to clue them in. There is one other reason why I want to be there. I want to see their faces when we get them, especially Foreman's. It's childish, I know, but—"

"Never mind, I understand," Slater said.

"You've given me the bad news. What's the good news?"

"Ah, I haven't finished with the bad news yet. Greenfield has identified IAS payments to that Cayman Islands account, but we've had no luck so far tracing who's making the withdrawals. The good news was getting the phone."

Tom waved at him. "Go away. You're no good to me."

Slater grinned and stood up. "Has Greenfield told you what he wants to do?"

"He's taking the Boston job and I already told Garry Strand. Johnston will be your 2IC. Will that cause friction in the team?"

"If it does, I'll handle it. Have fun in the Big Apple," Slater said and made for the door.

"I'll send you a postcard," Tom told him.

He hated letting Slater down, but there was simply no way he could justify the two of them going to New York. There would be enough local FBI bodies involved as it is. After all, it was Werner Saul's turf. Talking of turf…

Eyeing the HTC, he picked up the phone and was about to dial when a tingle ran down the back of his spine.

Postcard!

Amazing how things can sometimes work themselves out. He smiled and punched in a direct number.

"Julian Briggs."

"It's Tom. Can you be in New York on Monday?"

"I can fly in on Sunday night and be ready by morning. We're going after Kessler?"

"And Foreman."

"How do we handle it?"

"You'll like this. We'll mail Kessler a letter. When he comes in and reads it, the contents will make him call Foreman and our little bug will have the ensuing, and hopefully incriminating, conversation on tape."

Briggs laughed. "Pay Foreman in his own coin, eh? I like it. And if this doesn't work?"

"I have a fallback option. I'll brief Werner Saul to have men outside both offices in case either of them tries to get away."

"We know that Foreman is in New York?"

"Saul is keeping an eye on him."

"Sounds good. I tell you, I'm looking forward to ending this. Saxon's been after me and I haven't had much to show him lately."

"Hancock's been on my case also. This should make both of them happy."

"There's no justice, is there. Ah, there's been a development, Tom. Miss Spiteri is back in Laramie."

"Christ! Why the hell did you let her do that? If things go belly up on Monday, we could have more bodies on our hands."

"Krafter will be released from hospital this afternoon and the protection detail you sent can watch both of them. If Foreman is in New York, we're in a low risk scenario. Besides, she'll be staying at his house and wasn't in any danger at work."

Tom shrugged, not liking it. "Well, we'll see what happens on Monday."

"Where do you want to meet?"

"If you can be at Werner Saul's office by eight, we'll go from there."

"See you then," Briggs said and rang off.

Tom glanced at his watch: 5:20. He needed to brief Saul and arrange a flight for himself. He got up, hoping Marsha was still in.

* * *

Wide awake, even though he had to get up early to catch his six a.m. flight out of Ronald Reagan, Tom was thankful it was only an hour to LaGuardia. As he checked in at Terminal C, he was not surprised to see lots of business types dressed in severe suits, carrying expensive briefcases, queuing for their boarding passes. His e-ticket had an attached pass and he was spared the crush. He just had enough time to gulp down a coffee before they announced boarding of US Airways flight 2158. Comfortable in his business class seat, waiting for everybody to settle in, attendants banging shut overhead lockers, he was eager for the Being 757-200 to be pushed back. Twelve minutes late, they were finally on their way.

His weekend had been pleasant, especially the Saturday afternoon barbecue. Mark was a bubbling host and Melissa took to him instantly, much to Tom's relief. She gaped when Mark told her something of their adventure in Israel to nab Matan Irian, the Mossad man who conducted the sabotage of the Valero refinery. Afterward, Tom took her to his place for a nightcap. Nothing naughty happened, but the couple of kisses they exchanged got to be pretty steamy.

All in all, it had turned into one of his better evenings.

Dawn had already broken as the narrow-body jet began its descent into New York. At least they were spared the numbing ritual of holding in a stacked pattern and came straight in. With a jolt and a squeal of tires, they were down and the pilot engaged reverse thrust. Bright sunshine bathed the terminals as the aircraft turned onto a taxiway.

As usual, it took a while for the Yellow Cab to thread its way from LaGuardia up Broadway to the Federal Plaza tower in lower Manhattan. The traffic along the busy thoroughfare heavy, but flowed steadily. The sidewalks were crowded with office workers, winos clutching brown paper bags, the homeless pushing an odd shopping cart containing their worldly belongings, and some merely wandered along the shadowy canyons without purpose. New York had a lot to offer its citizens, but it also hid a lot of darkness along the way.

The cab stopped opposite 26 Federal Plaza. Tom grabbed his small bag and got out, leaving the cabbie with a fiver for a tip. With the sounds of a busy metropolis suddenly loud around him, he dashed across the street and entered the sleek tower. He bypassed the round reception information desk and made straight for the elevator banks. Inside, he pressed a white metal button for the twenty-third floor. The electronic display reeled off floor numbers as the high-speed elevator surged up. Underneath it, the clock said 7:55 a.m., Monday, October 17.

His stomach sagged as the car slowed, then stopped. A pleasant female voice announced, 'Twenty-third floor, FBI Reception' and the double doors opened with a hiss. He walked out and faced a large open cubicle walled off from the rest of the floor by heavy glass panels. Many of the desks were already occupied. He stepped to the counter as a stern individual made an appearance.

"May I help you, sir?" the man growled, not looking in the mood to help anyone.

"Thomas Meecham, Supervising Special Agent, Washington, to see Werner Saul."

"Can I see some identification, please?"

Tom produced his ID wallet and held it up. The man gave it a thorough look and nodded. "Just a moment."

Tom felt like a criminal by the cold reception as he eased

himself into one of the three beige cloth couches that surrounded a low wooden coffee table cluttered with morning papers. Before he could properly relax, a sprightly, gray-haired short man opened the glass door on his right.

"Meecham?"

Tom stood up and held out his hand. "That's right."

"Werner Saul." They shook hands and Saul held the door open for him. "How was your flight in?"

"Routine," Tom said. "It's the getting in and out of airports that's a hassle."

Saul laughed as they walked toward offices along the east side of the building. "I know what you mean."

He stopped before a ceiling-high white door, opened it and walked in. The bulky man inside immediately stood up. Saul strode to a seat behind a wide executive desk positioned before a glass wall with Manhattan's skyline as a backdrop, sat down and faced his guests.

"Tom, meet Special Agent Julian Briggs. I guess you two have met."

"Only over the phone," Briggs said with a smile.

"Sometimes even that was too close," Tom added as they shook hands, sizing up the man. Briggs was just over average height, but he held himself with confidence and his dark eyes were clear and penetrating.

"Coffee?" Saul inquired and Tom nodded. Briggs already nursed a cup.

"Thanks, I wouldn't mind one."

Saul pressed a button on his multi-function phone keyboard. Moments later, a youngster opened the door and peered in.

"How do you want it?" Saul asked.

"Black with one sugar, please."

Saul glanced at the youngster, who nodded and closed the door behind him.

Saul straightened and crossed his arms over the desk. "All

right, let's get comfortable and go over this."

Tom sprawled into a soft chair positioned in front of the desk and waited. The SAC clearly knew what he was doing, and that made him happy. A smart operator meant an efficient execution with a minimum of fumbles. Besides, they had talked it through on Friday at length.

"The van eavesdropping on Kessler's bug is already near the IAS offices," Saul said briskly. "Both of you will be given ear implants to keep you in real-time contact with the technicians inside and each other. I've got men covering the main entrance and back exit in case Kessler decides to run for it. You got everything you need?" he said, glancing at Tom's bag.

"The letter is ready. The HTC smartphone is backup in case Kessler fails to take the bait. It was my first choice, but without Kessler's code word, I'm reluctant to use it."

"I can understand why," Saul agreed. "Let's hope your letter gambit works. My men are also watching TriCon, but we're not tailing Foreman directly. As a former CIA field operative, there was a real risk that he would spot a tail, and I didn't think you'd be pleased about that. Even if he doesn't show up this morning, we've got alerts out to all airports, rail and bus terminals. There are lots of other ways he could disappear, but I believe we should be all right. After all, he doesn't suspect a thing."

"Sounds good," Tom said and glanced at Briggs. "Do you have anything?"

Briggs shook his head. "Between you two, everything seems to be covered, but I do have one question. The bug planted in Kessler's office, is it powerful enough to pick up both sides of a conversation?"

"I wondered if someone was going to raise that," Saul said, when a knock interrupted him. "Come!"

Tom's coffee arrived and he nodded his thanks as the youngster held out the cup and saucer. He took a sip of good, strong coffee and leaned back against the chair.

"The mike is planted under the lip of Kessler's desk," Saul was saying, "and has excellent pickup up to six feet. With some post-processing, we found we can hear both sides of the call quite clearly, and we get an even better reception from his cellphone speaker." Saul darted a look at Tom. "You agree?"

Tom nodded. "The audio recordings you've been sending me are first rate," he said and took another sip. It was exactly what he needed.

"Discussing this with Meecham, as soon as Kessler makes his call to Foreman, and I guess that's the critical point, the guys in the van will alert the watchers around the TriCon building, move to the twelfth floor and block all exits. If Kessler doesn't make his call, you'll have to fall back on your backup plan, Tom."

"I guess we've covered it all." Tom finished his coffee and stood up. "Might as well get on with it. My thanks, Werner, for setting everything up."

"You can thank me once you have your guys under lock and key," the Intelligence Division SAC said dryly as he stood up. "It's been a while since I've been out in the field and I wouldn't mind going with you. That's what happens when you get chained to a desk." He gave Tom a sharp glance and smiled. "It wouldn't surprise me if that's the reason why you're here instead of sending one of your agents."

Tom grinned at Saul's perceptiveness. "I wouldn't have missed it for anything. I'm still getting used to running a section instead of being a senior field operative."

"It'll grow on you," Saul said comfortably. "You'll even get to like it, not that you've been wasting your time since coming to Washington."

Tom winced at the reminder, figuring it would take a while before his involvement with the John the Baptist Scroll died down. Seeing his expression, Saul laughed.

"I don't blame you one bit, and I'd steal a chance to be out there myself if I could. Wrap this up and we'll pick it apart over lunch." He leaned across the desk and pressed a button.

The youngster who served Tom coffee came in and Saul waved at his guests. "They're all yours, Kurt. Bring them back in one piece."

"Yes, sir. If you will follow me please, gentlemen, we'll go to the basement and pick up our car," Kurt said politely. Tom took his bag and followed him out.

The black Chevy Suburban eased onto Broadway, then went up a block and turned onto the Avenue of the Americas. Tom was thankful that IAS and TriCon had their offices relatively close to each other. Despite all the planning and preparation, he was aware that in the field, things always happened which could upset an ops. He did not need further setbacks on this one.

He turned to Briggs sitting beside him in the back seat. "Ready for this?"

"I want to wring the bastard's neck," Briggs growled and Tom smiled, liking his attitude. "I just hope this letter gag works," Briggs added.

"We'll find out soon enough," Tom said.

As they passed Bryant Park on the corner of 42nd Street, Tom prepared himself mentally as they approached the IAS building. Kurt slowed, then eased to a stop a few cars behind a parked nondescript white Toyota van. The three of them got out, slamming the doors shut, and walked toward the van. Kurt banged once on the back door and waited. The door opened a crack and a face peered out, then swung fully open.

Inside, the thing smelled like an electrical shop. The entire right side was taken up with electronic equipment and screens. The seated man lifted off his headphones and nodded to his visitors.

"I'm Casey, technician in charge."

He picked up two skin-colored Bluetooth earpieces and held them out. Tom took one and fitted it into his left ear.

"You'll be able to hear me and I'll pick up everything you

say. If you get in trouble, yell and the men outside will be there in seconds."

"I don't think I'll need them for the first part," Tom said, "but they might come in handy once Kessler makes his call. Has he shown up?"

"Not yet. It's still a little early for him. He normally gets in around eight-fifty or so."

Tom turned to Briggs who was sitting on the bench positioned along the left side. "Right, let's do this."

The second technician opened the back door and Tom stepped into bright sunshine. Skyscrapers clawed at the sky around him. On the sidewalk, he mingled with other pedestrians and made his way toward the IAS building. The sound of rushing cars was a constant background noise.

The heavy glass door panels slid out of his way and he stopped in front of a curved reception station.

"Can I help you, sir?"

Tom fixed on a frown and stared through the young brunette, extracted an envelope from his jacket pocket and held it out.

"Please deliver this to Mr. Kessler as soon as he arrives," he told her sternly in a heavy, rasping voice and her expression suddenly turned serious.

"Of course, sir. May I ask who—"

"Mr. Kessler will know. Remember, as soon as he arrives."

Without looking back, he strode into the street and walked steadily toward the van, happy with the delivery. The frightened receptionist was not likely to forget him in a hurry, or her little task.

When he reached the van, the door opened and he climbed in.

"The package has been delivered," he said brightly and looked at Briggs. "As soon as he finishes his call to Foreman, you go in and grab him."

"It'll be a pleasure," Briggs assured him, his smile grim.

"Okay, Kurt. Let's go over to TriCon."

Walking toward the black Chevy saloon, Tom would have preferred delivering the letter earlier. If Kessler got in at his usual time, he could find himself still heading for TriCon and Foreman alerted.

Kurt made a right, then a block up, another right onto Fifth Avenue, and headed uptown with the traffic toward the Empire State Building towering into a blue sky. As they drove across 33rd Street, Tom tapped his earpiece.

"Approaching Fifth and Thirty-First. Tell the men to be ready."

"Acknowledged."

Kurt drove past their destination, made an illegal U-turn and stopped in front of a modern slab skyscraper. They were in a ten-minute loading zone, but Tom didn't worry about details.

"Has Foreman shown up?"

"He was seen entering the building nine minutes ago," Casey said. "Kessler just made an appearance."

Tom sat back, watched pedestrians crowding the sidewalk, and relaxed. The waiting was over.

It took another twelve minutes before his earpiece crackled. He wasn't surprised at the delay. By the time Kessler got his morning coffee, checked his mail and made himself comfortable before getting around to opening the envelope, it all took time.

"Kessler is dialing. I'm patching you in," Casey announced calmly.

The guy might be calm, probably having done this thing countless of times, but Tom felt a prickling of excitement.

After a couple of rings, a harsh electronic voice answered. "Identify."

"Raven." Kessler's tense voice came through clearly.

"Proceed."

"I got your note, Striker. I don't know how you identified

me, but I'm not paying for your bungled attempt to kill Krafter. It's not what I ordered."

"What are you talking about? I don't know who you are and I never left any note."

"It was hand-delivered minutes ago!" Kessler fumed. "Everything you touched has gone wrong: the murder frame-up, threatening to kill Krafter's girlfriend, and now an attempt on Krafter himself! And you have the gall to demand payment for that fiasco."

"Listen to me, Raven. I never delivered…you've been compromised," Foreman declared suddenly and cut contact.

Tom heard a sharp inhale as Kessler realized what was happening, the world about to cave in on him.

"Oh, my God," Kessler murmured weakly.

"That's done it. Briggs, move in," Tom ordered. He had them. He had them both.

"On the way."

"Casey? Block off TriCon."

"Already moving."

Tom reached for his Glock 22, 9mm holstered on his left hip, chambered a round, flipped on the safety and pushed the semiautomatic back into the holster. He glanced at Kurt and nodded.

"Let's go."

Kurt slapped an FBI sticker against the windscreen and scrambled out. They hurried into the glass-fronted building, crossed a large marbled double-story foyer, and headed for the elevator banks. Groups of office workers waited their turn to go up.

When the triangle above one of the elevators turned white and the door opened with a musical *ting*, Tom held up his ID badge and pushed through.

"FBI!"

People around him immediately stepped back. Inside the elevator, he punched the button for the twelfth floor and it turned amber. The door sighed shut and they surged up. The three men inside with them didn't look at them, staring straight ahead. When the door opened, a dark suited man stood waiting in the corridor. He tensed, then relaxed when he recognized Kurt.

"Mr. Meecham?"

"That's right. Any movement?"

"Nobody's gone into the office or left since we came up."

"Right. Let's go in."

As the three of them moved toward the ceiling-high glass entrance, the TriCon Security logo cut into the thick frosted glass, Tom figured the company occupied the entire floor, and probably more than one. He walked in and stopped before a low reception desk. The rest of the floor was walled off with dark paneling. The pretty receptionist smiled at them, then blanched when Tom held up his badge.

"FBI. We need to see Mr. Foreman."

Hesitating, she reached for the phone and hissed when Tom grabbed her hand.

"No announcement. Get up, open the door and show us to his office or desk. I don't want anybody getting hurt unnecessarily. Is he in?"

Color washed out of her face and she nodded. She stood up, stepped away from her curved workstation, and opened a side door. Tom followed her and found himself in a wide corridor flanked by closed offices. Clearly, TriCon considered that security applied to them as well. His footsteps made hollow sounds on the dark gray carpet as he walked after the girl.

She stopped beside a door and pointed with her hand. "This is his office. What's this all about?"

"Stand back," he told her softly and took out his Glock. The two agents beside him did the same and assumed a shooting stance. She gasped and pressed a knuckled hand against her mouth. "Call him and ask him to come out. Tell him the boss wants him or something."

She bit her lip, moved to the door and knocked. "Mr. Foreman? Mr. Lazars wants to see you right away."

Tom pushed her to one side and raised his weapon. He heard movement and the door opened.

"Freeze!" Tom barked and held his gun in a two-handed grip, chest high.

Foreman's eyes flickered, but he made no move. Studying the face, Tom thought he looked exactly like the computer-generated image: hard and used, without emotion, except for the eyes. Icy blue, they were empty windows into a soul that had lost all trace of humanity long ago.

"Kurt? Cuff him," Tom ordered without taking his eyes off his target.

Careful not to get in the line of fire, Kurt took out a set of cuffs and motioned Foreman to turn. "Hands behind your back."

With the cuffs in place, he shoved Foreman against the corridor wall. Tom stepped closer and pressed the Glock against the man's spine.

"Sean Foreman, you're under arrest for two counts of murder, one count of attempted murder, two counts of causing bodily harm, one count of financial fraud, and one count of conspiracy to murder. You have the right to remain silent. Anything you say can and will be used against you in a court of law. You have the right to speak to an attorney. If you cannot afford an attorney, one will be appointed to you. Do you understand these rights as they were stated?"

"I understand," Foreman grated, his voice heavy and full of menace.

"Having these rights in mind, do you wish to talk to us now?"

Foreman merely smiled. "Mira? Please tell Mr. Lazars what's going on, will you?"

"Certainly…sir," the ashen faced receptionist mumbled.

"Pat him down," Tom told Kurt, who quickly ran over Foreman's body. He looked up and shook his head.

"Casey? We got him and we're coming in."

"Briggs reported that he has Kessler in custody."

"Excellent. Tell him we'll meet at Federal Plaza and give a heads up to Mr. Saul."

"Acknowledged."

By now, several people had emerged out of their offices, staring silently at the FBI men and the drawn guns. A trim, youngish individual pushed through and stood before Tom.

"I am Lazars, TriCon CEO. Would you mind telling me what's going on and why one of my most senior officers is handcuffed?"

"Your senior officer is facing two murder one charges," Tom told him. "You'll be contacted in due course, I'm sure. Now, if you will excuse us?" He glanced at Kurt and the other agent. People slowly made way as he walked toward the front desk.

At ground level, they strode out of the foyer, followed by curious stares. Outside, a cop looked suspiciously at the FBI sticker on their car. Tom could forgive him the comical expression when he saw the small group marching toward him.

"Morning, officer," he said politely. "Casey? We'll need another car and more men."

"Already on the way, and they've been warned that your man is ex-CIA."

Tom nodded with approval at a smart piece of thinking. Cuffed or not, Foreman could still have a trick or two left and everybody had to be frosty.

Pedestrians paused momentarily to gawk, but quickly moved on, not wishing to be involved. Cars rushed by along Fifth Avenue to sounds of horns and occasional police siren in the distance. A black Chevy Tahoe saloon pulled up behind Kurt's car and two men stepped out.

Tom turned to Foreman. "It hasn't been fun, but it'll be even less so for you."

"Raven was a fool!" Foreman grated.

"Funny, but he thought you were the fool," Tom said, smiling broadly, then glanced at the two new men.

They grabbed Foreman and bundled him into the Tahoe. The third agent nodded to Tom and got into the driver's seat. A moment later the saloon pulled away from the curb.

Kurt holstered his gun and patted down his jacket. "What now, sir?"

A load lifted off Tom's shoulders and he grinned. "Now? Back to the office. We have forms to fill out."

* * *

Krafter checked through the last email in a lengthy list, most of them from students and colleagues wishing him a speedy recovery, logged off his university account and sat back. He reached for his mug and took a sip of barely warm coffee. Even convalescing, work wouldn't leave him. Although to be fair, he was doing it to himself. Instead of enjoying a bit of respite, he simply couldn't let go. Elena was the same and wanted to spend a few hours at Bartlett & Strong. Unless Krafter accompanied her there, Ross wouldn't entertain leaving him alone.

He stretched his arms and winced as the bandages pulled at his wounds. The forced inactivity did have its good points. Elena became all clucky and hovered around him during the entire weekend. Not used to being fussed over, he couldn't make up his mind whether to relax to the inevitable or insist on doing some things himself. In the end, they compromised, and Elena allowed him to do chores he was clearly capable of, like making himself a cup of coffee. Taking a shower was trickier as he couldn't do all the twisting it involved. Elena happily helped solve his problem, but not before ribbing him about taking advantage of her like that.

The pleasant part was having her snuggle up to him at night, head on his shoulder, running a sharp fingernail over his chest while they talked. After the autonomic erotic reaction of his body to her proximity, they overcame their initial shyness and awkwardness, and enjoyed simply being close. Krafter found himself telling her things he had kept locked away from everybody, and he found the experience of sharing both pleasant and daunting. He always felt himself complete, not needing anyone. With Elena beside him, it was akin talking to himself. She did not judge, happy only to talk, and in turn, shared something of herself. Last night, they fell into a satisfying sleep long after midnight.

The phone rang and he picked up. "Krafter."

"Hi, doc. It's Julian Briggs. You got a minute?"

"Sure, glad to hear from you. What's up?"

"Some welcome news for you. It's all over. We got your man and the one giving him the orders."

"You did? Hey, that's great! Who was it?"

"Raymond Kessler, IAS CEO."

Krafter sagged in his chair and let out a long sigh. He felt as if a fog had lifted and he could see clearly. A lot of things suddenly took on a sharp focus. The road he was looking at had its twists and dark turns, and his stomach tensed at the prospect, but he was determined to walk that road. Retreating into his comfortable shell no longer an option.

"I can't tell you what this means, Mr. Briggs. I owe you a lot."

"Glad to help, doc, although we all had our frustrating moments along the way. How's your side?"

"I won't be running around anytime soon, but I hope to be back at work next week; at least on limited duty. I'll have to wait for the surgeon's verdict."

"Don't rush it. If Frank Ross is there, can I talk to him?"

"Sure. Does that mean you're pulling out my minders?"

"There's no reason for them to hang around any longer, and

I suspect you'll be glad to see the last of them."

"Let's say it's been an educational experience," Krafter said dryly and Briggs laughed. "Hold on, I'll get him."

Krafter put down the phone and hobbled out of the study. Elena and Ross were seated around the living room table, nursing coffee and talking.

"Frank? I've got Briggs on the phone and he wants to talk to you."

Ross put down his cup and glanced at Elena. "Excuse me." He stood up and walked quickly past Krafter.

"Bad news?" Elena asked, her eyebrows arched.

"Far from it." Krafter pulled back a chair, sat down with a grunt, and took her hand. "The FBI caught them."

She inhaled sharply and clutched his hand. "When?"

"This morning, I guess. Briggs didn't go into the details."

"And the man who shot you?"

"Briggs didn't say, but I'm sure he'll tell me everything in due course."

"That's great, Larry," she gushed. "I am genuinely happy for you."

Ross came in wearing a grin. "This is it, I guess."

Krafter extended his hand. "Excuse me for not standing up—"

"Quite all right."

"—but thanks for everything, Frank. And please extend my thanks to Ernie and Walter."

"I'll do that," he said as they shook hands.

"Do you need a lift somewhere?"

"That won't be necessary. We've got a car and I'll call Ernie. He'll pick me up."

Ten minutes later, a white Buick pulled up outside and Ross left after giving them a friendly wave. With a stifled groan, Krafter pried himself up and shuffled to the front door. He watched the saloon drive off, closing an unsettling episode in his life. He took Elena's hand and they slowly walked into the kitchen.

Seated at the table, Krafter fought to break through the suddenly awkward silence. No longer under protection, both of them were now free to resume their normal lives.

Elena cleared her throat and patted back her hair. "Well, I guess I better be on my way."

"You don't have to go, you know," Krafter said softly.

"I need to go to the office and pick up my mail. I'll be back later in the afternoon. You still need looking after."

"That's not what I meant." Taking a deep breath, he took both her hands in his. "How would you like to move to Boston?"

"What would I do in Boston?"

"Practice law."

She tensed. "I'm already practicing law...here."

He stroked her smooth skin and made the plunge. "I'll be lonely in Boston without you, but it would be different if you were there with me...as my wife...if you will have me." He stared deep into her eyes and his throat tightened. "Will you marry me?"

After a moment, she relaxed, her face soft and radiant.

"You're a dope, Larry Krafter."

About the author

Stefan Vučak has written twenty-one novels, which include eight SF books in the Shadow Gods Saga. His *Cry of Eagles* won the coveted Readers' Favorite silver medal award, and his *All the Evils* was the prestigious Eric Hoffer contest finalist and Readers' Favorite silver medal winner. *Strike for Honor* won the gold medal.

Stefan leveraged a successful career in the Information Technology industry, which took him to the Middle East working on cell-phone systems. Writing has been a road of discovery, helping him broaden his horizons. He also spends time as an editor and book reviewer. Stefan lives in Melbourne, Australia.

To learn more about Stefan, visit his:
Website: https://www.stefanvucak.com
Facebook: https://www.facebook.com/StefanVucak/Author
Twitter: @stefanvucak

More Books by Stefan Vučak

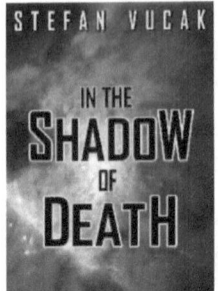

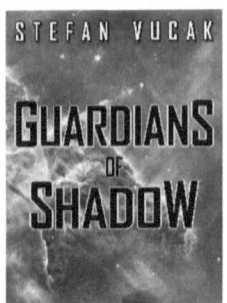